Missing Youth

A NOVEL BY

John Thomas

Copyright

Dedication

Also by John Thomas

Protected Arms
The Innocent Thief

CHAPTER 1

Pine Mountain, Georgia Late September, 1959

Henry Watson saw the boy walking alone on the highway shoulder, on the other side of the road, headed in the opposite direction. As he slowed down his rusty, gray 1945 GMC truck, he realized the boy was carrying a set of golf clubs on his back. From his size and looks, he appeared to be about thirteen years old. He was a skinny little fellow, wearing a green and white striped, short sleeve polo shirt and khaki shorts. There was a determination in the boy's step. Like he was running away or towards something.

Watson glanced at his rearview mirror. Not seeing any vehicle approaching from the rear, he slowed to a stop, put his truck in reverse and backed up to where he could see the boy's face. As the young boy neared the truck, Watson leaned his head out of the window and yelled, "Hey kid. You looking fer that there golfing place?"

Tommy Harrison stopped. He was so absorbed in his own thoughts that he hadn't seen or heard the truck.

"Uh … oh … yes sir."

"Well, you're going the wrong way. It's about a mile the other way."

Tommy turned and looked back at the direction he had come. Surely he hadn't overshot the golf course that much. David Rutledge, his friend since the third grade, would be at the golf course, waiting on him.

"Do you happen to have the time?" asked Tommy, hoping the old man had a watch.

Watson reached into a top pocket of his bib overalls and pulled out his daddy's gold-plated pocket watch.

"9:35."

Tommy looked back towards the golf course. All he saw was the bridge he had earlier walked under. There was no way that he was going to make his 10 o'clock tee time. At least, not on foot.

"If you need a ride, I'm heading that way," offered Watson with a country twang in his voice that reminded Tommy of his cousins in Marietta, Georgia.

"Yes. That would be great! Thank you. Thank you."

"Jest throw them sticks in the back and hop in."

Tommy ran across the road, slid the clubs off his shoulder and carefully lifted them over the tailgate and onto the truck bed. Then he ran to the passenger's side of the truck and climbed in. It was only then that he really noticed the man behind the wheel. He looked old. Maybe fifty or sixty. He was deeply tanned, and his face was wrinkled… most likely from the sun, quite possibly from smoking or maybe both. His hair was mostly gray and cropped close to his head. He wore faded blue bib overalls over a long-sleeve, red checkered shirt. Stuck between two yellow-stained fingers of his rough, left hand was a cigarette butt with about a half-inch of ash just waiting to fall. His equally rough, right hand had a firm grip on the steering wheel. And he smelled 'ripe' as his dad would have said. When the man smiled at Tommy, he noticed a couple of his bottom teeth were missing. *Not a golfer*, thought Tommy.

As the truck roared off, Watson flicked the cigarette butt out the window. In less than a couple of minutes, Tommy saw the entrance to Callaway Gardens. Instead of turning into the resort, the old man gunned the engine and sped off.

"Hey! That was it! Right back there. Where are you going?" yelled Tommy, looking through the back window as the entrance to the resort kept getting farther and farther away. "You need to turn around," he hollered looking at the grizzly-looking driver who paid him no attention and said nothing. Tommy knew he was in trouble. He looked at the door ready to jump out the first time the truck came to a stop. But the door handle and the window crank were missing. It was the first time that he was really afraid.

"Let me out of here," Tommy screamed while banging on the window.

"Boy… I know what you been up to. You best keep that yapper shut if you know what's good fer ya," hollered the old man, looking at the road and the frightened boy, alternately. "I ain't gonna hurt you unless I has to."

Tommy stared straight ahead. He was afraid. But he was more mad than afraid. Mad that he had made the wrong turn. Mad that he was going to miss his tee time. And especially mad that he had gotten into this truck with a complete stranger. Especially, with all the warnings from his parents.

CHAPTER 2

David Rutledge sat on the large leather sofa in George Russell's office. Russell was the Head Pro at Ida Cason Callaway Gardens Golf Course. While Russell waited impatiently for a call back from Pine Mountain's Police Chief James Broome, David looked in awe at all the autographed pictures that covered the better part of two walls of some of the world's most famous golfers including Sam Snead, Ben Hogan, Byron Nelson and Jimmy Demaret. The diversion helped numb the angst that he felt for his missing friend.

Shortly, the phone rang on Russell's desk. As the tanned, dark-haired pro quickly picked up the phone, David stopped looking around and focused his attention on the pro's side of the conversation.

"George… What's this I hear about a missing golfer?" asked Chief Broome.

"It's a young boy. And I don't think he's missing. I think he's lost. The boy... his name is… uh…" Russell looked at the notes on his desk. "His name is Tommy Harrison. He's from Atlanta."

"Lost? What do you mean by *lost*? How can anyone get *lost* on a golf course?"

"He and another boy… David Rutledge… camped over at Roosevelt Park last night. They were supposed to play golf today at ten o'clock. For some unknown reason, the two boys went separate ways when they walked from the park to the course. The Rutledge boy stayed on the highways. The Harrison kid took off through the woods. He hasn't shown up, so I think he's still somewhere out in the woods, wandering around."

"That sounds just like something a dang city boy would do. Have you sent anybody out to look for him?"

"Yes. One of my assistants. But no luck. He said he drove the perimeter of the park and into the park but didn't see anyone. I just sent him back out to check one more time."

"Okay. I'll be there shortly."

Russell hung up and looked over at the boy.

"The police are on their way. They'll find your friend. So don't you worry."

"Is he going to be in any trouble? I know he didn't mean to get lost."

"No, son. But Chief Broome will give him a tongue lashing that he'll never forget. I'm sure of that."

Within ten minutes, a shiny 1957 Chevrolet Bel Air black and white police car drove up to the pro shop and parked just outside the front entrance. Out of the Chevy stepped a big, burly man, dressed in a dark blue police uniform with his peaked cap in his hand. His bushy salt and pepper hair matched his wiry eyebrows. His craggy face sported a serious scowl.

"George in his office?" Broome bellowed out as he entered the building.

Will Bennett, one of the two assistant pros, immediately recognized the voice even before laying eyes on the man. "Yes sir."

Not needing directions, Broome turned left and headed to a closed door between the shelves of golf shoes and racks of polo shirts and plaid pants. Without knocking, he opened the door to find the head pro sitting at his desk. Russell immediately stood up, rounded his desk and shook hands with the chief. The two men had been friends since Russell became head pro four years ago. Broome eyed a young, black hair, blue eye boy sitting on the couch.

"Is that him? The lost boy?" Did I drive all the way out here for nothing?"

"No sir. That's David Rutledge. He's the lost boy's friend."

"And you're sure he's not somewhere on the property?"

"We've looked everywhere… locker rooms… men's and women's, practice areas, restrooms, dining areas and on the course. If he's here, we can't find him. Anyway, the Rutledge boy said they were to meet here at the pro shop. I think he's lost, plain and simple."

"Yeah. Probably so. Have you called the boy's parents yet?"

"Not yet. But I've written down both boys' parents' names, addresses and phone numbers… just in case." Russell returned to his desk, picked up a pad, tore off the first sheet and handed it to Broome.

Broome scanned the information, folded the paper and stuck it in his top pocket.

"No need calling them unless we have to."

"What's he look like… the boy?" Broome's question directed to Russell.

"I don't know. I didn't ask. We're just looking for a kid carrying a set of golf clubs."

The chief looked over at the boy who was staring straight ahead. "Son. What does your friend look like? Color of hair, eyes, clothes he was wearing."

The loud rough tone of the man's voice reminded David of his father when he was mad and about to give him a spanking. His voice trembled as he answered. "He's got brown hair… a flattop, like mine. And he's got brown eyes. Uh… he's wearing khaki shorts and a new green and white golf shirt. It looks just like mine except different colors. We bought them together at Rich's."

"Is he skinny like you?" asked Broome.

"Yes sir. Maybe more. And shorter. Oh… and his golf bag is red canvas, his clubs are Wilson K-28's and he's wearing his Kangaroo's."

"Kangaroo's?"

"Yes sir. They're his new, black and white golf shoes. He got them for his birthday. I don't know anybody else who wears them but him."

"Aren't y'all a little young to be left alone in the woods?"

"No sir. I'm fifteen and Tommy's sixteen. We've camped out before, just not here."

"With y'all both walking to the golf course, I'm guessing y'all don't have a car."

"No sir. All I've got is a learner's license, but Tommy can drive. He can drive anything… straight stick… automatic… truck… you name it. But his car's not safe to drive on the highway. It's a '53 Buick with a bad transmission. It works okay until we get to a hill, and if we don't get a running start, it will stall. Then we have to get a push or let it roll back down to level ground." David talked a lot when he was nervous, and he was nervous. "Not only that, he's too short to drive this far. He has to sit on a pillow to see over the steering wheel. So… to answer your question. Tommy's mom, Mrs. Harrison, drove us."

Broome had heard enough. "George… hand me your phone."

The pro pulled up the cord on the black rotary phone and pushed it over to the far side of his desk.

The chief picked up the receiver and dialed dispatch.

"Betty… Call Lewis. Have him meet me in the parking lot at Roosevelt Park. Tell him to bring Buddy." Buddy was Lewis' hunting dogs, a bloodhound. "We got a boy lost in the park." Without waiting for a reply, he hung up the receiver.

Broome looked over at the Rutledge boy. "Son. I want you to come with me. I want you to show me where you two boys camped out last night."

"Yes sir," said David and immediately stood.

"George… if that boy shows up or your assistant finds him, call Betty at the office. Have her get in touch with me so we're not out there wasting our time."

"Yes sir."

Broome put on his cap, turned to the door and headed out of the office with David following close behind. Once they were outside and as they were walking over to the chief's car, David did a quick look towards the driveway that led from the highway to the pro shop. He prayed he'd see Tommy with his golf clubs hung over his shoulders slowly walking up the gravel road.

That didn't happen.

CHAPTER 3

"Sit up, boy," barked Henry Watson to the frowning, young boy who sat slumped down in the truck's passenger seat with his arms folded and his feet resting above the glovebox. "And git those ga'dang spikedy shoes off my dashboard. It looks bad enough as it tis."

Tommy looked at the man and felt something inside him that he had never experienced before. Intense hatred. There were people and things he didn't like. Broccoli, sand traps and Jack St. Claire, the class bully, to name a few. Those feelings paled in comparison to how he felt about the man sitting next to him who was lighting up another cigarette.

Doing as the old man had asked, Tommy sat up, dropped his feet to the floorboard and looked straight out the right front windshield. There was no hiding the grimace on his face.

"What's yer name?" asked Watson, but there was no reply.

"Boy… I asked you, what's yer name?" This time he gave the young lad the stink eye. It was the same contortion of the eyes that Tommy's dad did when he was doing or saying something wrong.

"Tommy."

"You ain't got a last name?"

"Harrison. Tommy… Tommy Harrison."

"You from around here?"

"No sir."

"Where you from?"

"Decatur."

"That's a fer piece from here," said Watson, thinking Decatur, Alabama not Decatur, Georgia which is what Tommy meant.

"Any of your people living down here?"

"If you mean relatives, no," answered Tommy, looking over at the old man, wondering why the questions. And why had the man taken him. Why the man had ruined his golf game with his best friend. Whatever the reason, he knew it couldn't be good. While his abductor railed on about his dislike of big cities like Atlanta and Birmingham, Tommy considered his options. His door and window were inoperable. His only way out of the truck was the driver's side, and the sooner, the better… before he was too far away to ever find his way back to the camp ground. As his dad had always said, 'Son, you got yourself into this mess. Now you can get yourself out.'

"Where are you taking me?" asked Tommy, now watching the man's every move.

"You'll know soon enough. Jest so you know, I ain't gonna hurt you unless I has to."

Tommy didn't believe the man, and like his daddy said, he was ready to get himself out of this mess.

He had noticed that his abductor would always check the side mirror just before flicking the ashes from his cigarette out the window. He could have used the ashtray in the dashboard had it not already been filled to capacity with old, discarded cigarette butts. The next time Tommy saw the old man look to the side mirror, he slid his body towards the middle of the bench seat, leaned back towards the right door and with his left leg began kicking him in the right arm, shoulder and hand with all his might. Simultaneously, with his right leg, he began kicking at the gearshift. Both actions caused the old man to drop his cigarette onto the seat and roll down against his overalls.

Watson immediately slammed on brakes causing Tommy to slide into the floorboard, butt first. Ignoring the pain and the blood coming from his hand and arms, Watson killed the engine, jerked the key out of the ignition and jumped out of the car. Before the cigarette could do any real damage to the seat, he swept it off the seat and out onto the road. Luckily, his overalls were unharmed.

Furious at what had just happened, Watson stomped over to the passenger's side of the truck where he angrily flung open the door. He saw Tommy tenaciously, yet unsuccessfully, trying to right himself. Before the boy could pull himself up, Watson shoved the boy's neck into the elbow bend of his right arm and with his left arm began applying pressure to the back of his neck… a chokehold technique he'd learned as an MP (Military Police) to control unruly and usually drunken soldiers. Tommy instinctively grabbed Watson's arm which allowed the old man to apply even more pressure. Within fifteen seconds, Tommy went limp.

"Ga'dang it. See what you made me go and do?" yelled Watson at the unconscious boy as he grabbed a small nylon rope from the glove compartment and tied the boy's hands and legs. There would be no more attempts to escape.

Before returning to his side of the truck, the old man pulled off Tommy's new Kangaroo golf shoes and tossed them into the nearby ravine. The same fate awaited Tommy's golf clubs but not before Watson used the attached golf towel to wipe the blood off his arm and shirt sleeve mumbling to himself as he did.

Shortly, he and his unconscious captive were back on the road. With no radio in the truck, the remainder of the trip was silent and uneventful, other than the sound of the wind blowing into the cab of the truck which suited Watson just fine.

CHAPTER 4

With the Roosevelt State Park camping grounds only three miles from the pro shop, the trip was only a five minute drive. On the way over, Broome noticed the Rutledge boy's fascination with his car. Without saying a word, he flipped on the roof's flashing red light. Then he picked up his mike and called Betty.

"Betty… is Lewis on his way?"

"Yes sir. Him and Buddy. They should be there real soon. Also, George Russell from the golf course called. He said his assistant just returned from their search but found no sign of the boy."

"Okay. 'Preciate it." Broome saw David's shoulders slump. Immediately, he flipped off the mike and flipped on the siren.

David stared in awe at the large man. He was no longer afraid of him, just fascinated with him, the car and the whole experience. If anybody could find Tommy, this man could.

Once the Chevy hit the gravel road, David looked out the window to see that they had arrived at the entrance to the State Park. Broome slowed his car down, turned off the flashing dome light, the siren and pulled into the first parking spot next to the Visitor's Center.

"Wait here. I'll be right back."

He stepped out of the car, put on his cap and headed into the cinder block building. The attendant who had heard the siren blasting greeted the chief at the door. When asked, he said he had not seen anyone matching the boy's description come into the building, so the chief left.

He shook his head as he got back into the car and placed his cap on the bench seat between him and the boy. As he did, he could see the worried and lost look on his young passenger's face return.

"Son… don't you worry your little head off about your friend. These woods are big, and it's easy to get lost. But Lewis… he's one of my deputies … he's bringing Buddy, his hunting dog. Ol' Buddy can find anything. And I mean anything. You and Tommy will be out there golfing before lunch. Everything's gonna be all right."

David answered with a "Yes sir." But the chief's reassuring response did nothing to calm David's fears. They wouldn't go away until he saw his friend's face. He was a worrier. That was his nature, just like his mom. But not Tommy. He never worried about anything. Not even now, as he roamed the vast wooded area, he probably wasn't worried about anything except missing his tee time and losing the bet.

"How long have you known your friend?" asked Broome, as he rolled down his window, hoping the conversation would ease the boy's distress.

"Ever since the third grade when the Harrisons moved to Decatur. Tommy and I sat next to each other in Mrs. Gibbs' class. We hit it off that first day and became best friends. He lives just around the corner from my house. We do everything together. Golf, basketball, football, tennis, Ping Pong. We even have a paper route together. We used to deliver the papers on our bikes until Tommy got his dad's old '53 Buick. He gets paid fifty cents more than me for the gas and all, but it's worth it. We can get the papers out in half the time. Plus we don't have to worry about the Mitchell's Dobermans. During the summer, we also work at the Venetian swimming pool. This year, we worked in the snack shop making sandwiches, selling candy and things like that. It's a lot harder than last year when we worked as bottle-boys."

"What the heck is a bottle-boy?" asked Broome.

"We go around the pool and pick up all the soda bottles that are lying around and put them in the racks. That way they don't get broken and people get cut. Plus the Baker's… they're the owners… they get their deposit back. It's two cents a bottle. But, like I said, we don't do that anymore."

"My guess is that y'all are really good swimmers. Do I have that right?"

"Oh yes sir. We swim probably more than we work. And the Baker's don't charge us anything."

"So tell me… why'd you boys split up going to the golf course? Why did you take the road and your friend, Tommy, cut through the woods?"

"It was stupid. It was like a race to see who could get to the golf course the quickest. Everything with Tommy and me is a contest. We're best friends, but we're always competing. Don't ask me why. Anyway, he wanted to walk to the golf course through the woods rather than walking back to the highway. He said that the shortest distance between two points was a straight line, and that's the way he wanted to go. Not me.

Tommy's smart and all that, but when we got here yesterday, we walked around in the woods a little bit, exploring and all. It was so dense and there were all kinds of hiding places for snakes, bugs… you name it. And the spider webs… they were everywhere. So, no. I didn't want any part of that. This morning, he went his way and I went mine. The loser had to pay for the Cokes."

"Well, looks like you won."

"Yeah," replied David, not caring.

For the next few minutes, the two sat in silence until they heard the crunch of gravel of a car approaching. It was Lewis in his 1952 Ford Mainline patrol car. Buddy was in the passenger seat with his head stuck out the open window.

Once Lewis had parked, Broome leaned out the window and looking past Buddy whose slobber was streaking down the side of the car, spoke to Lewis.

"Follow me. Once we get to the campsite, you can take it from there."

"Will do," said Lewis, nodding in compliance.

Broome looked over to the young boy as he shifted the gear up into reverse, "OK. Which way?"

"Down that road," said David who turned and pointed down a dirt road heading towards Lake Delano.

Broome backed the car out of the parking space and headed towards the lake, driving slow enough for Lewis to easily follow. As they made their way down to the campsite, the chief and David checked out anybody or anything that moved, looking for Tommy but with no luck.

"That's it," said David, his voice elevated, while pointing to the tent just off the shoreline of the lake. Broome drove as close as he could to the campsite. He had hardly come to a complete stop before David had hopped out of the car. He ran to the tent, pulled back the canvas door and looked inside. There was no sign of Tommy or his golf clubs.

He looked up, solemn-faced and shook his head at Broome who had just gotten out of the car. He walked over to the tent, knelt down and did a quick survey inside the tent. He didn't exactly know what he was looking for but figured he'd know once he saw it. But he saw nothing out of the ordinary.

When the chief stood up, he saw that Lewis and Buddy had arrived, with the dog sitting patiently, waiting for his turn to help.

Lewis was young, in his late twenties and had been on the force for six years rising to the rank of sergeant. He was trim, tan and wore his brownish blond hair in a short Elvis Presley style. Just like the chief, his uniform was meticulous showing that he took pride in his clothes and job.

He walked up to David and introduced himself and Buddy.

David immediately began stroking the dogs head like they had been friends for years. He turned and looked at the young sergeant with hope in his eyes.

"David," said Lewis. "If your friend is *anywhere* in these woods, Buddy will find him. I'm going to need something that Tommy wore yesterday… like a t-shirt, underwear, socks… whatever, so Buddy can get his scent. Is there anything in the tent we might use?"

"His backpack has the clothes he wore down here yesterday. Will that help?"

"Yes. That'll do just fine."

David immediately turned and headed back into the tent, ducking his head down low as he did. Within seconds he reappeared holding a tan, canvas backpack and handed it to Lewis.

Lewis opened the bag and dug around until he found a pair of wadded up, previously worn white underwear and pulled them out. He then bent down and let Buddy sniff the garment enough times to get the scent of the lost boy. The dog barked three or four times and Lewis stood up. He placed the underwear in a plastic bag and inside his pants pocket just in case the dog needed a refresher. The dog then began smelling the ground in front of him, barking and pulling harder on his leash. He was ready for the hunt.

"David, can you hold Buddy for just a minute?" asked Broome. "I need to talk to Lewis for just a second."

David nodded and Lewis handed the leash over to the young boy but not before commanding Buddy to sit. The dog immediately sat, but the sad look on his face and the occasional whimpering showed that he was not happy. David, who felt the same, knelt down in front of Buddy and rubbed the dog's head. The dog's wet kisses on David's hand followed by an avalanche of kisses to his face was evidence enough for the boy to know the dog wanted to find Tommy as badly as he.

Broome waited until he and Lewis were out of earshot before speaking.

"I want you to be calm and reassuring with David before you take off. When he gets nervous, he talks… nonstop. And I need some peace and quiet so I can think."

"I got it. My mom's the same way, but she doesn't have to be nervous. It comes naturally." Lewis laughed. Broome didn't.

"The missing boy's name is Tommy Harrison. He's wearing khaki pants, a green and white striped shirt, black and white golf shoes and possibly carrying a golf bag," instructed Broome.

"Yes sir," answered Lewis, fidgeting. He was just as anxious to get started as Buddy. "Me and Buddy will find him if he's out there."

"Now… once you find him, fire a couple of shots in the air. Then bring him over to the pro shop or to the Visitor's Center, which ever one's the closest and then have Betty call me. In the meantime, I'm gonna be circling around the park, at least a couple of times before going back to the pro shop. If we find him or he shows up before you're finished, I'll do the same… fire a couple of rounds in the air to let you know he's here."

"Yes sir. Got it."

Lewis returned to the tent where David handed him the leash. Buddy was ready to go but remained sitting as he had been ordered.

"Can I go with you? Maybe I can help. You don't know what he looks like, but I do. I know a lot of Boy Scout stuff."

"Actually, I'd rather you go with the Chief. Me and Buddy know these woods so we are going to be moving really fast. I don't want to have to worry about you trying to keep up or falling and hurting yourself or anything like that."

"I'm fast and I promise I won't get hurt. Pleeeeease."

"I think the Chief is gonna need you more. While I'm out in the woods, he's gonna drive around the park a couple of times. He's needs you as a lookout. You know he can't see both sides of the road."

Lewis looked at the chief to see if he had said the right thing. Broome slightly nodded his head.

David was disappointed but understood. As he walked back to the chief's car, Lewis retrieved the plastic bag from his pocket that contained Tommy's underwear, leaned down and gave Buddy another sniff. He had hardly returned the underwear to its plastic bag and into his pocket before Buddy had the leash taut and was furiously jerking at Lewis' arm. Soon, the two were headed towards Lake Delano with Buddy's nose close to the ground with his head moving left, then right, repeating the sequence, like a windshield wiper as he smelled everything searching for his assigned odor. Every now and then, Lewis would pull Buddy to a halt to observe the dirt, sand and fallen leaves looking for the little holes left by the lost boy's golf shoes. They were easy to see. Buddy was on his trail.

CHAPTER 5

The chief and David stood outside the patrol car and watched Lewis and the dog make their way towards the lake. Broome was relieved to see them veer to the right and away from the lake and head straight towards the woods. As soon as the two were out of sight, Broome motioned for David to get in the car which he did. Then the chief drove out of the park and began their first of three slow counter clockwise trips around the perimeter of the park, driving twenty miles per hour. The normally talkative boy was silent as he stared out the window totally focused on finding his friend. The first two trips proved unfruitful with neither one seeing anything to cause them to stop. While it was upsetting to David, Broome wasn't worried, at least not yet, as Roosevelt State Park was the largest park in Georgia with over nine acres of mostly dense forest. It was easy for a person to get lost.

On their third trip around the park, about a mile past the entrance to the Callaway Gardens golf course, Broome spotted Lewis and Buddy just up ahead, on the opposite side of the road. He immediately sped up and then slowed to a stop, pulling off onto the shoulder of the road.

Broome looked over at David who was reaching for the door handle. "Stay here," he ordered and stepped out of the car.

David watched as the chief walked across the road, over to Lewis who was kneeling down beside his old bloodhound, rubbing its head.

"Sorry Chief. No luck," said Lewis standing to meet his boss. "The trail ends right there." Lewis pointed to an area in the road, close to the shoulder. "This is where Buddy lost the scent. You can see the scuff marks and some small holes in the pavement that had to be made by the boy's golf shoes. He came out of the woods about a half a mile back that way." Lewis pointed back towards the golf course entrance. "He must have gotten his bearings all confused in the woods because instead of heading straight out of the woods, he angled off to the left. Once he got to the road, he turned left and was walking *away* from the golf course."

Broome kneeled down and looked closely at the spot. Lewis was right. The marks had to have been made by the boy's golf shoes.

"Why would it end right in the middle of the road?' asked Broome, thinking out loud. He stood and looked over at Lewis. "Any chance the trail could have picked up farther on down the road?"

"Me and Buddy went almost all the way up to where highways 27 and 190 split," said Lewis pointing in a direction away from the golf course. "and way down yonder towards the railroad overpass." He pointed in the opposite direction. "There was nothing. No little holes in the ground and no scent that Buddy could pick up."

"Well, we know he didn't just take his shoes off in the middle of the road. This is not good," said Broome, looking at Lewis, purposely avoiding the wide-eyed gaze from the anxious boy in the car. Then repeating himself, "This is not good."

Both men stared in silence at the tiny holes in the pavement that could only have been caused by the golf shoes.

The chief continued. "I'm thinking… I'm thinking he might have gotten into somebody's car, needing a ride back to the golf course."

"Yeah. That makes sense. But you say he's not there. You think they took him?" asked Lewis.

"That's the only thing that makes sense. I mean, the boy can't just disappear into thin air."

"No sir. That's not gonna happen."

"Hmm. *Not* good. Not good at all. Okay. I'm going to take you and Buddy back to your car. Then I'm heading back to the office. I've got to let the boy's parents know he's gone missing. Then I'm gonna call the GBI. Let them take it from here."

The chief turned and headed to the driver's side of the car while Lewis and Buddy piled into the back seat. As they closed the doors, David asked the question whose answer he feared.

"Where's Tommy? Why couldn't Lewis and Buddy find him? You promised."

Broome didn't want to upset the boy but knew he had to tell him sooner or later. So he did. David sat in silence. He didn't know what to think or feel. He knew Tommy was gone. But it didn't seem real. He was just here… at the camp… acting the fool as his grandmother would say. He'd be back. He had to. Tommy was his best friend.

CHAPTER 6

Tommy awoke shortly to find both his hands and feet tied. And if that wasn't bad enough, gone were his brand new, black and white Kangaroo golf shoes. He didn't know how long he had been unconscious, but at least he was alive. Considering the nature of the attack, he figured he should be quite dead by now. But he wasn't. That meant that the old man must have other plans for him. But what were they and did they still include him dying? Tommy tried not to think about what *might* happen. Instead, he looked out the window trying to figure out where they were. Hopefully, somewhere in Georgia. After about ten or so miles down the road, he saw an Alabama highway sign… State Road 15.

Watson heard the boy shuffling around on the seat and looked over to see Tommy staring at him.

"Boy… you do something stupid like that agin and you'll find yourself at the bottom of a lake. I ain't putting up with none of your *shenanigans*," said Watson heavily accenting the first syllable of the word. "We ain't got much further to go. Jest enjoy the ride."

"Where are we going? Why did you take me? Where are my…"

"You best keep that yapper zipped and everything'll be jest fine," interrupted Watson. "Else, I'm gonna stick one of them funny-looking socks of yours down your throat."

Tommy knew not to challenge the old man again and nodded his head. Sadly, he looked out the window where all he saw was woods and farmlands in Somewhere, Alabama. He felt like crying, but crying was for sissies and he wasn't a sissy.

About a half hour later, Watson turned off the main highway and onto a lightly traveled, heavily wooded, densely thicketed county road. He'd only traveled only a few hundred yards when he made another right turn off the road and onto the two ruts that led to a dirt driveway. An old dented, gray metal mail box affixed atop a leaning wood post marked the entrance which, otherwise, would have gone unnoticed by the unobservant. But not by Tommy. He would never forget the hand painted numbers and name on the box: *Watson 14437.*

On either side of the dirt driveway, hidden by scraggly weeds, were two wooden posts which had a heavy, rusty chain hanging between the two. Multiple 'No Trespassing' signs were nailed to each post and two more signs with the same ominous message hung on the chain. Similar 'No Trespassing' signs and a few 'Keep Out' signs were posted on tree trunks to the left and right of the entryway making it quite clear that visitors were not welcome.

With the old truck safely off the highway and stopped just short of the chained entrance, Watson shut off the engine and removed the ignition key. He made sure the boy saw that the key was gone. He then climbed out of the truck, unlocked the padlock and lowered the chain to the ground. He returned to the truck, restarted the engine and slowly drove over the chains. Once the rear of the truck was clear of the two posts, he looked over at Tommy who was eyeing his every move.

"This is it. We're home."

Just as he had done when he entered the property, Watson secured the vehicle, climbed out of the truck, raised the chain and locked the padlock.

All the while, Tommy kept thinking what the old man had just said. *We're home.*

CHAPTER 7

"Ain't much further," said Watson as he started the truck, shifted the gear into first and began driving down the slightly winding, uneven dirt driveway.

Tommy said nothing, choosing not to acknowledge the comment. Instead, he took in the surrounding area just in case he could attempt an escape. All he saw were trees and scrub bushes that made him think of the dense forest of Roosevelt State Park that he had so stupidly chosen as his path to the golf course. If he had only listened to David…

Within seconds, the highway was out of sight and the first of many pot holes, ruts and bumps had Tommy bouncing all over the truck. Watson looked over and saw the boy bracing himself by pressing his feet against the dashboard and stretching his body so that his back was against the seat. He laughed at the sight but slowed the truck down. *Don't need no boy with broken bones. Won't be good fer nothin',* he thought. Once Tommy saw that the old man was either easing the truck over the potholes and bumps or avoiding them all together, he relaxed his body, dropped his feet back to the floorboard and pushed himself back to a sitting position.

Shortly, the forest gave way to lakes on both sides of the road. Neither were as big as Lake Delano in Roosevelt State Park. Nonetheless, both were sizable. When Watson reached what appeared to be the midway point of the two lakes, he stopped the truck. He looked over at Tommy who was staring out his side window, refusing to look at his captor.

"You see them there two lakes?" asked Watson. "Ain't nobody ever swimmed across them lakes. Nobody. Too big. Filled with snakes, too. Even seen a gator in 'em once or twiced."

Tommy looked out the front windshield and then out both side-windows of the truck. The lakes had a barbed wire fence running along the banks on either side of the road which would keep anyone from going into the lake or getting out of the lake depending on one's frame of reference. Covering the banks and the nearby shorelines were aquatic weeds of all sizes and varieties. Dead trees and tree stumps dotted the body of the two lakes. It reminded him of the pond where he, his dad and his granddaddy had gone frog gigging a few years back. They, too, were filled with snakes. He had not swum in *that* pond and he had no intensions of swimming in either of these two lakes. But why had the old man taken time to warn him about the lakes?

Watson watched the boy canvas the lakes. Once he figured the young lad had seen enough, he shifted the truck's gear into first, let out the clutch and gently pressed down on the gas pedal. Tommy continued to look out his side window at the lake as the truck slowly made its way down the road. But Tommy's mind wasn't on the lake. Instead, he was mentally bashing himself for having gotten into a truck with a complete stranger. *What kind of idiot…*

After a short while, the truck slowed to a stop and Tommy could see they were almost to the end of the two lakes. Straight ahead, blocking the truck was a rusted, old cow gate that had barbed wire stretched from side to side, top to bottom and diagonally. Fence panels, also laced with barbed wire, were to either side of the gate and extended about six feet into the lake. They acted as end-points to the barbed wire fence that ran along the banks of the lakes. It was obvious to Tommy that the old man didn't want anyone getting in *or* out of his property without his permission or knowledge. Watson turned off the motor, pulled the key from the ignition and stepped out of the truck.

"Gotta unlock the gate. Won't be but a minute. Now, don't you go runnin' off," said Watson, laughing.

The procedure with the opening and closing of the gates was the same as with the chain. Soon the lakes were behind them and the road was once again lined by overgrown bushes and trees whose canopies made the sunlight barely visible.

As the truck approached a large thicket of trees directly in front of them, it appeared as though they had come to a dead end. Instead, the road made a hard right turn which Watson navigated with ease. Suddenly, the darkness of the dense shrouded thicket was replaced with the brightness of the overhead sun in a cloudless sky revealing acres of open fields. Watson once again stopped the truck.

"You see them empty fields?" Watson pointed first to the left and then right side of the truck. "There ain't nothin' growing there 'cept some scraggly trees 'cause the gov'mint is paying me *not* to grow anything on them. How stupid is that? Paying me *not* to grow anything. And to tell the truth, that land ain't much good anyhow. Bad soil and too wet. So the jokes on them."

Tommy looked at the fields. If he wanted to say anything, he didn't. The old man had told him to keep his mouth shut and that's what he was planning to do. No sense in provoking him. Plus he had no interest in *them empty fields* or why the old man was getting paid not to grow anything on them. What did interest him was the sun and its position in the sky. It was almost overhead. Was it rising or setting? He'd learned from the Scouts how to estimate the time by the direction of shadows cast by the sun. Looking at the trees and their shadows, he knew it was either around 11 a.m. or 1 p.m., Georgia time depending on if they were traveling North or South… whether the sun was rising or setting. If it were rising, that meant they were not that far from Callaway gardens… maybe an hour and a half travel time. However, if it were setting, it meant he had been unconscious much longer than he thought and they were much farther away from Georgia.

Tommy continued to watch the sun's position as they slowly headed down the dirt road until he saw what looked to be large fields covered in snow.

"Boy… them's my cotton fields… my money crop," said Watson, proudly as they approached the fields. "Ain't got as many acres growing as I used to did. But that's okay. Ain't hardly got enough farm hands to pick what I got."

Tommy wasn't sure why the old man was giving him what seemed like a tour of the property, but at least he didn't feel threatened. At least not yet. And the sun was rising!

As the truck rolled past the cotton fields, Tommy saw to his far left in the middle of the field a deeply tanned, burly man sitting on an old tractor. He wore a wide brim straw hat and had a rifle laying across his lap. He seemed to be watching rows of heads that were bobbing up and down. Tommy had never been to a farm so none of this made sense, just like him being taken and tied up by the old man.

Watson honked the truck's horn, stuck his hand out the window and waved. The young man on the tractor looked over, waved his hat and then resumed his watch.

"That's my boy, Jesse."

None of the bobbing heads acknowledged the honk nor the wave.

Once they had passed the end of the cotton fields, vast acreage of cornfields came into view. Most of the fields had been harvested with only a few rows waiting to be picked. It wasn't long before the old man continued his discourse on how long it took to plant corn, how little money it brought in and how he needed a corn picker and sheller. But that was a few years off and until then, he'd have to use his boys.

"City boys think all that corn is jest fer eating. And it 'tis. Mostly by our farm animals… pigs, chickens and cows. But we git our fill, too. Can't let me or my boys go hungry." Watson patted his tiny round belly.

As Watson slowly drove by the few acres of peanuts, he seemed to be repeating himself… not enough money in the crop, how long it took to pick and shake the crop and the need for new machinery. While all of this was boring to Tommy, it kept the man talking which gave Tommy time to think about where they were… Somewhere, Alabama; and how far they were from Callaway Gardens… about an hour and a half; and how to escape… no plan whatsoever.

As Watson approached the end of the peanut crop, the road veered off to the right and then a hard left through another thicket of trees. Watson down shifted the truck into second gear and eased the truck through the maze. Once past the wall of trees and brush, the whole area opened up. Off to the left was a small pond surrounded by weeping willows and river birch. Off to the right was an old white clapboard, one-story, spraddle-roof farmhouse whose paint was cracked and peeling. And to its immediate right was a weathered, unpainted dogtrot style house with its breezeway enclosed. Growing between the two houses was a large magnolia tree.

Watson slowly drove towards the front of the farmhouse ignoring the chickens in front of the truck that were squawking and flapping their wings as they jumped out of the way to avoid being served up for dinner. The floundering chickens reminded Tommy of squirrels crossing the road, trying to dodge oncoming cars and trucks. He hoped the chickens were a lot more decisive.

Watson pulled to a stop only a few feet from the sagging porch, shut off the engine, shoved the gear into first gear and set the parking brake.

With no handles on the door, all Tommy could do was look outside. On the nearby porch, he saw a thin, old woman sitting in a rocking chair. She had grayish-white hair which was rolled up in a bun and partially covered by a white scarf. She looked to be about the same age as the old man. Her aquiline nose, high cheekbones, craggy face and dark, brown eyes made her resemble the Indian on the back side of the Buffalo nickel. She wore a long, wrinkled, almost floor length faded blue and white dress that looked to have come directly from a clothesline.

The old woman arose from her rocking chair and walked to the front stoop. When she saw the boy in the passenger seat of the truck, a big grin lit up her craggy face.

"I was a'feared you were gonna come back empty handed," she hollered to Watson who had left the cab and was rounding the back of the truck. Before he answered the woman, he opened the passenger's door, lifted Tommy out of the front seat and sat him on the truck's running board. For a scrawny man, Watson had the strength of someone much larger.

"The Lord was a looking out fer me," he said as the wide-eyed Tommy looked in all directions trying to take in everything around him. "Last time I went over to that orphanage, I suspected they was gonna close that place and I was right. All the windows was boarded up and there was chains and locks on all the doors. So I was headed back home and that's when I seen this here boy," smiled Watson while looking at Tommy. "He was running down a highway and he was heading right toward me. Right then and there, I know'd the Lord had taken pity on this old man."

"Why have you got him all hog-tied? He a runaway?"

"Yes ma'am. That and a thief. I seen him hightailing away from that golfing place over there near Chipley[1]. He had some golfing sticks in a bag on his shoulder. I figured he done stole them along with them spikedy shoes he was wearing."

"That's not true!" yelled Tommy. "Those …"

Watson reached over and grabbed Tommy's ear and began twisting it causing Tommy to wince in pain.

"Boy … don't you talk back to me. Ain't nobody ever taught you to respect your elders?" asked Watson giving the terrified boy a look that said *I mean it.*

Watson turned back to Sarah and continued. "Anyhows, I asked him if he wanted a ride. He said yes and he got into my truck. I jest didn't let him out."

"But you ain't explained why you got him all tied up?

"Me and the boy got into a little tussle while I was driving him home. He kicked me in the shoulder," said Watson, pointing to the blood on his shirt. "and he cracked my ga'dang windshield. But I learnt him a lesson

---

[1] In 1958, Chipley, Georgia changed its name to Pine Mountain when Callaway Gardens opened.

not to mess with Henry Watson. I put him down using my army training and then tied him up while he was out so I could drive home in peace."

"Don't sound like he ain't never had no discipline," said Sarah.

"That's what I figured. Them days are over."

Tommy listened as the old man and woman talked about him as though he wasn't even there. He wanted to speak up, but seeing that the old lady seemed to be on board with the whole abduction thing, he decided to listen and see what they had planned for him.

The old lady then moved in for a closer look at Tommy who couldn't help but notice the random white hairs sprouted from a couple of warts on her chin. And her teeth were yellow stained, but unlike the old man, none were missing.

"He's a skinny, little fella, ain't he? But he don't look sickly. Not like Little Eddie, bless his soul." Then she noticed the boy's feet. "Why ain't this boy wearing any shoes? They in the truck?"

"No, Sarah. Like I done told you, when he broke my window with them spikedy shoes he was wearing, I got mad. So after I put him down, I took them off and flung them in a creek."

Hearing that his new Kangaroo golf shoes lay somewhere beside the road in a ditch was more than Tommy could bear.

"No! No! Not my golf shoes!"

"Yep and them golfing sticks, too," replied Watson, smiling. "All in the ravine. The Bible says thou shalt not steal."

Instinctively, Tommy lashed out, flailing his bound hands at the old man while at the same time trying to kick him.

"That boy's got spirit," said the old woman, heading back to her rocking chair so not to be the recipient of Tommy's anger.

"Yep. A lot of giddy-up in him," responded Watson. Then using his right arm to protect himself from Tommy's wild, frenzied jabs and arm slinging, he grabbed the boy's right ear again and twisted it causing Tommy to immediately cease his protest.

"Stop! Stop! You're hurting me!" he yelled.

"He's had enough, Henry. Let him be," said Sarah. "What's your name, boy?"

Tommy was thankful for the woman's intervention and immediately spoke up.

"Tommy, ma'am. Tommy Harrison."

"Looks like you was raised with manners. I like that."

"Jest no discipline," said Watson, then added, "You watch the boy while I go git him some leggings."

Tommy wasn't real sure what the old man meant by *leggings*, but he knew it couldn't be good.

CHAPTER 8

"Betty… see if you can get Marty on the phone," barked Chief Broome, as he rushed through the front door of the Pine Mountain Police Department. Once inside the swinging gate that separated Betty's area from the visitor's section, Broome stopped, turned and looked back at David who had been tagging close behind.

"Son… you stay here, out front with Betty." The chief pointed to the two chairs just outside his office door. "Make yourself comfortable. I gotta make a couple of phone calls to see what we can do about finding your friend."

"Yes sir. And thank you."

Broome acknowledged the boy by nodding his head, but deep down he knew there was not much he or anybody else could do about finding the missing boy until the abductor made contact… if that ever happened.

Betty who served as secretary, dispatcher and Lewis' on and off girlfriend held the phone up over her head and began waving it to get the chief's attention.

"Sir. His secretary. She said he'd be there in a minute."

Broome immediately headed into his office, hung his cap on a nearby peg, sat down in his wooden, swivel chair behind his big oak desk and picked up the phone.

A few minutes later, Martin Stephens, head of the Georgia Bureau of Investigation, answered.

"Marty… Jim Broome. How are things up there in the big city?" Betty immediately disconnected her phone once she heard Stephens' voice.

"Couldn't be better, Jimmy. How about you?"

"Not so good down here. I need your help."

"I figured this wasn't a social call."

"I got a boy who's gone missing. From what I can gather, I think he's been abducted."

"White boy?"

What an ass, thought Broome. "Yeah. A white boy."

Martin Stephens had been director of the GBI since Sam Roper resigned to become Imperial Wizard of the Ku Klux Klan for the state of Georgia. Roper had been appointed Director of the GBI by Georgia's Governor Eugene Talmadge, an alleged Klansman, admitted crook and shrewd politician. Under Roper's term of office as director, the Klan had infiltrated most law enforcement offices in South Georgia and under Stephens' leadership, nothing had been done to curtail or discourage its proliferation. Broome, on the other hand, was not a racist and to his knowledge, none of his officers were members of the Klan.

"Tell me about it," said Stephens.

Broome went over everything he knew about the missing boy and what they had done to locate him. He also told him about the missing boy's friend, David, who was sitting nervously outside the chief's office, eavesdropping, listening to every word Broome said, hoping to hear something positive.

Stephens listened but had no intensions of helping Broome. He had bigger fish to fry. Finding a missing boy whose parents were simply owners of a small bicycle/lawnmower shop in Atlanta would not draw the public attention that he wanted. He wanted name recognition for when he ran for governor and having his men investigate an abduction that had little possibility of being solved would not bode well for his reputation.

"So what I understand, no one saw the boy once he left his campsite?"

"Not that we know."

"And this guy, Lewis. Is he any good?"

"He and Buddy, his bloodhound, are the best trackers in the county."

"Good. Good. And you think the boy got into somebody's car."

"We can't be sure but Buddy lost the boy's scent in the middle of the road. Not only that, the little holes made in the pavement by the metal spikes from the boy's shoes ended in the same place. So… that's the only thing that makes sense to me."

"What about their parents? Have they been any help?"

"I haven't called them yet. I was hoping you could handle that and, if possible, pick up his friend and take him home."

"Jimmy, that's not going to happen. I just don't have the manpower right now. J. Edgar has asked me to keep an eye on some colored preacher in Atlanta named King along with his commie friends. They're stirring up trouble everywhere they go. And you know when J. Edgar speaks, you jump. And you needn't call them … the FBI, either. They won't help unless the kid is twelve years old or younger, something they call the *tender years* rule. So you're gonna have to handle this one yourself. Anyway, from what you've told me, I don't think there's any more that you, *we* or the FBI could do until there's a ransom note. Once that happens, call me and if I can spare a man, we'll take it from there."

What a waste of time, thought Broome. He should have known that Stephens had no intensions of taking the case as soon as he found out that the missing kid's parents weren't *important* or *rich* or *famous*.

"Yeah. I'll do that. Thanks for your help." Broome hung up without waiting for a reply. He had a call to make and a trip to Atlanta. He dreaded both.

CHAPTER 9

Watson walked inside the screened door and gave out a yell as he headed to the kitchen, "Caleb … front and center." Watson was proud of his time in the service and tried to run his farm using the same philosophy.

Shortly, he was followed out of the house by a man who looked like the one that Tommy had seen on the tractor in the cotton fields, only heavier. He appeared to be in his late twenties to early thirties, dressed in clothes similar to the old man: blue bib overalls and a green checkered long sleeve shirt. His dark black hair was cropped almost to a stubble which was in sharp contrast to the beard and mustache that covered the majority of his face. Perched above the man's close-set, beady black eyes were two ropelike black eyebrows that were almost touching each other. The rest of his face was deeply tanned. Over his shoulder, he carried a burlap sack. He was struggling to keep up with the old man.

"Daddy… hold up. You *know* this bag ain't real light," said Caleb Watson, one of Henry and Sarah's twin sons.

Watson ignored his son and continued his fast gait off the porch and down the stairs until he was standing in front of Tommy. When the boy looked up, Watson could see the fear in the boy as his eyes began darting nervously back and forth between him and Caleb who was now hovering over his father's shoulder.

"Son," said Watson, talking to Tommy. "We ain't gonna hurt you. Jest don't do nuttin' stupid, ya hear?"

Tommy nodded. "Yes sir."

Watson then squatted down, shifting his right foot to balance himself only to trip over the sack that Caleb had laid down behind his feet.

"What in tarnation?" yelled Watson looking up at his son. "Don't jest stand there, boy. Help me up."

Caleb grabbed his daddy's outreached hand and pulled him up.

"I'm sorry, Daddy. I'm sorry." He then gently dusted off his daddy's backside.

"What was your mind thinking putting that bag behind me? You know I ain't got eyes in the back of my head. Now move that bag over where I can git to it without having to twist all around."

"Yes, Daddy."

Caleb looked to Watson's left, his right, and back to the left again before deciding where to move the bag. Once his mind was made up, he began sliding the bag over to Watson's right side but not before getting a nod of approval from his father.

"That's good. You ought to have done it that way the first time around. Now go git this boy some socks and shoes whilst I hook up his leggings."

"Yes, Daddy." He left, talking to himself as he did.

"Dumber than a stump, that one," said Watson, looking at Tommy, shaking his head at the same time.

Watson squatted back down and began removing Tommy's argyle socks, tossing them aside. He then untied the rope that bound the boy's legs while leaving his hands tied. From the burlap bag, he pulled out a pair of leg shackles that looked like police hand cuffs except with a longer chain. As soon as Tommy saw the leg irons, he fully understood what they had meant by "leggings. All he could think about was getting out of there. *These people are crazy.* Instinctively, he began kicking at Watson, hitting the old man a couple of times in the chest causing him to fall on his haunches and out of the way of Tommy's flailing legs.

Tommy pushed himself off the running board and turned towards the road leading out of the farm and started to run but ran right into Caleb's outstretched arms.

"Where you off to, little fella," said Caleb who sat him back down on the truck's running board.

Watson wasted little time getting to his feet and back in Tommy's face.

"I reckon you don't listen real good," he barked, grabbing the boy's ear and twisting it.

"Ouch! Stop! You're hurting me," yelled Tommy, falling down to his knees.

Once Watson felt he had made his point, he let go.

"Next time you do something stupid like you jest done, I'm gonna take out my cane stick."

"Yes sir."

"Now git yourself over to them steps and sit yourself down,"

Watson watched as Tommy struggled to get to his feet, pushing off the ground with his tied hands. Once he was upright, he slowly walked over to the porch, dodging unfettered chickens as he did. He could feel the eyes of Watson, his son and the old lady watching his every move.

"Caleb… bring me them leggings!"

As ordered, Caleb ran to the bag of shackles and lugged them over to his father making sure he put them on his right side and where his daddy could see them.

"Tommy," said Watson, addressing the boy by his first name for the first time. "You'll only be wearing these here leggings fer jest a short time… if you behave, that is. Jest so you know, a few years back, we had a couple of pickers who up and ran away jest two days after I brung 'em here. I didn't make nobody wear no leggings back then. Anyways, I had to send my boy, Jesse, after them. All he come back with was jest them boy's shoes. And that's all I'm gonna say about that."

Tommy understood the warning. He wondered what the old man meant when he said he'd only be wearing the shackles only a short time. How long was a short time?

While he sat there in silence, Watson slid some calf-high socks on Tommy's feet and attached the shackles around both ankles using a key attached to his keychain to lock them. Next, he slid on some old scuffed up, cut-off black army boots on Tommy's feet that were at least a couple of sizes too large and laced them up.

Watson checked the shackles to make sure they were secure, not too loose or tight. He then untied the boy's hands and returned the rope to the glove compartment in his truck. When he turned around, he saw that Tommy had his right hand raised high like a school boy wanting to ask the teacher a question.

"What do you want?"

"Sir… why am I here?" asked Tommy, lowering his arm.

"Because I brung you here… that's why." Then turning to Caleb, "Son, go git me three of them tall chairs from the house and set them next to mama. It's time fer Tommy's orientation." Watson made a point of pronouncing all five syllables in the word. Just how he had learned it while at boot camp in the Army Infantry during World War II.

CHAPTER 10

"Now Tommy," said Watson, taking the boy by his arm and helping him to stand. "Here's what I want you to do. Start walking slowly towards me. You need to git used to them leggings. If you try to walk too fast *or run*, you ain't gonna git too fer 'afore you fall. If you don't believe me, jest try it."

Tommy did what he was told and began slowly walking towards the old man. The first few steps were awkward as his natural stride was longer than the chain length between the shackles. After a number of steps, he had grown accustomed to his restrictive gait. He found that his walk was more like a shuffle, similar to the way his grandfather walked after his stroke.

Once Watson was satisfied that Tommy could walk wearing the shackles, he guided him over to the porch steps. As they negotiated the first of the three steps, Watson saw Caleb coming from the house, using his backside to open the screen door. Once he was on the porch, Watson began yelling at him.

"Caleb. You only *brung* us two chairs. I specifically *asked* fer three."

Caleb looked at the two chairs and nodded in agreement. "I'm sorry, Daddy." He turned around, opened the screen door and carried the two chairs back into the house. Watson didn't stop him. He just shook his head.

"Caleb ain't all there," he said in a somewhat apologetic tone. "When he was a young'un, he fell off the porch and hit his noggin' on one of them steps. Blood was a'gooshin' everywheres. Sarah bandaged him up and all. But he ain't been right ever since."

Tommy listened but chose not to acknowledge Watson. Instead, he continued his climb. By the time he managed the two remaining steps by himself, Caleb had returned with the same two chairs under one arm and a third under the other. Methodically, he set each chair down in a row next to his mother's rocker making sure each chair was perfectly aligned with the other. Satisfied with the results, he sat in the chair next to his mama.

"Tommy," said Watson. "Sit in that chair on the end."

Tommy did as he was told and Watson sat between Caleb and Tommy.

"I like Daddy's orientation talks." said Caleb pronouncing the word *orientation* just like Watson. He gazed out towards the pond with a big smile on his face waiting for his daddy to begin.

While Watson seemed to be gathering his thoughts, Tommy heard scratching on the screen door which he saw slowly open and a short-haired, black and brown terrier mongrel made his way out. The skinny dog walked over to Watson, laid down between his feet and began licking his paws and then his privates.

"Tommy," said Watson, turning and looking the boy straight in the eyes. "We are a God-fearing people. We trust in the Lord. Are you a believer? Do *you* trust in the Lord?"

"I do, Daddy! I do," said Caleb, excitement in his eyes.

"Shut up, boy. This ain't about you. This is about Tommy, here." The reprimand could be heard in the tone of the old man's voice.

Tommy had been baptized when he turned eight, so he was a Christian but maybe not to the extent as his abductor.

"Son … do *you* trust in the Lord?"

"Yes sir."

"Good. Then you'll believe what I'm gonna tell you. After I left the orphanage with nary a boy, I prayed mightily that the Lord would have favor upon me. That's when I seen you walking with them stolen golfing sticks hung on your back, I knew you was going the wrong way. Ain't nuttin' that way fer fifty miles so I know'd you was lost. And as the Bible says… once you was lost and now you was found. And I found you. The Lord had listened and he answered my prayers. So I took you. The Lord helps them that helps themself."

As Tommy listened to the old man using his religion to justify his actions, even at his young age, it became clear to him that verses in the Bible could be used for both good and evil. He wanted to interrupt and tell him that he had it all wrong, but he didn't think he could handle another ear twisting.

"We are the Watsons. I'm Henry and that there is Sarah, my wife, and this here is Caleb, my son. You'll meet Jesse, my other son and the other boys later." Smiling for the first time, he looked down between his legs and pointed at the dog. "That there is Tippy. He ain't good fer nuttin'."

From the way things were going, Tommy no longer felt afraid for his life. But why was he here? Why was he taken? Hopefully, he'd understand after this orientation… his mind mimicking how Watson and Caleb had said the word.

Watson continued. "A long time ago, this was the Twin Lakes Plantation. Two thousand acres large. It was owned by my great-great granddaddy George Watson. He growed more cotton than anyone in the county. Nearbout the whole dad-burn state. He had over a two-hunnerd fifty coloreds at one time or another workin' in the fields. You see them tall oak trees way, way over yonder?" Watson pointed to his far right.

Tommy nodded his head.

"According to my granddaddy, that's where the big house sat. Had four of them tall columns and all. A lot bigger than this old place. But it got burnt mostly to the ground… either by them ga'dang Union boys or them worthless coloreds that used to pick the cotton. Anyways, after the war… the Confederate war, my granddaddy's money weren't no good no more. The Yankees took over the banks and they only wanted U.S. dollars. He didn't have no proper money to pay the mortgage, so they took most of his land. Next came the depression… We lost even more land. Now, all we's got is about one hunnerd thirty acres. The rest is owned by some politician from Montgomery. And he ain't growing nuttin' and gitting paid by the U.S. gov'mint not to. But that's okay."

"Damn Yankees," interjected Caleb with a grimace.

"Caleb! You *watch* your mouth!" snapped Sarah, slapping her son on the arm.

"Boy … you know we don't talk that way. I hear you say that cuss word agin, I'm gonna beat the living tar out of you," said Watson, with Sarah nodding in agreement.

"But Daddy, Jesse…"

"Don't you Jesse me. He don't talk that way. He knows better." He looked at Tommy whose eyes were darting back and forth between the two. "Tommy. We have rules around here. We have *no* cussing and *never*… never take the Lord's name in vain, not if you know what's good fer ya'."

"Yes sir."

Before continuing, he leaned forward and pulled out a pack of cigarettes from his shirt pocket hidden by the bib of his overalls. Gently he tapped the bottom of the pack and on command a single cigarette popped up. He stuck the pack up to his mouth and pulled the cigarette out with his lips. He replaced the pack and pulled a small box of matches out from a top pocket of his overalls. He pulled out one of the wooden match sticks and with one long stroke against his pants leg, lit the match and the cigarette in one synchronized motion. It was a ritual he had done many times as was evident by his yellow teeth, fingers and nagging cough.

He took a couple of long drags, leaned down and blew the smoke between his legs engulfing the dog who ignored the white cloud and continued his licking. Watson looked at the boy who seemed disgusted by the whole ordeal.

"That's another rule. Nobody smokes around here but me. Can't take no chances of someone burning down the farm. Not only that, it ain't good fer you. I got a cough jest like my paw used to have. He told me not to smoke, but I got hooked in the Army. Hooked on Old Golds, jest like him. Anyways, enough said about smoking."

Tommy's dad had told him about all the scientific studies that linked lung cancer to smoking. He asked him never to smoke. But Tommy didn't need to be asked. He'd tried it once and didn't like the taste or smell. That one time was enough for him, scientific studies or not.

"Tommy… we here are farmers. Cotton is what we mainly grow. About twenty-eight acres. Used to be over a hunnerd. But twenty-eight is now alls what the gov'mint 'lows us to grow. They call it allotments. I call it stealing. Nuttin' we can do about it. Anyways… don't hardly have enough help fer what we got. We also grow some corn and peanuts, but that don't bring in enough to make it worth our while. You done seen all our fields as we drove in. We also got some pigs, chickens, a few cows and two mules. That's about all."

Watson stuck the cigarette in his mouth, sucked in the smoke, and blew it out, again between his legs and towards Tippy. This time the dog slowly stood up and moved over to Sarah's chair and under the old woman's skirt.

"You can see the pig pen over there past the chicken coop." He pointed his cigarette to a pen off in the distance and to the right of the house just beyond a small, wooden hen house. Tommy looked to where the old man was pointing, and nodded, still confused as to what this was all about… why his feet were chained and why he was being told so much about the farm. There was no fear… just questions.

"Off that away is the workers' cabin and beside it is the barn where we keep the tractor. The cows and mules also sleep in there if they don't want to stay outside."

Tommy looked left and saw the old dog-trot house he had seen when they drove in and to its immediate right was a large, old weather-beaten, dilapidated building, in worse shape than either house. If it *was* a barn, it didn't look like any of the ones he'd seen in books.

Watson stood up. "Caleb, help the boy git down them steps. I want to give him a good look at the place."

"Yes, Daddy."

Caleb stood, pulled Tommy up from his chair and he ushered him down the steps where Watson was already there, watching… waiting. Neither Sarah nor Tippy moved. She continued to rock and the dog continued to lick and bite at fleas.

"First place is the workers' cabin."

Tommy meekly raised his hand to ask a question, but Watson ignored it. Instead he continued walking towards the weathered building that sat adjacent to the main farmhouse separated by a large magnolia tree. The old man's gait was short and slow allowing Tommy who was still getting accustomed to the shackles to keep pace. Once they got to the dogtrot style house, instead of using a ramp that led up to the left side of the porch, Watson ambled up the front steps and waited on the porch until Tommy had successfully managed the two steps, unassisted. Caleb walked behind the young boy with his hands in the ready position just in case the boy's feet got tangled and he fell.

Tommy watched as the old man pulled out a ring of keys, found the one he was looking for and unlocked the front door.

"Y'all wait right here."

Watson walked into the enclosed breezeway, pulled the string attached to an overhead hanging lightbulb and waved the two into the dimly lit hallway.

The temperature in the house was stifling. Sweat began pouring down Tommy's forehead, under his arms and down his back. Neither Watson nor Caleb seemed to notice. Watson continued his orientation.

"These here rooms on the left and right are Jesse and Caleb's." Watson pointed to the two locked doors. "No one enters them unless they say so. You git that?"

"This is *my* room. Ain't it, Daddy," interjected Caleb, smiling while patting the locked door to Tommy's immediate right.

Watson ignored his son, but instead looked at Tommy who was nodding to acknowledge Watson's warning.

Watson walked a little farther into a much larger room where he pulled the string to one of the two overhead hanging lightbulbs. He then motioned Tommy and Caleb into the big room.

"This here is the mess hall." Tommy took notice of the long table and chairs that were centered in the large hallway. "This is where you boys eat your meals."

"Mama's a real good cook. Ain't she, Daddy," added Caleb.

"Follow me," said Watson, again dismissing his son's comments.

He walked about halfway down the hall and entered an open door to a room on his left.

Unlike the hallway, there was no need for Watson to turn on the overhead light. Three open windows, two on the far side of the room and one on its right, provided ample natural light. Nor was the room as hot and stuffy as the hallway given the slight September breeze that found its way into the room through the open windows. What caught Tommy's attention were the iron bars on all three windows. It was obvious that no one was getting in… or out.

Centered in the room were three metal bunk beds, each one covered with an olive drab blanket, neatly made. None had a ladder. At both ends of the bunk was an open foot locker. A dormant wood burning stove and a neatly stacked pile of wood sat between the two far windows.

"This is one of the boys' bunkrooms," said Watson as he went from bunk to bunk.

Tommy watched Watson as he carefully inspected each bed and foot locker, nodding his head in approval once he had finished.

"Follow me," ordered the old man as he left the room. Tommy and Caleb were quick to follow.

"This here is the new privy," said Watson as he opened a door to his left at the far end of the hall.

"You need to go?" he asked, looking directly at Tommy.

"No sir. I'm okay."

Watson crossed the hall and into a second room that was identical to the one they had just seen. Unlike the first room, only five of the six beds were made up. One was stripped down to the mattress.

As before, Watson began inspecting the bunks. The first two, both upper and lower beds, passed his scrutiny. But not so the third bunk. He turned around, stared Caleb in the eyes and with a raised voice asked, "Whose bunk is this?"

"Eugene's, Daddy."

"Did you inspect these beds this morning?"

"Yes, Daddy."

"Well … this one ain't up to snuff. Boy… you ain't lying to me, are ya?" Watson asked, now almost yelling.

"No, Daddy. Maybe Eugene throwed something on it after I left or … or maybe a squirrel come through the window and …

"Ga'dang it, boy," yelled Watson. "I ain't looking fer no excuses." He then began jerking the sheets and covers off the bottom bunk. When he had finished, he turned and stepped towards Caleb, his face within inches of his son's face. "Don't let this happen agin. When Eugene comes in from the fields, you send him straight to the house. Do I make myself clear?"

"Yes, Daddy. Eugene… uh… I won't fergit," said Caleb, trembling even though he was much bigger than his father.

"You *best* not." He stepped back from Caleb and turned back towards Tommy.

"Son… like I said earlier, we have rules. Everybody obeys the rules or …" He stopped in mid-sentence, paused for a second then continued, "Take a seat on that there bunk." Watson waited until Tommy sat down before sitting on the bunk opposite him. Caleb looked at Watson who motioned with his head for him to sit down next to Tommy.

"Was your Pa ever in the service?"

"No sir. During the war, he worked in the naval shipyard in Charleston building ships. He was a welder."

"Well, then you pro'bly ain't never heard of recruit training, like in the Army. It's now called basic training." Watson smiled at his current knowledge of military affairs.

"No sir."

"Well… listen up and I'll learn you a thing or two. Basic training is how the Army gits new recruits ready fer combat. They teach you to shoot, march, wear gasmasks, fling hand grenades, fight with bayonets, climb the obstacle course (which Watson pronounced it ob-sti-cle), and most importantly, take care of your weapon. Army folk say weapon… not gun."

As Tommy listened to the old man ramble on, it reminded him of his dad's *talks*… the ones he got in lieu of the belt. But his dad's talks were quick and to the point not like the sermon he was getting from the old man.

"Do you know why the Army has marching drills?"

"For parades?"

"*Nooooo!* That ain't why they do it. It's discipline. It learns you to take orders. Obey your leaders. See, I'm the leader here. Caleb and Jesse do what I say… what I order. And my boys … they obey me, Caleb and Jesse. That's how it works. And we all obey the Lord. No ifs, ands or buts. You understand?"

"Yes sir," replied Tommy, thinking that if he said *learn* instead of *teach* one more time, he would scream.

"Now this here bunk … the one that that I throwed the bedding to the floor? That's because Eugene didn't make it up right. There was wrinkles on his bed. That boy knows better. Making your bed the Army way is discipline. Now Caleb is going to show you how that's done. Caleb… go git the boy some sheets and a blanket… and bring him some work clothes."

Work clothes, thought Tommy. *Is that why he took me? To work on the farm?*

Caleb jumped up from the bed and headed out the door, repeating to himself what his father had just asked.

"Tommy… you see how Caleb did what I say. No backtalk. No sass. Jest doing what he was ordered to do. That, my son, is discipline."

Tommy nodded his head. He understood that … and much more.

CHAPTER 11

While Caleb was in the hallway, getting bedding and clothing from an old pie safe, Watson continued his orientation.

"Tommy … this here is a farm. And farms *need* workers. Most of the teeny, tiny farms like this one has their chilluns to work the farm. But the Lord only blessed Sarah and me with two kids… and one ain't much good fer nuttin'. Anyhows, we need our cotton picked, peanuts shaked and stacked, and the corn picked. We can't git tenants. Ain't none to be gotten. Most have all gone to work in the factories. Same with the sharecroppers. Besides, none of them gonna work my farm. Ain't big enough. Can't make enough money. So I has to git boys, like you, to work the farm. Do you understand?"

Tommy nodded as the image of the bobbing heads and the man sitting on a tractor with a rifle laying across his lap immediately came to mind. These workers… they were all kids! And he was about to join those bobbing heads.

"We work this farm every day, 'cepting Sundays, not counting the chores. We work mostly sunrise to sunset, Monday through Friday. Saturdays … we only work until a little past three. We feed you good. You have a nice place to sleep. And we now have a new indoor privy. No harm will come to you as long as you don't do nuttin' foolish like you done before. Most of the boys on the farm come from an orphanage in Georgia. But that done closed down. We have a couple of runaways, like yourself. You'll git to meet all them real soon. Ain't none of them wearing chains 'cause none of them wants to leave this here farm. They ain't got no place to go. They mostly like it here."

The loud growl coming from Watson's stomach caused him to stop his mini-sermon, pull out his watch and check the time. It was almost noon. He always ate lunch at noon. No exceptions. And Sarah always knew to have his food ready. As he stood, he saw Caleb standing at the door, his arms hugging the clothing and bedding.

"Caleb … don't jest stand there. Help git Tommy into his work clothes. Then show him how to make his bunk bed. After lunch, I want to take him down to the fields and you learn him how to pick cotton."

"But Daddy, you ain't done with your orientation. What about the barn… and the hen house… uh… and the…"

"Caleb. This orientation is done. I'm gonna go eat. Now you git on with your duties. Do I make myself clear?"

"Yes, Daddy."

Watson turned and left without saying a word.

Caleb stared at the bed for a moment as he tried to remember what he was supposed to do. Then he smiled, laid the bedding on the bunk and handed Tommy his work clothes. Using a set of keys he pulled from around his neck, he unlocked Tommy's shackles.

"Now you git youself dressed before Daddy gits back. He's a real fast eater."

Caleb turned his back to Tommy to give him some privacy.

"Tell me when you're done finished. I ain't gonna peek."

Tommy sat down and removed the boots he'd been given by Watson. He stood, dropped his khaki shorts to the floor and put on a pair of cut-off Army fatigue pants and tied the piece of rope that served as a belt. He then pulled his green and white striped, short sleeve polo shirt over his head and slipped on the T-shirt and field cap. Everything … pants, shirt and cap … were all olive drab in color.

"You done yet?" asked Caleb, fidgeting with his keys.

"Yeah. I'm done," responded Tommy, a sound of resignation in the tone of his voice.

Caleb turned around, picked up Tommy's old clothes, neatly fold them and put them in the bottom of his foot locker. He then grabbed the shackles, locked them around Tommy's ankles.

"Tommy … we has to make our beds every day but Sunday. And me and Jesse makes sure they is done right."

Caleb preceded to make the bed, mumbling instructions as he did. Every corner had a perfect forty-five-degree fold. When he finished, he took his keys and dropped them on the middle of the bed. They bounced up a few inches but not to Caleb's satisfaction. He adjusted the covers on the bed and dropped the keys again. He smiled.

"You see how them keys jump back at you? That's real good."

Tommy nodded, but he didn't care.

Caleb could see the sorrow in Tommy's eyes but misunderstood the reason.

"Tommy … making that bunk … it ain't hard. You want to watch me make it agin?"

"No."

"Then I reckon we best be heading out to the front stoop."

Caleb headed out of the bunkroom, keeping a slow pace so that Tommy didn't have any trouble keeping up with him.

Once outside, Caleb locked the front door and he and Tommy sat down on the top stoop waiting for Watson's return.

Tommy looked down at the shackles and then back up at Caleb who had a big smile on his face while he stared at nothing particular. Caleb was a happy man. But this was his home. Tommy felt lost. His mind kept going back to the day's events. Only a few hours ago, he and David were outside their tent, cooking breakfast on a Coleman single burner stove that David's father had borrowed from a neighbor. All they could talk about was golf and making the golf team at Decatur High. Everything was perfect. He was happy. Why did he have to walk through the woods? And why did he turn the wrong way? And why did he jump in old man Watson's truck? Everything seemed so unreal. And yet, here he was. He needed to find a way out and Caleb could be his answer.

"Caleb … how long do you think I will have to wear these leggings if I don't do anything stupid?"

"I'm a'guessin' about two weeks. Yeah … two weeks. Maybe less. If you pick lots of cotton, maybe Daddy might take them off early."

"What if I'm not a good cotton picker? Do you think your daddy will let me go?"

"Ain't nuttin' to picking cotton. Anybody can do it."

"But … what if … what if I'm really slow? You know … the worst cotton picker of all times?"

"Oh no. I'll learn you to be fast. Jesse … he's my twin brother … he watches over the fields. He don't take kindly to no slow pickers."

"Is he mean like your daddy?"

"Oh … Daddy ain't mean. Jest ornery excepting when he gits mad. Then, all he does is pull your ear or thump you on the head. I hate them thumpings. They hurt lots worser than the ear pulling."

"What about Jesse?"

"I love Jesee and all that, but he can be mean. Mama says he has one of them mean streaks in his body … somewheres. I ain't never seen it. Sometimes, he likes to use his cane. He ain't hardly got no toleration fer nuttin'. Daddy … I ain't seen him cane nobody fer a long time. If'n he does, it ain't nuttin'. Daddy and Mama … they like Jesse a whole lot better than me. When Daddy passes, Jesse will git all this farm. But he don't want none of it. He wants to go live in Macon or Columbus and work in a factory so he can git a new car and maybe a girlfriend. He don't have no girlfriend here in Willis."

Tommy liked Caleb. The more he talked, the more Tommy thought of David and how much he talked, especially when he was nervous. He missed David. He missed his mom and dad. He missed his home.

"Caleb … I like you."

"Back at you. You're gonna …"

Caleb stopped midsentence when he heard Watson's truck crank up.

"Daddy's coming. He don't like it none too much if he has to wait."

He stood and helped Tommy down the few steps just as Watson drove up.

"Caleb… give this sack of food to Tommy and help him git on the back of the truck. We need to git this boy out to the cotton field."

CHAPTER 12

Tommy and Caleb sat on the tailgate of the old truck as Watson slowly drove out to the cotton fields.

As they were about to drive over the first of many ruts, Caleb hollered out, "Lift your legs like me so them leg bones of yours don't git broke." He raised his legs as high as he could and Tommy did likewise just as the rear of the truck dipped towards the ground while it passed over one of the deeper potholes.

"How'd you know to do that?" asked Tommy as it was easy to see that his legs could have easily been pinned between the tailgate and the ground as the truck drove over the ruts.

Caleb pulled back his pants legs to reveal massive scarring to his shins.

"When Daddy was done with the war, he bought this here truck with his Army money. On Daddy's banking day, he took me, Jesse and Mama with him over to Willis. Whilst he was at the bank, me, Mama and Jesse headed off to the general store. We didn't have no boys then. Jest a tenant. On the way back, Daddy drove over some railroad tracks. Me and Jesse were riding on the back jest like me and you. Jesse raised his legs when Daddy drove over the tracks like I done showed you. I didn't and both my leg bones was squished by them tracks and this here tailgate. I thought it done broke both of my leg bones. All it done was mangle them both up real bad. It hurt like the dickens. I cried all the way home. Daddy told me never to do that no more. That's how I know."

"Caleb … you were really lucky. Why didn't your daddy take you to the hospital to get your legs bandaged?" ask Tommy thinking if he broke a leg and ended up in the hospital, he could get help there.

"Ain't nobody around here can afford no hospital. That's fer rich folks. Mama takes care of us all."

That's great, thought Tommy.

"I'm glad I didn't get hurt. Thanks for warning me."

"Ain't me and you friends?"

"Yes."

"Friends help one another.   Now you best be eating your food before we git to the fields."

Tommy opened the greasy brown paper bag and pulled out what looked to be a small pancake that was dripping in butter. He broke off a piece, smelled it and ate it.

"That there is a hoecake," commented Caleb.

"It's very good. Kinda tastes like cornbread."

"That ain't cornbread. It's a hoecake. I like to sop mine in sorghum."

Tommy pulled the second hoecake out and ate all of it. Then he pulled out a thick slice of fried meat and held it up for Caleb to see.

"Fried fatback."

Hoecakes? Sorghum? Fried fatback? Tommy knew he was in Alabama, but he might as well been in another country, never having heard of any of the food he was eating.

Tommy took a bite of the fatback. While it tasted similar to bacon, it was too salty for him.

"You want this?" he asked Caleb who wasted no time in accepting the offer.

"There ain't no better cook than my mama. And she's got a heap of ribbons from the county fair that say so. Used to be when I was a young'un, her cakes and jellies beat out everbody. But we don't go to the fair no more. Not like we used to did. Ain't got the money. Daddy says the bank took it all."

Tommy took in everything that Caleb was saying. Tommy's dad had always told him that you learned a lot more by listening than you did by talking. And he wanted to know as much as he could about who these people were, where they lived and how he could get out of there. Caleb seemed to be a valuable source and without a doubt, a talker.

Before long, Watson slowed the truck down to a complete stop and killed the engine. Caleb immediately jumped off the back of the truck and helped Tommy down.

"You won't be wearing them leggings long if you don't do anything stupid like run away," repeated Caleb as he helped Tommy to his feet.

"Has anyone ever done that? Run away?"

"Once or twiced."

"What happened to…"

"Okay boys. Times a'wastin'," said Watson as he stepped out of the truck, a newly lit cigarette cupped in his hand. Tippy was not far behind as he cautiously used the running board as a springboard to mother earth. "The cotton ain't gonna pick itself," continued Watson.

He leaned over the side of the truck bed, pulled up a six-foot canvas bag and threw it to Tommy who instinctively caught it.

"That there is your cotton bag. Holds about thirty to forty pounds. You pull it behind you and that's where you stow your pickins'. Caleb…"

"Yes, Daddy."

"Take him out to the field and show him how to pick. And Caleb… no more talking. Jest pickin'. Do I make myself clear?" Watson loved that phrase… *Do I make myself clear?* He'd learned it in Army boot camp. It seemed like all drill instructors used it after every order.

"Yes, Daddy."

Caleb turned to Tommy. "You see that there man on that tractor?" He pointed out towards the middle of the field. "That's my brother Jesse. That's all the fer we has to go." Sheepishly, he looked at his daddy and said, "That's all the talking I'm gonna do."

Watson nodded his head in approval. Then he and Tippy climbed in the truck and headed back to the farm.

Caleb ushered Tommy towards the turnrow, the end of the field where the tractor made its turn. The two walked slowly, side by side, for about twenty rows. Then Caleb turned left and headed down a particular row with Tommy now following close behind. To the left and about halfway down the row, Tommy began seeing other kids about his same age and younger. As he passed by the bobbing heads, a hushed talk began among them. They were all dressed in the cut-off Army fatigues, t-shirt, field cap and cut-off black army boots.

Once they had passed the last picker, Tommy saw Caleb's twin brother sitting on a tractor four or five rows over. Just as he had seen before, a rifle lay across his lap. It was hard to tell if he was asleep or awake with his straw hat pulled down over his eyes… until he yelled.

"Hey boy… what's your name?"

Before Tommy could answer, he heard his twin brother shout out, "Caleb."

"Not you, you moron. The boy."

"Tommy Harrison," answered Tommy.

"Tommy. I don't put up with no shenanigans out here," said Jesse, with the emphasis on *she* in shenanigans. "You are out here to pick cotton. Do I make myself clear?"

The apple doesn't fall far from the tree, thought Tommy, a phrase his mother used many times when he'd done something, good or bad, that reminded her of his dad.

"Yes sir."

"And by the by, this here Winchester thirty aught six, I use it fer hunting, killing snakes and shooting runaways and slackers. Do I make myself clear?" Jesse asked, pushing the bolt handle of his bolt-action rifle forward, searched the skies and quickly fired at a hawk that had been circling above, looking for prey.

The field mouse below whom the hawk had in his sight would live to see another day as the bird fell from the sky.

"Do I make myself clear?" he reiterated.

"Yes sir."

"That there is Jesse. He's my brother," said Caleb, always impressed by anything his twin did. "He's a real good shooter, ain't he?"

Tommy didn't need to answer the obvious.

Once they had reached the beginning of Tommy's assigned row, Caleb bent over the first stalk and began his lesson on the proper way to pick cotton.

"Tommy… you see how I done picked only the big ones? We pick them first then come back later, maybe like a week or so and pick them little ones when they've fully growed out."

Demonstrating again, he grasped a large cotton ball at the base of the plant next to him, twisted the large white fibre out of the boll and stuck it into Tommy's long sack. He did that a number of times with each effort ending in *See?*

"Ouch!" yelled Tommy on his first attempt and immediately jerked his hand back having incorrectly grabbed the prickly burr. He could hear laughter coming from the other pickers which immediately ceased when Jesse fired another load from his shotgun.

Caleb continues his lesson as if nothing ever happened. "Jest grab the big ole ball else you're gonna stick or cut yourself." Caleb demonstrated his technique again but slower. Almost in slow motion. "See?"

Tommy tried again, this time successfully. Then again. And again. It wasn't long before he'd gotten up some speed. Caleb was all smiles as he saw how his student had progressed… and so quickly.

After about an hour of picking and with Caleb's help, Tommy had caught up to the picker on the row adjacent to his.

"What's your name?" asked the young picker quietly as he continued to pick. The boys on the other rows listened in, but their picking never ceased nor did they stop to get a glimpse of the new boy. One warning from Jesse for laughing and not picking was enough.

"Tommy. Tommy Harrison. What's yours?"

"Leroy," he answered as he looked at the shackles on Tommy's feet.

"So you're a runaway. Most of us here came from the orphanage in Waverly Hall, Georgia except Sammy and Claude. Both of them are runaways, too."

"But I'm *not* a runaway," said Tommy as he stood to talk. "I was taken. Ol' man Watson saw …"

A blast from Jesse's rifle stopped him mid-sentence. Both boys and Caleb ducked *after* the bullet flew by taking out a large cotton ball between their rows and only inches from their bodies.

"Leroy," yelled Jesse. "Git your scrawny ass back to pickin'. And Caleb… tell what's his name that I meant what I said about slackers. I ain't got no use fer them."

For Leroy, there was no hesitation as he immediately began to pick as fast as he could.

"Tommy… Jesse ain't kiddin'," said Caleb.

"I can see that," said Tommy who returned to picking while Caleb watched. The banter between Leroy and Tommy had ceased. Jesse had made his point.

Tommy continued to pick for the next hour but without Caleb's help. His speed slowed as his fingers tired, but he was now officially a bobbing head.

"Tommy … I jest seen Daddy drive up. I need to go help him git ready fer the weigh-in. You done real good today. And I like that me and you is friends. Now when you hear Jesse crank up the tractor, that means you bring your bag up to that there cart." Caleb pointed to a tall wood-slatted wagon filled with cotton. "That's where you git your bag weighed." He then left and Tommy went back to picking.

Before long, Tommy heard Jesse's tractor start and watched as it headed towards the cotton wagon as did all the pickers. Tommy grabbed his sack and rushed to catch up with the other boys. Soon he was walking alongside a boy three rows over.

"Hi. I'm Tommy Harrison."

The boy slowed his pace just enough to turn and give Tommy the once-over.

"I'm Ronnie. You the new boy, ain't you?" Ronnie was deeply tanned, had bulging eyes and his eyebrows were arched in such a way that he always had a look of surprise on his face.

"Yes."

Ronnie continued to walk as he talked.

"I can see you ain't from the orphanage."

"No. I'm from Decatur. Decatur, Georgia."

"Seems like I heard Watson say he was gonna git another picker to replace Little Eddie. You must be it."

"Who's Little Eddie? What happened to him? Why did they let him go home?"

"We ain't s'posed to talk about Little Eddie. Ain't nobody knows what happened to him. Most say he done run away."

"Why did he runaway and how?"

"You best talk to Vernon. He knows more than most."

"Which one is Vernon?"

"You'll know when you meet him. Him, Eugene and Charlie are the smart ones of the bunch."

Can't be too smart if they're out here picking cotton, thought Tommy.

CHAPTER 13

Knowing David Rutledge's propensity to talk, whether nervous or not, Broome was well aware of what the two plus hour trip to Decatur, Georgia would entail. A non-stop, mostly one-sided conversation with the boy. And David didn't disappoint.

"My mom likes to say we're two peas in a pod, Tommy and me, because we're always together. We've been that way ever since the third grade. That's when Tommy moved from Atlanta. Mrs. Gibbs, our teacher, sat him next to me because he was the new kid and she knew I got along with everybody… everybody but Nelson Turner. Even though he was new to the class didn't mean he was scared… you know… shy. Before the week was out, everybody in the class knew Tommy Harrison. He made friends real easy. And he was smart. Really smart. I never saw him open his book or skim through his class notes before a test. And he seemed to always make an "A." I mean, I had to study *hard* just to keep up. I was glad to be his best friend. Like I said, we did everything together. Golf, tennis, basketball, ping pong. You name it, we played it… together. Always on the same team. But we didn't only play together. We worked together. Like I told you earlier, we were bottle boys at Venetian Swimming pool, ran a paper route… even tried to start a German Shephard breeding company. We got the male dog… AKC registered and planned to stud him out once he got bigger. Cost us $15. But the dog got distemper and died. Broke our hearts. So his mom went out and got a dog from the pound. His name is Rusty because he's red looking. He's a sweet dog, but we can't breed him because he's not pure-breed and not AKC registered. Last summer, Tommy talked his dad into letting me and him work at their shop a couple of days a week. I wasn't much good at it. I could sweep up and all. But Tommy learned how to repair lawnmowers, bikes, run the cash register. Everything. I only went because of Tommy and the hot dogs at Manuel's Tavern up the street from the shop. And he loved music. All kinds. He even taught himself to play the guitar. Never took a lesson."

David rambled on and on, jumping from one topic to the next. Before the trip ended, Broome felt he knew more about the two boys, especially Tommy, than anyone except their parents.

Once they reached Atlanta, David became more excited and animated as he pointed out familiar sites. The chief had scarcely turned into the driveway of the Rutledge's nice, well-kept, split-level home in Decatur, Georgia when he saw both of David's parents come running out the front door. David's mother had tears running down her face as she hugged her only son. David's father shook the chief's hand, thanked him and after introductions began peppering him with questions.

"So you think Tommy was abducted?"

Maureen Rutledge, David's mother, could see that just the first question upset her son, so she took him into the house and fixed him a bowl of butter pecan ice cream, his and Tommy's favorite.

"That's what little evidence we have points to," answered Broome once Tommy was out of earshot.

"Any chance this might not be a kidnapping but something worse?" asked J. N. Rutledge not having to explain what he meant by *worse*.

"Let's pray it's not." Then, using logic versus first-hand knowledge or experience, he continued. "If it's a kidnapping, the Harrisons should be contacted soon. The longer they... the abductors keep Tommy, the greater the chance of something going wrong or maybe them being caught."

"And if the ransom is paid, what's the likelihood that they won't release Tommy?"

Again, Broome understood the subtlety of the question."

"Being that this took place in South Georgia, I'm guessing... and I have to guess because I have never worked an abduction case nor has there ever been one in Pine Mountain to my knowledge... anyway I'm guessing there's a better chance of his safe release in our neck of the woods than if this had happened here, in Atlanta."

"No offense, but can the FBI, GBI or the State Patrol help? I think the more people looking into this the better."

"None taken. I have contacted the GBI and they are willing to get involved once a ransom note has been received. Until then, it's a wait and see for them. I have not contacted the FBI because unless it's what they call a *Tender Years* kidnapping, one that involves children twelve years of age or younger, they will assist but will leave it up to local authorities unless..."

"Unless the family is rich, famous or politically connected," said J. N. completing Broome's unfinished sentence.

"Unfortunately, Mr. Harrison is just an ordinary citizen, like the rest of us," replied Broome. "So I wouldn't expect much from the FBI. And as for the State Highway Patrol, kidnappings do not fall under their jurisdiction."

"How much do you think the ransom will be assuming this is a kidnapping?"

"I'm guessing it's going to be probably something less than a thousand dollars assuming the abductors are from my area of the state."

J. N. nodded and thought of his own son. The abductors could just as easily have taken him. *But there for the grace of God*, he thought.

"Chief Broome, we love Tommy. He's almost like a son. He and David are inseparable. What can we do to help?"

"With you being this far away, I'm not sure what you can do." Broome wanted to add, *I'm not even sure I know what I can do*, but showing any kind of weakness wouldn't help the situation.

"Do you think it would help if we went with you to see the Harrisons?"

"I appreciate the offer, but I think this is something I need to do… by myself. Speaking of which, I need to get moving. I've got to stop by the Decatur Police station before I see the Harrisons. I want the locals involved." He turned and headed towards his car.

"Just one last thing," said J. N., walking alongside the chief. "The Harrisons are good people… salt of the earth. I don't know if David told you, but they own a bicycle/lawnmower shop."

"Yes. He told me a lot about them… and Tommy."

"That sounds like my son. A talkative one, he is." J. N. paused to craft his next few sentences. "The Harrisons are not rich people. And they are very proud. When the ransom note arrives, I'm assuming they will show it to you."

"Yes. Me and the GBI."

"Regardless of the amount, the Harrisons are going to pay even if that means selling their house, business… everything. I know I would if I were them. But I don't want that to happen. This abduction… it's already *more* than any family should bear. If it's not asking too much, please let me help with the money. We have been most fortunate. The Good Lord has blessed us and I don't mind sharing. Do you think that's possible?"

"If I can make that happen, I will."

"Thank you. And it has to be anonymous."

"Understood."

The chief gave J. N. a business card with the phone number of the Pine Mountain Police Department with his home phone number written on the back, got into his car but not before retrieving David's golf clubs and backpack and setting them to the side of the car. That's when he saw David running from his house, yelling.

"Stop. Wait. I want to go with you! I want to help find Tommy. Please. Pleeeeaaaasssse!"

The angst in David's face and voice caused J. N.'s eyes to well up as did the chief's.

Broome put his arm around the boy. He wasn't sure what his next step would be in locating Tommy, but he knew for certain it didn't involve having a young teenager underfoot.

"David, I'm sorry, but this is a police matter. I know you want to help, but I can't take you back to Pine Mountain and I know your folks won't let me. You just stay put. I'll make sure you and your family know what progress we're making. I promise."

David nodded his head, but he wasn't happy. Nothing would make him happy except seeing his best friend.

As the chief backed the car out of the driveway, J. N. picked up the backpack and David slung his golf clubs around his shoulder.

"I hate golf," he said as he walked towards the house, his head hanging down. He looked like he had just lost his best friend. And he had.

CHAPTER 14

The City of Decatur is a four-square mile, bedroom community of 22.000 people, located six miles east of Atlanta. Its police department and the City Hall occupy the same red brick building found on the corner of McDonough Street and Trinity Avenue, just down the street from the DeKalb County courthouse.

Using a map that Betty had drawn, Broome easily found the building, parked his car in the back, near the side entrance and entered the station. Once inside, he engaged the desk sergeant who was standing behind a long counter. After a short wait, Broome was ushered into Chief Barry Manning's office. The two men shook hands, exchanged pleasantries and Broome relayed the details of the Harrison boy's abduction and the GBI's rebuff.

"*Is he a white boy?*" asked Chief Manning, rhetorically, while shaking his head. "That sounds like something Stephens (GBI Director) would say. I know both families. Good people. I'll be glad to help in any way. But I'm not sure what I can do."

"Just keep an eye on them, especially David. He's really upset which is to be expected. And, if it's okay with you, I am going to ask the Harrisons to contact you first, if and when they get a ransom demand and then have you call me. Hopefully I can get the GBI involved."

"That works for me. So you haven't seen the Harrisons yet?"

"No. I was going to call my office to get an update before talking to them."

"Good idea. You can use my phone."

The two exchanged business cards and Manning left his office to give his Pine Mountain counterpart some privacy.

"Betty. Any news on the boy?"

"If you mean has he been found? No."

"Is Lewis there?"

"Yes."

"Let me speak to him."

Broome paced back and forth going as far as the phone cord would allow until Lewis answered.

"Yes sir," answered Lewis, sitting in the chief's chair.

"Did you go back out to the campsite like I told you?"

"Yes sir. Stayed an hour. While I was there, I got to thinking. You know Buddy's not the dog he used to be. He's getting old. Could be his smelling glands are off. I wanted to make sure we didn't miss anything, so I called Wallace… he's my hunting buddy. I got him to bring his dog Radar out to the park. I had him and Radar follow the boy's scent. He ended up on the highway at the same spot as me and Buddy. I also had them check up and down the road for about a quarter of a mile both ways, hoping they might pick up the scent again. Nothing. But I did find a cigarette butt right where the scent ended. It might not mean a thing. Just in case, I saved it in an envelope for you."

"Lewis… you might make a good cop yet," said Broome laughing. "You did the right thing. When I get back, I want you to show me where you found it."

"Yes sir. Also, I checked in the golf shop, but they had nothing new to offer. So I guess we're no better off than when you left."

"Yeah. I know. Now I got to go tell that to the boy's parents. If anything changes, I want you to call Chief Barry Manning with the City of Decatur Police Department. He'll know what to do." Broome rattled off Manning's phone number from Manning's business card.

On the way out of Chief Manning's office, Broome found him in the common area and the two walked out to Broome's car. As they did, Broome told the Decatur chief about J. N. Rutledge's offer to help with the ransom.

"Like I said, good people. Plus, I'm sure J. N. has the money. He works for BellSouth. Some sort of manager there."

Broome drove out of the parking lot and once again, following Betty's detailed map, he found the Harrison's house. It was a gray brick, ranch style home… nice but not in the same class as the Rutledge's. If the abductors were looking for a large ransom, they had chosen the wrong boy. Tommy's parents were out the front door even before Broome turned into their driveway. What Broome had to tell them would not change the worried look on either parent's face.

Dorothy Harrison, the mother, was the first to reach Broome's car. Before speaking to the chief who had his window rolled down, she peered into the passenger side of the car and then the back seat. While she did not expect to see her son in the car, the fact that he wasn't actually there made the whole situation real. She began to cry and turned to hug her husband.

The chief stepped out of his car with his peaked cap in his right hand and an old Army leather satchel in the other.

"I'm Chief Jim Broome from Pine Mountain. I'm the one who called about your son."

"Tom Harrison," said the sullen, athletic looking man, shaking hands with the officer. Broome noticed the grease stains on a blue uniform shirt that had "Tom" stitched above the left shirt pocket and "Little 5 Points / Bicycle & Lawnmower" above the right pocket. An occupational hazard of working in a repair shop. "I'm Tommy's dad and this is Dorothy, my wife and Tommy's mother." Dorothy Harrison, a brown head, brown eyed, attractive woman, turned from her husband's shoulder and shook the chief's hand. Her eyes were red and had tears welled up in them.

"So you still haven't found Tommy?" she asked and afterwards wondered why she had, seeing that no one had been in the car but the policeman.

"No ma'am. Do you mind if we talk inside?"

Both husband and wife nodded, turned and headed up to their house. Once inside, Dorothy offered Broome a seat in a nearby stuffed, slightly frayed chair. The parents sat down on an adjacent sofa. Scattered on a nearby coffee table were a number of photos of Tommy... some framed, some not. Broome had asked the parents for a recent picture when he called them before leaving Pine Mountain.

The house was neat, clean but very average. It could very easily be a home in Pine Mountain. Broome told the anxious parents everything that he knew and what he didn't know. Nothing he said calmed the parents nor did he expect it would.

"What do we do now?" asked Tom Harrison. "Wait for a ransom note?"

"Yes... unless," said the chief thinking about what J. N. Rutledge had said, *Any chance this might not be a kidnapping but something worse.* He wished he'd just left it at *Yes.*"

"What do you mean... *unless?*" asked Dorothy Harrison, an even more worried look now cloaking her face.

"I'm sorry. That was a poor choice of words. Typically, most abductors just want money, plain and simple," said Broome, speaking off the cuff and trying not to upset the mother even more than he already had. "And if not, then usually the victim is a female and might have been taken for other reasons. My thoughts are, Tommy is being held for ransom."

"But what if we can't come up with the money? What if it's too much or we don't have time to get what they want. What happens then? We can't let our son die…" She then burst into tears. "I knew I shouldn't have let him and David go camping. Oh God! What was I thinking?" she asked rhetorically, wiping the tears from her eyes with her hands.

"Honey, you can't beat yourself up. If anyone's at fault here, it's me. I should have gone with them. They've never gone camping by themselves. I've always gone with them. And *I'm* the one who said that *nothing* could happen."

Broome felt he needed to step in. Laying blame wasn't going to help anybody.

"Neither one of you is at fault. Tommy just happened to be in the wrong place at the wrong time. And as far as the money goes, we have a fund that will cover the ransom."

It was the first thing that Broome had said that seemed to bring comfort to the parents.

"What happens when we get a ransom note or a phone call demanding money?" asked Tom. "What do we do?"

"I want you to contact Chief Barry Manning at the City of Decatur Police Department… immediately. Under no circumstance do you take matters into your own hands. Once you've contacted Chief Manning, he will call me and we will get the GBI involved. They are more experienced in handling these types of cases."

"Why aren't they involved now… the GBI?" asked Tom.

Good question, thought Broome. "Until there's a ransom note, there's not much any of us can do. My men have searched the park multiple times using two different tracking dogs. Each time, the scent ended in the middle of the same road at the same location. We even had them search the highway in both directions hoping the dog might catch a scent but with no luck."

"So all we do is sit around waiting for a ransom note?" asked Dorothy. Her sarcastic, yet concerned tone of voice did not go unnoticed by either Broome or her husband, Tom.

"I'm afraid that all we *can* do is just wait," replied Broome. "But I really don't think we'll be waiting long. Possibly less than seventy-two hours. Kidnappers like to act fast. The longer they have the victim in their presence, the more exposure they have and the more likely something might go wrong. I'm thinking they will contact you sooner than later. Believe me, I don't like this as much as…" Broome stopped midsentence. There was no way that he could compare himself to a mother or father who had just lost their child and might never get him back. He then reached over and picked up a few of the unframed pictures of the boy from off the coffee table. He silently examined them.

"Can I take these?"

"Yes. Take what you need," said Tom Harrison. Then pointing to one particular photo, he added, "This picture of him and David might be the best. It was taken this past April by Mr. Rutledge at a Master's practice round. Tommy's hair was long then. We don't have any of him with his flattop."

"Thank you. These are perfect." Broome slipped that one and a few more into his satchel and stood up. There was no more he could do at the Harrison's. "They will help… a lot. When I get back to Pine Mountain, I will make sure they get passed around to all my men. He didn't have the heart to tell them that he only had two men and one woman in his office. I'll also stick one up in my office, one in the lobby and another in the post office. Who knows, maybe somebody saw what happened. Maybe even recognize the vehicle. Pine Mountain isn't very large and most everybody knows everybody. Hopefully, something will turn up."

"Well, I can tell you one thing," said Tom as he and Dorothy stood. "My boy's a fighter. And he's smart. If there's any way he can get out of this mess, he will."

Broome pulled out a business card and pen from his satchel and wrote down Chief Manning's name and phone number on the back just under his own home telephone number. He handed the card to Tom's outstretched hand.

"Those are my phone numbers and Chief Manning's. Anytime you need to just talk or have a question, call me, collect, anytime, day or night."

That was all Broome had to offer. There was nothing he had said or could say to relieve the Harrison's angst. Unless the abductor contacted the Harrisons, the boy's body was found or he just showed up at the golf club or campsite, his investigation was finished other than passing around a few photos. This is not how he liked to work.

CHAPTER 15

Tommy's back, legs, arms, fingers … every part of his body hurt. It had been the hardest three hours of work in his young life. Yet, he had not worked nearly as long as the other eleven pickers.

It was Tommy's first weigh-in and he was last in line which gave him an opportunity to understand the process. If he was ever going to find a way out of this place, he needed to know more about farm life and where he might find an opportunity to escape.

Tommy observed that the boys would line up just to the right of a big, wood-slatted wagon that was filled with cotton. They would bring their sack to Jesse who would hang it on a hook attached to a scale. Watson would read the bag's weight and write the number in a gray ledger book. Once Jesse saw his daddy nod his head, he would return the sack to the boy who would carry it over to Caleb. Caleb would take the sack, climb a ladder attached to the side of the cotton wagon and dump its contents in with the other cotton. He would then throw the sack back to the boy who would then head to the back of the Watson's truck where they would stand around, drinking water from a large bucket which had about three dipping cups.

Unlike in the field where Jesse kept talking to a minimum, at the weigh-ins with Watson present, there seemed to be no restrictions on the incessant chatter or laughter.

When it was Tommy's turn at the scale, Jesse grabbed his bag and hooked it on the scale. Watson leaned over and looked at the needle until it stopped wavering.

"Tommy … you done real good today. Real good. I watched you from the truck. Son … you keep this up, you ain't gonna be wearing those leggings too long. I believe the Lord done sent me a good one this time." Then Watson smiled at him and nodded his head.

Tommy thought it was in his best interest not to tell the old man that Caleb helped fill his bag. Not if it meant the shackles would be removed sooner than later. So he didn't. Instead, he shuffled over to Caleb, handed him his bag and then shuffled over to the water bucket and pulled out a full dipping cup of water. He expected the boys to inundate him with questions once he had his fill of water. Instead, after Jesse had put the scale away, they ran to the slatted wagon, climbed the ladder to the top and jumped into the cotton like they were jumping into a swimming pool.

Tommy hung the dipping cup on the side of the water bucket and was about to head over to the wagon to join in the fun when one of the boys who had stayed behind put his hand out to stop him.

"Ain't no way you can climb in that wagon. Not with them leggings on. Me and you is gonna have to ride on the back of the truck," said a pudgy, black-haired boy with a hint of facial hair growing over his upper lip. "My name is Clarence."

"Tommy."

Clarence then jumped up on the back of the truck and reached down towards Tommy.

"Grab aholt."

Tommy extended his hand and Clarence who had strength along with girth easily hoisted him onto the tailgate. Clarence grabbed the empty cotton sack from Tommy's hand and threw it on top of the other sacks.

Watson, who was in the truck and had been closely watching the two boys from his rear-view mirror, waited until they were seated, then pulled the truck in behind the cotton wagon as it headed back to the farmhouse.

"Thanks for the lift. I appreciate it," said Tommy.

"I ain't that nice. Ol' man Watson told me I had to make sure you got on the truck. If you wanna know the truth of the matter, I'd druther have been on the cotton wagon. It's a heap more fun and a whole lot more comfortable. I fergit your name already, but mine is Clarence in case you done fergot. Just so you know, sometimes Jesse calls me Porky... you know... like Porky Pig 'cause I'm so fat."

Tommy looked at the boy. He was slightly overweight, but not so much that anyone should call him Porky.

"I'm Tommy."

Clarence looked at the shackles on Tommy's legs and then his hands that bore no callouses and were covered with dirt and traces of blood.

"You ain't never picked cotton before, has you?"

"First time."

"You'll git used to it … the picking, the sun, the dirt, the back pain and Jesse."

"How long have you been here?"

"Almost three years. Me, Charlie, Ronnie, JoJo, Larry and Clint was the first boys that Watson got after the tenants done left. Excepting Larry and Clint, we all come from the orphanage over in Waverly. Larry and Clint was runaways that Watson got at the po'lice station. But they ain't here no more. They stole off after only two days, during lunch break. I reckon they figured that they wouldn't be seen when they snuck off. But ol' man Watson … he sees everthing … at least when he used to work the fields. He had Jesse take off after them. Next thing we know, we heard some shots ring out. The only thing Jesse brung back was them boy's shoes. He hung them in the hall fer a couple of weeks. Nobody knows if they got away or not. But after seeing them shoes with what looked like blood on them, ain't nobody gonna run away no more. Just to make sure, the next thing we know, Watson had Jesse put iron bars on our windows and a lock on the front door. Then he made us all wear them leggings like you got on."

Tommy thought for a second. He remembered another boy … Ronnie … mentioning that someone named Little Eddie might have run away.

"What about a boy named Eddie? Didn't he run away?

"We ain't s'posed to talk about Little Eddie."

"Why? What happened to him?"

Clarence looked back over his shoulder at the truck's rear window to make sure the old man wasn't looking at them through his rear-view mirror. Then in a whisper even though his voice couldn't be heard over the loud noise of the truck's motor, he continued.

"Little Eddie… we called him Little Eddie because he were the smallest and youngest boy of the bunch. Anyways, Watson picked him up from the orphanage before the start of cotton planting time. That's when we put down the seeds. It ain't hard like picking the cotton. Anyways, nobody figured he'd last more than a few weeks because he were so small. Not only that, he looked like a girl. And *you know* girls ain't real good doing man's work. But he kept up with the best of us. Missus Watson liked him the best. Then one night, about a month ago, I heard him crying. Just after he'd taken his Saturday night shower and right after he had a little set-to with Jesse. Now … Little Eddie … he never took no guff off nobody, not Watson, Jesse… not nobody. I don't know what Jesse did or said to hurt that boy's feelings, but I heard him crying well into the night. Anyways, the next day, Sunday, I knew something weren't right with him. He were always a quiet boy, but that Sunday, he stayed to himself even more so and hardly ate any of the Sunday lunch. And that's the best meal we git all week. The next day, we all went to the cotton fields and he was left behind to do chores. A short time later, Missus Watson come running to the field. She, Watson and Jesse jumped into the truck and skedaddled back to the farmhouse leaving Caleb to mind us. About an hour or so later, ol' man Watson returned. He didn't say nuttin'. But later that night, Caleb told Vernon … he's the real smart picker. Anyways, he told Vernon that Little Eddie done run off. Out towards what's left of the old plantation. That he done got clean away. Now Vernon …"

Before Clarence could finish his sentence, the truck came to a halt just behind the cotton wagon outside the workers' cabin. Clarence immediately jumped off the back of the truck and turned to help Tommy making sure he didn't fall as he slid off the back of the truck.

"What did Vernon say about Eddie?" asked Tommy.

Clarence gave him a frown and shook his head as he saw Watson heading towards them.

"Clarence… make sure Tommy gits to the cabin alright."

"Yes sir."

Tommy tried to talk as they walked up onto the porch of the workers' cabin, but Clarence kept shushing him. They waited in line behind the last boy as Caleb did a count of every boy as they walked through the door."

"Ten," said Caleb as Sammy passed by him. "Clarence … you make eleven and Tommy, you make twelve. All present and accounted fer." Another military term Watson had instilled in his sons.

"Your daddy told me to bring Tommy to the cabin. So here he is," said Clarence and then he left.

"Plop yourself down in that there chair and I'll be right back," replied Caleb.

He watched Tommy sit and then walked over to the front door, pulled his keys from around his neck and locked the door. He checked to make sure it was secure and returned to Tommy. He then knelt down and removed the leg irons and hung them on a nearby peg that already held two other pair of shackles.

"I don't have to wear these anymore?" asked Tommy, surprised that Watson had let Caleb take them off so soon. Not the two weeks like he'd understood. Had Caleb made a mistake?

"Can't sleep with them things on. But I has to put them back on you tomorrow morning, right after breakfast. I'm sorry, little buddy."

"That's okay. I understand."

But he didn't understand. Not that, nor why Watson had kidnapped him. Nor why he had even gotten in the old man's truck. Nor how he could get himself out of this mess. But Little Eddie did.

He needed to talk to someone named Vernon.

CHAPTER 16

The sun was setting when Chief Broome pulled in to the parking lot of Pine Mountain's police station. The outside lights were on, but he knew by now that everybody would have gone home. Police stations in small towns did not stay open twenty-four hours a day nor on Sundays… not like the big cities. No budget and no reason. There was very little crime in Pine Mountain except of the few occasional unruly locals or misbehaving guests at the Callaway Gardens resort. But a visit by the chief or one of his deputies who'd show up with their patrol car's red dome light flashing and possibly their siren blaring, and everything would be back to small town normal.

On Broome's desk was a white envelope which had *Evidence* handwritten on the outside. Underneath the envelope was the police report on the missing boy. Lewis had filled in as much as he could. He was a good cop. He was going to make a fine chief one day… maybe sooner than later.

Broome opened the envelope and dumped out the spent butt. Instinctively he leaned over and smelled the contents. *Awful smell,* thought the non-smoker. Using the eraser portion of a pencil, he rolled the butt over and over, examining it as he did. There were no traces of lipstick which might indicate the smoker was a man… or not. He also saw a portion of the brand name that had not been smoked away. Old Gold. Using the pencil, he rolled the cigarette back into the envelope. He considered getting out the department's fingerprint kit, dusting the cigarette and lifting any prints found on the butt using the adhesive tape. But he'd never used the kit before. And he'd only had a ten-minute overview from the former chief, Warren Johnson. He had no qualms about calling Johnson and asking him for help with the kit and even the investigation, but the old chief had died less than six months after retiring. Not to mention, he wasn't real sure what he would do with the prints if he found any. Instead, Broome decided either he or one of his deputies would drive the cigarette butt to the GBI lab in Atlanta on Monday. There, the technicians could process the evidence and if any prints were found, store them for future comparison should a suspect be apprehended.

Broome sealed the envelope and set it in his right-hand top drawer. He picked up the police report and scanned it. Lewis had been very thorough in his work. Broome added a few notes from his talk with the Harrisons and Rutledges and filed the report in the fifth of the five filing cabinets that lined the wall behind his desk.

As he closed the drawer to the cabinet, he thought about all of the cases that had been filed while he had served as Pine Mountain's Chief of Police. Nothing like this had ever happened before. *Why now?* He thought. He wasn't trained nor did he have the experience to handle such an investigation. The job was only supposed to be *temporary* until the town council found a more qualified candidate. He was a retired Lieutenant Colonel having served in the U.S. Army for twenty years with his last assignment being at Fort Benning, Georgia as Commander of the Adjutant General Battalion. He handled new recruits as they entered basic training. He and his wife, Ruth Ann, had moved to Pine Mountain to be near her aging and ailing mother. It was Ruth Ann's brother who was on the town council who coaxed Broome into back-filling the job as chief. No more than six months was all he said. Now, four years later, he was still chief. The council had stopped looking for anyone else the day Broome put on the chief's uniform. And to be honest, he had enjoyed the work, the people and feeling productive.

Broome shook his head. *Water under the bridge,* he thought. He was the chief and he was responsible for the investigation. His mind wandered back to the Harrisons. They seemed like a fine family. And from what David had told him, Tommy seemed like the all-American boy. Why was he taken? Was it happenstance? Was someone driving down the road, saw him as an opportunity to make some quick money and snatched him? Or… Or… could it have been an accident? Could someone have hit him with their car and they carried him to a hospital? Why hadn't he thought of that earlier? It made perfect sense. Both dogs had lost Tommy's scent in the middle of the highway. Excited at his newfound theory, Broome picked up his phone, dialed the operator and had her connect him to Meriwether Memorial Hospital in Warm Springs, the newest hospital in the area and only about ten miles away. As he waited for an attendant to answer, the thought occurred to him… what if it *was* an accident, and the boy lay injured in the hospital and the GBI *had* jumped in to investigate an abduction. Talk about an embarrassment. And what about the Harrisons and the Rutledges? Had he caused unnecessary heartache, stress and angst in those fine folks? Talk about poor police work. Before he had time to berate himself anymore, an admitting clerk picked up the phone and informed Broome that no young boy had been brought into the hospital suffering from a vehicular accident or for any other reason for that matter. Not since Thursday night.

Broome hung up and immediately called the next two closest hospitals, City-County Hospital in LaGrange, Georgia and St. Francis in Columbus, Georgia. The same answer. Neither hospital had admitted or treated a young boy involved in any kind of auto accident in the last twenty-four hours. Broome felt guilty that he was relieved that his incompetent work would never be discovered. Then another thought occurred to him. What if it had been an accident and Tommy had been killed and the driver grabbed the body and dumped it some remote area in Georgia or Alabama, possibly never to be found. He didn't like that scenario at all, but it was one that needed to be investigated. Instinctively, he pulled out a yellow legal pad and began creating a list of things to do, starting with the trip to the GBI lab. Fortunately… or unfortunately, it was a short list.

Once he had finished, he opened up his satchel, stuck the legal pad into one of its pockets and pulled out the pictures of Tommy and spread them out on his desk. He was a cute boy, looking more like his father than his mother. And like David had said, he was small for his age. He could easily pass for twelve or thirteen. He grabbed his satchel, the picture of Tommy and David at the Masters and left his office, closing the door behind him. On the way out of the building, he stopped by the bulletin board and pinned the picture where anyone who entered the building could see. He would never forget that face. He hoped the boy was alive and the fighter that his father said he was. Otherwise…

CHAPTER 17

Ruth Ann Broome saw her husband's patrol car's headlights shine on the kitchen wall as he turned into the driveway. It was unusual for him to be coming home so late, but Betty had called her earlier and told her about the missing boy and Broome's trip to Atlanta, so it wasn't unexpected. Normally, dinner was at six, no sooner… no later… a habit he had acquired in the military and continued after his retirement. Knowing he would be late, Ruth Ann made his favorite meal, one that could simmer on the stove until he arrived, regardless of the time. Pot roast. This was normally their Sunday, after church meal, but she figured he needed it tonight.

"Something smells good," said Broome as he walked through the back screen door, holding his cap in one hand and his leather satchel in the other.

"Thought you could use a good meal after what you went through today. Any news on the boy?"

"No. None. It's like he just disappeared."

"I know his parents have got to be devastated."

"That's an understatement. Not to mention his best friend who reported him missing. The look on his face as I left his house this afternoon… I still can't get it out of my mind. It was so sad … it'd break your heart."

Ruth Ann had leaky eyes, so the tears came easily as she hugged her husband while thinking about the lost boy.

"Oh Jim, I'm so sorry. What do you do now?"

"Ruthie…" Broome thought for a second as he set his satchel and cap on the table and sat down in one of the gray-vinyl covered dinette chairs. "I just don't know. I'm really at a loss. You know I was never trained for this kind of work. And I can't get any help from the GBI. They're too busy helping the FBI chase down some black preacher man and forgetting about our Georgia citizens. I pray the boy is alive. That he's lost or at worse, kidnapped, and all they want is some ransom money. I know I'd pay if he were my boy."

There was a sadness to his face as he talked. He and Ruth Ann had never been able to have any children of their own. Each spouse bore the blame for their childlessness. She felt her age at the time of their marriage, thirty-eight, worked against her. He blamed his Army career, World War II and everything else other than Ruth Ann. But it wasn't because they didn't try.

He and Ruth Ann met at Fort Benning, Georgia in early 1941. She was a typist in the Women's Army Axillary Corp (WACs) and he was a sergeant, enrolled in the Infantry Officer Candidate's School. Six months later to the day, Saturday, December 6, 1941, Second Lieutenant James William Broome and Ruth Ann Freeman were married in the Fort Benning Infantry Chapel. The following day, the Japanese bombed Pearl Harbor and their Honeymoon to Daytona Beach was cancelled. Within months, he was shipped out to England. He distinguished himself on the battle field, fighting in the Battle of the Bulge where he earned a battlefield promotion to captain and a Silver Star for his heroism. His last war-time military duty was the Korean War where he was promoted to Major. Before retiring from the Army, he had reached the rank of Lieutenant Colonel.

Ruth Ann watched her husband's head and shoulders slump down as he sat in a kitchen chair. She felt somewhat guilty that her husband seemed so defeated. After all, it was she and her brother that had been the ones who pushed Broome to take the job as Chief of Police for Pine Mountain. The city needed a chief and Ruth Ann needed her husband to get out of the house and do something besides sit in his recliner watching TV.

"Can I get you a beer while I finish up dinner?" she asked, hoping to improve his mood.

"No. I just want to sit here and think." He pulled out the legal pad from his satchel and started reviewing his notes.

Ruth Ann left him alone and returned to the stove where she whipped up some mash potatoes, heated up some leftover butterbeans, placed the homemade biscuits in the oven and poured a couple of glasses of sweet iced tea.

Once they had blessed the food, Broome mowed through his dinner hardly saying a word as he ate. He finished it before Ruth Ann was half way through. The speed in which he devoured his food was another acquired habit leftover from the military. Only tonight, he seemed to be even faster… like he was in a race to get somewhere. But there was nowhere to go.

"That was delicious. Thank you," he said, then took a swig of his tea and sat the glass down, staring at the far wall, looking at nothing in particular.

Ruth Ann wondered if he'd even tasted her meal. Even though she had hardly finished half her meal, she couldn't eat any more for worrying over Jim's state of depression. It had been a long time since she had seen him this deeply worried about anything. She picked up both plates and took them over to the kitchen sink where she scraped the remains into a trash can. She then set them down in the sink and return to the table.

Jim who was in deep thought, still staring at the far wall, never saw Ruth Ann sit down beside him. When he laid the pen down, she reached over with her hand and placed it on his. He knew he wasn't alone. He looked over at her and smiled.

"You want to talk about it?" she asked. "It might be good for you. Something might come to mind."

Jim nodded. Ruth Ann had always been his sounding board, so he told her everything he knew about the case and what had been done including his visit to the two families in Decatur.

"This is awful," said Ruth Ann. "So no one saw the boy being taken?"

"Not that we know."

"And you're sure that he was taken and not lost in the woods somewhere?"

"Yes! Yes! He *had* to be taken," he said with a raised voice. "We had two different dogs at two different times follow his trail to the middle of the highway about a mile from the golf course and that's where it stopped."

He then looked up and saw the hurt look on Ruth Ann's face.

"I'm sorry, Ruthie. I shouldn't be taking my frustrations out on you. It's that … that I feel lost. I have this hopeless feeling and I'm not sure what more I can do."

Ruth Ann understood. It was the same feeling she had about being childless … hopeless.

"Apology accepted. Now let's move on." She thought for a second. "Have you checked with the hospitals? Quite possibly, he could have gotten hurt in the woods or hit by a car and someone carried him there."

"Ruthie… you're better at this than me. I didn't even think of that until about an hour ago. But no, I don't think that happened. I called every hospital in the area and nothing. Plus, there was no blood on the pavement where the dogs lost his scent."

"And they've checked the golf course? Maybe someone picked him up and let him out at the wrong entrance. Is there an employee's entrance or maintenance entrance?"

"There's only one entrance for guests and workers on that road. Not only that … they've turned the golf course upside down looking for the boy. He's not there. He has to have been abducted."

"What do you do now?"

Jim looked down at the yellow legal pad where he'd written down a 'to-do' list for him and his deputies, Lewis Phillips and Bob Galloway.

"Monday, I'm gonna have Lewis drive a possible piece of evidence to the GBI lab in Atlanta and have them analyze it … check it out for fingerprints. It's a cigarette butt that we found on the highway where the dogs lost the boy's scent. And Bob, I'm gonna have him drive over to the *Daily News* in LaGrange. Have them run the boy's picture in the paper for the next week or so. I'm hoping someone will have seen the kid. While Betty holds down the fort, I'm going to drive over to the Sheriff's department and see if they can help. Other than that, we wait for the kidnappers to contact the boy's parents."

"Jim… this would have happened regardless of who was chief. It just so happened to be you."

"Yeah … but *I am the chief* and whatever happens to this boy is all anybody will ever remember me for. Ruthie, I'm not feeling sorry for myself. I just wish I could think of something … do something more to help find this boy. You've been real helpful. I'm glad we talked. But I'm lost. Totally lost."

CHAPTER 18

Sarah and Henry sat alone at the dinner table, both having finished their supper. Neither of their sons ate with them on Saturdays unless it was Christmas. Jesse would dine on a sack lunch while he waited at the Willis Cotton Gin to have their cotton weighed and sold. And Caleb would eat at the workers' cabin with the pickers, making sure the boys had enough to eat and got their weekly shower. Only Tippy graced their presence as he lay on the wooden floor between the diners ready to pounce on any morsel of food that might be dropped . While his eyes were shut, his ears and smell remained on high alert.

Watson took out his pack of Old Golds, popped out a cigarette and then offered one to Sarah who accepted. She never smoked around her sons or any of the boys, but most knew she did. He pulled the matches from a top pocket from his bib overalls, lit his then used the same match to light hers. Neither spoke while they enjoyed their after-dinner smoke followed by a coughing bout by Henry.

"Them cigarettes gonna kill us, Henry. I hear you coughing more and more every day and I ain't much better."

"Sarah … you *know* the Lord ain't gonna take us until He's ready, so it don't matter what we say or do."

There was silence for a few minutes as Henry pulled out another cigarette, offering one to Sarah, who refused. Instead, she stood, took their plates over to the sink and began washing them. Watson made use of the time to look at the day's weigh-ins from his gray ledger book and add up the week's total pickings. When Sarah returned to the table, she found Tippy in her chair eating the leftovers from the dinner bowls.

"Git!" she shouted, shooing the dog down from the table. "Henry … I reckon you didn't see that ol' flea bag eating tomorrow's lunch, not with your head stuck down in that there book."

Henry looked up, oblivious to the dog or what Sarah had said, more interested in his numbers.

"What you yapping about, woman? Can't you see my brain's a'thinking?"

"When your brain ain't a'thinking, I'd like to know how that new boy done out in the field today? He worth keeping?"

Watson smiled. "That boy … Tommy … he done real good fer his first day." Watson elongated *real* to make his point. "Matter of fact, he nearbout outdid Sammy and Claude on the last weigh-in."

"Well … that ain't no surprise. 'Specially Sammy. All him and his brother wants to do is fish."

"You got that right."

Sarah sat back down, took the cigarette from Watson, took a puff and handed it back.

"Henry… I'm worried. You said that boy, Tommy, were a runaway and a thief. You sure you ain't got that wrong? He don't seem like none of them things to me. He's got manners. He don't look beat up. He weren't dirty and smelly like them other runaways you brung here. And he weren't in need of no haircut. What if you was wrong and the po'lice come looking fer him? We can't have that. I ain't sure we ought to keep him."

Watson hated it when he was challenged.

"Looky here, woman. I seen what I seen. I know he done stole them golfing sticks and spikedy shoes from that there golfing place in Georgia and was running away. I done him a *favor* by not turning him in to the po'lice. I brung him to the farm to set him on the straightening arrow. Besides, we got cotton to pick. And corn and peanuts. We need help and the orphanage is closed, so I ain't got no place to git kids no more. And finding runaways ain't easy. We done lost Little Eddie. I ain't gonna loose Tommy. He's a good picker, so we're keeping him. Be-ins how I found him in Georgia and this here is Alabama, ain't no po'lice gonna cross no state lines looking fer some runaway. Do I make myself clear?" Watson immediately wished he had stopped talking a sentence earlier.

"Henry Watson … don't you go talking to me like I'm one of them picker boys… or… or Caleb," she said giving Watson the evil eye. "I ain't that old and I ain't that weak. So you best watch your tongue if you know what's good fer you. And you best keep an eye on that boy."

Sarah had made herself perfectly clear.

CHAPTER 19

Once Tommy's shackles were removed, he made a dash for the privy line, awaiting his turn. When he exited, Caleb was standing outside the door. He ushered Tommy over to the long, wooden table in the center of the big hall that was filled with dishes of food. Other boys were already at the table, standing behind a chair with their field cap removed and hung on the ladder-back's post. Tommy could see how young looking they were. All of them were about his age although he knew he looked younger. And everyone had a buzz cut, similar to his flattop. What seemed strange to him was that they all seemed happy. Not like himself who couldn't keep from thinking about his mom and dad, his friend David and finding a way out.

Once all the boys were at the table, Caleb nodded and everyone sat down with their hands folded, ready for Caleb's quick prayer,

"The Lord giveth. And the Lord taketh away. Bless this food. Amen."

After the prayer, Caleb stood and pulled out a piece of paper with all the names of the boys scribbled down in the order of the total weight of their weekly pickings. He proceeded to call out the list, stopping between names to allow for the catcalls, groans and cheers from the boys. Tommy's name, to no surprise, was called out last.

Once Caleb had sat down, the boys immediately picked up the bowl of food in front of them, took a descent helping and passed it to the left. Tommy took notice and did the same. At first, there was hardly any talking among the boys as they began devouring the food like they hadn't eaten in a week. Caleb had been right about his mother's cooking. It was really good although Tommy wasn't really sure what some of the vegetables were.

As soon as the boys began taking second helpings, their silence ended with almost everyone asking Tommy questions. What was his name? How old was he? Where was he from? Why had he run away? Did he know his parents? Had he ever been in a foster home or orphanage? And even though he said that Watson had abducted him, a word most of the boys didn't recognize or understand, their questions seemed to err on the side of Watson … that he was a runaway, because of the shackles.

Caleb wasn't interested in the boys' questions or Tommy's answers, only eating which he did quite vigorously.

When the meal was over, so was the boys' interest in Tommy. Instead, they quickly lined up for their turn in the shower. The order of the queue was based on Caleb's list. Each picker was allowed five minutes in the bathroom, or privy as everyone on the farm called it. Caleb stood just outside the door with his watch timing everyone. When he knocked, they had about thirty seconds to finish whatever they were doing. With Tommy being last, his wait was nearly an hour before his turn at the facilities. This gave him plenty of time to understand the process.

Before each boy entered the bathroom, they would grab a clean t-shirt and a clean pair of underwear off a shelf just outside the door. When they exited, they would toss their dirty clothes in a large open box underneath the shelf. Then they would walk over to a large open pie safe which was positioned just outside each of the bunkrooms where they would pick up a set of clean work clothes before heading into their assigned room. It was very well organized.

Once it was Tommy's turn, he quickly stripped and hopped in the shower finding the rectangle bar of homemade soap just to the right of the door. Unlike the yellow and green tile in his shower at home that his mother kept spotless, this one had gray concrete walls and floors. It was very dark inside with the only light coming from a hanging bulb over the sink. He found the faucets, turned the left one on and waited for the water to turn hot. That didn't happen. The cold shower was very invigorating.

Once he heard Caleb's knock, Tommy dried off as much as he could with the lone towel that was almost as wet as he. When he emerged, he saw Caleb standing outside, naked except for a dry towel wrapped around his waist and his keys hanging around his neck.

"Nice … ain't it," said Caleb proudly of the new privy.

"Uh … yes. I like it," said Tommy not telling Caleb what he really thought. "But there's no more hot water."

"There ain't none 'til winter. Then we fire up the boiler out back with a bunch of corncobs. Daddy and Jesse put that in when they done the new privy."

Caleb grinned and disappeared behind the bathroom door leaving Tommy alone in the big hall.

He walked over to the pie safe and picked up his clean work clothes from the pie safe. Before he headed into his assigned bunkroom, he stopped and looked around. He couldn't believe everything that had happened to him. From a city boy to farm boy. All in one day. He felt like crying, but he didn't. Crying was for sissies.

His train of thought was interrupted when the front door flung open and Jesse walked in.

"Hey boy," yelled Jesse, his word slurred. "Ain't you s'posed to be in bed?"

"Yes sir," said Tommy over his shoulder as he quick-stepped into the bunkroom.

* * * * * *

The bunkroom was eerily quiet as Tommy tiptoed over to his bunk and crawled up and into the top bed. He slid under the sheet and pushed the blanket down to his knees. Even though he was tired from his first day on the farm, sleep did not come. Instead, he lay in bed staring into the darkness above him.

He had no idea what time it was or how long he had lain there when he heard the boy in the bed below whisper, "Are you awake?"

"Yeah. I'm awake. Can't sleep," answered Tommy.

"First night jitters. You'll get used to it. By the way, I'm Eugene."

"Tommy."

"I'm Vernon," said the boy on the top bunk next to Tommy.

Before long, it seemed that no one was asleep and they all told Tommy their names. Below Vernon was Leroy whom he had met in the fields. And in the first bunk were JoJo on top and Clarence on the bottom. Having talked to Clarence, he knew that Vernon was the smart one. So was Eugene.

JoJo's actual name was Joe. Because he stuttered, he hardly ever said Joe. Mostly J … Joe. So JoJo is what everybody called him, both at the farm and the orphanage. It was never meant as a slight and JoJo never considered it one.

Just like at the dinner table, everybody began to talk at once, albeit in hushed tones so not to wake Jesse, if that were even possible. Mostly, they asked Tommy, the same questions as they had asked before. Where was he from? Why did he run away? What orphanage was he from?

"I didn't run away," answered Tommy. "I've never been in an orphanage or a foster home."

"Are you saying that Watson kidnapped you?" asked Vernon, incredulously, somewhat skeptical of Tommy's answer. Otherwise, why the shackles?

"Yes. I thought the old man was just giving me a ride. But he never stopped. Instead, he brought me here."

"To replace Little Eddie," offered Eugene as an explanation.

"I don't doubt you, but I do find that hard to believe," said Vernon. "Watson is a grumpy, cantankerous old man, but he's honest, fair and very religious. He likes discipline. He likes rules. Sometimes he makes them up on the fly. But nobody here was taken against their will. Well … maybe Sammy and Claude. They didn't want to come, but it was either here or the orphanage. They chose the farm and now they like it here. And you'll find it's not so bad being here … at least not for the ones of us who came from the orphanage."

"How can you say that?" asked Tommy, mad that no one seemed to believe him and his louder and more aggressive voice showed his anger. "The old man choked me unconscious, twisted my ear so hard I thought I was going to pass out and put me in leg irons. And his boy, Jesse … he shot bullets at me. How could it have been any worse at the orphanage?"

"I can answer that," said Vernon. "The work … it's back breaking and tedious. But it takes no mental acuity. Simply repetitiveness. We don't get paid but, as you should know by now, the old lady cooks a good meal. And we have a roof over our head, a place to sleep and a place to take an indoor shower, albeit weekly. Whereas, at the orphanage, we were never guaranteed a bed. It was like a free-for-all every night to get a cot. The food was inferior with no second helpings … not that anybody wanted any. And we were beaten almost daily for no reason."

"What about the bullets and the shackles?" asked Tommy.

"Watson only puts shackles on new pickers he gets from the police or runaways. It won't last long. You have to gain his trust."

"And pick a lot of cotton," added Leroy.

Vernon continued. "Now the bullets. Watson doesn't know that Jesse is shooting at us. The gun is supposed to be for our protection against snakes. But Jesse's malicious. He does it for fun. You needn't worry, he's a good shot. He's not going to hit you. Today, with you being the new kid, he was just making a point."

"Well … he certainly made his point."

This first night was not going well for Tommy. If he had any hope of going home, he couldn't be so combative. He decided to temper what he was saying.

"How do I earn his trust? Watson?"

"Obey his many rules which I can narrow down to three rules. Number one… never challenge the Watsons on anything. Just keep your mouth shut. Number two… do the work they ask, how they ask and when they ask. And rule number three … the most important one … stay as far away from Jesse as possible."

"Vernon's right if you can understand what he was saying with all those highfalutin words he uses," said Eugene, reclaiming the conversation. "His mama and daddy were teachers, so sometimes you just have to ask him what he's talking about."

"Actually, Dad was a Professor of Literature at LaGrange College and Mom taught high school English. So I was doomed to be a voracious reader and to always be correcting everybody's grammar around here. Well… just the boys. And I must say, I've done a credible job with Billy. But Wayne and Leroy … they're hopeless."

"And it's really irritating. Ain't that right, JoJo," said Wayne not looking for an answer.

"Case in point," said Vernon, with everybody laughing.

Tommy liked his roommates, especially Vernon. Although he was one of the youngest, without question, he was probably the smartest.

"So Vernon… how did you end up in the orphanage? Where are your parents?"

"I *had* parents," said Vernon. "Both died in a fire at a hotel in Atlanta. It'll be three years this coming December. They were on the eleventh floor. The fire started on the third floor when somebody's cigarette caught the bedspread on fire. My parents didn't stand a chance."

"Why were they in Atlanta and how did you escape?" asked Tommy, saddened by Vernon's loss of his parents and thinking that he might never see his own parents again.

"They were supposed to be gone only two nights. I was eleven and pretty independent so they didn't worry about leaving me alone at the house. They were in Atlanta celebrating Daddy getting tenure at the college. We all were so proud of him. When the Dean of the college came to the house, I knew something wasn't right. Worst day of my life. The next thing I know, the courts had sent me to the orphanage."

"How did you end up here at the farm?"

"When I heard about boys being sent to a farm, I asked Mr. Bumble if I could go. I hated the orphanage. If that didn't happen, I was thinking about running away. But he didn't like me because I was the one who nicknamed him Mr. Bumble."

"Who's Mr. Bumble?" asked Tommy.

"Mr. Bumble was in charge of the orphanage. But that wasn't his real name. His real name was Phillip Bundy, but behind his back I called him Mr. Bumble, so named after a callous, pompous character in *Oliver Twist,* a book written by Charles Dickens. By the way, if you are interested, I do readings every Sunday afternoon from a number of my books that the Watsons let me bring from the orphanage. There is no schooling here. So I've sort of assumed the role as teacher. And besides the readings, I also teach a little math and grammar."

"So you *like* it here?"

"Yes. I do. The only really bad thing about this farm is …"

Before he could complete his sentence, the door swung open.

"Lights out means lights out. Do I make myself clear?" yelled Jesse, slamming the door without waiting for a response.

"is Jesse," said Tommy, finishing Vernon's sentence.

CHAPTER 20

After a restless, fretful night, Tommy had finally fallen sound asleep, dreaming he was back home, when he felt someone pushing on his shoulder. He awoke, sat straight up and turned to see the dimly lit face of one of the pickers … one of the bobbing heads that he had seen at the weigh-in and at dinner. He'd yet to meet the young boy peering over the side of his bed.

"Hey … uh … new kid. You gotta get up and dressed. We got chores to do."

Tommy ignored the plea and laid back down in the bed. The boy immediately began his pushing, prodding and shoving all over again but this time even more vigorously.

"I'm not kidding. You gotta get up. Pleeeeeeassssse."

Hearing the desperation in the boy's voice, Tommy slowly sat up, threw his feet over the side of the bed and rubbed his sleep-deprived eyes.

"Who are you?" he asked.

"I'm Charlie. I sleep in the other room. You need to get a move on. Me and you … we got chores to do."

"What chores? Nobody told me anything about chores."

"We gotta feed the chickens and the pigs. Then we got to milk the cows and gather the eggs. Caleb told me last night that I had to teach you, but I forgot to tell you. We gotta go before Caleb leaves. Pleeeeeasssse."

The plea was so pitiful that Tommy jumped down from his bunk and quickly dressed in his clean work clothes.

"Do I have to do this every day?" asked Tommy has he pulled on his boots.

"No. Everybody has to do it at least four times a month, including helping out Mrs. Watson in the kitchen. We do it in the morning and Caleb does it in the afternoon while we do our final weigh-in. But no more talking. We got to hurry. If Caleb has left …." Without finishing his sentence, he turned and headed out of the room with Tommy following close behind.

When they got to the front door, Charlie saw it was closed.

"Oh no no no no. This is not good. I should have gotten up earlier," said Charlie as he tried in vain to open the locked door. "Caleb's already gone. We can't get out unless we ask Jesse. He's not gonna like this … uh … what's your name?"

"Tommy."

"Yes. Tommy. Now I remember. Look. I'm gonna knock on Jesse's door. When he opens, *do not* say anything to him. Don't even look at him. Stand behind me. If he says *anything* to you, agree with him, no matter what."

Charlie turned to his right and Tommy positioned himself just behind Charlie's back as he knocked on Jesse's door. He then whispered over his back shoulder, "Never knock more than twice … and never loud."

Tommy was beginning to think that Jesse wasn't even in his room when the door swung open and there was Jesse, his eyes just barely open. He was still dressed in the clothes he had worn in the field.

"What do you want?"

Even though Tommy was standing behind Charlie, he could still smell Jesse's breath. It reeked of alcohol. Tommy immediately thought of his Uncle Scott whose breath often had the same foul odor.

"We need you to open the front door. Caleb's already left."

"Then you're late." He pushed the two boys out of the way and headed to the front door, removing the keys that hung around his neck.

When he turned back towards his bunkroom, he saw Tommy.

"Ain't you that new boy?"

"Yes sir."

"Well, Charlie ain't no new boy. He knows better." He then grabbed Charlie's ear and twisted it like Watson had done to Tommy but even harder. He let go and slapped the defenseless boy on the back of his head, not once but twice to make a point.

"Now you boys git out of here and don't you never wake me agin!" He turned and headed back into his room, slamming the door behind him.

"Are you okay?" asked Tommy as they walked out of the workers' cabin towards the barn.

"Yes," quivered Charlie, trying his hardest not to cry.

"I'm sorry I made us late. If I had known …."

"No. It was my fault. I should have gotten up earlier. I know better. Let's get this over so we're not late for breakfast or we won't get any."

Charlie picked up his pace while wiping tears from his eyes with the back of his hand. He hoped there was enough distance between the two that Tommy wouldn't notice. But he had. Vernon was right about Jesse. Stay as far away as possible.

"Go open that gate over there while I feed the pigs and chickens," ordered Charlie. "When the cows hear the gate squeak, they'll make their way to the barn. Once you see them coming, follow them in. I'll meet you there."

Tommy nodded and walked past the barn to an open field that was surrounded by barbed wire. Only as he pushed open the gate did he realize he wasn't wearing the leg shackles. Had they forgotten or was it because they were late? Regardless, this was his time to make his escape. He turned to look to see if he saw anyone up at the main house, the workers' cabin or the barn. He saw no one. What he did see was the old truck parked under an overhang just off the side of the barn. Thinking this might be his only chance to get away, he made a dash to the truck hoping he'd find the keys in the ignition.

The truck's door creaked loudly as Tommy opened it and crawled inside. Surely Charlie must have heard it. Tommy looked out the windows but saw nothing. He also did not see the key in the ignition. Nor was it above either visors or in the glove compartment. That's when he heard a voice call out.

"Tommy … is that you in Daddy's truck?"

Tommy froze. He looked out the front window to see Caleb. Before Tommy could answer, Caleb called out again, "Tommy … what you doing in Daddy's truck?"

"I'm looking for Charlie."

"Well he ain't gonna be in Daddy's truck," said Caleb, laughing.

Tommy climbed out of the truck, shut the door and walked over to Caleb, glad it hadn't been Watson or even worse, Jesse.

"Ain't you s'posed to be with Charlie?" asked Caleb.

"No. He told me to open the gate for the cows. When I did, I saw them running towards me. I got scared and ran to the truck to get out of their way. I was looking for Charlie for help." Tommy hoped Caleb didn't see through his lie.

Caleb laughed again, shaking his head. "Well … them cows ain't going to hurt you. They's only three of them. And they's old and nearly dried up … hardly giving any milk a'tall. Charlie is s'posed to learn you how to milk them cows, but if he ain't here, I reckon I gotta do it."

Caleb turned and headed towards the barn with Tommy following close behind.

When they got to the barn, the cows were in the stall and Charlie had already started milking the first one. When he saw Caleb and Tommy come into the barn, he nodded but said nothing as he continued his rhythmic pulling of the cow's teats.

Tommy did a quick glance around the old barn. It was old but clean and orderly, just like the workers' cabin. Taking up most of the right side were the cow stalls. On the left side, either hanging on the wall or lying against it were farming tools and equipment of all varieties, none of which he knew. Open at the back of the barn was another set of barn doors with the farm's only tractor more outside of the barn than in. And above the front third of the barn was a loft, partially filled with hay. A wooden ladder leading up to it was positioned in close proximity to cow stalls.

Tommy noticed that the barn didn't have locks on the doors which meant he would have access to the tractor whenever he had chore duty assuming Jesse left the key in the ignition and … if he knew how to drive one. At the next weigh-in, he would be more observant of Jesse's hand and footwork as he drove the tractor. Surely, it couldn't be any harder than a stick-shift.

His thoughts were interrupted when he heard Charlie ask, "So where'd you go?"

"I … uh …"

"He were in Daddy's truck, looking fer you. Them cows scairt him," said Caleb, smiling.

"I see," said Charlie, not believing Tommy's story for one minute.

"Tommy … this here cow is Sugar," said Caleb while rubbing the cow's backside. "And that one there, next to Sugar, is Essie. And that one there is Rosie. Ain't none of them is gonna hurt you."

"Now watch Charlie milk ol' Sugar. See how he grabs them two teats with his fingers? Now gimme your hands." Caleb first positioned Tommy's thumb and index finger of the left hand with the proper milking grip and then the right hand. "Once you has aholt to them, you pull them down real easy and squish them at the same time shooting the milk into the pail. See?"

Caleb grabbed a nearby stool and pail. He set the stool down next to Essie's side and stuck the pail under her udders.

"Now sit yourself down and give her a try."

Tommy watched Charlie a couple more times, sat down on the stool and grabbed two of Essie's teats as Caleb had demonstrated.

Just before Tommy's first pull, Caleb shouted out, "Don't shoot them first two pulls in the bucket. Shoot 'em at your foot."

"Why?" asked Tommy.

"'Cause Daddy said so."

"Keeps bacteria out," said Charlie over his shoulder while never losing his rhythm.

"How'd you know that?" asked Tommy as he timidly pulled on the teats with barely a drop squirting out next to his foot.

"I grew up on a small farm outside of Butler, Georgia," said the towheaded, deeply tanned boy who was a little taller than most of the other boys at the Watson's farm.

"So how'd you end up here?"

"Both my parents got killed in a car accident about three years ago while we were coming home from a church revival. I got thrown from the car. Ended up in a hospital in Columbus, Georgia for three weeks. I didn't have any kinfolk nearby that wanted me, so they sent me to the orphanage. When Watson came looking for boys to work on the farm, I volunteered. I hated the orphanage."

"I'm sorry about your folks," said Tommy not having any real success with Essie who kept mooing while looking at the boy.

"You ain't doing it right," said Caleb. "Them cows don't like they's teats being pulled the wrong way."

He kneeled down next to Tommy and demonstrated the proper method, going slow at first so Tommy could see.

Caleb moved aside and watched Tommy until he had milk flowing, only slowing his tempo when the cow moved or swished its tail.

"You done figured it out, Tommy," he said, excitedly. "But you don't has to be scairt of 'ol Essie. She likes being milked … jest not real hard."

He elongated the word *real,* just as Watson had. "If you wants, you can twist your hands to and fro, like this. See?"

Tommy watched Caleb's hands and mimicked what he had seen.

After Caleb was satisfied that his student was milking the cow properly, he grabbed another pail and stool, sat down beside Rosie and began gently and methodically milking the cow, smiling at every shot of milk into the pail.

Normally Tommy's competitive spirit would have kicked in and he would have tried to have his bucket filled before Caleb. Instead, he chose to use the opportunity to learn more about the farm and in particular, the tractor.

"Caleb," said Tommy through the open space between Essie's legs. "You seemed to know how to do everything on this farm. What's the most fun thing that you do?"

Caleb thought for a minute as he continued to steadily pull on Rosie's teats.

"I like eating my mama's food."

"I like it, too. What chore do you like best?"

"Oh … I reckon I l like milking these ol' cows 'cause they 'preciate it."

"You're really good at picking cotton. Why aren't you out in the field with us?"

"Daddy says Mama needs me more. I help with the cooking, washing clothes and all them things."

"Can you drive that tractor?"

"Oh … I ain't allowed on the tractor," said Caleb, shaking his head. "Only Daddy and Jesse.

"But is it hard to drive? Is it like driving a truck?"

"A truck ain't got but four gears. A tractor has a heap more, but it ain't hard to drive."

Tommy wanted to ask about the key to the tractor. Did it need one? If so, did they leave it in the tractor? If not, was there a spare hung somewhere in the barn? But he chose not to push his luck.

"Caleb … you know more about a farm than anybody I know," said Tommy, meaning every word.

Hearing Tommy's words made Caleb swell up in pride with a big smile creeping across his face.

"Thank you, Tommy. Ain't nobody ever told me that before."

It wasn't long before all three cows had their udder's emptied and were heading back out to the pasture but not before nudging Caleb in appreciation.

Charlie poured the milk from one of the pails into the other two, equalizing the contents the best he could.

"See you boys at breakfast," said Caleb, who grabbed a pail in each hand and headed back to the main house.

"Are we through?" asked Tommy.

"Gotta get the eggs and that's it," said Charlie. "While I do that, you go close the gate to the pasture and then meet me in the hen house. It's just off the left side of the main house. Oh … and if you *even think* about running away again while you're with me, don't. Vernon went missing for just a couple of hours the day after Little Eddie ran off. Jesse and Tippy found him heading back from the old plantation. They got into a shouting match and then Jesse caned him so bad on his backside that he bled for two days. Nobody ever told Watson. When he asked where the boy was, Jesse told him that he was sick in bed. But he wasn't in bed. Jesse threw him in the storm cellar. He stayed there for two days. So unless you want the same thing to happen to you, I wouldn't go missing for any reason. Not with Jesse around. Ask Vernon."

I will, thought Tommy.

CHAPTER 21

On most Sundays, if the doors to Chipley Methodist Church were open, Jim and Ruth Ann Broome were there. He was chairman of the administrative board and taught the Men's Bible Class. She was treasurer of the W.S.C.S. (Women's Society of Christian Service) and worked in the church's nursery every Sunday, the closest she'd come to having a child of her own. Normally, they both would be dressed in their finest Sunday-go-to-meeting clothes. But today, not for Jim. He was dressed in his Monday through Saturday chief's uniform.

Last night, as they sat in the living room, talking about the missing child, Ruth Ann suggested they take the pictures of the missing boy to their church and have them passed around in hopes that someone might have seen him or might possibly see him. Jim's depressed mood quickly changed.

"Why stop at our church? Why not visit the other two large churches in Pine Mountain?" he asked.

By the time they had kissed each other good night and turned off the bedside lamp, they had called the pastors of the three largest churches in Pine Mountain and had been given the green light to address their congregations. With the services at all three churches starting at 11:15 a.m., Ruth Ann would speak to the members at Chipley Methodist and Jim would speak at the other two churches.

Standing at the church's podium before the congregation, Ruth Ann began to speak. She had always been a stay-at-home wife and caregiver for her mother, so she had never had the need nor opportunity to speak before a large crowd. Her hands shook slightly as she held tightly onto the podium. And when she spoke, her voice trembled. She had hardly gotten Tommy's name out of her mouth when she broke down in tears. Her emotional meltdown wasn't the result of her public speaking nervousness. It was the thought of that young boy and the unimaginable possibilities of what might have happened to him. Many in the congregation had tears of empathy in their eyes. But she regrouped. She had to for the boy's sake. This couldn't be about her. So she calmly gave a brief summary of the case, a description of the child and what he was wearing. When she was done talking, she passed around pictures of the child to the parishioners with almost everyone taking a long, hard look with some shaking their head in disbelief. Nothing like this had ever happened in Pine Mountain. Ruth Ann answered a few questions, then she left the pulpit and returned to her seat on the first row, her eyes filled with tears. She prayed her efforts were not in vain.

Bethany Baptist Church, just off Georgia Highway 18, was Jim's first stop as it was closest to his house. Bethany was one of the oldest churches in Pine Mountain, its original building dating back to the 1800s. It had an all-black congregation, whereas the First Baptist Church, Jim's next stop, was all white. He never understood the separation of races. As a military man, he had fought and worked beside people of all races. All he cared about was that they did their job... not their race, religion, financial well-being or anything else.

The service began with the gospel choir singing two hymns making everyone in the church, including Jim, glad to be alive and in His presence. After Rev. Tom Davidson gave a long, impassioned prayer, he introduced the chief. It was not the first time he had been there. As an elected official, it was most important that he reach out to *all* the people of Pine Mountain, so he had visited *every* church at one time or another.

Unlike Ruth Ann, Jim was accustomed to talking in front of large crowds, so there were no public speaking nerves to conquer. Just like Ruthie, he too had tears in his eyes as he talked about Tommy as though he was his own child. Just before handing out the picture, a thought occurred to him. One that he wished he had discussed with his wife. Instead, he dove in head first.

"To help the community keep this missing boy in their minds, the police department is announcing a $500 reward for the first person helping us locate Tommy Harrison."

He thanked the congregation and looked over at Reverend Davidson who was now standing and shook his hand. But the good Reverend did not release his grasp. Instead, he looked Jim in the eye and then turned to the congregation.

"Chief Broome... the reward for helping locate one of God's children is very generous. But no member of Bethany Baptist Church needs a reward for doing the Lord's work. You pass around those pictures of the Harrison boy and we will do our duty as members of this grand temple of God and as citizens of this fine town of Pine Mountain to help locate him." He then released Jim's hand.

After passing out the pictures of the boy and afterwards collecting them, Jim realized he only had thirty minutes to make his next stop. With the siren blasting and the dome light flashing he sped down Georgia Highway 18, ignoring any red light until he pulled into the parking lot of the First Baptist Church of Pine Mountain. Carrying the pictures in his hand, he quick-walked up the steps, through the front doors and into sanctuary where he removed his hat. The preacher, Reverend George Dickert, looked up from his podium, saw the big chief and immediately stopped his sermon. He summoned Jim to the pulpit and introduced him. Just like at Bethany, he really didn't need an introduction.

As before, he discussed the case at a high level, keeping the details to himself. He described the boy and what he was wearing. But this time, he chose not to insult the good people of the First Baptist Church with the offer of a reward. *Fool me once...* Nor would he tell Ruthie about his faux pas.

Jim passed out the pictures and then stayed for the remainder of the service which interestingly enough was about the parables of the lost sheep, the lost coin and the lost son with the sermon ending with the preacher's reading of Luke, Chapter 15, verse 24. "For this my son was dead, and is alive again; he was lost, and is found. And they began to be merry." (King James Version).

Jim prayed that the preacher and God were talking about Tommy Harrison.

CHAPTER 22

Once the chores were done, Tommy and Charlie headed back to the workers' cabin just in time to join Caleb and the other boys for the Sunday morning breakfast feast consisting of eggs, grits, bacon, biscuits and gravy. Just like Saturday's meal, the food was excellent and plentiful, leaving little time for talking. Only eating. When the talking did commence, Tommy was now old news. Only Vernon who sat by Tommy had questions and vice versa.

"Am I to understand that you were abducted?" asked Vernon, now questioning his own skepticism.

"Yes. But Watson thinks that I'm a runaway … and a thief."

"Why would he think that? He's a very religious man. I don't think he would say that unless he really believed it. Tell me what happened."

Tommy told Vernon how his mom had taken him and a friend to Roosevelt State Park where they set up camp. That they were to play golf at Callaway Gardens the next day. He told Vernon about the bet and how he had trekked through the woods from the campsite to the golf course only to misjudge its location and get disoriented when he reached the highway. That he had turned the wrong way and was actually heading away from the golf course when Watson drove up.

"When he saw you, you were walking *away* from the golf course, carrying a set of golf clubs. Is that right?"

"Yes. Actually, I was almost running because I didn't want to miss my tee time."

Vernon thought for a second. There was no way a runaway could make up a story like this.

"So … Watson saw a boy … you … running *away* from a golf course carrying a set of golf clubs."

"And wearing a new pair of golf shoes," added Tommy. "I see where you're going. But don't you think the police would be looking for me?"

"Not here in Alabama. Here's what I think. If you do what you're told, pick as much cotton as you can and stay out of Jesse's way, once

Watson removes your shackles for good, we can try to figure a way for you to get out of here."

"You'd do that? For me?"

"Why not? This farm is for orphaned kids, like me. You have parents. Of course, I'll help."

"Did you help Little Eddie get out?"

"I don't want to talk about …"

Before Vernon could finish his sentence, the front door swung opened and there was Henry Watson with Bible in hand.

"Okay boys. Let's git this here table cleaned," yelled Watson.

He then rapped on Jesse's door. "Time to git up, boy. You done slept enough."

Watson waited a few seconds and rapped again.

"Okay. Okay. I'm coming," yelled Jesse from inside the room.

Satisfied his son was up, Watson made his way into the big hall. Shortly, Jesse emerged from his room, still dressed in yesterday's clothes and his eyes more shut than open. He shuffled over to his usual chair at the darkest, far end of the hall, sat down and closed his eyes.

Tommy turned to Vernon and asked, "What's happening?"

"Sunday morning worship service. It's mandatory for everybody except Mrs. Watson. Don't worry. They're not long."

Vernon grabbed up his cup, plate and utensils and headed over to the cart where he set them on top of the other boy's dirty dishes. Tommy was right behind him. By the time they had returned to the table, all of the seats farthest from Watson had been taken. Tommy and Vernon ended up getting the seats immediately to the left and right of the old man.

With everyone's head bowed and eyes closed except Tommy's, Watson began his prayer by thanking the Lord for his farm, family and his young pickers. He asked the Lord for a prosperous cotton crop, no rain while it was being picked and freedom from ill health or injury. Finally, he thanked the Lord for helping him to find his new picker, Tommy, and to be able to give this lost soul a home. He prayed that the Lord would help the boy to see the difference between right and wrong and that stealing was a sin. He closed with the Lord's Prayer which everybody recited in unison except Tommy who was fuming over what Watson had said even though he knew the prayer by heart.

Before the prayer ended, Vernon opened his eyes and glanced over at Tommy. He could see by the look on his face that he wasn't happy about being called a runaway and even worse, a thief. He knew that if Tommy challenged Watson, it would delay his chance of escape. He shot Tommy a quick look while shaking his head. He then laid three fingers of his right hand across the back of his left hand. Tommy nodded his head showing that he understood the significance of the three fingers. Vernon's three rules … mainly to keep his mouth shut.

With the prayer ended and Watson satisfied that he had all the boy's attention, he slipped on a pair of glasses and slowly opened his old, worn leather bound Bible … one that had been handed down for three generations … to 2 Thessalonians, Chapter 3, Verse 10. He began reading the verse.

"For even when we were with you, this we commanded you, that if any would not work, neither should he eat."

He looked around the table as he slowly closed the Bible, removed his glasses and stuck them in the top pocket of his freshly washed bib overalls.

"Any of you boys knows what that there Bible verse means?" Watson asked and looked around the table for a hand to be raised. He expected none and there were none.

Even though Tommy was angry at Watson, he so badly wanted to raise his hand because he knew the answer to the question. Again, it was his competitive nature. He had never been shy in school about raising his hand to ask or answer questions. But seeing that no one, including Vernon, had not raised their hand, he kept his hands under the table.

Watson looked around the table. Other than Tommy, Vernon and a couple of other boys, most had their heads down, looking at the table, hoping not to be called on. To their relief, Watson called out Tommy's name.

"Tommy … what do you think that there Bible verse means?"

"It means that if we don't work, we don't eat."

"That's right. Boys … you hear what he said … if you don't work, you don't eat." To get his point across, he repeated himself but much slower. "If you don't work, you don't eat. Some of you boys ain't carrying your weight around here. Tommy only jest learnt how to pick cotton and he nearbout outpicked a couple of you boys. I'm thinking that like the Bible says, if you ain't picking much, you ain't eating much. Do I make myself clear?"

Every boy, as well as Caleb, nodded. This time, their eyes all on Watson.

"Good."

Watson turned his Bible to Exodus, Chapter 20.

"Any of you boys know the Ten Commandments?" asked Watson and, as before, looked around the table for a hand to be raised. Again, there were none.

"JoJo. What is the eighth commandment?"

As soon as he had asked the boy, he regretted it.

"Mis … Mis … Mis … ter Wa … Wa … Watson. I … I … ain't re … re … real su … sure."

"How 'bout you, Vernon?"

"Thou shalt not steal," replied Vernon, immediately, who knew all ten.

"Did everbody hear Vernon? Thou shalt not steal. Stealing is a sin in the eyes of the Lord. Now our new boy, Tommy … before I brung him to our farm, I seen him stealing. It don't matter what he done stole. But like the Lord said, we don't tolerate no stealing around here. Ain't that right, Charlie?"

"Yes sir."

"Ain't that right, Claude?"

"Yes sir."

"How 'bout you, Leroy?"

"Yes sir."

"Tommy … this ain't my rule. It's the Lord's rule. There ain't no stealing on this here farm. Do I make myself clear?"

As soon as Tommy said *But Mr. Watson …,* every boy's eyes in the room turned towards Tommy with a look of disbelief, then at Watson to see his reaction. Every boy, except Vernon, who simply closed his eyes and shook his head.

Watson's response was swift as he thumped the back of the boy's head with his Bible. He then leaned down and looked at his wayward boy straight in the eyes. He was so close, that Tommy could smell the tobacco on his foul-smelling breath and see the anger in the man's eyes.

"First Timothy, Chapter five, Verse 1. Rebuke not an elder, but treat him as a father, and the younger men as brethren. Boy … that means respect your elders. Do I make myself clear?"

"Yes sir. I'm sorry," said Tommy having realized he might have spoiled his chances of a quick escape.

Jesse, who had drifted off to sleep, was awakened by the disturbance. He instinctively jumped to his feet to see what was happening. When he heard his daddy shouting, he saw that he and the new boy were having some sort of confrontation. He rushed to his father's side to offer his assistance.

"What's this boy done to you, Daddy?" he yelled, looking alternately between his daddy and Tommy. "I'm gonna go git my cane."

Watson stood up and looked Jesse square in the eyes. "Son … you ain't in charge here. Ain't nobody gonna do no caning around here. You go back to that there chair where you been sleeping and leave me and Tommy be."

Don't nobody talk to me like that, thought Jesse as he turned and headed back to his room and slammed the door.

Watson ignored his son's insolence. Instead, he focused his attention on his wayward picker. Every boy was watching Tommy except Vernon who could only stare at the table and shake his head at his friend's impertinence.

"Tommy … what is the eight commandment?

"Thou shalt not steal."

"That's right. There ain't no stealing on this here farm. Do I make myself clear?"

"Yes sir," said Tommy as he looked at Vernon who didn't look back.

* * * * * *

"What'd I tell you?" asked Vernon as he and Tommy headed back to the bunkroom after Watson had abruptly ended his Sunday sermon.

"I know. I know. Remember the three rules," he sighed. "But I couldn't just sit there and let him accuse me of stealing in front of everyone. I'm not a thief. I've never stolen anything in my life."

"I believe you, but if you want to get out of here, you can't make enemies with the man who literally has the key to your freedom. And I don't care what he says, *do not* challenge him. You're not going to win. Hopefully, you'll only be in those shackles for just two weeks."

Tommy understood. He could handle anything for two weeks.

Vernon continued to talk as both boys climbed into their bunks.

"I don't know if you heard Jesse, but he was ready to cane you and he didn't even know what you had done. When Watson's mad, he's a yeller and an ear twister. If he's really mad, he gets out the cane. But honestly, the caning isn't as bad as the ear twisting. In fact, it's almost like a rite of passage. Everybody has to be caned by Watston to be one of the guys. But he doesn't want to hurt you. He's just trying to make a point. It's all about discipline. Now Jesse … he's mean. Really mean and I should know. I'll show you my back if you don't believe me."

Tommy hesitated but decided to brave a response.

"I heard that happened when you went looking for Little Eddie?"

"I don't know who told you that, but we are not supposed to talk about Little Eddie. Especially around Jesse. Do I make myself clear?" He laughed as did Tommy but nothing more was said about Little Eddie.

CHAPTER 23

Sarah Watson had always prided herself on her cooking skills. As she grew older, she felt they had somewhat diminished, but nobody else on the farm felt that way. Everybody, Watson, Jesse, Caleb and the kids, always looked forward to the week-end meals, especially Sunday where she always outdid herself. This Sunday, the mid-day meal had fried chicken, hominy, collards, okra, sweet potatoes, biscuits, gravy and sweet tea, topped off by a cobbler of some variety. Today's choice was apple cobbler. Henry's favorite. No one went hungry.

The Watson twins took turns eating with the pickers. Today was Caleb's turn which always pleased the boys as no one wanted to eat with Jesse and likewise. Instead, he would be eating with his folks at the main house.

Besides Jesse, also eating with the Watsons was JoJo. Each Sunday, one of the pickers ate with the Watsons. It was not a request. The designated picker was based on bedroom rotation and bunk position, starting with the lower bunk nearest the door, moving to the top bunk, then to the next bottom bunk and so on. With JoJo being on the top bunk nearest the door, Leroy who had the bottom bunk on the second row would be the next to have the "honor."

The Watson's magnanimity was not heart felt. There was an ulterior motive behind their kindness.   Early on, when Watson began taking on boys from the orphanage and runaways from the Columbus Police Department, the two runaways, Clint and Larry, sneaked off during a lunch break during planting season and, other than their shoes, were never seen again. The Watsons felt they were caught off guard and couldn't let that ever happen again. Jesse wanted to have a weekly beating to put the fear of God in the boys. Henry wanted the pickers to wear shackles or leggings as he called them. Caleb had no thoughts about the situation, whatsoever. Regardless, they felt they needed to know at all times what the boys were thinking, planning, conspiring especially when new boys were brought in.

Sarah had another idea. She told them, "You can catch more flies with honey than with vinegar." An Italian proverb she had to explain to the

Watson men. Her idea was to have the top picker come to the main farmhouse for the Sunday mid-day meal. That way, they could subtly ask questions while plying the boy with dessert. But Henry was smart enough to know that being the top picker and having to have Sunday lunch with his family was like winning the lottery but losing the ticket. He knew that none of the boys would want that 'honor' and their pickings would suffer, so he liked his idea of the leggings the best.

As a compromise, a modified version of each idea was adopted. Sarah agreed to the shackles but just for new runaways and only for two or three weeks. In return, Watson agreed to have a picker at the main house for the Sunday meal but on a rotation basis.

Within a few weeks after implementing the plan, the Sunday inquisition ceased but the rotation of the 'guest' picker continued.

This Sunday would be different. With a new runaway picker on the farm, the Watsons, especially Henry, were most curious as to what the other pickers were hearing from Tommy even though he had only been on the farm for less than two days.

When JoJo arrived, Watson was waiting for him at the door.

Of all the pickers, thought the old man knowing JoJo's struggle with his stuttering. He ushered the boy into the dining room where they saw Jesse already seated at the table, his right leg bouncing impatiently.

"Hey, JoJo," said Sarah as she brought in the hot-off-the-stove fried chicken.

"Hi … hi … M … M … Mi … Mis … Missus Wa … Watson," said JoJo, standing behind the assigned picker's chair.

Once the Watsons were seated, JoJo sat down. After the blessing, the food was passed around starting with Henry, moving clockwise to Jesse, Sarah and JoJo. There was plenty of food and the leftovers would be served again on Monday.

The conversation among the Watsons centered on Tommy and how appreciative they were that the Lord had helped Henry find the lost boy. They talked about how quickly he had learned to pick cotton and how much he had picked for the last weigh-in. JoJo listened but did not participate in the discussion. Instead, he just ate. Jesse also remained silent, only looking up to ask for more food to be passed.

It wasn't until after JoJo's second helping of Sarah Watson's famous apple cobbler had almost been consumed that Watson began his questioning of the unsuspecting picker, starting off by complimenting the boy.

"JoJo… I'm proud of you. I jest looked at my cotton numbers and you done outpicked all them other boys. Like I done told you in today's sermon, if you don't work, you don't eat. I'm telling you, boy, you ain't one of them slackers."

"I … I… ap … ap … apre … preciate tha … tha … that." The more nervous or frightened JoJo got, the worse his stuttering became.

"So … what do you think of that new boy, Tommy? Do you like him?"

"Ye … yes si … sir. He … he's ver … very ni … ni … nice."

"Does he like it here?"

"I .. I do … don't kn … kn … know."

"What do you mean *you don't know*? Ain't you got no brain?" barked Jesse, ready to get the inquisition over so he could go fishing.

"I … I … I … I … thi … thi …" said JoJo, now more nervous than ever.

"Spit it out, boy! We ain't got all day," said Jesse, glaring at the boy.

"Now Jesse. Let the boy finish," intervened Sarah who was clearing the dishes. "Now, JoJo, what were you trying to say?"

"He … He … ain … ain't rea … rea … real ha … ha … happy," answered JoJo, looking up at the old lady who had a motherly smile on her face.

"Does he want to leave? Did he say that?" asked Henry.

"Not … not that I … I … ca … can re … re … re … mem … mem … ber."

"Henry, I think we need to let the boy finish his cobbler." There was no push back from anyone as the short conversation had been frustrating to all.

But JoJo was too exhausted to eat any more. So he excused himself from the table and hurried out the front door, glad his time with the Watsons was over. Jesse wasn't too far behind.

Watson sat back, pulled his Old Golds from his top pocket and lit one up. He knew what was coming next.

Sarah sat down in a chair next to Henry who offered her one of his Old Golds. She lit the cigarette using Henry's, inhaled the carcinogenic smoke and blew it out through her two nostrils. She repeated the process while Henry waited for her verbal attack.

"Henry … I'm telling you … that boy's gonna be trouble. And I ain't talking about JoJo. If you know what's good fer you, you best keep an eye on him or he's gonna be like them other boys who done run off."

"I ain't worried about that boy. But seeing how you is, I'll make sure that he don't go nowhere."

CHAPTER 24

According to the Bible, the book of Exodus, after six days of labor, the seventh day was to be a day of rest. For Christians, that day was Sunday. Being a religious man, Watson would never knowingly disobey the word of God. But like most laws, rules, statues and even the word of God, there were exceptions. Sarah Watson was one. After all, *someone* had to cook. Even on Sunday, working men had to eat. Watson also assumed that the Lord turned a blind eye to the boys who did chores on Sunday because the chickens, cows and pigs didn't know what day of the week it was. And they, too, had to eat.

While none of the boys liked doing the chores on *any* day, they hated doing them on Sunday the worst since they would lose the only day of the week they could sleep in. On the other hand, Sarah didn't mind preparing any meal, Sunday's included. In fact, she loved to cook even though she no longer had any real good help now that Little Eddie was gone. None of the other boys liked working in the kitchen. It was just another chore to them. But Little Eddie had taken to the kitchen like the other boys did to fishing and swimming, oftentimes taking their turn helping Sarah.

By four o'clock, Sunday's mid-day meal and dish detail were over and Watson's regimented, military-style schedule that he used to run his farm was over for the day until "lights out." The boys were free for the rest of the day. They could lay around on their bunks, go fishing or swimming with Jesse, or attend a reading/learning session conducted by Vernon. Only Sammy and Claude, the Poston brothers, were brave enough to go to the pond with Jesse. They loved fishing more than learning and would keep their distance from their adversary. The rest of the boys including Caleb stayed for Vernon's reading session.

Vernon began his reading/learning sessions not long after he arrived at the farm. Like most of the other pickers, he came from the orphanage, so he knew that hardly any of them could read or write nor perform basic math calculations as most had dropped out of school at the age of 15 which was the minimum legal age in most states including Georgia and Alabama. And there was no incentive for the orphanage to encourage the boys to stay in school as it cost them money to educate them.

Being that Vernon's parents were educators, it was only natural for him to follow in their footsteps. After a few months on the farm, he defied his own rule of keeping his mouth shut and asked the Watsons if he could hold learning sessions on Sunday's during the boy's free time. The Watsons were reluctant at first but eventually approved. Initially, only Charlie, Eugene and Billy stayed for the sessions. Within three months, every boy other than the Poston Brothers chose learning over sleeping or fishing. While the literacy rate was still very low, it was gradually improving.

Vernon's sessions were held at the meal table with him standing at the head of the table just as Watson had done when he preached his sermons, the main difference being that Watson's attendance was mandatory and boys didn't have to fight to keep their eyes open.

Once everyone, including Caleb, had gathered around the table, Vernon opened his book and began to read. He learned early on that he needed to stop at the most exciting part of the book to teach the English or math session before he returned to reading, otherwise he would lose half his audience to the bunks.

Currently, he was reading *Treasure Island* by Robert Lewis Stevenson. The boys loved it, especially when he acted out the parts or used different voices for the different characters, especially his low Captain John Silver's voice. When he got to Chapter 29, "The Black Spot Again", he stopped reading to change hats, figuratively, from reader to teacher.

"You can't stop now," groaned Wayne. "That ain't fair."

"N … no … it … it ain't," added JoJo who had earlier returned from the Watsons.

"Okay, guys. I don't want to hear the word *ain't* again," lectured Vernon.

"You jest done said it yourself," said Caleb, jumping into the conversation then laughing.

"How many times have I had the lecture on *ain't*, Leroy?" asked Vernon, knowing that it was about once a month.

"Too many," replied Leroy to the sound of laughter from the other boys.

"Charlie … can you conjugate the present tense of the verb *to be*, please?"

Charlie had been a quick learner and one that had pleased Vernon the most.

"I am; you are; he, she, it is. We are; you are; they are."

"Excellent. Now everybody repeat after me." Vernon then repeated the conjugation along with the rest of the boys. It was though it was a song or poem that they had memorized.

"Excellent. So Caleb, why not use the correct verb instead of using *ain't?*"

Caleb thought for a minute.

"I reckon they's jest too many choices."

All the boys, as well as Caleb, broke out laughing at his answer.

"Good point," said Vernon, he, too, laughing. "But I want you all to try. Wayne … instead of saying *that ain't fair*, what would you say if you didn't use the word *ain't* in that sentence?"

"That is not fair?" answered Wayne, questioning his answer.

"Excellent! Doesn't that sound better? Now repeat what you just said three times. You too, Billy."

As both boys repeated the sentence, Caleb who was at the far end of the table had his hand raised, waving it frantically in the air.

"Yes, Caleb?"

"I got a sentence. Sometimes my daddy calls me an idjit, but I *is not* an idjit." Caleb made a point to emphasize *is not*. Before Vernon had a chance to correct the verb, Leroy spoke up.

"Caleb *is not* an idjit."

Then Wayne chimed in followed by JoJo who did not stutter. Before long, everyone in the room was chanting, "Caleb is not an idjit. Caleb is not an idjit."

Tears welled up in Caleb's eyes as he looked around at his friends.

Once the chanting had stopped, Tommy spoke up.

"Caleb … I've only been here one day, but you are the kindest Watson … no … kindest person on this farm. Your daddy is mean to say that. I think he's just jealous that everybody likes you more than him."

"Well said, Tommy. Okay … let's finish up this lesson and get back to reading. I want everyone to repeat after me. Caleb is the best."

"Caleb is the best," yelled everyone until Vernon raised his hand signaling for everyone to stop.

He looked up and down the table. He had everyone's attention … for a lesson in English! His mother and father would be proud.

"Okay, students. Repeat after me. I am the best."

In unison, every boy repeated the sentence with the same enthusiasm as before.

"You are the best." Then Vernon pointed to each one of his students as they repeated after him.

"He is the best," said Vernon and pointed to Caleb as everyone joined in, pointing to Caleb.

"Best lesson ever," yelled out Leroy. "I ain't … I mean … I *am not* ever going to forgit it."

Vernon only wished that were true, but he knew the lesson would be short-lived. *Ain't* was never going to go away. Not with these boys. But that didn't mean he was going to quit trying. There was always hope. When he reached down to pick up Stevenson's novel, the room went quiet in anticipation.

For the hour or so, Vernon weaved himself in and out of Stevenson's characters with his voice. Everyone in the room listened to his every word. Once he had read the last page of the last chapter, he laid the book down.

"Read us another!" called out Ronnie with everybody chiming in, chanting, *read us another,* while at the same time banging their fists on the table in tempo.

To gain the attention of the boys, Vernon held up another book in the air. Almost immediately, there was silence.

"The next book that I plan to read is *The Call of the Wild* by Jack London. It's a story about a dog named Buck who is kidnapped from his home. I think everyone will really enjoy this one." He then opened the book to the first chapter.

Before he could begin, Tommy blurted out, "Just like me. I was kidnapped. That's why I'm here!"

Immediately, the buzz in the room about the new book went dead silent as everyone looked at Tommy. While a number of the boys had heard Tommy's earlier objections to being called a runaway, his outburst about being kidnapped took everybody by surprise.

"It's true," said Tommy to his rapt audience most of whose faces he now recognized. He stood and told them of his plight. How he got lost heading to the golf course. How Watson had given him a lift thinking he was a runaway and had stolen the golf clubs he was carrying and the shoes he was wearing. He told them he had a home in Decatur, Georgia, just outside of Atlanta. He had a mom and a dad. He said he missed them and wanted to go home. Tears began to well up in his eyes and as hard as he tried, he couldn't keep them from running down his face.

"That ain't right … uh … I mean that *is not* right," said Leroy, correcting himself upon seeing a frown from Vernon which turned to a smile when the proper wording was used.

"N … n … not r … right," repeated JoJo.

Then Clarence jumped into the mix. "He shouldn't even be here. He ain't no runaway like Sammy and Claude. Watson done this boy wrong, I tell ya."

"Maybe we should give Watson the black spot like them people did to ol' Long John," suggested Leroy.

"Yeah. Give ol' man Watson the black spot," responded Billy, the normally quiet, red-headed, freckled face kid.

"And give one to Jesse, too," said Clarence. "He's way worse than Watson."

Vernon watched as every one of the boys were either nodding or vocalizing their agreement. He now wished he had chosen a different book for his next read. Tommy wouldn't have gotten upset and the boys wouldn't have gotten riled up. He had to squelch this and fast or there would be repercussions.

"Okay, guys. Listen up," barked Vernon, silencing the uproar. "Do any of you *even remember* what's the significance or meaning of the black spot?"

No one answered. Not even, Tommy who knew. So Vernon continued.

"In the book, a member of the crew gives Long John Silver a torn page from the Bible with a black spot on one side and the word *Deposed* on the other. If you recall, deposed means ousted … removed … thrown out. That's what the pirates wanted to do with Long John. They wanted to depose him … get rid of him. Is that what you want to do with Watson? Get rid of him? Do you know what would happen to us and this farm if that happened? Leroy? Clarence? Billy? Anybody?"

Again, no one answered.

"Let me tell you. Without Henry Watson and knowing that women don't normally run farms, it would have to be either Caleb or Jesse ..."

Before he could finish his sentence, Leroy yelled out, "I want Caleb. Caleb, yes."

Clarence who sat directly across from Leroy shouted out, "Jesse, no!"

"Caleb, yes!" returned Leroy.

"Jesse, no!" hollered Clarence who looked at Leroy and laughed.

Vernon considered trying to halt the friendly banter but decided to let the boys have their fun.

With the two boys being egged on by the others, the next thing anybody knew they were both standing on their chair shouting at each other, stomping their feet in rhythm to the words.

Soon everyone in the room was standing, including Caleb, Vernon and Tommy, as they clapped their hands and stomped their feet in synchronization while Leroy and Clarence continued to shout back at each other, "Caleb, yes. Jesse, no."

The shouting, clapping, stomping and jumping had just reached a crescendo when Leroy stopped his bellowing in mid-sentence, looked at Clarence and flicked his head towards the back of the room. When Clarence turned and looked back to where Leroy had been gesturing with his head, his face turned ashen and his mouth dropped open. Both boys jumped down from their chair and found their seat causing the other boys to stop their chanting and look to the back of the room. Just like Leroy and Clarence, they, too, sat down with many of them with their heads bowed. Everyone, that is, except Caleb who had his back to the door as he continued to sing out, "Caleb, yes. Jesse, no."

When he finally did turn around, he smiled.

It was only Sammy and Claude. Then he saw Jesse.

CHAPTER 25

"Caleb!!! In my room … *now!*" yelled Jesse standing just inside the door with fishing rods in one hand and a rifle in the other. "And you … you … boys … lights out in five minutes. Do I make myself clear?"

There were smatterings of *yes sir* among the boys all of whom had worried and scared looks on their faces as they scurried to their bunks with none looking back at Jesse. Caleb, on the other hand, was all smiles as he lumbered to his brother's room. Jesse hardly ever let him into his room, so Caleb was full of anticipation.

He paused just outside the open door as he watched his brother hang the rifle in a rack next to his bed and slide the fishing rods under his bed. He then saw him pull out a brown paper bag out from under his bed.

"Don't jest stand there like a bump on a log. Git in here and shut the door!" yelled Jesse as he pulled a mason jar from the brown paper bag, unscrewed the lid and took a big swallow.

Caleb did as his brother asked, waiting patiently with his hands behind his back as he watched Jesse take a second drink.

"You know I git this tickle in my throat from all that cotton dust," barked Jesse, closing the now empty jar and sliding it under his bed. "This ain't nuttin' but medicine. But don't you go telling Mama or Daddy. There ain't no sense in worrying them."

"Jesse … Vernon said there *is not* no such word as *ain't*. He said …"

"Vernon's a fool, jest like you. Now … what in tarnation was all that laughing, stomping and shouting about?"

"Them boys was jest having some fun," said Caleb, still smiling.

"And jest what kind of fun was them boys having?"

Caleb thought for a minute.

"I can't rightly remember."

Jesse knew if he pressed too hard, his brother would clam up, cross his arms in front of his body and start rocking his body back and forth. He had to use a gentler approach which was not part of his normal demeanor.

"What did Vernon read to y'all today?"

Caleb got all excited as he relayed what little he remembered about the book, *Treasure Island.*

"You see … this pirate named Long John he wants to find a treasure on this island. But he don't have no map. This other man and a boy named Jim has the map. Somehows Long John gits the map from this man and him and his men go live in this fort. But them pirates ain't … are not happy with Long John. He must of done them wrong. So they give him a black dot on a Bible page which means they wants to dispose of him which means git rid of him. Anyways, Long John give them pirates the map so him and Jim can git away. When the pirates find the cave whereabouts the treasure was hidden, it was *all* gone. Ol' Ben Gum done stole it. Somehows Long John gits back on the ship with Jim. He finds himself a tiny boat, steals some of the treasure and sails away never to be seen by nobody."

None of Caleb's ramblings made sense to Jesse, except the part about the black dot.

"Tell me agin about that there black dot on a Bible."

"Them pirates … they done give Long John the black dot on the Bible which meant they wants to *dispose* of him … *git rid* of him," said Caleb much slower so Jesse would understand.

But he understood alright.

"Did any of them boys want to give me or Daddy a black dot?"

Caleb could tell he was getting into real trouble and wasn't sure how to get himself out.

"I figured they was jest kidding."

"Who was kidding?"

"All them boys. You know … Clarence, Leroy. They done got upset when Tommy told us all that Daddy done stole him. That he weren't a runaway." Unlike Jesse who had no qualms about lying, Caleb couldn't help but tell the truth. It was his nature.

"That Tommy boy is lying!" screamed Jesse causing Caleb to take a step back knowing that when his brother got mad, he usually took it out on something or somebody. "Daddy done told us he found that boy on the street, running away after he done stole some golfing things. And Daddy don't never lie."

"Jesse, them boys was jest having fun."

"So why was they yelling *Caleb, yes* and *Jesse, no?*"

"It weren't nuttin'."

"Boy … you take me fer a fool?" he asked as he reached forward and jerked Caleb's face towards him using his hand, squeezing tightly as he did. "I ain't asking agin." He then let go.

Caleb rubbed his jaw trying to ease some of the pain, both physical and mental.

"I ain't saying," said Caleb, fergetting his earlier English lesson from Vernon.

Jesse balled up his fist, ready to punch his brother. Instead, he pushed him away from the door, yelling, "Then git outta my way. If you won't tell me, I can find out fer myself."

Caleb followed his brother out of the room and watched him as he walked over to the door to the bunkroom on the left and opened it. He then walked over to the door to the bunkroom on the right, flung it open and just stood.

Most of the boys in both rooms pretended to be asleep, some with the sheet pulled over their head. The boys in the right bunkroom who were brave enough to look over to the doorway saw something more frightening than any nightmare they could imagine. The silhouette of Jesse holding a whipping cane in his hand.

CHAPTER 26

"Clarence … Leroy … Tommy!! Git yourself out of bed and come out here, right now. Do I make myself clear?"

All three boys immediately jumped out of bed while responding, "Yes sir." There was no waiting for another warning.

Vernon wanted to whisper something … anything to the boys that they might say or do to placate Jesse, but nothing came to mind. He felt whatever happened to the three boys was his fault. It was on him. He should have shut the festivities down before Jesse had returned from fishing. But everybody was having so much fun and that rarely happened on the farm.

Jesse watched the boys come out of the bunkroom, their heads hung low trying not to make any eye contact with the man. Jesse was mad, but at the same time, he relished the fear he saw in the boy's body language. This is where he and his daddy differed on how to run the farm. His daddy tried to instill discipline by preaching, yelling, twisting of ears and an occasional swat with a cane on the hind side that didn't even raise a welt. Jesse also believed in discipline but only when accompanied with fear. He didn't care if the boys liked him or not. He just wanted them to fear him. That's why he opened the doors to both bunkrooms. He wanted all the boys to hear how he handled discipline.

Once the three boys were assembled just outside their bunkroom, Jesse slapped the whipping cane against the door frame. He wanted their undivided attention.

"Boys … when I come back from fishing, I seen all y'all hooping and a hollering and jumping around like a bunch of wild animals. Now … I ain't gonna ask y'all this but once. What was all this *Caleb, yes* and *Jesse, no* nonsense about? You first, Leroy."

"I ain't real sure," he replied thinking a non-answer was better than the truth.

Without any hesitation, Jesse whacked the back of the boy's legs with his cane.

"Owwwwww! That hurt!" yelled Leroy, rubbing his leg.

"Porky … you want to tell me?" asked Jesse, looking at Clarence.

"I ain't rightly sure neither," he answered, figuring he was going to get a caning regardless of his answer.

And he was right as he felt the cane lash across the back of his legs, not once but twice. Unlike Leroy, he refused to give Jesse any satisfaction by acknowledging the intense pain by yelling out.

Jesse turned to Tommy. "Okay, new boy … if you know what's good fer you, you best give me an answer."

Being last, Tommy had time to think of what to say.

"Sir … uh … we were playing a game called *Treasure Island*. It's where you give out black spots to the person you think has the treasure map. Leroy thought ..."

Before Tommy could finish his story, Jesse's cane came down hard against his back side. Unlike Clarence, Tommy made his hurt known as he yelled out in pain.

"Boy … don't lie to me. I ain't no fool. I heared you said that Daddy done stole you. Is that right?"

"Sir … it was part of the game. We …"

Jesse popped Tommy again, but he was too close to get in a hard whack.

"My daddy don't lie. You hear me?"

"Yes sir," answered Tommy, realizing his Treasure Island game answer wasn't gaining much traction.

Jesse thought for a minute. He could see the fear in the boys' eyes but not so much that they would tell him anything. He needed to push harder.

"I want you boys to turn them chairs around and stand on them like I seen you when I come in from fishing." He slapped the cane against the dining room table to make his point and the boys did what he said.

"Now I wants you boys to start hollering, *Caleb, yes … Jesse, no* jest like you done before." He slapped the table again, this time much harder.

Leroy started the chant followed by Clarence and Tommy. *Caleb, yes. Jesse, no. Caleb, yes. Jesse, no.* Their quivering voices hardly made a sound.

"Louder. I can't hear you," yelled Jesse, followed by a rap of the cane on the table.

As the chant got louder and quicker, Caleb who had been sitting in his room heard the boys and came out of his room and into the big hall chanting and clapping his hands. *Caleb, yes! Jesse, no!*

Jesse turned to see his brother walking towards the boys with a big smile on his face as he kept his chant in time with the boys but much louder. *Caleb, yes! Jesse, no! Caleb, yes! Jesse, no!*

"Stop that, you stupid moron," he yelled, so mad that veins in his temple were pulsating. He so badly wanted to whack his brother. Instead, he turned and began smacking Clarence across his back and legs with his cane until blood began to seep from the wounds. The caning was quick but violent and this time Clarence could not muffle his cries as he fell off the chair.

Fear. That was what Jesse wanted. And he could see and feel it in the other two boys knowing they were next. His mind wandered to the two bunkrooms. He wished he could see the other boy's reactions … their faces … their trembling bodies.

Feeling invigorated, he began to swat Leroy. As he raised his hand for the third time, he felt the cane pulled from his fist. He looked around to see Caleb breaking the cane across the back of a chair.

"Leave them boys alone. They ain't done nuttin' to you," yelled Caleb.

"You stupid, stupid moron," yelled Jesse, punching his brother in the stomach so hard it doubled him over.

While he and Caleb were identical twins, he hated the forever linked association. He never got over the fact that when they were young, people would always get them confused. Caleb was the fool. Not him. Caleb was the one who always had a goofy smile on his face. Not him. Caleb was the one who had drool running down his face. Not him. He hated his brother more than he hated himself.

"Don't you NEVER do that agin. These boys need to be learnt a lesson."

As Caleb reached for an empty chair to sit, Jesse turned to see that Leroy and Tommy had jumped down from their chairs and were now huddled around Clarence trying to comfort the boy who couldn't seem to stop crying.

"They've had enough," said Tommy, standing up and positioning himself between Jesse and the other two boys.

"Well, looky here, looky here. Ain't you jest something, trying to be the hero and all. Well … them boys done learnt their lesson. But you ain't."

He reached over and grabbed Tommy by the arm, pulling him up against his body so close that he was looking down at the young boy's determined face. Before he could say anything, Tommy began hitting him in the stomach with his free hand. The blows took Jesse by surprise causing him to throw Tommy to the ground. Other than Vernon, he had never had a boy to confront him or to challenge his authority. He needed to punish Tommy just like he had done to Vernon.

As Tommy lifted himself up to his hands and knees and tried crawling under the table, Jesse grabbed him by the collar of his T-shirt and jerked him back up to a standing position.

"Boy … you're going with me."

As Clarence and Leroy watched, afraid to offer any help, Jesse marched Tommy towards the front door grabbing a pair of shackles off one of the nearby pegs as he did. He pushed him out to the front porch and onto the steps where he shackled the boy's legs. He then shoved him towards the big magnolia tree that separated the farmhouse and the workers' cabin and towards the lone, dimly glowing light bulb that hung on the farmhouse's back porch. When they neared the light, instead of turning towards the house as Tommy had hoped, they kept walking straight until they came to a big mound of dirt. One that looked like an Indian burial that he had seen in one of his history books at school.

Tommy closely watched Jesse as he moved over to the mound of dirt, kicked away a long board, reached down and pulled open a door.

"This here is where you sleep tonight," he said in hushed tone while pointing to the door.

Tommy looked down and saw steps that led down to a big hole in the ground.

"Now git."

Tommy crawled on his knees to the opening, swiveled his feet around and down to the first rung. The next step was just in reach of his shackled foot so he was able to climb down the steps.

Before reaching the bottom, the door closed.

He was alone. And it was dark.

CHAPTER 27

"Hello? Anybody out there?" Tommy called, not expecting a reply and glad there was none. He had never been afraid of the dark. At least not that he could remember. But this was different. He had never been locked in a deep pit. It was as though he had been thrown into a large grave. As he stood at the base of the steps in complete darkness, he began to conjure up images of his new prison. What came to mind was the dungeon in the book, *The Pit and the Pendulum* by Edgar Allen Poe where the cavernous walls were closing in on the victim of the story and a swinging axe was ready to cut out his heart.

He knew that was fiction, but this was real. Where was he? Then he remembered what Charlie had told him about Vernon. How Jesse had caned him and thrown him into the storm cellar for two days. When Charlie made mention of the storm cellar, he had assumed it was like a basement. But this pit had to be what he was talking about.

While Tommy clung to the steps, he had time to think about his short time at the farm. He no longer feared Watson. Other than the chokehold the old man had administered in the car, the few ear twistings and the thump on the back of the head with the Bible, he posed no threat. The work wasn't hard, the food was really good and he liked all the boys he'd met. He especially liked Caleb. He was as good as they come. But, Jesse was another story. He seemed to enjoy dishing out punishment. If Caleb hadn't stepped in and broken Jesse's cane, Tommy felt certain that his back or legs or maybe both might have been as bad or worse than Clarence's. Being sent down into the storm cellar had to be Jesse's way of showing Tommy and all the other kids who was the boss. That he should be feared. And it worked.

Then a thought occurred to Tommy. If Jesse planned on leaving him down here in the cellar for two days like Vernon, he wouldn't be expected to be out in the fields, in the cabin or doing chores. If he could get out of the cellar, he had two days to escape from the farm and find help. With him wearing shackles, he probably needed at least that much time.

Excited over the possibility of escape, Tommy began climbing up the steps hoping that Jesse who had been drinking might have forgotten to shove the door-locking board back in place. The steps were tricky considering the shackles, but he managed. When his head hit the door, he pushed up but it only moved about three inches, just enough of a gap to let in some of the light from the lone bulb on the farmhouse's back porch. At least there was no sign of Jesse. Nor anybody else, for that matter.

He stuck his arm out the gap and contorted his body in such a way that he could reach back across the door hoping he had enough arm-length to reach the locking board. As hard as he tried, he couldn't stretch his arm far enough. His hopes of escaping were dashed.

He pulled his arm back in, pushed the door back up with his head and cried out for help through the open gap. But no one came. After a while, his head began to hurt from the weight of the roof door.

Dejected, he eased the door down and began his descent back into the darkness. Once he reached bottom, he held firm to the steps with both hands. He was alone, but at least he was safe … for now.

Before long, Tommy grew tired of clinging to the steps and staring out into darkness. Boredom had begun to replace the fears he had of the dark abyss. Feeling brave, he released the vice-like grip that his hands had on the steps, shuffled a foot or so to his right and quickly re-gripped the steps with his left hand, not wishing to lose his lifeline. With his right hand, he felt directly in front of him. As expected, nothing but a dirt wall. Waving his arm to the right and behind him, he felt nothing. Feeling braver, he shuffled a couple of feet more to the right, keeping the dirt wall in front of him but having to let go of the steps. Again, he waved his arm in all directions. Nothing. Feeling less brave with the steps no longer in reach, he decided he would slide two more paces to the right. If he felt nothing, he would return to his home base, the steps. But this time as he reached out to his right, his fingertips hit something and it wasn't dirt. Out of curiosity, not bravery, he turned and let both hands explore.

He found shelves! Multiple shelves with glass jars, stacked three deep, on every one that he could feel. He grabbed one of the jars and from its shape and size, he felt quite sure it was a mason jar. One like his mother used to can fruits and vegetables, a holdover from the rationing days of World War II. His suspicions were confirmed when he unscrewed the top and the lid stayed sealed to the jar. He placed the open band on the shelf, pried open the lid and took a sniff. It smelled like peaches and a sampling proved him right.

Tommy returned to the steps and placed the jar on the rung that was approximately eye-level. He then ventured off to the left side of the steps where he found more shelves and more mason jars. These were filled with green beans. He took that jar back to his home base and set it next to the peach preserves. If he was going to be in the cellar for a couple of days, at least he had some food. Just no water except the liquid from the jars.

He moved to the left of the steps and slid his body down along the dirt wall to where he was sitting on the dirt floor, his legs splayed out in front of him.

He wished he were sleepy, but too many thoughts were running through his mind. He realized that he'd been so consumed by his own troubles, he hadn't even taken time to think about his parents and their angst. Surely by now they knew he had been abducted. Or did they think he was still lost or maybe drowned? After all, the park was large with acres of woods and a huge lake. Regardless, he knew his mother would be blaming herself for letting him and David go to the park alone. She had wanted her husband to go with them. And if not him, then David's father. They had always gone camping with them when they were younger. But they were now sophomores in high school. Neither Tommy nor David wanted anyone "babysitting" them at the park. They could take care of themselves. *Nothing could happen to them,* they said.

He wished he could reach out to his parents and to David. Let them know that he was alive and safe. Anything to keep them from worrying. But he couldn't and they would worry but in different ways. When his mother worried, she would sit in her favorite chair and read the Bible looking for a comforting passage. When his dad worried, he would work, either around the house or at his bicycle/lawnmower shop. Work was his therapy. David, on the other hand, would talk. The more nervous or worried he got, the more he talked. Tommy couldn't help but laugh thinking about his best friend.

Then he cried.

Then he slept.

* * * * * *

Jesse returned to the cabin to find that all the lights had been turned off. He pulled a match from his bib overalls, struck it across the seat of his pants, and used the glow of the flame to find the pull string to the overhead light just inside the small corridor that separated his and Caleb's room. Once he had light, he doused the flame with his fingers and tossed the burnt match to the floor. *Let the boys sweep it up. It's their job*, he thought.

The dimly lit 60-watt bulb revealed that Caleb's door was shut. He never slept with his door shut. He didn't like being enclosed. Yet, it was closed. Jesse turned the knob and pushed. It was locked. He wanted to knock, go into Caleb's room, hug him and tell him that he was sorry. Instead, he headed into his room, closed and locked the door.

As he lay in the bed with the lights out, he could still see Caleb in the chair, bent over with tears running down his face. He wished he hadn't hit him. He hadn't felt this much guilt since he was eight years old. When he and Caleb were racing to see who could make it to the top of the steps. Caleb was just about to reach the porch first when Jesse grabbed one of his legs causing him to fall backwards. He fell down the steps and hit his head on the corner of one the boards. He should have been taken to the hospital, but they didn't have the money. His mama patched him up the best she could, but his brother was never the same after the accident. Nor was he. Caleb had always been a happy boy before the accident and that didn't change after the accident. What did change was his memory, his common sense, his ability to reason.

The guilt of that day hung over Jesse like a dark cloud. Afterwards, he was never happy even when he should have been. He became hateful and mean-spirited to everyone, especially Caleb, calling him idjit, moron, fool. He knew it hurt and upset Caleb, but he couldn't stop. Psychiatrist would label it as low self-esteem or perhaps jealousy. Deep down, he wished he could be like his brother. Happy. Always smiling. Not a worry in the world. Everybody loved Caleb. That's why the boys were yelling *Caleb, yes* and *Jesse, no.* They wanted Caleb, not him. They loved Caleb, not him.

Why had he hit his brother? He had never done that before. *Tommy,* he thought. He's the reason. He'd been a trouble-maker ever since coming to the farm. Yet … he reminded him of Little Eddie. Sweet Little Eddie. Both were small in stature, had an almost angelic face, and was smart. *Too smart.* Daddy should have never taken him in. Not a liar and a thief. If Tommy hadn't gotten those boys all riled up, needing discipline, he would have never hurt his brother.'

It was all Tommy's fault.

CHAPTER 28

Chief Broome had always been an early riser, a prerequisite for his military service. And it had carried over to his civilian life. This morning, he was the first to arrive at the office which was no different from any other work day other than the fact that he was an hour earlier than usual.

As he waited on the coffee to brew, he thought about yesterday and how well the day had turned out considering the fact they had yet to find the boy. Getting the word out about Tommy through the different churches had been a good idea, thanks to Ruth Ann.

The chief had just poured himself a cup of Maxwell House's finest, when he heard the front door open. He looked up to see that it was Lewis. Obviously, he hadn't slept much either. He normally made his presence known around 8 a.m.

"G' morning," said Broome.

"Back at you, Chief."

"Looks like you could use a cup." Without waiting for a reply, the chief found Lewis' favorite turquoise mug and filled it to the brim. Just plain black coffee was all he ever wanted.

Lewis thanked the chief, blew on the hot brew and took a gulp.

"I'm sorry that me and Buddy couldn't help out anymore," he offered.

"You and Buddy did all you could. That's all anyone can ask."

"And no help from the GBI?"

"Not with the investigation but once Betty gets here, I want you to take that cigarette butt you found to their lab in Atlanta. Have them check for fingerprints."

The two walked into Broome's office where he pulled the "Evidence" envelope from his desk drawer. He handed it to Lewis along with directions to the lab.

By 7:00 a.m., Betty and Bob had both arrived and Lewis left. Unlike big city police departments, there was no hustle and bustle, no suspects being interrogated and no week-end crime reports to fill out. Just a laid-back, small-town police station.

"Bob!" yelled Broome through the open door. "Come in here. I need you."

Within seconds, Bob Galloway stood in front of the chief's desk, coffee cup in hand.

"I want you to take this picture of the missing boy over to the *Daily News*. Have them run it for a week. Front page, if possible. Don't take no for an answer. Have them bill me if they won't do this as a community service."

"Yes sir." Within minutes, he was heading out the door with Tommy's picture in one hand and his cap in the other.

With Bob and Lewis gone, the only sound in the office was the clicking noise coming from Betty's typewriter as she typed up the weekly payroll … until the phone rang.

"I've got Will Zachary on the phone," said Betty on the intercom. "He wants to talk to you. He says it's urgent."

Broome clicked off the intercom and picked up his phone on the first ring. Phone calls this early in the morning were hardly ever good news. The last thing he needed was another problem, especially coming from Will Zachary.

"Will, what do I owe the pleasure of such an early call?"

"Jim … a neighbor called me this morning. He told me one of my cows was out in the middle of the highway. But that's not what I'm calling about. I had my boy, Will Junior, drive down there and he herded the cow back into the pasture. After mending the fence, he was supposed to check out the rest of the fence. He wasn't gone that long when I heard his tractor stop in front of the house. He came running into the house hands a'waving and talking up a storm, jabbering about that missing boy we heard Ruth Ann talk about at church yesterday."

Broome's heart leaped. He hoped it was good news. He prayed it was good news.

"Anyway, Will Junior saw some golf clubs laying in the ravine between my property and the highway. He said he left everything just as he saw it. Just thought you might want to know."

"Will… I don't know what all this means, but you and your boy did the right thing. I can't tell you how much I appreciate this. Now … if you don't mind going back down there and watch over things, that would be most helpful. Don't let anybody touch anything. I'll be there shortly."

Broome placed the phone down on the receiver, leaned back in his chair with his hands behind his head and thought about what he needed to do. Crime investigations were not an everyday occurrence in Pine Mountain. He wished the GBI had taken the lead on this case. But they hadn't. So it was up to him, like it or not.

"Betty! Call Lewis," yelled Broome while simultaneously sliding open the second drawer on the right side of his desk. "Tell him to turn around and meet me at the Zachary's farm. Tell him to bring Buddy and go by the hardware store and pick me up a painter's tarp."

From the open desk drawer, he pulled out Pine Mountain Police Department's official camera, a Kodak Brownie and the plastic bag that contained Tommy's underwear. From a nearby storage closet, he grabbed a box labeled "Crime Scene Investigation Stuff" which contained rubber gloves, flares, paper bags, envelopes, tape measurer, a flashlight, a fingerprinting kit, three bags of casting material, a large bucket, a stirring stick, some pencils and an inch thick instruction manual. The box hadn't been opened since the former chief's last day in office when he showed Broome the box and gave him a ten-minute lesson on how to use the fingerprinting kit.

He placed everything in the CSI box, grabbed his cap and headed out of his office, stopping at Betty's desk to tell her where he was going. He didn't need directions to the Zachary's farm. Both families attended the same church, both men were church ushers and Will Zachary was his boss... the mayor of Pine Mountain.

CHAPTER 29

The Zachary's farm, located off Georgia Highway 18, was less than a fifteen-minute drive from the police station. Just as he passed the farm's main entrance, Broome saw Will and Will Junior up ahead, standing behind their fence and both waving their hands. He slowed and pulled off to the side of the road, stopping about three car lengths from the spot where the Zachary's were pointing. He turned off the engine leaving the car's dome light flashing, stepped out of the car, donning his peaked cap.

"That's them. Right there. Near the creek," yelled Will Junior moving closer to the barbed fence and pointing more emphatically.

"Thank you. I'll get to them in a second. I want to check out the highway first."

"But the golf clubs are over here. Right under those bushes," countered the boy.

"Hold your horses, son," said the boy's father. "The chief knows what he'd doing."

If only that were true, thought Broome as he began a slow and methodical walk up the highway going from one side of the road to the other looking for any spike marks. There were none. But there, in the middle of the highway, near the painted highway dividing line, almost directly across from the Zachary's, was a half-smoked cigarette butt. He leaned down to get a closer look and saw that it was an Old Gold. *Not a coincidence,* he thought. He hustled back to his car where he pulled out a pencil and an envelope already labeled "Evidence" and from "Crime Scene Investigation Stuff" box. He returned to where the cigarette lay and using one of the CSI pencils, rolled the butt into the envelope. He then sealed it, returned it to the CSI box and headed back to the spot where he had found the butt.

"What are you doing?" asked a curious Will Junior, now leaning on a post of the wire fence.

"Looking for evidence," responded the chief.

"But the golf clubs are over here. Right in front of me." Will Junior pointed down to the creek. "I can go get them if you want."

"Thank you, Will Junior, but I need to do that myself. I have a uh… a procedure to follow," said Broome, an off the cuff response.

"Jim, do you need us for anything else?" asked the mayor, knowing the chief needed to be left alone to think. "If not, we got chores to do and we don't need to be interfering with your investigation."

"I'm fine, sir. This is going to take a while. And I want this done right," he answered while thinking, *Plus I have no clue what I'm doing.*

The two hopped on their tractor and headed back to their farmhouse, leaving Broome alone to do his police work. He liked the Zacharys but was glad to see them leave. He was beginning to feel like an actor who had forgotten his words and was improvising and not doing a very good job at it.

Broome continued his search for spike marks. When he was satisfied there were none, he returned to the section of the highway directly across from where Will Junior had been pointing… where the golf clubs lay. With all of the dense brush and bramble, the bag could hardly be seen from the road unless one was actually looking for the clubs. As he searched for an easy access to the farm side of the ravine, he noticed a long tire track and some footprints left in the dried mud on the shoulder of the road. Thinking back, he remembered that the only rainy day that week was Friday night, the day before Tommy went missing. More than likely, the footprints and the tire tracks had to be the abductor and his vehicle … assuming that's what this was. An abduction.

With summertime showers popping up at their whim, the golf clubs could wait. Besides, they weren't going anywhere. For the third time, he headed back to the car and this time brought back the entire CSI box.

He pulled out the CSI manual, found the section with step-by-step instructions on how to cast tire tracks and footprints and began the process.

The first step was to take multiple photos, just in case the footprints or tire tracks were damaged or destroyed or if the casts weren't usable. Using the always reliable Kodak, Broome took multiple pictures from different angles and distances.

The second step was making the actual casts of the potential evidence. Using water from the nearby creek, he filled the CSI bucket up to a measured line and returned to the highway. There he poured the whole CSI bag of plaster of Paris into the bucket and stirred it until it looked like pancake batter. Lastly, He poured part of the mix onto a small section of the tire track and the rest in nearby left and right footprints.

While the casts were hardening, he slipped on a pair of rubber gloves and headed down the ravine where he took a large step over the small creek onto the Zachary's property. These were the times when he wished he was smaller as there was little property between the barbed wire fence and the creek. While the clubs had been hard to see from the highway side of the creek, they were clearly visible from the Zachary's property.

After rolling up both pants legs, he straddled the creek and walked over to where the bag lay. He eased the bag out of the thicket pushing the splayed clubs back into the bag as he did. He was careful not to grab the bag by the handle or strap just in case there were fingerprints. Holding the bag by its collar, he turned around and began to straddle the creek back to the highway. That's when he saw the cleated soles of the boy's black and white golf shoes. Both were upside down in a bush near the creek bed and only visible from that direction. Broome understood why the golf clubs were tossed. But, why the golf shoes? That made no sense at all.

He reached down, grabbed the shoes and, one by one, tossed them to the side of the road.

Broome had just begun to climb up the ravine with the golf bag when he saw Lewis drive up and park behind his car. When the sergeant exited, he was carrying the painter's tarp as Broome had requested. He stopped long enough, put on his cap and to pat Buddy on the head who was leaning out the open rear window with his paws perched on its ledge waiting to pounce at the first call.

"Lewis, I'm glad you're here," said Broome as he reached the road. "I'm sorry I had to call you back but something more important came up. I hope you hadn't driven too far."

"Actually, I had stopped at Pearl's boarding house to get some breakfast and ..." Lewis stopped mid-sentence when he saw the golf clubs and came running towards the chief. "Hey! Are those the boy's golf clubs? Where'd you find them? What about the boy?"

"Slow down. I'll tell you everything I know. First, yes, they are the boy's clubs. They match the description given to me by his friend. Plus, the bag has a tag with his name on it. Will Junior found them in the ravine next to his property while he was looking for a stray cow. I also found his shoes." The chief pointed over to the side of the road where they lay.

"Oh … and I found another cigarette butt in the middle of the road. And you'll never guess what brand."

"You're kidding me.

"Nope. Old Gold. Just like you found Saturday near Callaway Gardens. And I don't think it's a coincidence. And while I'm thinking about it … that was a fine piece of detective work you did finding that cigarette stub. Most people would have overlooked it. Good job, Lewis."

Receiving compliments always embarrassed Lewis. "Thank you," he mumbled, nodding his head in acknowledgement.

"What about the boy?"

"Nothing. That's why I wanted you to bring Buddy. Maybe he can pick up his trail."

"You want me to call Buddy now? He's raring to go."

"No. Not just yet," said Broome who reached down into the CSI box and pulled out another pair of rubber gloves."

"Here … put these on. Then I want you to spread that tarp out in the back of my trunk so I can lay these clubs and those shoes on it. The gloves keep us from contaminating the evidence."

"Makes sense."

Lewis slipped on the gloves, headed over to the chief's car and unfolded the tarp in the trunk. He stood back as Broome carefully laid the golf bag on top.

"Is that blood?" asked Lewis, pointing to the bag.

"Where?"

"On the towel hooked to the bag."

Broome bent over and looked down at the golf bag. He then spread out the green and white Masters towel that lay on top of it and thoroughly examined it.

"Good catch, Lewis," said Broome looking over at his deputy.

"You think it's the boy's?" Lewis.

"Good question. We won't know until I get this to the GBI lab in Atlanta. One thing's for certain, if this is blood, there isn't enough on that towel to make me think that a person bled out. *I know* what that looks like." Broome was recalling his days in the service on the battlefields during World War II and the Korean War where he had seen lots of blood and lots of deaths.

"So now you're going, not me?"

"Yes. Besides going to the lab, I want to see the Harrison's and Rutledge's and fill them in on our progress. It's not much, but we owe it to them. Now follow me. I want your young eyes looking at our next piece of evidence."

Broome headed back up the highway to where the golf shoes lay. He bent down, picked up the first shoe and examined it. He handed it over to Lewis who also gave it a once over.

"You think this is blood?" asked Lewis pointing to some reddish-brown spots he'd found.

"Yes. Or maybe mud. Again, that's something for the GBI lab to determine."

Lewis handed the shoe back to the chief who set it down and picked up the second shoe. Reddish-brown spots were also found on it. An uneasy feeling came over Broome. Everything they had found had blood on it, if that's what it was. He prayed it wasn't.

Broome picked up the first shoe and he and Lewis headed over to the chief's car and carefully placed the shoes on the tarp, next to the golf clubs. He then led Lewis over to the white casts on the side of the road.

"What are those?" asked Lewis.

"They're casts of tire tracks and footprints that I found in close proximity of where the golf clubs and shoes had to have been thrown into the ravine."

"How'd you know how to do all this stuff?"

"Everything I know I read from a book in that box." The chief pointed to the CSI box. "When you become chief, I will give you the box and you can read it yourself." Then the chief laughed.

Lewis would have laughed except his mind was focused on what the chief had just said, *when you become chief.*

Once all the evidence, casts and the CSI box were in the chief's car, Lewis got Buddy and they met the chief at the approximate location on the highway where the half-smoked Old Gold had been found. Buddy got a good smell of the cigarette from the "Evidence" envelope and immediately began jerking the leash. At first, he seemed to want to go into the bushes where the golf clubs had been found. But changed his mind and ended up at Broome's closed trunk, barking non-stop.

"Hush Buddy." The dog ceased his steady bark but continued to vent an occasional bark intermixed with a low guttural whimper. "Chief, he's barking at the golf bag."

"Well, it was worth a try."

Broome closed the trunk of his car and accompanied Lewis and Buddy back to their car with both men in deep thought. Once Lewis had let Buddy into the back seat, he turned to Broome. "You know, I've been thinking. What if it was the boy who was smoking those Old Golds? Not the abductor. If so, we might be chasing our tail."

"Good question. I like your thinking, but I hope you're wrong."

Broome made a mental note to ask the Harrisons.

"Unless you can think of anything, I think we're done here."

"No sir."

"While I'm gone, here's what I want you to do. Drive towards the Alabama state line. And drive real slow. Maybe you'll find something."

Both men had the same thought, *I hope not THAT something.* Meaning the boy's body.

The two men headed out going in different directions but with one goal in mind: Finding Tommy Harrison. Alive.

CHAPTER 30

Tommy wasn't sure if it was the sudden light or the sound of the squeaking roof door swinging open that awakened him. Regardless, he saw Caleb looking down at him from the cellar's entrance. When he looked around, the cellar didn't seem as menacing as he had thought. Certainly not like Poe's dungeon. Just shelves on every wall, mostly filled with stacks of mason jars.

"Tommy! You need to git yourself up here right now. Daddy's gonna be coming around with the truck in jest a minute. I brung you your clothes and shoes."

"Does Jesse know you're letting me out?" asked Tommy as he climbed up the steps.

"He ain't … is not up right this minute. Besides, he might'n not remember anyways. Last time, when he throwed Vernon in the cellar, he plumb fergot about him fer two days."

Once Tommy had reached the last rung, Caleb extended his hand and pulled him from the cellar. While Tommy watched, Caleb closed the door and placed the locking board back in place.

"I brung you some biscuits and fatback since you done missed breakfast." He pointed to a greasy brown sack sitting on a small wood pile next to the cellar. "Now … let me unloose them leggings."

Tommy sat down on the cellar door and Caleb slipped his keys from around his neck and unlocked the shackles.

Tommy could see apprehension in Caleb's eyes, so he dressed as fast as possible.

"Won't your Daddy be mad at you for letting me out?"

"Oh, he don't know what Jesse done. He don't know he beat the tar out of Clarence and Leroy and throwed you in the cellar. If'n he did, Jesse would be in a heap of trouble."

"Then, why are you doing this? Jesse *should* be in trouble."

"He's my brother. I love him. And he don't usually act real mean like he done to you boys 'cepting when he's taking his medicine."

"Yes, but …"

"Tommy, we best be leaving. Daddy don't know I'm gone."

As Tommy was shuffling back to the workers' cabin, he looked at the farmhouse just in time to see Mrs. Watson back away from the screen door. She had been watching them.

CHAPTER 31

Caleb held his hand out to stop Tommy behind the big magnolia tree when he saw his daddy's pickup truck in front of the workers' cabin.

"Shhh," he whispered with his index finger held vertically in front of his lips.

The two watched as the boys from the first bunkroom filed out the front door and jumped into the back of the truck. As always, Sammy and Claude sat on the tailgate. They were bigger and older than the other pickers, so there was no discussion.

Once Watson had driven off and was out of sight, Caleb motioned for Tommy to follow him. Even though Tommy had been wearing the shackles for only three days, he had become accustomed to their gait limitations and easily kept pace even as he downed the biscuit and fatback.

"You only got about ten minutes to use the privy and make your bed before Daddy's back," cautioned Caleb as they neared the cabin. "I'm gonna go sit out front. I'll holler when I see him."

"Okay. And thank you for letting me out. You are a kind man."

Caleb was taken aback as he had never been called a man. Idjit, moron, boy, dummy and many more derogatory names but never *man.*

"I 'preciate that." He then gave Tommy a big smile.

When Tommy walked into the main hall, he saw Leroy, Wayne, Charlie and JoJo sitting around the meal table and they were telling knock-knock jokes.

"Dishes who?" asked Leroy.

"Dishes Caleb. Ain't you glad I ain't Jesse," laughed Wayne.

"T … T … T … Tommy," stuttered JoJo when he saw his friend enter the room.

"How'd you git out?" asked Leroy with a surprised look on his face. "I figured you'd be in fer at least two days like Vernon."

"Caleb got me out. Where's Jesse?"

"He left right after Caleb. Headed out to the barn to git the tractor. He looked bad. Eyes all red and swollen."

Tommy looked at Leroy's legs.

"You don't look too good yourself. Your legs are a mess."

"It ain't nuttin'. Now Clarence … his legs and backside are all messed up. He ain't working today in the fields. He ain't fit to pick cotton today. Instead, they got him doing the chores instead of Claude. He might be out tomorrow, too."

"I should have kept my mouth shut," said Tommy. "This is all my fault. You boys were fine until I showed up.

"It weren't your fault," said Leroy. "And we weren't fine before you showed up. Jesse's done this before, 'specially lately when he's been drinking. Look at them scars on Wayne's legs."

Wayne turned around so Tommy could see the back of his legs.

"I ain … ain't nev … never been be … be … beat," added JoJo.

"Neither have I," said Charlie. "And don't intend to."

"Aside from the beatings me, Tommy and Clarence got, all I can say is I ain't had that much fun since I come to this place," said Leroy.

"You got that right," said Wayne.

Tommy was about to head to the bunkroom when he saw Vernon and Eugene walk out the door.

"Just one day? Aren't you the lucky one," said Vernon.

Tommy thought about how much time he had.

"I gotta go make my bunk before Watson gets back or else …"

"It's already done," interrupted Eugene. "Vernon and I didn't want you to get into any more trouble, so we took care of it."

"I owe you guys. Now I have to excuse myself or I won't get in my bathroom time." He left, not waiting on any responses.

* * * * * *

When Caleb heard his daddy's truck and saw its headlights break through the rapidly dissipating ground fog, he pushed himself off the bench where he had almost dozed off, hurried to the front door, flung it open and yelled out, "Daddy's here."

By the time Watson pulled to a stop, all the boys from the second bunkroom, minus Clarence, were waiting at the foot of the steps.

Even though the boys never dallied as they climbed into the bed of the truck, Watson never failed to harass their efforts with his favorite admonition.

"Time's a'wasting. That cotton ain't gonna pick itself."

Caleb, JoJo and Leroy claimed the tailgate while Tommy, Vernon and Eugene sat down in the truck-bed with their backs to the rear window.

"Were you scared?" asked Vernon, directing his question to Tommy who was in the middle.

"Can he hear?" Tommy asked, while motioning with his hand towards Watson.

"No. You can talk. The engine makes too much noise for him to hear."

"Yeah. I was scared. At first, all kind of weird and scary thoughts passed through my mind. But after a while, when nothing had happened, I ventured away from the ladder."

"You find the canned goods Mrs. Watson stores down there?"

"I did. Peach preserves and green beans."

"Actually, the cellar isn't really that bad. You just have to get used to the darkness unless it's winter time."

"It's certainly a lot better than getting beaten by Jesse," said Tommy. "Why doesn't his daddy do something about that ... the canings?"

"Even though Jesse is the favorite son, I don't think Watson is turning a blind eye," said Vernon. "He believes in discipline but not corporal punishment. I honestly don't think he knows. Jesse's always been mean, quick to slap one of us around. Even a caning now and then but nothing like what he did to Clarence, Leroy or even me. The canings have only become a real issue since Little Eddie ran away."

"Why doesn't somebody tell him?"

"Like who? Not me. I've already suffered the wrath of Jesse. And believe me, he *would* find out who snitched. I tell everybody to adhere to my rule number three. Stay as far away from Jesses as possible and life on the farm will be good."

"How many times has he caned you?"

"Just that once. Most of the boys have never been caned. Just Wayne and now Leroy, Clarence and you. Like I said earlier, the canings and excessive drinking have only been going on since Little Eddie left."

"Why do you think …"

Tommy stopped mid-sentence when he felt the truck come to a full stop and heard the engine shut off.

"Later," said Vernon.

* * * * * *

By the time Watson stepped out of the truck and closed the door, all the boys except Tommy had left the vehicle. He smiled as he saw them hustling over to the cotton wagon to grab their cotton sack. He liked the discipline they exhibited, especially without him having to enforce it. When he reached the tailgate, he saw Caleb helping Tommy jump to the ground.

"Boy … how'd you like to be out of them leggings by Saturday?" asked Watson, looking at Tommy.

"Very much so, sir."

"I seen how quick you done learnt how to pick. Nearbout outdid Sammy and Clarence on your first day."

"Yes sir. It's not that hard once you get your rhythm."

"Looky here. If you out pick five of my boys by Saturday, you ain't gotta wear them leggings no more. You reckon you can do that?"

"Yes sir!!"

"But Daddy, that ain't … is not fair," offered Caleb.

"Don't Daddy me," snapped Watson. "Mama said that Clarence ain't feeling too good today. Said he got all tangled up with a mess of yellow jackets and got welts all over his legs. She's got him doing chores and helping her in the kitchen. Sissy work. So I'm one boy short. I need Tommy. I want you to put him next to JoJo this morning and next to Eugene in the afternoon. See if he can keep up with my best pickers."

"I can, sir," assured Tommy.

"Good boy. Now git your hiney out there and git pickin'."

Without waiting for Caleb, Tommy headed over to the cotton wagon and grabbed a sack. Watson watched until Caleb had caught up with the shackled boy and saw them walking down the row next to JoJo where Leroy was working. *That's a good boy,* he thought while nodding. *Sarah's wrong. He ain't gonna be no trouble.* He then returned to his truck and drove back to the farm.

"Your mama told you to let me out, didn't she?" asked Tommy.

Caleb looked to see that his daddy was gone. He stopped, turned and looked at Tommy who almost bumped into him.

"Don't you tell nobody, 'specially Daddy."

"What about Clarence? She told your daddy that he got stung by bees. Why is she protecting Jesse?"

Clarence turned and looked towards the end of the rows where Jesse sat on the tractor, rifle in hand and hat covering his eyes just to make sure he, too, was out of earshot.

"You ain't never seen Daddy git *real* mad," said Caleb, forgetting to correct his English. "That ear pulling and head thumping ain't nuttin' like he used to did before he went into the army. He'd give Jesse a whacking with a paddle fer no reason a'tall. But he never got after me. He always said I didn't know any better. He jest called me an idjit which hurt me worse. Now since he come back from the army, he's done changed. He don't git mad like he used to did. But Mama's ain't taking no chances. She don't tell Daddy nuttin' that might git Jesse or me in trouble. Ain't that what mamas s'posed to do?"

"Yes, Caleb. That's what mamas are supposed to do. And you're not an idjit. You're the best farmer I know. You can pick cotton. You know how to milk cows, feed the chickens, help with the meals … everything. All Jesse does is sit on the tractor and sleep."

Caleb smiled as he and Tommy walked down the cotton row to where Leroy was picking.

"Leroy … Daddy wants Tommy picking next to JoJo," said Caleb. "If you would kindly move over a few rows, I'd 'preciate it."

JoJo stopped picking when he heard his name mentioned and looked over at Caleb, Tommy and Leroy who had picked up his sack, and was holding it above his head as he slid past the cotton plants being careful not to step on any of the stems. Tommy couldn't help but stare at the welts on Leroy's legs and wonder how bad Clarence must look.

"H … h … hey, Tom … Tommy," stuttered JoJo.

"Hey, JoJo," responded Tommy.

"You ain't fergotten how to pick cotton, has you?" asked Caleb.

"No. I remem …."

"Caleb," yelled out Jesse, his nap being interrupted. "What in tarnation is going on out there? Them boys are s'posed to be picking cotton, not jibber-jabbering. This ain't s'posed to be no social shindig. Y'all git back to work. Do I make myself clear?"

Before anyone could answer, he recognized Tommy, even though his hat and work clothes made him look just like all the other pickers.

"What's *he* doing out here?" asked Jesse, pointing his rifle at Tommy. "I thought I throwed him down in the cellar. Who let him out?"

"I did. We ain't got enough pickers with Clarence being too sick to work. You know that cotton ain't gonna pick itself," said Caleb, mimicking his daddy.

"You stupid moron …"

"He's not a moron. Stop calling him that," yelled Tommy knowing the consequences of his backtalk.

"Caleb ain't no moron," yelled Leroy. "He's the best."

"Caleb's the best," echoed Vernon followed by Eugene, JoJo, Wayne with the rest of the boys joining in.

"Caleb's the best! Caleb's the best! Caleb's the best."

Jesse had had enough. He jumped down from the tractor, leaving his rifle laying across the seat. He found a nearby stick and was marching towards Tommy when a faraway bell began to toll causing Jesse to stop dead in his tracts, the boys to stop their chanting and Tommy to wonder what was going on.

CHAPTER 32

Without the young Rutledge boy in the car, the trip to Atlanta this time was long, boring and uneventful. There was no sound except the blowing of the wind through the front windows. However, the silence gave Broome an opportunity to think. Think about what he knew. Think about what he didn't know which was more than what he knew. And to think about what he was going to say to the Harrisons and the Rutledges. He had hoped that the Harrisons would have already heard from the abductors. But since he hadn't received a call from the Decatur police chief or the Harrisons, he assumed that it hadn't happened. So the responsibility of the investigation still lay on his shoulders. And all he had was the box of evidence and the golf clubs with the blood-stained towel. Hopefully, the state lab could at least determine if it was the boy's blood before he visited the Harrisons. Assuming it was the boy's blood, what did that mean?

The GBI lab, officially known as the State Crime Lab, was located in the new Department of Public Safety building on East Confederate Avenue in Southeast Atlanta. The lab was relatively new only having been established in 1952 when the Georgia State Legislators approved a bill and signed by Governor Herman Talmadge transferring the Fulton County Scientific Crime Laboratory to the state. Dr. Herman Jones became its first director.

As the Chief of Police for Pine Mountain, Georgia, Broome had never had reason to use the services of the state lab so when he arrived at the multi-level, elongated building complex with its huge parking lot, he felt lost. This seemed to be a common thread in his investigation.

The woman receptionist in the lobby couldn't help but laugh when she saw the ruggedly, handsome officer enter the building carrying a box out in front of him, his peaked cap under his right arm, and lugging a set of golf clubs across his shoulders.

"Are you sure you have the right place," she asked. "Candler Park Golf Course is about five miles north of here." She then laughed again.

At first, Broome seemed confused by the woman's comment but he, too, began to laugh when he considered how he must look.

"Actually, I'm looking for someone to examine some evidence in a kidnapping case. My name is Jim Broome, Chief of Police, Pine Mountain, Georgia. Can you direct me to that person?"

"Well, you've come to the right place. Let me see what I can do. Have a seat ... well ... never mind," she said as she looked at the golf clubs strapped to the man's back.

Within a few minutes, a young, bespectacled man with a military buzz cut and wearing a white lab coat came from a door behind and to the right of the receptionist. He walked over to the chief and introduced himself as Dr. Gordon Barrineau, forensic scientist. Broome shifted the box to his left arm, extended his right hand and introduced himself as they shook hands. The sight of the chief and his entourage of evidence did not draw laughter from the man as it had the receptionist. Instead, he was all business when he spoke.

"Please follow me." There was no offer to help with the chief's load.

On the second floor, Barrineau opened the door to his office and sat down behind a gray metal desk that had only the basic necessities on its top. He pointed to an empty chair in front of his desk.

"Have a seat and tell me what brings you to our facilities."

The chief set the box down on the floor next to his chair and placed his cap on top. From his right coat pocket, he pulled out a pair of rubber gloves and slipped them on before pulling the golf clubs from his shoulder. While he held the bag with one hand, he pulled out the painter's tarp from the box and wrapped it around the clubs before laying them down next to the box. He then removed the gloves, slid them in his pocket and sat down in the chair facing the forensic scientist who had watched the entire ordeal, once again, offering no help.

Broome saw the man look up at the clock on the wall. Not wishing to waste any more of his valuable time, Broome told the story of the missing boy and the evidence he'd found. The cigarette butts, the golf clubs, the golf shoes and the towel with blood stains.

Barrineau took notes as the chief spoke, never looking up until the officer had finished talking. Afterwards, he slipped on some protective gloves he'd pulled from one of the desks drawers and walked over to the evidence and gave it a cursory examination. He returned to his desk and then he spoke.

"I believe this is a first ... you know ... the golf clubs. Just so you don't think that I was being rude, I purposely watched you put on the protective gloves and carefully wrap the golf clubs. I can't tell you how many times we've gotten contaminated evidence. Your attentiveness to detail in preserving the original condition of the evidence is commendable. You had a very good teacher." Broome couldn't help but smile at the compliment. "So let me tell you what we can do," continued Barrineau. "The blood on the towel … we can analyze it to determine if it's human or animal. We can also determine the approximate date of the stain. However, most parents don' know the blood type of their children as it's not recorded on anyone's birth certificate, so we won't be able to tell if it's the boy's blood or his abductor's or someone else's. And the tire tracks from the mold, which by the way are excellent … all we will be able to tell you is the size and brand. Assuming the tires are originals, that same tire is used on a number of different vehicles built by a number of different car manufacturers. As for the fingerprints … if we find any on the golf bag or the cigarette butts … they will be useful only if we find the abductor and can use them for comparisons. Same with the shoeprints. And just so you know, you will probably be looking at three to four weeks or more before we can even start the process as forensic examinations from crimes committed in city of Atlanta take priority."

This is not what Broome wanted to hear, especially the delay. He had hoped that when he left the lab, he would be able to put out an alert to other nearby police stations and sheriff's departments in southwest Georgia the make and model of the abductor's vehicle. At the very least, he hoped he would know if the blood on the towel was Tommy's or not. He had no idea that blood types weren't recorded on birth certificates. He'd known his blood type since he joined the Army. It was on his dog tag which he still wore. The whole trip seemed a waste of time.

The young forensic saw the chief's disappointment in his face and body language.

"I'm sorry I couldn't give you any better news, but I'm a scientist. I believe in absolutes. I think it's better that you leave here knowing the facts rather than giving you false hopes."

"I understand. I am disappointed, but it's always better to know the truth. I appreciate your time." Broome leaned over and carefully picked up the golf clubs. "What should I do with these things and the box of evidence?"

"Leave them there. I'll have one of my assistants catalogue them and place everything in the evidence room."

As Broome reached down for his cap, Barrineau asked, "I'm curious. Why haven't you gotten the GBI involved?" asked Barrineau. "I thought they handled most kidnappings … them or the FBI."

"Oh, I asked. Got turned down. Not enough manpower according to Director Stephens. Too busy helping out the FBI keep tabs on some colored preacher named King," replied Broome staying calm, trying not to take his grievances out on Barrineau.

"I see," said Barrineau as he stood and walked around his desk and picked up the box of evidence. "Didn't you say the boy is from Decatur?"

"Yes sir. Nelson Ferry Road."

"That's close enough to the City of Atlanta for me. Grab those clubs and follow me." Barrineau was well aware of the GBI's involvement with the FBI, its obsession with the Reverend King and its drain on the GBI's resources, both agents *and* forensics.

Barrineau did a quick-walk down the long hallway to the first door on his right which had an opaque glass panel with "LAB A" imprinted on it. By the time he had shifted the evidence box to his left arm, pulled out his keys and unlocked the door, the chief had caught up with him. Once both men were inside the lab, Barrineau locked the door.

"We are very security conscience. We can't have the guilty set free because of a technicality, not on our part. So we are very protective of any evidence left in the room."

Broome nodded in agreement, but he was not familiar with that side of the law where technicalities could set a guilty man free. Not in Pine Mountain.

As he looked around, he was immediately impressed with what he saw. The room had the sterile feel of a new hospital. And it was very bright with eight windows on the far side of the room overlooking the old Confederate Soldiers Home and a ceiling covered with rows of fluorescent lights. The black and white linoleum square tiles that covered the floor were spotless. Scientific instruments of all kinds could be seen on the long, black counters that ran along three of the four sides of the room and in the glass-door wall cabinets that hung on either side of the room.

Barrineau walked over to the counter on the left side of the room and set the box down next to one of the lab's many microscopes.

"Put the golf clubs over there," he said pointing to the counter on the far wall. As he did, a young Black man wearing a white lab jacket entered the room from one of the three right-side offices.

"Grady. I didn't know you were here. Are you busy?"

"Not anything I can't do later. What do you need?"

"Grady … this is … uh …" Embarrassed, Barrineau picked up his notes off the top of Broome's evidence box. Before he could find the chief's name, Broome spoke up."

"I'm Jim Broome, Chief of Police, Pine Mountain, Georgia."

"Grady Johnson. Pleased to meet you." Grady moved towards the chief and the two shook hands.

"Grady … the chief has brought us a golf bag that belonged to a child that was abducted this past Saturday. There's a possibility that the abductor's fingerprints are on the bag. There's also a towel attached to the bag with some blood stains. Can you check for fingerprints and analyze the blood. Once that's done can you run the vacuum?"

Barrineau saw the baffled look on Broome's face and realized how his instructions must have sounded to a non-forensic person.

"Chief Broome. Vacuuming is one of our investigative tools. Grady will be using our *very expensive* trace evidence vacuum on the golf bag and towel. It captures hairs, glass, fibers, paint, drugs and other minute particles. We never know what we will find, but the results can be very useful. For example, our findings from the vacuum last month helped put a known drug dealer in jail for a long time."

"That's amazing."

"Yes, it is," replied Barrineau. "Especially to a layman. Grady and I work with these forensic tools every day. Yet, like you, I am still amazed at how far our science has come in the last few years with advances in fingerprinting and hair analysis, the use of chromatography …" Barrineau stopped his mini-lecture, seeing that he was losing his audience. "Obviously, I love my work."

"We all should be so lucky."

"Chief, this is going to take some time before we can get you some preliminary results. Unless you have some place to go, if you want, you can wait in the office next to Grady's. It's empty, but there's a phone if you need to make any calls."

"Actually, I do."

Barrineau walked Broome over to the office.

"When you pick up the phone, Jenny, our receptionist, will connect you to any number, local or long distance. I'm just outside if you need anything. I can close the door if you want.

"Yes, please."

Broome thanked Barrineau and took a seat behind the government-issued, gray metal desk. As he watched Barrineau close the frosted glass door, he couldn't help but think how professional and well trained the man was with his multiple college degrees in science and forensics. Unlike himself who was running his department and this investigation by the seat of his pants. He, like most of the other rural police departments, had little to no training in the science of police investigations. Not like the big city police departments where their recruits were given classroom and field training before becoming a police officer.

He had never felt so out of place.

CHAPTER 33

Sarah first realized that Clarence was missing when he didn't show up with the two pails of milk as scheduled. Normally, that would have been Caleb's job, but Henry had him keeping a watch on Tommy with it being only his second day of picking.

After waiting fifteen minutes and Clarence was still a no-show, she knew something wasn't right. It reminded her of the time when Little Eddie went missing. Rather than worry, she decided to go looking for him. She headed for the workers' cabin, but when she saw that the gate to the pasture was open, she changed her mind and headed straight for the barn, thinking accident.

The cows were in their stalls, but the milk pails sat empty stacked on top if each other. But there was no sign of Clarence. She left and headed to the workers' cabin and found one of the lockers opened and most of the clothes were gone along with the pillow case from the bunk. It had to be Clarence's. He had run away.

Watson saw Sarah quick-walking back to the main house while at the same time waving him down. Seeing her outside the house at this time of morning was not normal. So he hit the gas pedal and they both arrived at the house at about the same time.

Watson leaned his head out the window. Before he had a chance to say anything, Sarah blurted out, "Clarence is gone. Done run away."

"What do you mean, he done run away?"

"He's gone. Packed up his clothes and skedaddled."

Watson bolted from the truck, up the porch steps and over to a large black bell that hung from the roof's overhang. He jerked the cord hooked to the bell five or six times.

He then ran back to his truck, yelling, "Go back to the cabin and find something of the boy's that Tippy can smell. If he took all his clothes, bring his sheet. I'm going to round up the boys. And git me my whipping cane."

Watson pulled the gear shift into first and sped off, back to the field. He was not a happy man. He had a runaway on his hands that would have to be disciplined once he was found. And the punishment would have to be more than an ear pulling or head thumping. He had to make an example out of him. He never enjoyed reprimanding any of his workers. It was bad for morale. But it would be worse for morale if he didn't. The army had taught him that.

As he drove off, he couldn't help but wonder why Clarence had run away? It made no sense. He seemed to enjoy farming and the farm life. He had *never* been a problem. What changed?

It had to be the new boy. It had to be Tommy.

CHAPTER 34

Watson had said nothing about a bell during his orientation, but everybody else seemed to know what it meant. Tommy saw Jesse heading back to the tractor, Caleb running towards the cotton wagon and all the pickers heading towards the turnrow with their cotton sack flung over their shoulders.

"What's going on? What's with the bell?" Tommy asked JoJo.

"E … E… E …"

"Emergency," said Eugene coming to JoJo's rescue. "Grab you sack and follow me."

"What's the emergency?" asked Tommy struggling to keep up with both JoJo and Eugene.

"Don't know. We'll find out when we get back to the cabin."

Tommy and Eugene were the last of the pickers to reach the dirt road behind the turnrow where they saw Jesse tossing the sacks to Caleb who in turn was emptying the contents into the slatted cotton wagon with nothing being weighed or recorded.

"Drop the sack on the pile and wait over there with the rest of the boys fer the truck," ordered Jesse but not in a mean-spirited way.

As Tommy and Eugene neared the boys at the corner of the main dirt road and the cotton field, they could see everyone talking excitedly among each other except Sammy and Claude who never had anything to say much less get excited about anything unless it was fishing. The talk centered around what the emergency might be. Because a tornado had passed by the farm a couple of years ago, having another one seemed to be the most probable reason yet the skies were clear and the wind was almost at a standstill. Another possibility was an injury to one of the Watsons. Also being bantered around was the possibility of a fire in one of the buildings.

All the talk ceased when Watson's truck appeared on the horizon and he was driving. When he reached the intersection where the boys were milling around, he slowed but did not stop. Instead, he drove over to the cotton wagon, parked the truck, leaving the engine idling and walked to the rear of the wagon where Jesse and Caleb were pulling a tarp over the cotton.

"Y'all hurry up. We got a missing boy. Most likely, he done run away. I'm gonna git them boys in the cabin. Y'all meet me at the farmhouse. Do I make myself clear?"

With a runaway, Watson needed Jesse and Caleb with him, leaving no one to watch over the boys in the fields which made him vulnerable to more runaways. One leaves and they all might want to leave. As a precaution, all the boys would have to be locked in the cabin while he, his sons and Tippy searched for the missing boy. This meant that no one would be picking cotton and that was time lost which couldn't be made up. But he couldn't have a mutiny on his hands. He had to maintain control of the situation.

Watson didn't wait for a reply. Instead, he backed his truck all the way over to the boys who had seen everything but couldn't hear anything because of the engine noise. So the emergency was still a mystery to them.

Before Watson had come to a complete stop, he was yelling out the window.

"Y'all git in the back of the truck … now! Times a'wasting!"

Tommy watched as the boys did what Watson had ordered with no stopping to ask why or what was happening. That was the discipline that Watson had talked about. It had worked on Tommy as well as he, too, shuffled over to the truck without saying a word.

The old man stood on the running board, counting heads until everyone was seated in the truck. Of the eleven boys, eight sat crammed next to each other on the truck bed with their legs either crossed or knees pulled up to their chest. The other three boys, Tommy, Charlie and Billy, sat on the tailgate ready to extend their legs at the first bounce of the truck so not to risk injury.

Watson slid back into the truck, shifted the gear lever into first, and the truck seemed to leap as it took off down the dirt road back to the farm. Everyone held on tight as the old man seemed to ignore the ruts and bumps.

"Where are we going?" asked Tommy, looking first at Billy, then Charlie.

"I reckon the cabin 'cause I ain't seen no storm clouds," said Billy.

"I just hope nothing has happened to Mrs. Watson," said Charlie. "She's the only one who can really cook around here."

"Charlie's right," said Billy. "Caleb done all the cooking a whilst back when Missus Watson was gone fer a few days when her sister in Macon took ill. He done his best cooking and all, but it weren't fit fer even them hogs out there."

Before long, they arrived back at the farm and to everyone's delight, they saw Sarah, standing on the front porch with her arms folded across her chest and her right foot tapping the floor. Tommy could see the anxious look on her face as they slowly passed her by.

Once they reached the cabin, the truck came to an abrupt stop and Watson climbed out of the cab, leaving the engine running. He headed over to the cabin where he unlocked the front door and waited until the boys began filing into the building. As they did, he counted heads, making sure there were eleven boys. After the last boy, Tommy, had entered the cabin, Watson closed the door and locked it. He returned to the truck and drove back to the farmhouse, waiting for Jesse and Caleb.

Except for the few boys that lined up to use the privy, most went to their bunks and laid down or sat on their foot-locker waiting to find out why the emergency bell had been rung.

Tommy was shuffling towards his bunkroom when he heard Leroy yell out.

"Clarence is gone! All his clothes, his blanket … all gone!"

Within seconds, everyone had converged in the right-side bunkroom where they found Leroy sitting on his footlocker, visibly upset.

"I should have know'd he was going to run away. He was hurting so bad last night after Jesse had done beat him. He kept saying that weren't never going to happen to him agin. But I thought … I don't know what I thought."

"Leroy … there was nothing you or anybody could have done," said Vernon.

"I hope he gits clean away," said Wayne.

"That's not going to happen. Y'all hush and listen," said Vernon cupping his ear with his hand.

"Li … li … listen wh … wh … what?" asked JoJo.

"Tippy. You hear him? He's baying."

With no one talking it was easy to hear the dog.

"Does that mean they've found him?" asked Tommy once Vernon put his hand down.

"No," replied Vernon. "When the dog is baying, which is that deep-throated, drawn out, moaning sound that you're hearing, it means that Tippy has Clarence's scent and he's on his trail. Now, if the dog starts barking or intermixing the baying with the barking, that means he's found Clarence."

"Maybe they won't find him," said Tommy.

"Oh … they'll catch him, alright," said Vernon. "Nobody can hide from Tippy."

"Little Eddie did," said Leroy.

Vernon said nothing.

CHAPTER 35

Chief Broome had Jenny, the receptionist at the GBI Lab, place a call to Barry Manning, Chief of Police of Decatur, Georgia. With neither Manning nor the Harrisons having called him, he could only assume the abductors had yet to make contact. But it was only Monday and if the ransom demand had been sent by mail rather than hand delivered, it might not arrive until late Wednesday or Thursday.

Broome's call was answered by the duty officer who transferred it to Manning.

"Jim … I hope you're calling with some good news."

"I'm afraid not. But no bad news either. I just wanted to give you an update. I'm over at the State Crime Lab waiting on some preliminary results of some evidence we found this morning."

Broome proceeded to tell Manning about the golf clubs, shoes, cigarette butts and blood-stained towel that they'd found near the Zachary's farm.

"Excellent work. Unfortunately, there's been no activity here. You asked me to keep an eye on them and I have *literally* kept an eye on them. After you left, I set up a 24-hour surveillance of the Harrison's house with my men using their personal cars for the stake-out so not to attract attention. They were to be on the lookout for any suspicious or out of state cars. So far, they've seen nothing. My plan is to keep watch for about a week. What do you think?"

What do I think? thought Broome. *I think I dropped the ball. I should have thought of setting up surveillance.*

"A week should be fine. I appreciate you staying on top of things," said Broome.

"Actually, it was one of my officers that suggested the surveillance. He lives down the street from the Harrisons. He knows the family well. In fact, he pulled the first watch."

"Sounds like a good officer."

"He is. Probably my replacement in a few years."

Broome immediately thought of Lewis who was most likely his replacement but probably sooner than later considering the way the Harrison investigation was going.

"And David … how is he doing?" asked Broome.

"Not too good from what I hear. I had breakfast with his dad, J. N., this morning. He said David didn't go to school today and won't even come out of his room, except to eat."

"That's really sad. But we're at the mercy of the abductor. All we can do is wait."

Broome wished there was something he could tell the boy and tell Tommy's parents that would ease their pain. But the evidence he had and the expected lab results offered none.

Broome ended the call and had Jenny place a long-distance call to his office. Betty answered and transferred the call to Lewis.

"You find anything?" asked Broome, referring to Lewis' highway search from the Zachary's farm to the Alabama border.

"No sir. And I drove real slow like you told me. Did Betty tell you we got a call from J. N. Rutledge, David's daddy?"

"No, she didn't."

"He wants you to call him when you get a chance. You need his number?"

"No. I've got it. Did he tell you what he wanted?"

"No sir. I guess I should have asked. How's it going up there … at the lab?"

"I'm still waiting on results. It's a slow process."

The call ended and Broome placed the phone back in its cradle. He wondered what Rutledge wanted. With his son being so depressed, maybe he wanted to hire a professional. A private investigator. He couldn't blame him if he did. Or maybe he knew some people who had pulled some strings and gotten the GBI involved. Or maybe … Broome's thoughts were interrupted when he saw the shadowy image of someone approaching the frosted glass door and then knock.

"Chief Broome. This is Dr. Barrineau. May I come in?"

"Yes. Please."

Barrineau opened the door, took a seat in the visitor's chair and opened his notepad.

"We're still running tests, but I thought you might want to know what we've found out so far."

"I do," nodded the chief.

"The spots on the towel and shoes are definitely blood and is recent. No older than a week. And it's human … type B which is fairly rare." Barrineau flipped the page of his notes. As he did Broome spoke up.

"So how does that help me? I thought you said that the boy's and the abductor's blood type could be the same. And even if they weren't the same, you said most people don't know what type of blood their kids have. That it's not on their birth certificate. So I'm confused."

"I did say that, didn't I? I guess I should have made myself clearer. Now that we know the blood type from the stain, we just need to get the blood type of the missing boy's parents. Once we have that, we *might* be able to rule out either the boy, his abductor or anybody else."

"How's that?"

"Blood types are hereditary. So the boy …. uh …"

"Tommy Harrison," offered Broome.

"So, depending on Tommy's parents' blood type, genetically speaking, he can only have certain blood types. Now … knowing that the blood type found on the towel is B, my hope is that the parent's blood types are either A or O or a combination of the two. If that's the case, we will know for certain that the blood on the shoes and towels are not the missing boy's because it is impossible for that combination to have a child with blood type B. Have I made myself clear or have I confused you even more?"

"I think I understand," said Broome. "What if one of the boy's parents has a B blood type like you found on the towel?"

"Good question. Unfortunately, we'd be back to square one. On a positive note, we did find partial matching fingerprints and thumbprints on the two unfiltered Old Gold cigarettes. And we found the same prints on the leather strap on the golf bag and the boy's shoes. So unless the boy smokes, we know for certain these must be the abductor prints. Once you have a suspect in custody, we can use our findings to identify the abductor."

Barrineau's words gave Broome hope. Not that he had any suspects.

"Now for the molds … you're going to have to wait on the molds. We haven't had time to study them, but we should be able to match them up with their manufacturer. Even so, unless we have the vehicle to do a tire match to the mold, I don't think they will be much help. Any questions?"

Broome had none. Barrineau then stood and closed his notepad.

"In that case, we're pretty much done here. The other test results won't be available until tomorrow or Wednesday at the latest. I'll call you once they're done. If you have work to do or need to use the phone, stay as long as you want." The two exchanged business cards, shook hands and Barrineau left.

Broome's next call was to J. N. Rutledge.

"Any news on Tommy?" asked J. N.

"Nothing on the boy, himself," said Broome. He then told him that they had found some evidence possibly related to the case but chose not to disclose what they had found, where they had found it or how it related to the case. J. N. understood the privacy issues. He also told J. N. about the visits to the largest churches in town and how they had passed Tommy's pictures around the congregations asking for their help.

Broome continued. "In fact, that's why I'm sitting in the State Crime Lab as we speak. One of the church members, who happened upon the evidence, remembered our description of the boy and called me."

"I say the more people who know about Tommy, the better. And that's what I want to talk to you about. David ... my son ... is having a really tough time with all of this. The two boys were inseparable. Tommy was like another son to us. And I'm sure the Harrisons feel the same way. Anyway, I feel like I need to help, somehow."

Broome wondered where all of this was going.

J. N. continued. "The other night I began thinking and I've come up with a similar idea to the one you had passing out Tommy's picture to the different congregations. I asked David what he thought and he liked it ... a lot. So here's what I was thinking ... and please let me know if I'm interfering or if you don't think it's a good idea. I work for Southern Bell and my main responsibility with the company is the installation and maintenance of telephone equipment throughout the southeast. This includes telephone poles. Having said that, what do you think about me having a poster with David's picture and a reward of $3000 for his return placed on both sides of every tenth pole on the major highways in a twenty-mile radius from where Tommy was abducted? That's approximately every half mile. Upper management has given me the go-ahead as long as I pay for the posters and the cost of placing and removing the posters."

"I *like* it. I like it a lot. But that's a lot of reward money. Who's funding it? I know that Pine Mountain Police Department doesn't have that kind of money in their budget."

"That's all been taken care of. We just want Tommy's return."

Broome chose not to push any further on the source of the reward. Unless he was terribly mistaken, J. N. Rutledge was the donor.

"Just so you know, I'm also having the local paper run Tommy's picture. If it's okay with you, I can have them add the reward money to the article. Between the two of them, word of the missing boy should spread quickly. However, you should know that if the abductor sees the posters or reads the paper, he knows how much money he can demand."

"I understand. And the Harrisons need not worry about coming up with the money. Like I said, that's all been taken care of."

"Have you talked to them … the Harrisons and gotten their approval?" asked Broome.

"Not yet. I was hoping that you could do that so my involvement could be kept anonymous."

"I can. In fact, that was my next call."

"Assuming they agree, I should be able to have all the details worked out and the posters out to my foremen by Wednesday morning, Thursday at the latest."

"While you are still in the planning phase, I think you should change the coverage area," offered Broome as he considered where the golf clubs had been found and the direction the kidnapper had to be traveling. "From what I know, I think the abductor was heading west. Possibly into Alabama. I think you would get better coverage if West Point, Georgia was the center of your radius. And you're also going to need contact information on the poster. I suggest you use my department's address and phone number."

"I was hoping you'd say that," said J. N. while making notations of their conversation.

The two said their good-byes and the chief immediately called the Harrisons' home phone but got no answer. He then dialed their business phone.

"Little Five Points Bicycle and Lawnmower," answered Dorothy Harrison.

"Mrs. Harrison?" asked Broome.

"Yes. This is she. How can I help you?"

"This is Chief Jim Broome from Pine Mountain. I'm …"

"Have you found my son?" She asked, interrupting the chief. "Is he alright?"

"No ma'am. We haven't found him. I just wanted to give you and your husband an update."

Broome could hear a despondent sigh during the slight pause before she replied.

"Wait just a minute. Let me get Tom on the other line."

Within seconds, both of Tommy's parents were on the line.

"Okay. We're here," she said.

"I'm sorry that we haven't been able to locate your son. I can assure you that our department is doing everything we can. This morning, we found some evidence alongside of a road that goes to West Point, Georgia. We know it belongs to Tommy. It's his golf clubs and shoes." Broome could hear the woman gasp. "They were thrown into a ravine about ten miles outside of Pine Mountain. I don't want to alarm you, but there were some blood stains on a towel that was attached to the golf bag. We don't know if it's Tommy's or the abductor's. What I can tell you is we didn't see any blood pools on the highway where we found the evidence. Nor was there enough blood on the towel to indicate that there was a deadly encounter. We also found a cigarette butt at the location where we feel Tommy was taken and one where the golf clubs were found. All of that evidence is currently being analyzed by the State Crime Lab. They have found fingerprints on the cigarette butts and the golf bag that are identical. To help advance this investigation, I need to ask you some questions. Some you may find offensive. Please understand that I am only doing my job."

"Anything we can do to help," answered Tom Harrison. Tears streamed down Dorothy Harrison's face as she held her hand over the phone's mouthpiece to keep anyone from hearing her cry. Knowing that her son's golf clubs and shoes had been found had dashed the faint hope that she had that her son was lost.

"Does your son smoke and if so, does he smoke Old Golds?"

"Oh no," said Tom. "He hates smoking. I've never smelled smoke on him. Even so, you might want to ask his friend, David, just in case they were experimenting while they were camping. You know boys will be boys."

Dorothy was shaking her head. "I … I've never found any cigarettes in his clothes when I wash. He's not that kind of boy. He's … he's …" She turned her face away from the phone as she wept. Even so, her husband and Broome could still hear the broken-hearted woman as she sobbed.

Broome waited a few moments to let Mrs. Harrison compose herself and continued.

"Do you know Tommy's blood type or do you know both of your blood types?"

"Not Tommy's but both of our blood types are O," said Tom. "I know that because we are blood donors. We both have been giving blood to the Red Cross since World War II and they put your blood type on the donor card."

Remembering what Dr. Barrineau had said about the A and O blood types, Broome felt a ray of hope depending on the answers to his next two questions.

"By any chance is Tommy adopted?" asked Broome.

"No sir," answered Tom. "But why …"

Broome interrupted. "Is Tommy yours and Mrs. Harrison's child or is he a child by another marriage or possibly an affair?"

"Tommy is *our* child," said Dorothy in disgust not understanding the rude questions by the chief. "What does this have to do with our Tommy?"

"I'm sorry. I should have prefaced my questions with their reasoning. I apologize. But based on the lab test results, information I received from Dr. Barrineau at the State Crime Lab, your two blood types and the fact that Tommy is your child, I can tell you without a doubt that the blood stain on the towel is not Tommy's."

"Thank you, Lord," said Dorothy Harrison almost simultaneously as Tom Harrison said, "Thank God."

"Amen," said Broome. "Now let me tell you what we are doing to help find your boy. If all goes as planned, starting tomorrow, Tommy's picture will be in the local paper and by Wednesday … Thursday at the latest, missing person posters will be placed on telephone poles every mile along the major highways in parts of Western Georgia and Eastern Alabama both offering a three-thousand-dollar reward for Tommy's safe return. As requested, Broome kept Rutledge's involvement confidential.

"A reward of three thousand dollars!   There's *no way* we can come up with that kind of money. At least, not anytime soon," said Tom.

"Don't worry about the money," said Broome. "That's taken care of. We have sources available to us for emergencies such as this and the money doesn't have to be repaid. As for the amount of the reward, we wanted it large enough that either the abductors or someone who might know something will come forward."

"Shouldn't we have waited for the ransom demand?" asked Tom. "They might have only wanted a few hundred dollars which I could handle. Afterall, he is my son."

"We considered that and there's a chance you'll get a ransom demand for much less than the reward. But we're willing to take that risk. We want Tommy back and we think the large reward money will incent them to act sooner than later."

"We trust your decisions," said Tom.

"Thank you, Chief Broome. I'm sorry for my outbursts. I think if anybody can find Tommy, you can," added Dorothy.

The phone conversation ended. Broome appreciated their confidence in his abilities even if he didn't.

CHAPTER 36

Jesse struggled to hold tight onto Tippy's leash as the dog moved faster and faster away from the farm and towards the remains of the old plantation house. Watson, using his cane as a walking stick, and Caleb stayed close behind but gave Tippy and Jesse their space. From the look on dog's face, it was obvious that he enjoyed the hunt more than any of the Watsons except maybe Caleb who thought of the search as a game of hide and seek.

Tippy had picked up the scent just past the pig pen using the smell from the sheet that Sarah had pulled from Clarence's bed. The boy made no efforts to hide his tracks as he made his escape from the farm. Until the road past the plantation became covered with overgrown weeds and bushes, Tippy was hardly needed. All he had to do was point his nose in down the road towards his prey. Once the road was covered with underbrush, Tippy's skill as a tracker was the Watsons' only hope of finding the boy.

About thirty minutes into the search and maybe a mile from the farmhouse, Tippy pulled Jesse away from the overgrown road and over to the top of a small ravine. There he began to bark incessantly and claw at the dirt in front of him in an attempt to jump down into the ditch.

Jesse pulled back on the leash, grabbed the dog by the collar and peered down into the gully.

"Well … looky here, Tippy. Look who we done found," said Jesse, having to restrain the dog from jumping down into the gully. "Daddy … over here," he yelled. "We done found ol' Porky."

Watson and Caleb who had fallen behind Jesse and the dog rushed over to the ditch and looked down. There was Clarence with his body pressed up against the dirt wall and his eyes closed as if hoping that if he didn't see the old man or Jesse maybe they wouldn't see him.

"Let's git him out of there," said Watson over Tippy's never-ending bark. "And shut that dog up."

Jesse pulled Tippy away from the gully and kneeled down and affectionately patted the dog on his head and rubbed the dog's back which had a calming effect on the animal.

"Good ol' Tippy. See … you ain't too old."

Watson looked down at the scared boy who had yet to acknowledge that he had been caught as he refused to look up. Instead he kept his face pressed against hands.

"Clarence. Give me your hand."

"Yes sir," answered the boy, his voice so soft and meek that Watson could barely hear him.

"Caleb … help me git this boy up."

Caleb and Watson leaned over and both extended their hands towards Clarence. When the boy looked up, they could see the tears in his eyes.

Clarence was a heavy-set boy, so it took all the strength of both Clarence and Watson to pull him up from the ravine. Once Clarence reached the top of the gully, Watson immediately began his lecture on discipline.

"Son … you ain't never given me no trouble before. Did that new boy, Tommy, talk you into running away?"

"N … no sir," quivered Clarence.

"So why did you run away?"

"I don't know, sir."

"I thought you liked living on the farm."

"I … I do, sir."

"You know this means I got to punish you. I'm gonna have to put them leggings on you like Tommy."

"Yes sir."

"And I'm gonna have to cane you."

"Yes sir."

Clarence was not afraid of Watson's canings but knew that was part of the penalty for running away. Usually, it was just two or three swats that were never hard enough to raise welts. That would be torture, not discipline.

Watson had Clarence turn his back to him so to get a good angle on the boy's behind. That's when he saw that the back of his legs was covered with welts and dried blood. Watson knew that these wounds were not bee stings as he had been told. He then lifted the boy's shirt and saw more welts and dried blood.

"Who done this to you?" asked Watson, the anger in his voice scaring Clarence and Caleb who stood nearby.

Clarence looked up and saw Jesse, who was standing not too far behind the old man, begin slowly shaking his head, his piercing eyes staring him down. So he lowered his head and said nothing.

"Son … I asked you, who done this to you? Did that new boy have anything to do with this?"

"N … no sir," said Clarence, his lower lip quivering.

"What about any of them other boys?"

Before Clarence could respond, Jesse jumped in, hoping to keep the truth from his daddy.

"It was a bunch of them boys, Daddy. They was whipping up on ol' Porky … uh … Clarence with their rope belts last night. I came into the room and shut it down real quick. I never thunk he would run away."

"Don't call this boy Porky ever agin. Do I make myself clear?" barked Watson, giving his son the stink-eye.

"Yes sir."

"Clarence … what boys done this to you and why?"

"I don't know … sir," said Clarence, never looking up.

Watson could tell that Clarence didn't want to get any of the boys in trouble for fear of further retaliation. But he couldn't let this act of violence go unpunished.

"If you don't know or ain't willing to tell me who done this to you, then I guess *all* them boys has to be punished. So ain't nary a one of you is gonna git to go to Turner's after the cotton is done picked."

Turner's was the general store in Willis where Watson would take the boys after the crops were planted and picked. Each boy got a dollar to spend however they wished. Taking that away was worse than a beating. But discipline had to prevail.

"That ain't fair," said Caleb who had said nothing in hopes that the whole situation would come to a peaceful end. But it hadn't and he couldn't stand by and let all the boys take the blame for something that

Jesse had done. "Them boys didn't do nuttin' to Clarence. Jesse beat him up. Plain and simple. And … and … he beat up on Leroy and …"

"What in tarnation are you jabbering on about, fool?" asked Jesse interrupting his brother. "If you ain't an idjit, then you're a moron." He then began laughing nervously.

"Son … was Jesse the one who done this to you?"

Caleb's bravery seemed to inspire Clarence just enough that he nodded and said, "Yes sir."

"Ga'dangit, Jesse. What's gotten into you?"

Without warning, Watson lashed out at Jesse's legs with the cane, causing him to drop Tippy's leash. The dog ran off and laid down behind Caleb with his front legs stretched out and his head laying down between them.

Before Watson could deliver a second blow, Jesse reached out, grabbed the cane from his daddy's hand and flung it into the ravine.

"Don't you *ever* do that to me agin, you stupid old man," screamed Jesse, staring angrily at his father. "I ain't one of your little orphan boys."

He then turned and walked away, mumbling, "I hate you. I hate this farm."

But the words were not out of Henry Watson's nor Caleb's earshot.

Watson stood, but said nothing. He just stared out into the wilderness, hurt.

Caleb moved quickly to his daddy's side and put his arms around him.

"Daddy … Jesse didn't mean nuttin' by it. He jest ain't been right lately."

Watson said nothing for a while then he looked over at Clarence who was mesmerized by what he had seen and heard.

"Son … what Jesse done to you ain't right. That weren't discipline. That were pure meanness. That won't happen never agin. Not if Jesse wants to live on this here farm. Fer the next couple of days, I want you to help out Missus Watson in the kitchen. No chores or pickin' until she says you're able."

"Yes sir. I appreciate that, sir."

"And no more running away. Do I make myself clear."

"Yes sir. Actually, I was fixin' to turn around and go back home when I heard Tippy. Then I got scared. But you don't have to worry about me running away no more. I learnt my lesson."

The three with Tippy leading the way headed back to the farm.

Even though Watson had found his runaway, he was not smiling.

CHAPTER 37

The sound of the lock on the cabin door being opened had all of the pickers' attention. It wasn't that they were ready to head back out to the field. They wanted to know what had happened to Clarence.

When the door swung open, Jesse stormed in, slamming it behind him. He stopped long enough to lock the door and stare down the boys who were in the main hall.

"What are you looking at?" he yelled at no one in particular. The boys scattered and headed to their bunkroom with no one uttering a word. Jesse watched until all the boys were gone and then went to his room, slamming the door behind him and locking it.

Until they heard the front door of the cabin being unlocked and opened again, no one dared venture out of their bunkroom or say anything for fear of a possible confrontation with Jesse. But the familiar creaking sound that could only be made by the front door when it was either opened or closed was like an all-clear signal and everyone came rushing out of their room hoping to see Clarence. Even Sammy and Claude. Instead, they saw Caleb walk in, followed by his daddy. No Clarence. Had he alluded the always reliable Tippy and found freedom? Had they found him and Jesse had thrown him into the storm cellar like he'd done to Vernon? Muffled rumors of his whereabouts were flying everywhere and none were good.

Caleb who was smiling, as always, walked over to the large dining table and sat down in the chair at the end of the table. Watson came up behind him and grabbed hold to the chair's top slat. The chatter among the boys came to an immediate halt.

He slowly looked around the table at each one of the boys. He could see the apprehension in each of their faces.

"I reckon y'all are worried about Clarence. Well, he's fine. He's up at the house helping the missus with the garden and some light chores. He won't be picking fer the next few days until his wounds heal. Jest so you know, he told me that he weren't really running away. But he done got scared of Jesse and didn't want to git caned no more. Well … I'm here to tell you that won't never … ever … happen agin. Never … never … never. What y'all boys done, right or wrong, caused Jesse to git overly agitated. And things got out of hand. But what he done to Clarence, Leroy and Tommy is wrong. Wrong … wrong … wrong. That ain't discipline. That's pure meanness. I don't run my farm thataway. Now, I need you boys to git back out to the field. That cotton' ain't gonna pick itself." Then pointing to the first cluster of boys, "You six hop on the truck. I'll be back shortly to git the rest of you. Caleb … you go with me."

Everyone filed out of the cabin with Watson leading the pack. He and Caleb climbed into the truck's cab and the first six boys found a seat on either the truck bed or tailgate. Those left behind, Tommy, Leroy, Vernon, Sammy and Claude, found a seat either on the steps or the edge of the porch.

"Boy … did Jesse looked mad," said Tommy to anyone that would listen.

"Yeah … and in a couple of days he'll come out and he'll be meaner than ever," said Vernon. "I suggest we tread lightly around him. Better yet, stay as far away from him as possible. Rule number three."

"How come you didn't run away like Clarence?" asked Tommy looking at the welts on Leroy's legs.

"I ain't got no place to go," replied Leroy. "If the truth be told, I got beat up worse at the orphanage. It's way better living here on the farm, excepting fer Jesse. I ain't never gonna git him agitated no more. I learnt my lesson."

"There's something I don't understand," said Tommy. "Why did they ring the emergency bell when Clarence ran away but not Little Eddie?"

"Who told you that?" asked Vernon.

"Clarence."

"I really don't remember," said Vernon.

"Tommy's right," said Leroy. "Don't you remember Missus Watson come ruuning out to the field all flustered and everything. Her and Mr. Watson and Jesse headed back to the farm. They left Caleb to watch over us boys. That's what they done, alright."

"Then she must have forgotten our emergency protocols … procedures," said Vernon. "She was supposed to ring the bell. That's all." He stood and looked down at Tommy and Leroy. "Watson will be here in a minute."

Tommy could tell that Vernon didn't want to talk about *anything* that had to do with Little Eddie. Maybe he had "learnt his lesson" from the beating he had gotten from Jesse. He looked at Vernon's legs and could see the scars. He understood.

Watson returned shortly and drove the five remaining boys out to the field.

Caleb stayed out in the fields long enough to make sure Tommy hadn't forgotten how to pick. He was pleased to see that he hadn't and had even picked up speed in removing the little white puff ball from the hard boll. Tommy was on a mission to out pick at least five of the other boys so he could get the shackles removed from his legs. He looked up at Watson who was sitting on a chair in the back of the truck. Unlike Jesse, he wasn't asleep and there was no rifle.

CHAPTER 38

Chief Broome's trip home from Atlanta had been uneventful and gave him time to reflect on the case. So far, he was pleased with the progress they had made considering the fact that neither he nor anyone on his staff had any experience with major crime investigations. As he considered his next step, nothing came to mind. Even though it was early in the investigation, with no ransom demand, he had a bad feeling about the boy.

He arrived back at the office a little after four. Betty was at her desk working a crossword puzzle when he walked in and removed his hat.

"Where's Bob and Lewis?" he asked.

Betty slid the crossword into her desk's top drawer.

"Bob's out on patrol and Lewis had the early shift, so he's off. And you got two calls. One call from Dr. Barrineau at the State Crime Lab. He wants you to call him back as soon as you can. He said he'd be in his office until 4:30. The other one was from J. N. Rutledge. He also wants you to call him back. She then picked up a slip of paper with the two names and telephone numbers written down and handed it to Broome. "So what happened in Atlanta?"

Broome looked up at the large circular clock that hung on the wall just behind Betty's desk. 4:09.

"Not now. I'll bring everybody up to date on what I know tomorrow morning. Can you make sure that you, Lewis and Bob are here by 7:00? I don't want any stragglers."

"Yes sir."

Broome headed over to an old wooden table just to the left of his office door, stuck his hat under his left arm and picked up one of the clean coffee mugs, all of which were unique. When he reached for the handle of the aluminum coffee pot, he noticed it was not on the small hot plate. There was either no coffee or if there was, it was cold. After his long drive, he needed a cup.

"Betty … there's no coffee."

"No sir. I didn't think you were coming back to the office, so I didn't make any this afternoon."

"Well … I did come back. Any chance you could make some, please?"

Without waiting for a reply, he went into his office, hung his cap on a peg just to the right of the door and headed over to his desk. He sat down, picked up the phone, dialed "0."   and had the operator make the long-distance call to the State Crime Lab. The receptionist at the lab immediately transferred the call to Dr. Barrineau who skipped the normal exchange of pleasantries and got straight to the point.

"Chief Broome … I've got some preliminary results from the golf bag you brought in today. Besides the fingerprints which I told you about earlier, we also found traces of calcium arsenate, Dichlorodiphenyltrichloroethane, commonly known as DDT, some soil residue and cotton dust. The chemicals and cotton dust lead me to believe the person who drove the truck was either a cotton farmer, tenant or sharecropper. Or it could be someone who works with cotton such as a county agent, a cotton buyer or possibly someone who borrowed a farmer's truck. The soil residue we found on the bag came from an area that includes the Coastal Plains region, the Black Belt region and possibly the Piedmont Plateau region, all three in Alabama. The soil from the Coastal region is sandy with a clay-like sub-soil and the soil from the geological Black Belt region is thick, dark, fertile soil. The reason why we can't be certain about the presence of soil from the Piedmont region is because it is also clay-like just like the sub-soil of Coastal Plains. Am I losing you?"

"Not yet."

"Do you have a map near-by?"

"I can get one. Hold on."

He laid the receiver down and opened the right-hand middle drawer of his desk and pulled out a Sinclair Oil map of Georgia and Alabama. As he spread it out over his desk, he saw a freshly brewed cup of coffee being set down on the open corner of his desk.

"Thank you," he whispered to Betty. "I need this. It's been a long day."

Betty nodded and left, closing the door behind her. She returned to her desk and the crossword puzzle she had nearly finished.

Broome drank a couple of swigs of coffee and picked up the receiver.

"Okay. I got it."

"Do you see Russell and Macon Counties?" asked Barrineau.

After a brief search, Broome responded. "Yes sir."

"That's the beginning of the counties in the geological Black Belt region. Now … do you see Lee County?"

"Yes sir."

Lee County is the beginning of the Coastal region in Alabama and it's also the southern tip of the Piedmont Plateau region. I've seen some maps where the Black Belt also extends into the county.

Broome circled the three counties.

Barrineau continued. "What makes our job more difficult is that soil doesn't know where county lines exist, so one might find sand, clay and black soil in all three counties. I'm not a detective, but based on these soil samples, their geological location and the fact that I believe we are dealing with a cotton farmer or somebody associated with cotton farming, my educated guess would be to concentrate your search for the boy starting with Lee County and maybe the southern part of Chambers County, then move westward."

Broome then circled Chambers County.

"That's what we're going to do," said Broome. He understood that Dr. Barrineau wasn't a detective. But he was a genius and a logical one at that. What he said made sense.

"I want you to know that I really, really appreciate everything that you've done for this small-town policeman."

"I'm glad we could help. I hope you find the boy … alive."

Broome hung up the phone and studied the map, primarily the four circled counties. He then traced the highways from where the abduction occurred to the spot where the golf clubs and shoes were found on Georgia State Highway 18. From that point, he traced highway 18 over to West Point, Georgia where it fed into U.S. Alabama State Highway 15 in Lanett, Alabama which was just across the Chattahoochee River from West Point, Georgia. From there, he traced highway 15 down through Willis, Alabama on to Opelika, Alabama and stopped when he heard Betty's voice on the intercom.

"Yes?" barked the chief, his voice tinted with irritation at being interrupted.

"Mr. Rutledge is on the phone. You want to take it?"

"Yes," he answered, much calmer.

When the first square button on the phone base lit up, he quickly grabbed the phone's receiver, pushed the button and identified himself.

"Thanks for taking my call," said J. N. "I hope I haven't called at an inconvenient time."

"Actually, I was just about to call you. How are the posters coming along?"

"I'm glad you asked. We're ready to go to print once we get your approval. But it wasn't as easy as I first thought. Fortunately, I realized early on that I didn't know *what* should or shouldn't be on the posters, so I called in our head of security, here, at Southern Bell. He's a twenty-year, retired assistant police chief with the Atlanta Police Department. He was familiar with missing person posters but not so much kidnappings. His advice was to put just enough information on the poster about Tommy so that he could be easily identified but no more."

J. N. proceeded to describe the layout and composition of the posters. As he did, Broome couldn't help but think of the old FBI *Wanted* Poster that had been pinned to the bulletin board by the last chief. It had remained there more for police ambience than anything else. Other than the reward and the front-on facial picture, the posters were nothing alike.

"I like it," responded the chief.

"One last thing. My security guy said with that large amount of reward, it was going to generate a lot of attention and you'll probably get calls from places you've never heard of. So not to interfere with your daily operations, I'd like to add another phone line that is dedicated to Tommy's missing person calls. No charge to you or your department, of course."

Broome had never even considered there would be bogus calls. After all, this was South Georgia, not Atlanta. In order for his staff to filter out these disingenuous calls, they were going to need some personal information about Tommy that only he would know to help cull the calls.

"An excellent idea," offered Broome.

"Well … I guess I'm ready to go. The printers are local and they know the Harrisons. They said I should get the posters by Wednesday at the latest. My plans are to get them out to my men Thursday morning. And as far as the reward is concerned, I talked to my bank and they will coordinate setting up an account at Farmers & Merchants Bank in Pine

Mountain that allows you to withdraw the funds should the reward be collected."

Broome was impressed with how detailed and thorough Rutledge had been with the design of the posters and how expertly he had handled all the baggage it had brought along. Before the chief could internalize his own inexperience, his own incompetency, his own lack of direction, J. N. interrupted Broome's deep dive into the emotional abyss by adding, "My guy … the ex-assistant chief … he was most impressed with how professional and well organized you've handled this investigation. And I totally agree."

Broome was so taken aback by Rutledge's unexpected words of praise, he was almost speechless.

"Those are very kind words. I appreciate the vote of confidence. Before we hang up, I would like to share with you some findings by the State Crime Lab that might limit the area where you hang the posters."

He then proceeded to tell Rutledge about the residue found on the golf bag and its implications.

"Why would a cotton farmer abduct Tommy? Never mind. Don't answer that," said Rutledge, having a terrible thought cross his mind.

Broome had the same thought.

"What level of confidence do you have with these people at the Crime Lab?" asked Rutledge.

"The utmost confidence. I watched Dr. Barrineau and his team. They do amazing things. If it were me, based on the findings from the lab and at Dr Barrineau's suggestion, I would hang the posters starting in Chambers County and work my way down through Lee County."

"That's good enough for me."

The call ended with Broome asking Rutledge to have a few posters brought to the office when the crew came to install the new phone line. His spirits had been lifted by the call.

"Betty," said the chief, holding down the intercom button. "Did you tell Bob and Lewis about the meeting tomorrow morning?"

"Yes sir. They'll be here."

"Good."

"Is that all? Can I top off your coffee?"

Broome checked his watch. It was past quitting time.

"No, but thank you. I think we both need to go home."

Betty left, but Broome stayed, studying the map. But his mind couldn't shake the question that Rutledge had raised. *Why would a cotton farmer abduct Tommy?*

There were no good answers.

CHAPTER 39

At precisely 7:00 a.m., Chief Broome began his meeting in his office with all three employees standing on the other side of his desk, coffee mugs in hand. No one dared to be late. For Bob and Lewis, normal working hours were from 7 a.m. to 3 p.m., Monday through Saturday, with the two officers alternating days for the remaining work hours from 3 p.m. to 5 p.m. Betty worked 7 a.m. to 5 p.m., Monday through Friday, with Saturday and Sunday off. Normally, those work hours were considered suggestions. Not today.

"I'm sorry to have made all of you come to work on time …" He stopped and looked at each of his employees to see if they saw the humor in his remark. There wasn't a hint of a smile. The chief was not known for his levity. Nor was he a meeting kind of guy. When he did have them, they were short and to the point. Today was no different.

"I want to bring all of you up to date and I didn't want to have to do it three times. I think we've made some progress although we've yet to hear from the abductor."

The chief proceeded in describing the evidence, where it was found and the findings of the lab. He discussed Dr. Barrineau's conclusion that the abductor was either a cotton farmer or someone associated with cotton farming living most likely in Eastern Alabama.

"I've done some hunting over in those parts," commented Lewis. "There sure are a lot of cotton fields, so that makes sense."

Broome then told his staff about the posters that J. N. Rutledge planned to print and that they were to be hung on telephone poles on highways in Lee and Chambers Counties with a reward of three thousand dollars.

"Three thousand dollars!" said all three, almost simultaneously.

"Who's ponying up that kind of money?" asked Bob. "The boy's parents?"

"No. An anonymous donor. That's all I know and all you three need to know. Now back to where I left off. Because of the size of the reward, there's a good chance we'll be getting a lot of calls. Calls from people who will claim to have Tommy but are just trying to get the money. Later this morning, I'm going to call the Harrisons and get some personal information about Tommy that only he would know. That way, we can eliminate the bogus callers. Also, this afternoon, we're going to do some training on how to take the calls, what to ask, what not to ask, et cetera."

Broome looked down at his yellow tablet and checked off the items he'd just discussed.

"One last thing. So not to cause any interference with our daily operations, we're having another telephone line brought in to just handle these calls. It will be a different telephone number which will be on the posters. I'm gonna want that phone manned from 7 a.m. to 10 p.m. for the next couple of weeks or until we find Tommy. I will post the schedule later today. Just to be clear, I will also be on that schedule. Now as far as the overtime is concerned, I will get the city to authorize it."

"We don't need the overtime," volunteered Bob. "We can do it on our own time."

"Bob's right," added Lewis with Betty nodding her head in affirmation.

"I appreciate the offer, but that's my call. Overtime it shall be. And that's all I got to say this morning. Any questions?" He paused a few seconds, but there were none. "Okay. Back to work. Lewis … can you close the door on your way out?"

"Got it, Chief."

Once everyone had left, Broome checked off his last item for the meeting. He then picked up the phone, dialed "0" and had the operator make a long-distance call to the Harrison's home. With no answer, he had the operator call the Harrison's shop.

Tom Harrison answered.

"Mr. Harrison, this is Chief Broome." So not to raise Harrison's hope, Broome immediately gave a current status on the missing boy. "We still haven't found Tommy, but I wonder if I could ask you a few more questions, if this is a good time?"

"Yes. Please. Anything we can do to find our boy. But if you also want Dot … Mrs. Harrison on the phone, she's not here. She's gone to Stovall's to pick up some parts."

"No sir. I think we should proceed. As I told you and Mrs. Harrison earlier, posters of Tommy are going to be hung on telephone poles in parts of Eastern Alabama. Once they're hung, we expect the reward money is going to generate a lot of calls. In order for us to weed out the bogus callers … those that are just trying to cash in on the reward but offer no real information, we're going to need to know a few things about Tommy. That way we can quickly tell if we're talking to the abductor."

"You mean people will do that?"

"Not as much here in rural Georgia. But word will get out."

"What do you need?"

"Let's start with Tommy's middle initial. We will *not* put that on the poster nor anything else you tell me about Tommy. That way, the only way the caller could know that information is if Tommy, himself, tells them." Broome started to end his sentence with *assuming* but wisely chose not to.

"Tom P. Harrison the third. Tommy for short. I'm a junior, but I've never used the suffix."

"What does the P stand for?"

"Powhatan," said Mr. Harrison, then pronounced the name in syllables. "Pow … hat … tan."

"Interesting name. Indian?"

"Yes. Powhatan was the chief of a group of Indian tribes in the Virginia area, one of which was named after himself. Chief Powhatan was the father of Princess Pocahontas."

"So you're related to Chief Powwahatatatatan … er … Pocahontas?"

"No. Not that we know of. And we're not offended by your mispronunciation. Tommy couldn't say or spell his middle name until he was about twelve. I don't know why we did that to him. *Paul* would have been a simpler name to say and spell. But, we were young and Dorothy and I wanted to make Tom senior happy." Then he laughed while tearing up at the same time, thinking about his son who was missing and his father who had passed.

"That's perfect. I know that he and his friend, David, were going to play golf at Callaway Gardens. Who is his favorite golfer/"

"That's easy. Sam Snead."

"Do y'all have a dog?"

"Yes. Rusty. He's a mixture of golden retriever and Irish setter, so he's very red in color. While Tommy's gone, we're keeping him here at the shop. The dog misses Tommy as much as we do. You can see it in his eyes. They're very sad."

"What month and day is Tommy's birthday?"

"September 8th. This year, we got him a pair of black and white golf shoes. They had to be a certain brand. Kangaroo."

Broome was well aware of the golf shoes.

"Just a couple more. Where was Tommy born?"

"Charleston, South Carolina. We moved there during the war so I could work for the naval shipyard. I tried to enlist, but because I had asthma, they wouldn't accept me. After the war, we moved back to Atlanta."

"Does Tommy have any distinguishing marks on his body? Like a mole or birthmark?"

"Yes. A birthmark on the back of his neck that looks like a strawberry."

"I think that should be enough. I hope we hear something this week. I will keep you and Mrs. Harrison posted."

"Thank you, Chief Broome. I know you are doing everything possible to bring Tommy back and we appreciate it. I will tell Dorothy that you called."

Broome hung up the phone. The day had been very productive, but not rewarding. There would be no reward until Tommy was found, alive and well.

CHAPTER 40

The next two days in the field were uneventful and certainly less stressful with Watson watching the boys. Talking and even laughter, which Jesse never allowed, could be heard coming from the bobbing heads. Even without Clarence, the amount of cotton picked had been the farm's highest since the beginning of cotton season.

By Wednesday, Tommy had found his rhythm and his total weigh-ins reflected his increased picking speed. Watson had not failed to notice the new boy's results and at Wednesday's final weigh-in when he saw Tommy in his shackles shuffle up to the slatted wagon toting a nearly full cotton sack, he reminded him of his offer to remove the 'leggings.' Tommy had not forgotten.

Vernon and most of the other boys were aware of Watson's offer. So when the old man seemed to nod off or step away for a nature call, anyone close enough to Tommy grabbed a handful of cotton from their bags and stuck it in Tommy's. Those leggings would be gone by the week-end.

Knowing that Jesse might be making his presence known at any time, Vernon cornered Tommy right after dinner, Wednesday night.

"We need to talk."

He then led Tommy into the bunkroom where he sat down on one lower bunk and had Tommy sit on the one across from him.

"If Watson keeps his word which I have no doubt he will, your chains will be gone by Saturday after the last weigh in."

"I hope you're right."

"I am. I'm doing this because you don't belong here. Like you said, you have a home. You have parents. Watson was wrong in taking you. I understand he needs his cotton picked, but what he did to you was illegal. He could be thrown into jail if anyone were to find out."

"Well, once I'm out of here, I'm gonna tell everybody. Nobody ..."

"No! No! You can't do that! If you did, we would all be sent off to some orphanage or some state institution in Alabama. That would be worse. Much worse. You've never lived in an orphanage. The beatings are almost daily, the food is almost inedible and sleeping conditions are what you can find. Once you're there, you're going to be there until you turn eighteen unless you run away or somebody like Watson comes along. And *nobody* wants to take on a teenager, except Watson. And believe me, we all were happy to go."

"What about Jesse?"

"If everyone would simply remember my rules, especially when he's drinking, there wouldn't be a problem. But since you're leaving, that doesn't concern you. If I am going to help you, you must forget about the Watsons. Forget about where the farm is located. When asked, claim that you didn't know who took you or where. Otherwise, I can't help you. As they say, it's for the greater good."

"I understand. I just want to go home."

"Good. Now, here's what's going to happen. Leroy is scheduled for chores on Sunday. There are some wire cutters hanging in the barn. I will get him to slip them into one of the milk pails and as he heads up to the farm with the milk, toss them under the big magnolia tree. Then on Monday, he'll pick them up and pass them to you on the way out to the field."

"I'm confused. Why the wire cutters? Won't I be heading out towards the old plantation like … uh." Tommy paused knowing that he wanted to say, *like Little Eddie.* He caught himself and instead said, "like Clarence?"

The pause did not escape Vernon and he appreciated Tommy's prudence.

"Did you ever get Watson's orientation?" asked Vernon, enunciating the word in Watson's vernacular.

"Yes. Most of it. His lunch time interrupted the full sermon."

Both boys laughed.

"That sounds like the old man. Meals are the most important part of his day. Anyway, did he tell you the history of the plantation? That his granddaddy grew more cotton than any other farmer in the county? That the plantation used to be over two thousand acres? And that a politician from Montgomery now owns the property and nothing was growing on it?"

"Yes. In so many words."

"Well, two thousand acres is over three-square miles. That's a lot of territory to be rambling about trying to find a way out. Not only that, we don't know what's beyond those two thousand acres. Is it more farmland? Marshes? Lakes? You could end up getting lost or even circling back around to the Watsons'. We can't deal in unknowns. We have to work with what we know and we know that the dirt road by the cotton fields will take us to the highway."

"What about Tippy? Won't he be able to track me down like he did Clarence?"

"Yes, he can. But Tippy won't be here when you make your escape. He'll be with ol' man Watson. Every Monday, except those that Jesse can't watch the boys … like today … Watson goes to the bank in Willis. He *always* takes Tippy. And he leaves just before the first weigh-in and is gone for about two hours. Here's what going to happen. After you take your bag up to the cotton wagon and it's dumped, you will return with your empty bag to where you left off in the field. Eugene and I will be close behind. Once we begin picking again, you will make your break. I'll get JoJo who will be on the first row to take your row since he's approximately the same size and build. Neither Jesse nor Caleb should notice that you are gone because Jesse will be busy weighing the sacks of the other boys and writing down the amount. And Caleb will have his hands full emptying the sacks into the cotton wagon. Are you with me so far?"

"Yes."

"Head away from the cotton wagon, towards the gate and stay in your row. No zig-zagging. No running. And stay low. Don't do anything that might attract any attention. You should have plenty of time because after the weigh-in with his daddy gone, Jesse usually goes behind the wagon to smoke a cigarette. He doesn't want any of us to see, but we all do. After that, he takes a nature break and we can count on that because he's a creature of habit. He'll be gone at least ten to twelve minutes. I'll get Charlie to distract Caleb which should be easy. Once you reach the end of the cotton field, you will walk straight ahead through the open field and into some wooded area until you reach the road. Once you get to the gate at the beginning of the two lakes, cut the barb wire on the gate so you can crawl through. Make sure you cut the barb wire completely off the gate and toss it in the lake. Don't just cut enough for you to squeeze through and leave it hanging. Otherwise, Watson might see the dangling wire when he returns and will know something isn't right. Hopefully, they won't know you are gone until after lunch. Who knows, they might not know you're gone until the next day when Watson drives us to the fields. Now once you leave the property, turn left at the mail box. Stay on that road until it dead ends. There, you will turn left again. That's highway 15. It takes you away from Willis. Then either hitch hike to West Point which is in Georgia and go to the police station or stop at the first house and ask for help. Like you promised, you cannot tell them that you were kidnapped by the Watsons or *we* will feel the repercussions, not you."

Tommy thought about Vernon's plan. It was so well thought out, so detailed, he wondered if it was a plan that he had for his own escape.

"I understand. If I can just get home, that's all I want. But why can't you go with me? You could live at my house. I'm sure my mom and dad wouldn't mind."

"That won't work. It's going to be hard enough to sneak you out of here without being seen. But for both of us, there's no way. Plus, who would be there to teach the boys … to read them books? They would miss me and I would miss them. Let's just concentrate on getting you out of here."

Tommy nodded.

"This is the last time we talk about your escape until Monday unless we have to call it off for some reason. Understood?"

Tommy nodded, thinking Monday couldn't come fast enough.

CHAPTER 41

Normally, Watson's trip to the Farmers & Merchants Bank in Willis was the highlight of his week. There, he would deposit the check from the Willis Cotton Gin and make a payment on his mortgage or tractor, depending on the week of the month. Afterwards, he would head over to Millie's Diner where he'd eat lunch with some of the locals and they either talk about their crops, or they would trade lies about their service time during World War II.

But since his regularly scheduled Monday trip had to be moved to Thursday because of Jesse, there would be no lunch. No jaw-jacking with his ex-service buddies. Jesse had remained shut up in his room until Wednesday night when he finally traipsed up to the main house his head hung low like a dog with his tail between his legs and apologized for his mean and aggressive behavior. Watson eagerly accepted. He was too old to sit out in the sun all day watching the boys and helping with the weigh-ins. He needed his son back on the job.

When Thursday rolled around, Jesse was back in the field, on the tractor, watching the pickers. Watson waited until after the mid-day weigh-in and lunch to make sure his son's hot-temper was at bay before heading out to the bank. Tippy was confused by the day and the time but was always happy to take a ride as he curled up next to Watson with his head on his lap. For Watson, while it wouldn't be the same as his normal Monday banking day, it did allow him to get away from the farm with all its responsibilities and enjoy just being alone for an hour or two.

Thursday was a slow day at the bank and Watson quickly finished his business. After making a payment on the tractor, the teller told him that he was less than a year from paying it off.

"Is that right? What month?"

"August, if you continue to make your payments on time."

"That's jest before cotton picking season starts. That's good. Real good. Thank you, ma'am."

As Watson left the bank, he couldn't help but think that by next year, he might be able to buy that used cotton picker he'd been dreaming about.

With Sammy and JoJo turning eighteen soon, they could leave the farm if they wanted. If they did, he would be shorthanded and he would *need* the mechanical picker. Finding new boys was getting harder and harder now that the orphanage was closed. He had been most fortunate this year. With Little Eddie gone, finding Tommy like he did had been a Godsend. Otherwise, this year's cotton wouldn't be harvested on time and its weight, color and luster would be compromised as would be the money he got per load. There wouldn't be any mechanical picker in his future.

As he crossed the railroad tracks and turned right onto the main highway, all he could think about was the mechanical picker. He figured he'd learn to drive it and teach Jesse or maybe vice versa. They could have the crop picked in no time. And instead of picking the field three times, they could pick it four times. Maybe even five times. They could get the scrubs they normally tilled under. Scrub cotton was worth something. With Jesse on the picker, maybe Caleb could learn to drive the tractor though he doubted seriously that would ever happen. He was a good boy, but he was still an idjit.

With the wind blowing on his face through the truck's only operable window, an Old Gold cigarette hanging from his lips, a good old dog lying next to him and a mechanical cotton picker in his future, he was a happy man. Only when he neared the rural road that led to his farm did that all change.

Hanging on a telephone pole on his side of the road was a poster with a picture of a boy that looked like Tommy but with longer hair. The words, *MISSING PERSON*, was just above the picture and a *$3000 REWARD* below. He took a big drag from the cigarette, tossed the butt out the window, pulled over to the side of the road and jammed on the brakes. There was no calm in the old man as he killed the engine, shoved open the door and headed straight to the pole. There he yanked down the poster and read it in its entirety. The description of the boy and the clothes he was last seen wearing confirmed that it was Tommy.

Sarah had been right when she had said, *that boy's gonna be trouble.* She just didn't know how much trouble. In hindsight, he should have never picked him up. It hadn't been the Lord's doings. It was Satan's. But it was done. Now he had to figure out what to do next. The boy was turning out to be a good picker. And they really needed him to finish up the cotton crop on time. But could they risk having him around for another month?

Before returning to his truck with the poster, he pulled down the one from the other side of the pole, ripped it up and tossed it in the ditch. The less people who knew about the reward, the better.

Watson was not a happy man as he headed back to his farm with the poster partially stuck under his leg so it wouldn't blow out the window. He hardly remembers the ritual of unlocking and locking chains and gates and driving past acres of land, lakes and crops. He drove faster than normal causing Tippy to take refuge on the floorboard bracing himself from the unexpected bumps and bounces. There was no waving to Jesse as he drove by the bobbing heads, leaving a trail of dust behind him.

When he pulled up to the front of the house, he grabbed the missing person poster in one hand and Tippy by the collar with the other pulled the normally slow and methodical dog from the truck. He had no time to waste as he headed to the kitchen where he knew Sarah would be.

"Well, I reckon I shoulda listened to you. You was right about that boy being trouble. Nearbout drove off the road when I seen this here poster," said Watson as he flung the open poster onto the kitchen table.

Sarah picked up the poster, studied it and tossed it back on the table. She then pulled his pack of Old Golds from his top pocket, popped out a cigarette and stuck it in her mouth. Watson quickly pulled the box matches from his overalls and lit hers. He did the same for himself. They both sat at the kitchen table with Tippy staying close to Sarah.

"I ain't gonna tell you I told you so … but I told you so."

She then took a puff from her cigarette, tilted her head back and blew the smoke into the air.

CHAPTER 42

"Where do you think you're heading off to?" asked Sarah as she saw Watson suddenly grab the truck keys from the kitchen table.

"Me and Tippy are fixin' to go fer a drive. I need to think about this Tommy boy thing and I do my best thinking whilst I'm driving."

"Guess you won't be gone long."

Watson ignored the comment.

"Come on, Tippy. Git your little hiney up."

The dog did as commanded.

"Satan got us into this mess and I'm gonna figure a way to git out."

He left Sarah, still smoking and fuming, and headed out to the truck with Tippy following close behind.

Once Watson reached highway 15, instead of turning right towards Willis, he turned left, heading towards Lanett. It wasn't long before he spotted another pair of posters, one on each side the telephone pole so that traffic from either direction could see the picture of the boy.

Seeing no vehicles coming from either direction, he stopped, slid the gear in neutral, jammed on the emergency brakes and exited his truck. He headed straight for the posters. He looked up and down the highway. Seeing no one or no oncoming traffic, he reached up and pulled the posters down from both sides of the pole. He then ripped them apart and tossed them to the side of the road. He ran back to the truck and took off down the road.

About a mile down the road, there were another pair of posters that he pulled down. He drove almost all the way to Lanett and found that there were posters everywhere. He decided pulling them all down was not feasible. Whoever wanted Tommy, wanted him really bad.

He made a U-turn and headed back towards Willis where, once again, he was inundated with posters.

He'd been gone almost a half an hour and this was supposed to be a thinking trip. But so far, he had thought of nothing. As always, Sarah was right. Word would get out. With that kind of money for finding the missing boy, there would be riff-raff from all parts of Alabama and beyond descending on the town, harassing all the farmers. He had made up his mind. The boy had to go. And the sooner the better. But, how? He hadn't thought that through.

Back at the farm, he saw Jesse sitting on the tractor at the end-row of the cotton field, watching the bobbing-heads. He slowed, turned, pulled over next to him and leaned his head out the window. All the bobbing-heads paused just slightly out of curiosity but when Jesse stood, they immediately went back to picking.

"Who's eating dinner with the boys tonight? You or Caleb?" asked Watson.

"Me."

"Then I want you to change. We need to talk. You, me and Sarah."

"Daddy, I've already apologized fer …"

"This ain't about you, boy. We got a problem. Can't talk about it in front of the pickers. But I want you to keep an eye out on Tommy. That's all I'm saying."

Watson didn't wait for an answer. He shoved the truck into reverse, backed up to the main road and headed back to the farmhouse. He had done a lot of thinking but had no answers except that Tommy had to go.

CHAPTER 43

Sometime around 5 p.m. Central Time, Southern Bell lineman, Jake Tatum drove the company's truck into the phone company's equipment substation parking lot in Lanett, Alabama. He and his partner, Jimbo Martin, headed straight to their supervisor's office removing their yellow hard hats as they did.

"Boss … I think we got a problem."

"What kind of problem?" asked Lanny Vickers, Southern Bell Area Supervisor while thinking, *downed line, broken pole, wrecked vehicle.*

"Those posters."

"Did you run out? I thought you had extras."

"Not that. We put them up all the way to Opelika like you told us to do while visually checking the lines. But that ain't the problem. When we were heading back to the substation, somewhere between Willis and Lanett, we … well Jimbo noticed that some of the posters were gone. We stopped at one of the poles and found this." Jake then showed his boss one of the posters that had been ripped in half. "I'm guessing at least three, four or five more of them ain't hanging on the poles no more."

A puzzled look came over their supervisor.

"And no damage to the lines or poles?"

"No sir."

"That doesn't make any sense at all. I could understand if a couple of the posters were pulled down if someone thought they knew something about the missing boy and wanted the reward. But five? You think it's vandalism? A bunch of kids up to no good?"

"Could be. But why? Not only that, they would have to be driving. Too much distance between the posters."

"Right. Got to be something else."

Vickers thanked his men and as soon as they left, he immediately called his boss who relayed the incident to J. N. Rutledge who then called Chief Broome.

"There was no evidence of malicious damage to our equipment," offered Rutledge after telling Broome about the posters. "You think it has anything to do with Tommy?"

"Possibly. But having *multiple* posters ripped apart doesn't make any sense. If the person who did this knows about Tommy, I think they would have already contacted us. But we haven't had a single call about the boy all day, so I'm at a loss. Oh … and by the way. Thank you for the additional phone line. It's very much appreciated."

As Rutledge relayed his plan to replace the missing and ripped posters with the morning crew, Broome couldn't help but think about the words that Rutledge had said earlier, *there was no evidence.* Maybe not with his telephone equipment, but the posters might provide some evidence.

"How far away are your men from those missing posters?" he asked, excited about what had just come to mind.

"I'm guessing about fifteen or twenty miles."

"I know this is an inconvenience, but is there any chance you could have one of your men go back today to where the posters were torn down and bring what's left of them back to me?"

"I can do that," replied J. N., hearing the excitement in Broome's voice. "But what do you expect to find?"

"I know this is a longshot, but I want to have them analyzed for fingerprints to see if there's a match between the prints on the posters and the evidence we already have. If it does …," Broome said even more excitedly. "there's a really good chance the abductor lives somewhere in that area."

"Jim … say no more. I'll have them bring whatever they find to you sometime tonight. Your office or home?" The two men were now on first name basis with a friendship bonded by a common cause.

"Home. And tell them not to worry about what time it is. Also … most important … please have them wear gloves when they pick them up. I would appreciate it if they could they give me an approximate mileage from Lanett where they saw the first posters missing and the approximate mileage from Lanett where the last poster was missing."

"They will have that information when they bring you the posters."

Broome gave J. N. the address and directions to his house and ended the call.

Broome's hand almost trembled with excitement as he reached in his desk and pulled out the Sinclair Oil map of Alabama and Georgia. He looked at the previously drawn circle around Lee County. Were they getting close or was this just a wild goose chase? Regardless, this was going to be another trip to the State Crime Lab.

CHAPTER 44

Something wasn't right. Tommy could sense it. Ever since Watson stopped and talked to Jesse that afternoon, neither Jesse's nor Watson's eyes never seemed to leave him. Whether he was in the field or riding on the back of the truck heading back to the workers' cabin. Did they somehow know about his escape plans? He needed to talk to Vernon. Alone.

With most of the boys either lined up at the privy or resting on their bunks, he found Vernon mulling through one of his books in the main hall. He pulled him aside and out of earshot of Caleb who was busy setting up the evening's meal.

"Did you see how Jesse was staring at me all afternoon? And old man Watson, checking me out through the rear-view mirror?" asked Tommy, almost whispering.

"Yes. It was hard not to notice."

"You think they know about my escape plans?"

"No. Only you and I know. I haven't even had a chance to talk to Leroy, Charlie or Eugene. It's got to be something else."

"I need to find out. I can't have anything interfering with our plan."

"No. *I'll* find out. *You* go back to your bunk. I'll go talk to Caleb. See if he knows anything."

Tommy headed to the bunkroom and Vernon walked over to Caleb who was setting the last two bowls of food on the table.

"Caleb … is Tommy in trouble?" asked Vernon, figuring the direct approach was the best. Possibly catching him off guard.

"Tommy in trouble? No siree bob. Matter of the fact, Daddy done told me that Tommy *is not* gonna has to wear them leggings no more come Saturday. Who told you Tommy was in trouble?"

"No one. But Jesse seemed to be watching Tommy a lot today. Nobody else. The same for your daddy when he came to pick us up after the last weigh-in."

"Maybe they was lookin' how good Tommy done learnt how to pick cotton. Or maybe they was lookin' at Leroy, making sure he ain't … is not wanting to run away like Clarence. Weren't he picking next to Tommy?"

"Yes he was. You might be right."

Vernon appreciated Caleb's attempt at using the proper English as much as it was.

"Caleb … just in case we're wrong, I know that Tommy would appreciate you finding out if he's in some sort of trouble. I would, too."

"You know Jesse ain't talking to me since I done tattled on him."

"Maybe you can try talking to him when he's taking some of his medicine," offered Vernon.

"I reckon I can do that, 'specially fer Tommy."

Vernon returned to the bunkroom where he found Tommy lying on his bed.

"Caleb doesn't know anything. He says he thinks Jesse and Watson might have been keeping an eye on Leroy. He was picking in the row next to you. So that's a possibility. I guess we'll find out soon enough."

CHAPTER 45

Jesse walked into the kitchen to find Henry and Sarah already seated at the table.

"It's past six. We done started eating without you," said Henry, slipping a piece of the cured ham to Tippy.

"I was watching Tommy like you done asked me. Weren't nuttin' different about what he did in the fields. Matter a fact, he picked more cotton than a lot of them boys today. If he didn't have them leggings on, he'd probably done even more."

"Anything else?"

"No sir," answered Jesse respectfully. "After he done finished with his pickings and the weigh-ins, he went straight to the house to eat. He didn't bother nobody. He didn't hardly talk to no one, excepting maybe Leroy and JoJo. He sure don't look like no problem to me."

"Well … his picking ain't what I'm talking about," said Watson who then slid the *Missing Person* poster over to the end of the table for Jesse to see.

"Is that Tommy? He ain't got the same hair, but it sure looks like him," said Jesse as he viewed the poster.

"It's Tommy alright," said Sarah

"Daddy … I thought you done told me and Mama that you picked up that boy off the road. I was thinking he was a runaway like Sammy and Claude."

With Monday's reprimand still fresh on Jesse's mind, he couldn't help but lash out verbally at his daddy while at the same time fighting back the smirk that his face beckoned.

"I'm guessin' you done lied to me and Mama. That boy ain't no runaway. You done *stole* him. The Lord ain't had nuttin' to do with that there boy being here. You jest needed another picker and the orphanage was closed, so you took him. Plain and simple. You done put us …"

Jesse seemed to be enjoying himself too much at berating his father, so Sarah stopped him mid-sentence.

"Jesse … you best hold your tongue if you know what's good fer you. Your daddy done what he thought best fer this family and this farm. We needed a picker and he found one. A good one. Now sit yourself down and I'll go fix you a plate. We can talk about this once we all have ate."

Jesse pulled out a chair at the table and sat down between his daddy and his mama. While he might challenge his daddy every now and then, he knew better than confront his mama. Instead, all three ate in silence, never looking up from their plate except to get more food. Once the meal was over and Sarah had removed the dishes, Watson took charge.

"I done a lot of thinking about this whole situation," said Watson, pronouncing the word, sit-ye-a-shun. "Sarah was right about that boy when she first laid eyes on him. She said he was going to be trouble and she were right. And Jesse was right when he said it weren't the Lord that spoke to me when I laid eyes on that boy. It was Satan that sent me down the wrong path. He tricked me. I should have never taken that boy. Irregardless, what's done is done. Can't go changing what can't be changed. What we need to do now is figure out what to do with that boy. We don't want no po'lice gitting themselves involved, coming out to the farm, asking questions. And we don't want no riff raff showing up here or anywhere else looking fer the boy fer that there reward money."

While Watson talked, Jesse couldn't take his eyes off the poster and more specifically, the reward money.

"Well, I got it figured out," said Jesse. "That boy's worth three thousand dollars. We jest call that number on the poster, tell them we found the boy and git the money."

"Jesse … Ain't nobody taking no money fer that boy," said Sarah. "It ain't right."

"You listen to your mama. You don't pile one sin on top of another. And taking that money is jest that. Another sin. It's the Devil's money."

"But Daddy …"

"Jesse … you heard what your mama said. We ain't taking no money fer that boy. That's the Devil trying to tempt us jest like he done to Jesus in the desert. We ain't having none of it."

"So what do we do with him?" asked Jesse, disappointed in his father's decision.

"He's a good picker, so I'm gonna keep him until cotton season is over. Then …".

This time Sarah interrupted. "Henry … you'll do no such thing. Everbody knows we use them *orphan* boys to pick our crops. Ain't no hiding from that. Come Monday, you're taking that boy back to where you done found him. If we don't ask fer no reward money, the po'lice ain't gonna do nuttin' to nobody."

"But Mama … three thousand dollars."

Sarah looked Jesse in the eye with a look that said, *I have spoken.*

Jesse stood and immediately left, slamming the screen door on his way out.

"Henry. You keep an eye on that boy. That money's done gone to his brain."

CHAPTER 46

"What do you want?" yelled Jesse as he opened the door to his bedroom to see Caleb standing outside with a sheepish look on his face.

"I ... uh ... I ..." stammered Caleb, trying to get his thoughts together.

"Spit it out, ya dummy. I ain't got time to listen to you jibber jabbering about nuttin'."

"Is Tommy in trouble?"

"What! Why'd you ask that?"

"I seen how you was looking at him in the fields today after Daddy done talked to you. Jesse ... Tommy don't want *no* trouble. He ain't gonna run away like Clarence."

Jesse knew that someone had put Caleb up to this inquiry.

"I ain't worried about him running away. Matter of fact, I ain't worried about nothin'," said Jesse thinking about the reward money. "You tell Tommy he ain't in *no* trouble."

Then he slammed the door.

CHAPTER 47

By 5:30 a.m., Chief Broome was already on the road heading to Atlanta. Destination: Georgia State Crime Lab. Riding in the front passenger seat was a box of the remains of five posters with his leather satchel lying next to it. Broome wanted them closeby so he could keep an eye on them.

The Southern Bell workers had shown up to his house a little after eight last night with a box containing the potential new evidence along with a sheet showing the mileage from Lanett, Alabama to the first and last telephone pole. Ruth Ann offered them some pie and a cup of coffee as a courtesy, not a reward, but they respectfully declined and left.

As he continued to glance over at this potential evidence, the more excited he got at the prospect of what *might* be lying next to him. He couldn't get to Atlanta fast enough. He reached down and turned on the siren, the red dome lights and sped up to sixty miles per hour, ten miles over the limit. With no calls on the missing person's phone line, the posters with their possible matching fingerprints were the only new lead they had.

The receptionist at the Georgia State Crime Lab immediately recognized Chief Broome as he walked into the lobby area carrying a small box with his peaked cap under his arm. He was the only man who had ever come walking into to the building with a set of golf clubs slung over his back. Not even those employees who played the game had ever done that.

"So what are you bringing us this time? A bowling ball," she asked with a big smile on her face as Broome neared her desk.

Broome was too wrapped up in the purpose of his visit to recognize the lady's attempt at humor.

"Is Dr. Barrineau available?" he asked, the serious tone of his voice mirroring the look on his face. It was hard for the receptionist not to take notice.

"Let me check," she responded, her mood now matching Broome's."

Instead of sitting in one of the four chairs that hugged the nearby wall, he paced back and forth in front of the door that led to the labs. Shortly, Dr. Barrineau appeared.

"Back again so soon? What have you got for me this time?"

As they walked back to the scientist's office, Broome told Barrineau about the reward posters and how a number of them had been ripped apart and thrown alongside the highway in Lee County, Alabama.

"We're hoping that some of the fingerprints found on the posters might match what you found on the cigarette butts and golf bag," concluded Broome.

"When you said Alabama, didn't you mean Georgia? See, we don't have legal authority to work on evidence found in Alabama without their permission. Just Georgia. And to get permission, that takes time and I know you don't want to drive all the way to the lab at Alabama Polytechnic Institute[2] in Auburn, Alabama."

"Right. Right. I misspoke. I meant Georgia."

Once in the lab, Barrineau slid on some protective gloves and took the box from Broome and placed it on a nearby table. He carefully lifted the first poster remnant with some metal tweezers and placed it on a brightly lit counter under a fume hood.

Barrineau looked over at Broome who had not taken his eyes off of the forensic doctor.

"This could take us a little while. You can use my office if you'd like or you can stay here and watch."

"If you don't mind, I'd rather stay here. I just spent the last two plus hours sitting behind the steering wheel of my patrol car and I think I need to give my rear-end a break. Plus, what you do here is fascinating."

Barrineau was pleased that someone would actually take interest in his or his team's work. Hardly ever did they receive any recognition or credit for the work that they did in solving cases with most going to the GBI Director and every now and then, the agents.

He motioned the chief over to the counter, reached into a drawer and pulled out two sets of masks and goggles. He handed a set to Broome and the two slipped them on.

---

[2] Renamed Auburn University in 1960.

As he began preparing a solution of Ninhydrin in a large glass beaker, Barrineau took the opportunity to give Broome a brief history of the science of fingerprinting.

"Fingerprinting has been used for identification for centuries. Archaeologists have found bricks in Jericho, near the Jordan River that date back as far as 7000 BC that contain thumbprints that identified the bricklayer. Chinese documents from around 3000 BC have been found with clay seals bearing thumbprints used as their signature on legal documents. Classifying fingerprints, however, has only been around since about the 1800's."

Barrineau turned to see if he had lost his student.

"Am I boring you?"

"Oh no. Please continue."

"In the late 1800's, Dr. Henry Faulds, a British physician, missionary, teacher and scientist, published a research paper suggesting that fingerprints could be used for an individual's identification. As part of his study, he and some of his medical students shaved off the ridges of their finger and discovered they grew back in the same exact patterns as before. In an effort to advance his idea of fingerprint identification, he solicited the help of Charles Darwin, the famous naturalist. Darwin felt he was too old to become engaged in the project and passed it on to his half-cousin, Sir Francis Galton who years later published a book on fingerprints, aptly titled, *Finger Prints* in which he identified and named the different ridges of the finger as whorls, arches and loops. He advanced the idea that no two fingerprints were alike and were permanent. Around 1900, Sir Edward Henry, a British Inspector-General of Bengal, developed a mathematical system for classifying fingerprints. Today, we use a modified version of the Henry system. And to conclude my history lesson for today, Sir Henry returned to London where he would become Commissioner of the Metropolitan Police. A little-known fact about Sir Henry … he introduced police dogs to the force."

"Most interesting," mumbled Broome through his mask. "Not sure I could pass a test. Too many Henry's."

Surprisingly, the usual stoic Barrineau laughed at the comment. Continuing with his process, Barrineau slowly poured the solution into a large glass tray. Using metal tweezers, he dipped the first remnant into the Ninhydrin solution making sure the entire surface was covered by the liquid. After a few seconds of submersion, he pulled the remnant out allowing the excess solution to drip back into the tray. Because there could be prints on both sides of the paper and as a faster way of drying the solution, he hung it on a string-line that stretched the length of the overhead cabinets using ordinary clothespins. Once again, using the metal tweezers, he pulled out another remnant. Before he could begin to repeat the processes, Broome spoke up.

"Can I ask you a question?"

Barrineau nodded.

"Why aren't you using fingerprint powder?"

"Fingerprint powder is used for non-porous materials like glass, handguns, cars. Paper is porous, so we use a Ninhydrin-based solution." Barrineau repeated the pronunciation of the chemical.

"Makes sense. I'm glad I didn't waste my time with the fingerprint kit I found in my Crime Scene Investigation box."

"You did the right thing bringing it to us. I can't tell you how many pieces of evidence are inadmissible in court because of a botched test."

Barrineau saw Broome walk over and looked at the first sample as it dried and at the purple images that were forming.

"It's called Ruhemann's purple after Siegfried Ruhemann, the man who discovered Ninhydrin. And before you ask … yes, the prints will become darker and clearer over time."

"How long are we talking?" asked Broome.

"Twenty-four to forty-eight hours when letting the Ninhydrin dry naturally. But because we know you want the results before you leave, we're going to use a quick-dry method that one of my FBI colleagues taught me." Barrineau pulled open the door to one of the cabinets, pulled out an ordinary steam iron and plugged it in to a nearby electrical receptacle. As he added water to the iron, he continued. "The application of heat and steam from the iron will accelerate the reaction of our chemical solution and the amino acids left by the fingerprints. Hopefully, we will see something in minutes."

Broome moved to get a better angle as he watched Barrineau hold the iron about two inches from one side of the wet remnant then to the other side. As if magic, a number of purple fingerprint images began to appear. This excited both Barrineau and Broome.

While the first samples dried, Barrineau began to pull other pieces of posters from the box and repeat the chemical process. He would let these samples dry naturally. No steam iron. Afterwards, he would photograph all of them and place the remnants with the developed pictures in the evidence room.

Once he had finished applying the solution to the last poster remnant, he checked the first piece to make sure it had completely dried. Satisfied that it had, he removed his mask and goggles, leaving just his glasses.

"Chief, I'm going to go get the pictures we took of the fingerprints from the cigarette butts. When I get back, I'm going to compare them to the prints on the posters and see if we have a match. I'll be back in a second. You can now take off your goggles and mask. Just don't touch anything or breathe." He then laughed at his lame attempt at humor which was rare.

While he was gone, Broome studied the hanging piece of evidence. There were a number of fingerprints. Some almost perfect. Others smudged to the point they were almost unrecognizable.

It wasn't long before Barrineau returned holding some 8x12 photographs of the enlarged prints found on the cigarette butt. He laid them on the counter, pulled the dried piece of poster from the string-line and laid it next to the photographs. From the top cabinet, he retrieved a large magnifying glass and began comparing the two.

"Do you see anything?" asked Broome, anxious for results.

"Yes. Fingerprints but none that match our earlier prints. It's a process. It takes time."

Broome checked his watch. Time was his enemy. Tommy had already been gone too long without any contact from the abductor. That didn't bode well for the young boy.

Barrineau seemed to take forever studying each print comparing the whorls, arches and loops. After about five minutes into his search, Broome heard Barrineau yell out. "Ah ha! A match."

"Are you sure?"

"Positive. It appears that your Old Gold man is the one pulling down the posters. Well … at least this one. When the other fragments of the posters are ready, I will also check them out, but I think this is your man."

"Dr. Barrineau … I … I …"

"You're welcome." he said, pushing up his wire rimmed glasses.

"So what's your next move?"

"I'm not sure, but I have over two hours of drive time to figure it out."

Broome left a happy man, but as he slid behind the wheel of his car, he wasn't sure why.

Missing Youth

CHAPTER 48

It had been a very long day for Chief Broome with most of it spent driving and the day wasn't over. He pulled into his "Chief" designated parking space, one of the few luxuries his position afforded and saw Lewis and Bob's squad cars parked in nearby spots alongside Betty's '53 Chevy 150. With no other cars in the lot, it was a good sign that all was right in the little town of Pine Mountain. All except the missing boy.

The sound of the front door opening had all eyes in the room on the chief as he entered. No one spoke, but they all were thinking the same thing. *Did the prints match?*

"It's our guy," said the chief while removing his cap.

As everyone either clapped or cheered, Broome could feel the sense of relief in the room like they had found the boy. They hadn't, but at least they knew who they were looking for.

Broome continued. "Dr. Barrineau, the forensic specialist at the crime lab, nicknamed him the Old Gold man. So that's who we're looking for. The Old Gold man."

Broome looked over to the desk where the missing person's phone had been installed. Lewis was manning the phone.

"Any calls?"

"Just a wrong number, sir. That's all."

Not the answer Broome had hoped for.

"I've got to make a couple of calls. Afterwards, I want to have a team meeting. Betty, can you get Mr. Rutledge on the phone?"

"Yes sir."

Broome headed into his office, hanging his hat on the nearby peg. By the time he had sat down, Betty had Rutledge on the phone.

"Thank you, Betty," he answered through the intercom. "Now can you find me the phone number of the Lee County Sheriff's Office and get me the name of their chief?" Without waiting for a reply, he picked up the phone.

The two men exchanged greetings and Broome got right to the point of the call.

"Just wanted to give you a quick update. So far, only one call on the missing person line and it was a wrong number. The money doesn't seem to be ferreting out anyone, but it's still early. However … the posters that your men brought to me last night had fingerprints that matched the prints found on our earlier evidence."

"That's great. So it's the same person?"

"Yes. The Old Gold man as we now call him. That's the name Dr. Barrineau, the forensic scientist at the State Crime Lab, gave him."

"Appropriate."

"And we feel quite confident he lives somewhere in Lee County just as Dr. Barrineau suggested."

"Does that mean the Alabama police will now take over the case?"

"No, but it does complicate matters."

Broome had no idea who would be in charge of the investigation once he called the Lee County Sheriff's Office. Regardless, he would stay involved until the end … whenever and whatever that might be.

"Let me know if there's anything else I can do," said J. N. "If my men find any other posters missing or compromised in any way, I'll get back to you."

The call ended and Broome hit the intercom button.

"Betty … did you get the phone number to the Lee County Sheriff's Department?"

"Yes sir. Their chief's name is Nick Carson."

"See if you can reach him." He looked up at the clock. 3:47 p.m. Alabama was in the central time zone, an hour earlier.

Sheriff Carson who was not the type to keep people waiting regardless of their position in life was most prompt in answering Betty's call. He had been the head of the department for over nine years.

Once the two men had exchanged greetings and introductions, Broome gave Carson a short narrative of the kidnapping, the missing person phone line and the evidence they had found, both in Georgia and Alabama.

"So, based on what you told me, you don't really have *any* evidence that the child was actually taken to Alabama. And the fingerprints that you found only show that the man that you think abducted the boy might live in Alabama."

"That is correct."

Chief, has there been a ransom demand?"

"No sir."

"Any credible phone calls regarding the missing boy?"

"No sir."

"So, you really don't know if the boy is dead or alive or in Georgia or Alabama?"

"No sir."

"And the GBI can't or won't help?"

"No sir."

"Unless there's concrete evidence the boy was taken across state lines, the FBI won't get involved."

"That is also correct. Not unless the child is twelve years old or younger."

From Carson's line of questioning, Broome could see how an outside observer would have a different perspective on the case. But Carson hadn't met the Harrisons and hadn't seen the sorrow on their faces. Nor had he listened to the angst in David Rutledge's voice as he told about his missing friend. There was no way for him to know the sadness that those involved felt.

"Chief … I know I sound critical, but in my twenty-four years working in the Sheriff's Office, I've never had a kidnapping, so I wouldn't even know where to begin with that kind of investigation nor would any of my officers. I commend you for your efforts and your diligence. But I don't see how my office can be of any help to you. What I can do is to give you authorization to conduct your investigation in my county. In essence, I am deputizing you and your officers. I can have one of my officers drive the authorizations to you this afternoon. You can fill in the names. Also, if you find that you need a warrant, I will help you get one and I will send out one of my men to serve it. I'm afraid that's all I can do until we know a crime has been committed in our county.

"Actually, your authorization is more than enough and I really appreciate it."

The call ended and Broome pulled out his map of Georgia and Alabama. Using the information from the sheet the Southern Bell workers had given him, he marked with an 'X' the approximate location of the missing and torn posters and circled the county roads closest to his marks.

He then pressed down all three buttons on the intercom and hollered out, "My office. Everyone."

Bob, Betty and Lewis quickly assembled around Broome's desk. Rarely did he call a team meeting and now they were having a second one in just one week.

"I'm going to Alabama tomorrow. Actually, Lewis, Buddy and I are going. Kind of a field trip. I want us to check out the locations of where those torn-down posters were found. I'm not sure what we'll find, if anything. But the evidence we have leads me to believe the Old Gold man lives somewhere nearby. It's a long shot, but it's all we got."

"If that boy's anywhere within ten miles of the posters, ol' Buddy should be able to pick up the boy's scent," added Lewis.

"That's what I'm hoping," said Broome.

Broome turned to Betty. "Just in case I forget, first thing Monday, I want you to call the Lee County courthouse. I want you to get the names and addresses of the first ten property owners along Alabama highway 15 starting just outside of Willis, Alabama, and working your way towards Lanett. I also want a list of the first three property owners on Lee County Roads 262, 266, 270 and 830 as they feed off highway 15. If I'm confusing you, I've got them marked on my map."

Betty nodded. She knew exactly what to do having worked almost two years for the Harris County Superior Court in Hamilton, Georgia before coming to work for Sheriff Broome.

Then looking at Bob, Broome continued. "While we're gone, you'll be in charge of the office. Make sure either you or Betty are manning the missing person phone. Once we get to Willis, I will call to get an update assuming we can find a phone we can use. Any questions?"

Broome looked at the two officers and Betty. All three shook their heads.

"Let's hope tomorrow is a good day."

CHAPTER 49

Thursday and Friday seemed to drag on forever for Tommy. Monday couldn't get here fast enough. It wasn't as though he hated the farm or even the work. He enjoyed the new friends he had made and even the competition in trying to pick the most cotton. But he missed his mom and dad, his home, his friend, David. Surprisingly, he missed school.

Caleb had talked to Jesse Thursday night and Tommy was told that he wasn't in trouble. That Jesse wasn't worried about anything. But Friday, he could feel that something wasn't right. Something had changed. Jesse normally slept or appeared to be sleeping while watching over the pickers. But Friday, he had stayed alert and kept his eyes mostly on Tommy. Leroy thought he might have been watching Clarence now that he was back in the fields, worried that he might try running away again. But that didn't hold true as Tommy's row was nowhere near Clarence's.

And it couldn't be that Jesse thought that he was slacking off because his picking speed had increased to the point where he was now picking more than half the pickers. Strangely enough, Jesse had even complimented him at Friday's last weigh-in on the amount of cotton he had picked. Even smiled.

Watson seemed even stranger. He no longer seemed to care about the amount of cotton that Tommy picked. And he no longer mentioned the deal they had made about the leggings whereas at every weigh-in prior, he was all smiles. Not Friday.

Vernon was also aware of Jesse's uncharacteristic behavior.

"You think they know?" asked Tommy once he had Vernon alone in the bunkroom.

"I don't see how. None of this makes any sense. If they thought you were planning on running away from the farm, why remove your shackles? Why treat you so differently than they have before. Something is up. It's Leroy's turn to have Sunday dinner with the Watsons. Maybe he can figure out what's going on. In the meantime, keep a low profile … meaning don't do anything to attract unwanted attention from Jesse or the Watsons."

"Don't worry. I won't mess up," said Tommy.

"And remember my rules …"

"I know. Never challenge, keep mouth shut, do what they ask and stay away from Jesse."

"You got it. You should be fine."

"Yeah. It's only three days. What could happen in three days?"

CHAPTER 50

As the outside temperature continued to rise, all four windows and the two vents of Chief Broome's patrol car were open to allow the outside air to swirl throughout the car. Broome and Lewis occupied the front seat while Buddy laid claim to the entire back seat with his head hung out either of the two windows depending on his mood. There was no rhyme or reason to his selection.

Broome had hoped to get an early start, but the mayor had called that morning and wanted an update on the missing boy. Late morning breakfast meetings with the mayor at Woody's, a local diner, weren't uncommon, but they were never held on Saturday. And rarely was any real business discussed. Usually, the time was filled with stories by the mayor about hunting, fishing, farming and Will Junior. But this morning, he wanted to know more details about the missing boy and the chances of him being found dead anywhere near Pine Mountain. While the mayor was concerned about the boy, he seemed more concerned about the bad publicity that the kidnapping could bring to the town. It was bad for business, especially for Ida Cason Callaway Gardens whose tax dollars pretty much supported the entire town.

To the mayor's relief, Broome told him that he didn't know the fate of the boy. He then went into detail about the Old Gold man and the evidence they had found which seemed to suggest the abductor was from Alabama which seemed to placate his boss even more.

Broome left Zachary sitting at the booth and headed back to his office where he found Lewis and Buddy waiting anxiously in the parking lot.

The trip to Lanett only took about thirty minutes which gave Broome enough time to discuss with Lewis what he hoped to accomplish. Besides checking out the locations of the missing posters where the Old Gold man's fingerprints had been found, he wanted to give Buddy a chance to pick up the scent of the missing boy at those locations. If nothing came of that, he wanted to drive into the nearby town of Willis and talk to some of the locals. Maybe they could offer some help.

Using the information from the sheet that the Southern Bell lineman had given the chief, he drove until the calculated mileage on the speedometer had been reached. Lewis who had also been counting telephone poles between posters yelled out just as Broome put on his blinker.

"Chief … I think this is it!"

Broome slowed the car to a crawl, turned on the car's flashing red dome light and parked safely on the shoulder of the road. Both men exited the car with Broome carrying his leather satchel. They headed over to the telephone pole where they saw on one side what looked to be a small piece of a poster hanging from the small tack.

"This has got to be it," said Broome.

"Yes, sir. I believe so."

"Go get Buddy. Let's see if he can work some magic."

"Yes, sir."

While Lewis ran over to the car, Broome opened his leather satchel and pulled out the plastic bag containing Tommy's worn underwear.

When Buddy saw Lewis approaching the car, he stepped back from the window and waited patiently until Lewis pulled on the handle. Immediately, the dog began nudging the door open as he had other business on his mind. Once free from the car, he began marking his territory on nearby bushes, trees and even the telephone pole.

"Okay, Buddy. Enough," ordered Lewis. "Come here."

The dog immediately stopped what he was doing, trotted over to Lewis and sat.

Broome handed Lewis the plastic bag.

"What's the chances of Buddy picking up the boy's smell?"

"A few years back, I'd say darn good. Back then, he could sniff something out eight … ten miles away. But, I'm afraid that now, five … six miles is the best we can hope for especially with this wind and rain clouds approaching."

Lewis opened the sack, let Buddy get a good smell of the briefs and held on to his leash waiting for the dog to spring forward. But Buddy just sat there with his nose pointing to the sky, sniffing in all directions. After a few minutes, the dog curled up next to Lewis' feet. It was hard not to see the sadder than normal look on the dog's face.

"That's okay, Buddy. That's okay," said Lewis kneeling down to let the dog give him a slobbering kiss on his hand.

"You tell Buddy that we got more places to visit. His job isn't done yet," said Broome looking at the two carrying on like it was their last days. "Let's get back into the car."

Broome made two more stops along highway 15, where posters were missing. Buddy tried his best but couldn't pick up the scent of the missing boy.

"Next time, maybe we should have Wallace bring Radar," said Lewis. "He's not nearly as old as Buddy. Maybe he could track the boy down."

"Maybe. Let's see what we can find out in Willis first. There's always somebody in these small towns that knows everybody's business. We just need to find out who that person is."

"Yeah … we got a few like that in Pine Mountain, but I'm not naming any names."

"You're learning fast, Lewis."

About four miles down the road and on the left, Broome saw a large Coca Cola sign painted on the side of a dirty, white clapboard building. On the front of the building underneath a swinging blue and white Pure Oil sign was another sign, one not so new. *Turner's General Store.* The "t" in *Store* was almost gone, so the sign seemed to read, *Turner's General Sore.* An American Flag hung on a rusty gray pole to the right of the store giving evidence that it also served as the local post office.

Broome drove across some railroad tracks that divided the town's main street and pulled up to one of the gas tanks, killed the engine, grabbed his cap and stepped out of the car. As he slipped on his cap, he saw a slender, young women, in her late twenties throw open the screen door to the building, walk down the steps and head over to the pump.

"How much, sir?" she asked as she viewed the man's uniform and the Pine Mountain Police emblem on the door of the car.

"Four dollars. And I need a receipt."

"Are you going inside?"

"I am."

"Ask my mama for one. She's the lady behind the counter."

Broome handed the young attendant four one-dollar bills and then leaned in the driver's side window and looked over at Lewis.

"I'd like you to come inside with me and bring one of the posters. Leave Buddy in the car."

"Yes sir."

Lewis grabbed the first of many posters from off the bench seat and stepped out of the car donning his cap as he did. The young woman who had begun pumping the gas couldn't keep her eyes off the young officer as he rounded the car. *There's just that something about a man in a uniform,* she thought. There was no reciprocating thought by Lewis as he hurried to catch up with the chief.

Before Broome had a chance to reach for the handle on the screen door, Lewis had it pulled open allowing his boss to enter first into the store. Once they both were inside the building, the slamming of the screen door caused a brown-hair, heavy set woman behind the counter to immediately rise from her chair while slipping on a pair of browline glasses. The scowl on her face made it clear to Broome that she wasn't happy about leaving the breeze of the fan that gave her some comfort from the ninety-degree heat. Once she saw the uniforms of the two men, her frown turned into a smile, albeit fake.

"Can I help you?" she asked looking only at Broome.

"I hope so. I'm Jim Broome, Chief of Police of Pine Mountain, Georgia. And this is my assistant, Sergeant Lewis Phillips."

"Lurleen Turner. And that's my daughter, Rachel, out there pumping your gas." She then picked up a nearby church fan and began a slow but methodical sweeping action. "Are you looking for anything in particular?" she asked as her hand motions seemed to pick up speed.

Broome turned to Lewis. "Show her the poster."

Lewis set the poster on the counter with the picture of Tommy facing the lady.

"Have you ever seen this boy around here? His hair is shorter than it is in the picture."

Lurleen leaned over, adjusted her glasses and studied the picture up close.

"Cute little fella. I've seen this poster before. On one of the poles just outside my store. But I paid no attention to it because I've never seen this boy before."

She shoved the poster back towards Broome.

"Didn't you say you were from Pine Mountain? Pine Mountain, Georgia?" she asked and looked at the Pine Mountain Police Department patch on the sleeve of her visitor's shirt.

"Yes ma'am."

"Why are you *here* … in Willis? Is the boy a runaway? Or lost? And you think he could be *here*?" she asked, an excitement in her voice that had not been there before.

"The boy's name is Tommy Harrison and he was *kidnapped* in Pine Mountain, near Ida Cason Callaway Gardens and we have good reason to believe that he was brought to Alabama."

"You don't mean Willis, do you?"

"Possibly."

"Well, even if I had seen that boy, I probably wouldn't remember him. We always have a lot of boys running around the store, especially when cotton picking season is over. You know with the sharecroppers, tenants and all that. But they all look the same to me. Smelly and dirty. Always trying to sneak a candy or soda."

About that time, Rachel entered the store, talking as she did.

"Mama, did you give this man a receipt for his gas?" She asked, while eyeing Lewis. "That your dog in the car?"

"Yes ma'am," answered Lewis.

"He seems real sweet and friendly," said Rachel while she handed the gas money to her mama who counted it, rang it up on the register and slipped the ones into the till.

"Yes ma'am, he is. His name is Buddy," said Lewis.

"Rachel, dear. While I write up this man's receipt, look at that poster. See if you recognize that boy."

While Rachel examined the poster, Broome took time to take in his surroundings. The store was small with a large window on either side of the front door. Can goods, coffee, cigarettes, ropes, pots, pans, buckets and a sundry of other products occupied shelves that hung on every wall except the far back wall which carried an assortment of farming tools, fishing gear and rifles. In the middle of the store were two tables which had overalls, shirts, dresses, socks, hats neatly arranged. Stacked on the floor under the table were large bags of sugar and flour. And just in front of the counter were a number of small bins filled with penny candy. For a small town, the store was fairly well stocked.

Broome had his back to the counter when Rachel spoke up.

"Sir?" Broome immediately turned around to see the young woman shaking her head.

"No … uh uh. I've never seen him. His parents must be somebody real important with that kind of reward money. Why are you looking here in Willis?"

Lurleen chose to answer. "Honey … the boy was kidnapped and the chief thinks that maybe somebody here in Willis might have taken him."

"Well, not necessarily Willis," said Broome. "But maybe someplace close by. We're not real certain."

Lurleen handed Broome his receipt.

"Thank you, ma'am." He started to turn but thought for a second. "I notice you sell cigarettes. Do you happen to sell Old Golds?"

Without her mother having to ask, Rachel turned and pulled out a pack from the stack and set them down on the counter in front of her mother.

"We sell them all," said Lurleen. "Farmers love their cigarettes probably more than they do their wives. That'll be thirty cents."

"I'm sorry. I wasn't really looking to buy any cigarettes. I don't smoke. But the person we think abducted the boy does smoke and he smokes unfiltered Old Golds. Do you have many people around here who smokes that brand?"

While Lurleen thought for a second, Rachel piped up. "Not many. Only the ones …"

Lurleen looked sternly at her daughter who stopped talking mid-sentence.

"Actually, it *is* a fairly popular brand around here with a lot of the farmers because it was one of the brands of cigarettes that were packed in their C rations during the war. I know because my husband was in the war."

Rachel's interrupted comment had not gone unnoticed by Broome nor Lewis.

"I see." Once again, he started to turn for the door.

"Sir. Your poster," said Lurleen, holding it out to him.

"I can leave it here if you think the owner of the store wouldn't mind hanging it where the good folks of Willis might see it?"

"You are *looking* at the owner," said Lurleen, miffed at the slight.

"My sincere apologies," answered Broome. "We don't have many women business owners in Pine Mountain, if any, and I made a bad assumption. Again, my apologies. You have been most helpful and I should not have assumed."

"Actually, I'm used to it," said Lurleen, happy to put the man, any man, in his place. "Women aren't supposed to own stores. Just cook and have babies. Everybody in Willis thinks Jimmy, my husband, owns the store because he's the manager of the cotton gin and because he's a man. But my mom, dad and I opened the store during the war while Jimmy was overseas. I worked the shop and raised two girls while he was gone. Now, both my mom and dad are dead. I'm an only child, so now I am the sole owner." Lurleen paused for a second to fan herself a few times, then continued. "You asked if the owner of the store would mind hanging that poster. And no, she doesn't. If it's okay with you, I'm thinking I should hang it on the back of the cash register. That way everybody sees it."

"I really appreciate that," said Broome.

"I think we've taken up enough of your time. You have been most helpful." Turning to Lewis. "You see anything that you need?"

"Yes sir." He then took four Mary Janes, four Charleston Chews and two atomic fireballs that he had been eyeing from the wooden bins and laid them on the counter.

Rachel scooped them up and placed them in a small brown bag all the while wishing she had put on some make-up this morning before coming to work.

"That'll be ten cents."

Lewis laid a nickel and five pennies on the counter. As he did, Broome looked at his watch. It was 12:50 p.m., Eastern Standard Time. Way past either his or Lewis' lunch time. Hopefully there was a boarding house close by. Most had good food and were home to the local busybodies.

"Any chance there's a place we can catch lunch around here?"

Lurleen looked at a clock that hung over the screen door. Almost noon, Central Standard Time.

"Millie's Diner. Less than a half a mile up the road on the right across the tracks. Good food. Try their meat loaf."

CHAPTER 51

Saturday had finally come and to Tommy's relief, nothing had happened. But out in the field, Jesse's intense scrutiny continued as he seemed to watch Tommy's every move. He wondered if Clarence might have said something to cause their concern. Vernon, however, attributed it to Watson's paranoia about runaways, which Tommy had been labeled.

Even with the heightened vigilance, Vernon had decided that they should hold a practice run during the first weigh-in. He wanted to make sure that everything went smoothly Monday. He had told Charlie, Leroy and Eugene about the escape plan and they all were on board and each understood the role they played.

Tommy's hands seemed to be in overdrive as he filled his bag on what was supposed to be his last full day of picking. Only the shackles stood between him and freedom. He wasn't going to give Watson any reason not to remove them as he had promised.

The practice run went well. Once the weigh-in began, Jesse's focus was on weighing the bags of cotton. And Caleb was kept busy hoisting and dumping the full bags into the wagon. Because Watson was there to do the accounting of the cotton weight and not at the bank as he would be on Monday, there was no smoke break for Jesse. But, as predicted, he did take a nature break which Tommy mentally counted as about four minutes.

When Jesse did return to the tractor, he scanned the field paying no attention to any one person. Not even Tommy. He then sat down, laid back the best he could and closed his eyes. Everything seemed back to normal. Vernon who was in the row next to Tommy gave him the thumbs up. Monday was a go.

About a half hour after the weigh-in, Tommy heard Vernon say, "Oh no." He was looking towards the sky.

"What?" asked Tommy who looked to the sky but only saw the dark clouds that had just started to roll in. They were a needed relief from the hot baking sun.

"The clouds. They look like rain clouds."

"Why is that a problem? I like the cool air they bring."

"If it starts raining, we stop picking. Then we have to wait for it to stop raining and the cotton to dry before we start picking again."

"I can pick in the rain. That's not a problem."

"It's not about us. It's about the cotton and the cotton gin. If any of the cotton in the wagon is wet, the gin will deduct a certain percentage for the extra weight caused by the rain. Watson thinks they cheat him when they do that. Plus, they downgrade the quality of the cotton because of the discoloration caused by the water. If it rains today, tomorrow or Monday, we'll have to postpone your escape for a week."

"Oh no. That can't happen. Please … don't rain. Please," begged Tommy as the clouds grew darker and darker.

CHAPTER 52

Once Lurleen saw the patrol car drive off, she sent Rachel to the house to make them lunch. It was earlier than normal, but her daughter went willingly. She wouldn't come back this time without makeup … just in case. Lurleen then called her husband.

"Willis Cotton Gin," answered Rebecca Turner.

"Becky … this is your mama. Let me speak to your daddy."

"He's out in the yard. Something about a problem with the scale."

"Tell him I need him to come to the store as soon as possible. It's important. Real important."

Lurleen sat back down in front of the fan and picked up the poster. She didn't look at the picture. She stared at the three thousand dollars reward money. Even though she had the only general store in town, for the last few years, she had been losing business to the bigger, lower priced Jewish dry good stores in Opelika and to catalog sales from Sears Roebuck. Her business stayed in the red most of the year until the crops were harvested and the farmers paid off their credits. But with the price of cotton shrinking, the credits seemed to get bigger and the debt payments less frequent. She had made a big deal out of owning the store to the police chief from Pine Mountain. She also owned the house behind the general store. Both were mortgaged up to the hilt. She was only one bad crop from filing bankruptcy. To make matters worse, Jimmy didn't have a clue about the debt. All of her banking business was done at the First National Bank of Opelika where her parents took out the initial loan on the house and store. Jimmy banked at Farmers & Merchant Bank in Willis where the bank manager was one of his hunting buddies. If she could sell the business, she would. Three thousand dollars could make all that go away.

It wasn't long before the phones at the store and her house began to ring simultaneously. Lurleen listened to the rings. One long ring and one short ring. That meant the call was for her. Any other kind of ring sequence meant it was one of the other three phones on their four-way party line. Rural towns like Willis did not have the luxury of having two-way party lines or private lines for house phones. She picked up the receiver.

"Turner's General Store."

"It's Jimmy. What's so dang important that I gotta come to the store? You know it's my lunch time."

As he spoke, Lurleen heard a click sound on the phone which meant that one of the other three subscribers had picked up their phone and was listening in on their conversation. This was a common occurrence in Willis where everybody wanted to know everybody's business.

"Wait a minute, Jimmy," said Lurleen. "Rachel … is that you on the phone?" Immediately, the other listener who was not Rachel hung up.

"Jimmy … this is not something I want to discuss over the phone. It's important, so get yourself over here … now." Without waiting for a reply, she hung up the phone.

Lurleen and Jimmy Turner had been married for twenty-one years. Becky their oldest child was twenty years old and Rachel, nineteen. The children were three and two when the U.S. entered World War II. Jimmy could have been exempted from the draft, but he chose to go to war not out of patriotism and love of country but because all his buddies thought it the manly thing to do. When he returned home from the war a wounded soldier, he went to work for the cotton gin as a scale operator. Ten years later, he was the manager. The promotion was more in title than in money as most farmers made more than he. But considering he had only an eighth-grade education and was partially disabled, he had done well for himself.

Lurleen didn't have to wait long before a light blue 1953 Ford station wagon pulled up in front of the store. A portly man with receding black hair jumped out of the car and walked aggressively up the steps, threw open the screen door and entered the building.

Seeing no one else other than Lurleen in the store, he bellowed out, "Okay. I'm here. So what do you want?"

"Close the door and flip the CLOSED sign around."

Jimmy did as he was told. While he was king of the cotton gin, Lurleen ruled the house.

"You remember telling me about these?" She held up the poster. "And how *stupid* those people in Georgia must be for hanging them all over

Alabama? Well, I had a most interesting customer here today … the Chief of Police from Pine Mountain, Georgia."

"Are you sure it wasn't one of them revenuers?"

"Jimmy, the man was wearing a uniform."

"Why'd he stop here?"

"He got some gas and then he came inside and showed me the poster. He asked if I'd ever seen the boy here in the store. I told him no and I asked why was he looking here in Willis. *You're* not going to believe what he told me."

"What Lurleen? I ain't got time to play games. This is my lunch hour and I got a cotton gin to run."

Lurleen gave Jimmy a look that said he should have kept his mouth shut and he wished he had.

"Sorry, honey. What did he say?" asked Jimmy.

"He *told* me that they have reason to believe that the boy was *kidnapped* by someone who lives somewhere around here."

"That don't make no sense at all. We ain't got no kidnapper living in Willis. Did he tell you how he knows he live here?"

"No. But he did say the man smokes Old Golds. Unfiltered Old Golds."

"Well … that narrows it down," said Jimmy, sarcastically.

"Actually, it does. There's only about ten people around here who smoke that brand and if you think about it, who in Willis is always bringing in boys from that orphanage in Georgia to do his picking?"

"You can't be talking about ol' Henry Watson. He ain't no kidnapper."

"I *am* talking about Henry Watson."

"Shouldn't you have told that officer?"

"And what? Get Henry arrested?"

"I guess I wasn't thinking straight."

"No, you weren't. But I was. There's a three-thousand-dollar reward for that boy and I want it."

"But if Henry has that boy …"

"Then you need to figure out how to get him away."

"But … what if he's already done called this number here on the poster and told them he had the boy?"

"Jimmy … if Henry has that boy, he's not going to call that number and be put in jail as a kidnapper. He's not that stupid. Nobody's called. Otherwise, why was that policeman here in Willis looking for the boy?"

"Yeah. You're right."

"Of course I'm right. Jimmy … that money's ours for the taking. All three thousand dollars." Lurleen elongated all three words. "Don't you want that money?"

"Yes ma'am."

"Then you just need to find out if Henry has him and work out a plan to get him."

"I can do that," said Jimmy, now excited at the thought of getting a big payday. "His son, Jesse, will be bringing his cotton to the gin this afternoon. I can talk to him then. See what he says. If they have that boy, I'll know. I'll know."

"That's good, Jimmy. Real good. Now the first thing you need to do is to get yourself over to Millie's Diner. That's where I sent those policemen. I don't want them talking to anybody about that boy but you. That's my three thousand dollars."

She then turned around, grabbed a pack of unfiltered Old Golds and handed them to her husband.

"If that cop says anything about Old Golds, you show him that pack. Say you smoke them like a lot of other farmers and old war veterans. Don't say *anything* about Henry. And don't go running your mouth. You might say something you shouldn't. Let *them* do the talking."

Jimmy Turner took the pack and stuck them in his shirt pocket even though he had never smoked in his life, not even during the war. He had never been one to hurry. But three thousand dollars was calling.

CHAPTER 53

Millie's Diner, a white cinder block building with four large plate glass windows, green and white striped awnings and a double-sided Sealtest Ice Cream swing sign hanging over the door's entrance, was located on U.S. Highway 29 (Alabama State Road 15) just across from the cotton gin. It had been a mainstay of the town of Willis since 1935. The current building was a far cry from the original roadside wooden shack where Millie and her husband, Harold, began serving boiled peanuts and bar-b-que to the locals and motorists on their way to Florida. As word spread of their good food, so did their facilities, from the original walk-up, take-out operation, to their current building which had sixteen stools and twelve booths.

Broome had no trouble finding the place, but not so with a parking space as the diner's parking lot was packed. After about a five-minute wait, a young Black man was seen coming out of a side door with a couple of sacks of food. When he pulled out of his parking spot, Broome pulled in.

Buddy could hardly wait to exit the car and mark a tire … any tire. While Lewis waited patiently for the dog to do his business, Broome pulled out a couple of the posters from his leather satchel. After the dog had checked out a number of the vehicles, Lewis whistled, Buddy returned and he was tied to the car using a ten-foot rope. The back door to the car was left open so the dog could enter and exit at his will.

Once the two men were inside the building, there was an almost immediate hush to the vibrant conversation that filled the diner. The near silence caused by the two strangers wearing police uniforms only lasted a few seconds before the locals continued their discourse on the weather, cotton, fertilizer, … farming stuff.

Broome and Lewis along with three locals waited just inside the door for a place to sit.

"We got a couple of tables opening up soon," barked a skinny, middle-aged woman behind the counter to the group.

"That's Millie," said one of the three locals to Broome. "It won't be long. She gets them in, gets them out. She plays no favorites. Uniform or no uniform. Farmer or banker. Black or white. Whatever."

"Good woman," replied Broome.

True to her word, within three or four minutes, two tables opened up and were cleaned. The three locals took the first table to the left and Broome and Lewis took the far-end table to the right.

Broome and Lewis had just opened the menu when a young teenage girl came to their table.

"What can I get y'all to drink?"

"Tea," responded both Broome and Lewis. There was no need for them to say sweet tea as all tea served in the South was sweet with ice. "And a large cup of water. I need to take some out to my dog."

As the young teen headed over to the server's area, Jimmy Turner walked into the diner.

"Hey Millie! Harold! What's cooking?" he bellowed out over the noisy eaters.

"The usual," offered Harold over his shoulder while cooking burgers on the grill. Millie was too busy to respond. Jimmy looked left and then right for the police officers from Pine Mountain. Seeing them to his right, he headed that way, glad-handing and stopping for quick chats with the local patrons along the way.

When he reached the last booth, he stopped and looked at Lewis, then Broome.

"I'm Jimmy Turner, mayor of this here town. My wife, Lurleen, said you might be here. She's the owner of the general store." He stuck out his right hand to Broome who shook it and introduced himself. Lewis did the same.

"You mind if I join you?"

"Please do," said Broome.

Lewis slid out of the booth and sat down next to the chief.

As Turner took his seat, he noticed the two men looking at his partially missing left arm. Something he had grown used to over the years.

"War injury. Lost it in Normandy. But I survived unlike many of my friends."

"Difficult times," said Broome, not wishing to bring up his memories of the war.

The young waitress who had heard Jimmy come into the diner brought three teas and a large paper cup of water.

"Y'all know what y'all want?" she asked.

"If you've never eaten here before, I recommend the meat loaf or fried chicken. Best in the county," said Turner.

"Meat loaf it is," said Broome. "That and mash potatoes, gravy, field peas and turnip greens."

"Same here," said Lewis.

"Make that three, sweetheart," added Turner.

"Peach cobbler comes with the meal unless you want to pay extra. Is the cobbler okay?" she asked.

Everyone nodded and she left.

"Chief, I need to take this out to Buddy," said Lewis, picking up the cup of water.

"I think he'd appreciate that."

Lewis slid out of the table, apologizing to Turner as he left.

"Who's Buddy," asked Turner.

"Lewis' hunting dog. We use him for tracking. We hope he'll be able to pick up this missing boy's scent." Broome then slid one of the posters of the missing boy over to Turner who glanced at it.

"I seen this when them guys starting putting them up on the telephone poles. I figured that being the posters were for a Georgia boy, the boy was lost or a runaway. But Lurleen said that you think that this boy was kidnapped. Is that right?" Turner's voice was somewhat hushed as he talked.

"We do," replied Broome. "The boy's name is Tommy. Tommy Harrison.

"And you think the person who stole him is someone from *around here*?" asked Turner, his voice even more hushed.

"We do."

Turner leaned in as close as he could get to Broome. "Just so you know … most of the folks around here would offer up their first born for that kind of money. If they knew anything, they'd already done called that number. Being that you two officers are here in town, I suspect that ain't happened. But I may be able to help. Besides being the mayor, I'm manager of the cotton gin. And … I'm also the town's constable. I know pretty much everybody around these parts. Other than the bootleggers, they're all good Christian folks. Mostly farmers. I can't see none of them wanting to take that boy for any reason."

Turner seemed to be a talker, the town's busybody. That's what Broome was looking for.

"Like I told your wife, Mayor … we have sufficient reason to believe the abductor is most likely from this area."

"I don't understand. Is there something you ain't telling me that I should know?"

Broome thought for a minute about how much he should tell this complete stranger. Although he was mayor and constable of the town, he decided to keep it to a minimum, at least, at first.

"We've done some forensic testing of evidence which I am not at liberty to reveal. It points to this region and this area." Broome leaned in, motioned for Turner to do the same and in a hushed voice said, "We think he's a farmer. And we believe this person smokes unfiltered Old Gold cigarettes."

Broome leaned back as did Turner.

"Well … that narrows it down to about a few hundred people. Even I smoke them." He pulled out the unopened pack and showed it to Broome. "You want one?"

"I don't smoke." Broome glanced at the mayor's fingers that grasped the pack. Typically, smokers of any unfiltered cigarette had yellow stained fingers. Turner's were dirty but no signs that he was a smoker.

About that time Lewis returned and sat down next to the chief.

"How's Buddy?" asked Broome trying to change the direction of the questioning. He wanted to be the one asking Turner and not the other way around.

"He was in the car when I got there, laying down on the back seat. When he saw me pouring water in his bowl, he jumped out of the car like he had seen a squirrel."

"Don't care so much for dogs myself," said Turner. "And they don't seem to care for me either. I've probably gotten bit four or five times by dogs that ain't never bit nobody before. Lurleen says it's cause dogs can sense my fear."

"Your wife is right," said Lewis.

"Mayor … you said that you pretty much know everybody in this neck of the woods."

"I did say that."

"Do you think there's anybody around here that is known for liking young boys?" asked Broome as delicately as he could.

"No sir. Not here. Not in my town," said Turner, indignantly. "We don't allow queers here."

"I understand," said Broome, happy with the answer but uncomfortable with the mayor's choice of words.

"Like I said, we're good Christian folk in this town.

"And mostly cotton farmers?"

"Yes. They also grow corn and peanuts around depending on the time of the year."

"Do you know …"

Before Broome could finish his sentence, the young waitress arrived at the table with the plates of food. If the quality was as good as the quantity, the chief could see why the diner was filled.

With a mouth full of meatloaf, Turner spoke up.

"When was the boy taken?"

"A week ago, Saturday," said the chief, waiting to swallow his food before answering.

After washing the food down with some tea and before taking another bite of food, Turner continued.

"Now I ain't never been involved in no kidnapping, but I'm thinking that if that boy were still alive, whoever took him would have already asked the boy's parents for some money or called about that reward money on them posters. I'm just guessing you're here in Willis looking around 'cause you ain't had any genuine calls." Turner enunciated each syllable of *genuine.*

"Good guess."

"Now … if that boy *is* alive and you think he could be somewhere near Willis and the man who took him smokes Old Golds, I'll get Lurleen to make you up a list of everybody she knows that buys them things … er … other than me. I don't think it'll do you much good, but I'm offering."

"Thank you. That would be *most* helpful."

Broome thought about how he could take that list and match it to the list of land owners that Betty was getting from the county. It could possibly narrow his search to just a handful of people.

Turner continued. "Now before you go accusing any of my constituents, I got to tell you … most of them smokers are local farmers and I know it ain't none of them. No good reason." He then leaned in again towards the two officers. "Now there's a couple of them so-called farmers up past Beulah near the Osanippi Creek and the Chattahoochee River feeders … the Gilbert's and Perkin's … they mainly do moonshine. Not so much farming. And from what I hear, moonshine sales ain't what they used to be. Not since the county went wet. I wouldn't be a bit surprised if they ain't the ones who stole that boy. And maybe they're waiting a little while longer hoping to get more money. It's got to be a lot easier than making shine, not that I would know."

"Where is Beulah?"

"It's just up the road a piece, past my wife's store, heading north towards Lanett. If I'm not mistaken, I believe it's County Road 270. But there ain't nothing there except a church and a school. No law enforcement of any kind. Not even a post office. If I were you, I'd stay as far away from those people as possible. They're mean and don't take kindly to any lawman setting foot on their property. Matter of fact, they don't want nobody trespassing on their property. I heard rumors that they shot a hunter last year who'd got lost and wandered onto their property. The sheriff in Opelika turned a blind eye. He said the hunter should have known better. At least, that's the rumor. If your dog gets scent of the boy up there, you need to get the state troopers or revenuers involved."

Broome thought about what Turner had said about the moonshiners and the sheriff. He couldn't tell if the man was lying or embellishing the truth. Nor could he tell if he was suggesting that he and Lewis go there to look for Tommy or not. If it was too dangerous for the Lee County sheriff, how smart would it be for just him and Lewis to check it out? But he was there to find Tommy, so his decision was made.

"How soon do you think your wife can get a list of the people who smoke Old Golds?"

"I'll call her once I get back to the gin. Shouldn't take her too long. Maybe an hour."

"Fair enough. Against your advice, Lewis, Buddy and I are going to head on over to Beulah. See if the dog can pick up the boy's scent. If he does, we'll get help. That'll also give your wife more time to get the list together. Tell her we appreciate anything she can do and we'll meet her at the store sometime after two. Mayor Turner, I appreciate the information and the advice you've given us. You've been very helpful."

The chief reached over and shook Turner's hand signaling that the meeting was over.

"Can I have this?" asked Turner, pointing to the Poster that was next to his plate but his mind was on what Broome had said. *I appreciate the information and the advice you've given us.* Had he run his mouth too much? Had he said something he shouldn't? If so, Lurleen would never know.

"Take it. By all means."

All three men slid out of the booth. Almost simultaneously, Turner and Broome pulled out business cards and exchanged them.

"I'll keep a watch out for the boy. If I see or hear anything about him, I'll give you a call," said Turner. "I could sure use that reward money."

"I thought you said you are the town's constable."

"I am. Mayor, too."

"If you're the constable in this town, you can't collect any reward money because finding that boy is your job. You're paid to enforce the law."

Broome could see the immediate disappointment in Turner's face.

"You know they don't pay me much of nothing to be Constable or Mayor. It's more of an honorary position. But if that's the law, then that's it." All the while, Turner's mind was looking for ways around this legal and moral dilemma.

"Do we pay at the register?" asked Broome.

"It's already been taken care of. Compliments of the town of Willis. You and the good sergeant are our guests. And this ain't against the law in the state of Alabama."

"Thank you," said both Broome and Lewis almost at the same time.

Turner led the way to the door and stopped at the register where he saw Millie cutting a slice of coconut pie from one of her daily made desserts.

After clearing his throat, he hollered out, "Listen up, everyone." After some shushing, the diner was quiet other than the whirring of the overhead fans. "I know most of y'all have seen this poster on the telephone poles all around town." He set the poster down and put his good arm around Broome. "This here is Chief Broome and next to him is Sergeant Lewis. They are from Pine Mountain, Georgia where the boy in this poster was stolen. They have reason to believe the person who took him lives somewhere near here. I want all of you to keep a lookout and if any of y'all see or hear anything about this boy, I want you to either call the number on this poster or call me at the gin. There's a huge reward for finding him. That's all I got to say."

"We appreciate that," yelled out one of the diners with everyone laughing at the comment. "Shortest speech ever," yelled another, jumping on the bandwagon. Before long, the previously silent diners were yakking up a storm again, laughing but mostly talking about what Turner had said.

Turner turned to Millie.

"You mind taping this poster to the back of your register?"

"Sure thing. Right after the lunch crowd leaves." She took the poster from Turner and set it next to the register.

Turner turned to Broome. "That should help. Gossip is our fastest means of communications in this little town." He then laughed, shaking his head, all the while thinking he had to act fast.

As they headed towards their cars, finding the boy was the only thing on their minds but for different reasons.

CHAPTER 54

Turner waited in his car until he'd seen Broome's car turn left out of the restaurant's parking lot and onto the highway, heading towards County Road 270. Once the patrol car was out of sight, using the knob on the steering wheel, he wheeled out onto the highway and drove straight to the general store where he parked next to the side of the building.

When he walked in, he flipped the OPEN sign to CLOSED and headed towards the counter. He saw only Rachel.

"Where's your mama?"

"She's still at the house. Said she had some thinking to do."

Turner went back to the screen door, flipped the CLOSED sign to OPEN and headed to the rear of the building and out the back door. As he walked the dirt path to the house, he saw Lurleen sitting on the swing on the front porch, fanning and swinging.

"Whatcha doing?" he asked.

"Thinking."

"Thinking about what?"

Lurleen had been thinking. To use that three thousand dollars to reduce her debt meant she would have to tell Jimmy about it and how much. She wasn't sure she could handle the humiliation. She had always been her own woman. No one controlled her. She was an equal. This would all change if her financial situation was disclosed. Maybe a better solution would be to chuck it all and move to Florida. Rent was cheap. She and Jimmy could find jobs with regular paying salaries and there would be less pressure. The girls could fend for themselves. She wouldn't have to tell Jimmy anything. Three thousand dollars could make that happen.

"Lurleen … what are you thinking about?" asked Jimmy again.

"That three thousand dollars," said Lurleen. She then used her feet to stop the swinging but continued to fan.

"Jimmy … I *want* that money real bad, Jimmy. And I *know* that Henry Watson has to be the one who stole that boy." She then patted the open seat next to her. Turner sat down and patted her knee. They hadn't been this close or of like-minds in years.

"You ain't the only one, baby. Three thousand dollars would be real nice."

"What if …," said Lurleen, her eyes and voice filled with excitement. "What if we do get that money? What do you think about us moving down to Florida, like Miami or Fort Myers … even Jacksonville? It would be fun … exciting … new. We could …"

"What! And leave Willis? Leave Alabama? That ain't gonna happen. I left here one time before and didn't come back but with one arm. No. We ain't moving to Florida. Now … here's what I was thinking," said Turner, now his voice and eyes filled with excitement. "I was thinking we could buy you one of them RCA color TVs like Cora Mae has that you been wanting and I could get me a new fishing boat with one of them twenty-five horse power Evinrude engines."

Lurleen pushed herself off the swing not looking at Turner.

"Yeah. That would be nice," she said but all the while thinking, *that man already has half the money spent. And no telling what else he's thinking of buying. There's hardly enough left to make a dent in my debt. I'm no better off than before. I guess I might be going to Florida by myself.*

Lurleen continued, but the excitement was gone. "So what did you tell them? I hope you kept them as far away from Watson as possible."

"Oh yeah. I did good. *Real* good. I told them most likely them moonshiners over past Beulah probably took the boy. You know … for the money. I told them moonshine sales were down which I should know and they saw the boy as easy money."

"Jimmy, that is good. How'd you think of that?"

"Just come to me. And if that police officer gets the state troopers involved like I told them and shut them Beulah boys down, I'm the only game in town."

Lurleen chose not to comment on Turner's moonshine activities. She did not approve but eagerly accepted the money made from the sales. It kept the general store afloat more that he knew.

"What about the Old Golds. Did he mention them?"

"Yes. But I told them that none of the farmers around here who smoked them Old Golds would never steal any child. There was no need. That's when I told him about the moonshiners."

"So you think that's the last we'll see of them?"

"No. Chief Broome is coming back here before he leaves. Sometime after two. I told him that I would get you to make a list of everyone you could remember that smoked them cigarettes ... them Old Golds. Excepting Henry, of course."

"Why would you *do* such a foolish thing? There aren't probably ten farmers around here including Watson that smokes those things. It won't be any time before he's showing up at their front doorsteps."

Turner knew what Lurleen was thinking. *There he goes again. Running his mouth off.* He had to think of something quick.

"If you would just let me finish. I told him that to make him think that we were trying to help with his investigation. But I knew you wouldn't even be here when he came back. You've got to go do your hair at two. So just put down a few names and tell Rachel to tell him that you'll mail the rest. By then, we should have that reward money sitting in the bank."

Lurleen liked Jimmy's new found confidence. If she was going to get that money, she needed him to take charge, with her direction, of course.

"How are you planning on doing that?"

"Working on a plan. Once I got it all figured out, I'll run everything by you to make sure I ain't left nothing out."

"Jimmy ... I don't want to lose that money. You hear me? I want that money. We aren't ever going to have another chance *in our lifetime* to get that kind of money."

Turner nodded. "We won't lose it, honey. I promise."

CHAPTER 55

A couple of miles down the road, Broome pulled over to the side of the road.

"What did you think of Jimmy Turner?" he asked.

"What do you mean? Like as a person or what he said?" asked Lewis.

"Both."

"I think he was full of himself. But everybody there seemed to like him. And they must if he's their mayor."

"And constable. It's just that I got this feeling that he wasn't being completely honest with us. And I felt the same about his wife."

"How do you mean?"

"All this stuff about those moonshiners out past Beulah. That they were the ones who most likely kidnapped Tommy. The more I thought about it, it seemed as if he was pushing us away from Willis and towards Beulah. I don't know if that was intentional or not."

"I didn't get that feeling at all I thought he was trying to help us. Matter of fact, he told us to keep away from the moonshiners."

"Exactly. He told us he thought that if anybody had the boy, it was them. Then he told us that they were dangerous and we should stay away from them. Like playing one end against the other."

"I see what you're saying."

"Another thing. While you were outside with Buddy, I told Turner that we had reason to believe that the abductor smoked Old Golds. He said that he and a lot of farmers smoked them and pulled a pack from his shirt pocket and offered me one. The pack was unopened and upside down. Not only that, I noticed that his fingers weren't yellow-stained like most people who smoke unfiltered cigarettes."

"Chief … not all smokers have yellow-stained fingers. My daddy smokes. His fingers aren't yellow-stained. Dirty, maybe. But not yellow stained. I don't get it. We just met these people and for whatever reason you seem to feel they are working against us. Like they are protecting or hiding the abductor. Why do you think they would lie to us? He's offered to have his wife get us a list of all the Old Gold smokers. He's even tried to rally the people in the diner."

"You're right. Maybe I am just grasping at straws."

Broome slid the gear into *Drive* and headed towards Beulah. They stopped a number of times, pulling off the side of the road to let Buddy use his tracking skills but to no avail.

Once they had driven all the way to the Chattahoochee River with no luck from Buddy, they turned around and headed back to Willis where they checked out the entire town. With only five businesses and one church, it didn't take long. They also found the only payphone in town where Broome checked in with Bob. There had been no calls on the missing person phone.

Broome turned around in Benson's Feed & Seed parking lot and headed back to Turner's General Store where he stopped and parked the car next to the side of the building.

"You don't need to come in unless you want. I'm just going to run in and get that list of Old Gold smokers."

"No. You go. I'll take Buddy out, so we won't have to stop on the way home."

Both men and dog exited the car with Broome heading towards the door of the general store and Lewis and Buddy heading to the nearest tree.

When Broome walked in, the screen door slammed behind him causing Rachel to jump off her stool. When she didn't see the good looking, young sergeant, there was a look of disappointment that Broome immediately recognized and understood why.

"Is you mother here?" he asked as he walked to the counter. He could see the poster taped to the register as Lurleen had promised.

"No. She's at Sally Davis's house, getting her hair done. She does this every Saturday afternoon. She'd just plain up and die if she didn't get her hair fixed before Sunday church. Becky, my sister goes on Monday. But I like my hair natural … not that beehive looking thing that Becky wears."

That's all very interesting, thought Broome sarcastically, but he'd come back for a list, not a dialogue on hairdos.

"Did your mother happen to leave a list of names for me?"

"Yes sir, but it's not finished. Daddy clean forgot it was her hair day."

She handed Broome a list of twenty names.

"She said she would have the rest of the names ready by Monday and would mail it to you. She just needs your address."

Broome handed Rachel his business card.

"Tell her that I appreciate this," he said holding up the list. Then he turned and left with Rachel following close behind. She needed one more look at the young sergeant.

"You get what you need?" asked Lewis once Broome had returned to the car.

"I'm not real sure. I got a list of names, but I also think I got the runaround."

CHAPTER 56

It was the final weigh-in for the week. The dark clouds had come and gone without a drop of rain. Not even a sprinkle. Jesse stood by the scale weighing each of the picker's bags while Watson logged the totals into his gray ledger book.

When Watson saw Tommy shuffling up to the scale, he scanned his ledger book and looked at the boy's totals.

Tommy handed his sack to Jesse and waited as he hung it on the scale and weighed the contents. Watson viewed the results, logged it in and added it to the previous total.

Because Watson had been so indifferent about Tommy's Friday's totals and had said nothing about the promise he had made, Tommy expected the same response. He was surprised when he slipped the book under his arm and spoke up.

"Boy … you done good and I'm a man of my word," he said and bent down and unlocked the shackles on Tommy's feet.

"Thank you, sir. Thank you," replied Tommy while thinking, *now if the rains will hold off for a couple more days.*

"You learnt quick," said Watson, looking at the scale. "I wish I had more like you. Come Sunday, I want you to have dinner with me and the missus. I know it's Leroy's time, but I already done told him that I want to talk to you."

"Yes sir," replied Tommy.

Jesse pulled the bag down and threw it down at Tommy's newly-freed feet. He then shot his dad a look that made Tommy cringe.

Something wasn't right.

CHAPTER 57

Like every Saturday afternoon for the last seven cotton growing seasons, Jesse drove the tractor pulling the cotton wagon to the Willis Cotton Gin and waited in line for his turn to have his cotton weighed and vacuumed into the gin. While he ate his sack dinner, his mind would normally be on getting the check, making sure it was correct and getting his mason jar of Turner's home brew. But today, all he could think about was the three thousand dollars. His daddy had said that taking the money was a sin, Satan's handiwork. Jesse thought differently. *I didn't take that boy. Daddy did. If that's a sin, then it's on him. Not me.* As far as he was concerned the money was *his* for the taking. All he had to do was to figure out a way of getting it.

Once the last boll of cotton had been sucked out of the wagon, Jesse drove over to the office where he parked just past the front door. He turned off the engine, jumped down to the ground and headed straight to the nine-paned window door. The total process from the time he drove up to the line at the weighing station to the time he parked at the office had taken about an hour. This gave the office plenty of time to record the transaction and cut a check.

Willis Cotton Gin's office was a small, dirty, white clapboard building with three of the four sides consisting mainly of windows which appeared to have never been washed. It sat back behind the scales and to the left of the covered rail cars where the weighed and classified cotton bales were stored, ready for shipping.

The shop-bell attached to the front door rang out as Jesse entered the building and immediately closed the door behind him. A young girl in her early twenties, sitting in a chair behind a long wooden counter, set her *Photoplay* magazine aside and quickly stood when she saw who it was. Her hands immediately went to her backside where she smoothed down the non-existent wrinkles on her waist high denim jeans.

"Hey Jesse," she cooed as she checked her highly teased bouffant for any misplaced strands which was impossible considering the amount of aerosol hairspray she had used to hold it in place.

"Hey Becky," replied Jesse.

"So what do you think of my new hairdo? My hairdresser says I look like Connie Francis. What do *you* think?"

"I don't know who you're talking about."

"You know … the singer. She sang "Who's Sorry Now" and "Stupid Cupid. You want to hear them? I got the 45's back at the house."

"I ain't got time. I jest come fer my check and a jar of hooch."

"It'll be just you and me. You know …"

"Becky … I ain't got time fer this."

"Don't you like me? Or do you just not like girls? I've heard rumors …"

The look Jesse gave Becky made her glad that there was a counter separating them.

"Jest give me my check."

"Daddy wants to see you first."

"Huh? What fer? Why does he want to see me?"

"I don't know. He just said he wanted to see you. And *he* has your check."

Mad that she had been scorned, she returned to her seat, picked up her *Photoplay* magazine and turned back to the article about Elvis Presley.

Jesse stood there with a confused look on his face. Jimmy Turner, manager of the Willis Cotton Gin, had never, ever asked to see him. Not once in the seven years he had been in charge of bringing the cotton to the gin.

"Well, don't just stand there," said Becky. "And knock before you enter."

Jesse pushed through the counter-high wooden swing door and walked past Becky to the closed door that had a "PRIVATE" sign hung at eye level. He raised his hand, paused, then timidly knocked a couple of times.

Jesse waited a few seconds and when no one answered, he was ready to leave. He'd have his daddy come by and pick of the check when he made his weekly trip to the bank. Just as he was about to turn around, a loud voice rang out from behind the door. "Come in."

Jesse opened the door and peered at the middle-aged man sitting behind a large desk. The man's amputated arm disturbed him, so he chose not to look at it. Only at the round face of the gin's manager.

"Jesse, my boy," barked the man, elongating the boy's name, making it into two syllables. "Come on in and shut the door."

Jesse did as he was told.

"Have a seat," said Jimmy Turner, manager of the Willis Cotton Gin. "Care for a nip?" he asked as he opened the right-hand drawer and using his thumb and index finger, pulled out two clean glasses.

"Yes sir. I'd like that."

"How long has it been since I last seen you?"

"Not quite sure but it's been a while."

While Jesse was answering, Turner pulled out a mason jar filled with his personal, finest brew, twisted off the lid and filled the empty glasses. He slid one glass over to his guest, picked up the other and took a small sip.

"How's your daddy and mama doing?" asked Turner not caring one whit about Jesse's family. He did, however, take notice of Jesse's trembling hand as he picked up his glass and took a swallow of the brew. Turner liked having the upper hand.

"Good. Real good."

Turner then picked up Watson's cotton receipt book off his desk. It showed by date, the total weight of the cotton received and the amount of money paid out. Turner had a similar book for each farmer.

"Looks like y'all had a real good week. Your cotton is up by almost four hundred pounds over last week." Using his finger, Turner perused down the book until he reached the bottom. "Matter of fact, this is the best week you had in quite a while. Did your daddy get himself another one of them orphan boys?"

"No sir," said Jesse, looking at his drink and not at Turner. "The weather's been good and all them boys been a hustling."

Using his feet, Turner rotated his swivel chair one hundred eighty degrees, pulled a manila folder off an old wooden bookcase and swiveled back. He opened the folder, pulled out the poster that Broome had given him showing the missing boy and set it down next to Jesse's drink.

"What about this boy? You ever see him before?"

"Jest on them posters hanging on all them telephone poles," said Jesse hardly looking at the poster, his right leg nervously twitching. He took another swig of Turner's home brew and then wiped his mouth with the sleeve of his shirt.

Turner could tell that the boy was scared, either of him or his daddy or both. He also knew he was lying. He considered threatening to cancel the Watson's ginning privileges or withholding the check but knew that without good cause, that wouldn't go over well with the other farmers and that would be bad for business. He also considered telling him about the visit from the Pine Mountain Police but decided to keep that information to himself unless he had to meet with Watson.

"Are you sure that this boy ain't working on your daddy's farm? I'm thinking you might need another look."

Jesse stared down at the poster.

"N… n… no sir. I ain't never seen him before excepting on them posters."

"If you seen them posters, you seen that there boy is worth three thousand dollars. Being the constable of this town, if your daddy has that boy, then he has broke the law. He ain't entitled that reward money. Matter of fact, if he has that boy, they're gonna throw him in jail and you, too if you ain't telling the truth."

"Da … Daddy done seen that poster jest like I did only he was going to the bank. He said that reward money is the Devil's money. That it would be a sin to take it. Them's his exact words."

Turner had had enough of Jesse. Talking to him was a waste of time. He had no doubt that Watson had the boy. He needed to talk to him and the sooner the better. Without saying another word, he stood and looked sternly at Jesse who stayed seated.

"Jesse. You tell your daddy that I want to see him Monday after he done finished his banking business. You got that straight?"

"Yes sir, I do," he responded while standing.

Turner walked around the desk and handed Jesse an envelope containing a check for the cotton. Jesse immediately stuffed it in his most secure pocket of his bib overalls.

"What about my jar?" asked Jesse.

"Becky has it on her desk."

"Thank you, sir."

Turner ushered the boy to the door and just before turning the knob, an idea came to him.

"Oh … and if by any chance *you* come upon that boy, I'm willing to pay a finder's fee out of the reward money. That is … if you're interested."

"What's a finder's fee?"

Turner had him … hook, line and sinker.

"Well … let's say if *someone* was to somehow find that boy but was scared that the police might think he done stole him and might put him in jail for a long, long time, he might let someone else … say … uh … someone with authority … like a constable or mayor turn him in. Then the person who turned him in gets the reward money, but he shares it with the person who done actually found the boy as a finder's fee. That way nobody gets in trouble."

"When you say share, you mean like fifty-fifty?" asked Jesse, thinking half was better than nothing.

"Something like that."

"That sounds like a fair deal."

"It is, my boy. It is."

CHAPTER 58

"Call me back," said Turner who then hung up without waiting for a reply from Lurleen. He wanted privacy and calls made to his house/store phone, a four-way party line, afforded none. Whereas calls to the gin were on a business private line, something the owner of the gin had paid extra for.

Turner had hardly hung up the phone when he heard Becky call out.

"Daddy … Mama's on the phone."

"Got it," yelled Turner and waited until he was sure Becky had hung up.

"Well … you were right about the boy," said Turner. "Watson has him."

"You find that out from Jesse?"

"Yes ma'am. I talked to him when he brought in his cotton today just like I said I would. I showed him the poster. He said he didn't know nothing about the boy, but I could tell that he was lying. He was shaking and trembling."

"Assuming you've found the boy, what's your next step?"

"My next step is to have Jesse bring me the boy. By then, I should have it figured out how to get the money. Uh … I do have one slight … uh … little problem," said Turner, thinking back to what Broome had said about officers of the law not being eligible to collect any reward money.

"Always a problem. Jimmy … I want that money. I don't care what the problem is or what you have to do to get it. Am I understood?"

"Yes, Dear. Don't you worry. I'm gonna get that money. One way or another."

CHAPTER 59

After leaving the office building, Jesse sat on the seat of his tractor and considered Turner's offer. The finder's fee sounded good. Half was better than nothing since he didn't have any real plan on how to turn the boy in and get the money without being put in jail. But did he really want Turner involved? Not only that, could he even trust the one-arm man to share the reward money? Regardless, he had to do something quick. Or else, by Monday, the boy would be gone. He could feel the three thousand dollars slowly slipping away.

He cranked the tractor's engine, squeezed his legs together to secure the brown paper sack containing the moonshine filled mason jar and slowly eased the cotton wagon out onto Lee Street. He crossed the railroad tracks that ran through the center of town and was about to turn onto South Main when he spied the only pay phone in town. It sat in the corner of the parking lot of Benson's Feed & Seed. Posters of the missing boy were on both sides of the telephone pole whose wires fed down to the phone booth. Seeing Tommy's face on the poster, the reward money and the telephone number below were all it took to help Jesse know what he needed to do.

Instead of making the turn, he pulled into the dusty parking lot just far enough so that the cotton wagon was out of the street, yet within a few feet of the phone booth while at the same time avoiding the small roadside drainage ditch. He killed the engine, left the brown paper sack on the tractor's seat and jumped to the ground.

Then, he walked, head down, over to the telephone pole and did a quick look in all directions to make sure there was no oncoming traffic and no locals close by. He then reached up, ripped off one of the posters and slipped into the small, rectangular booth, closing the folding door behind him. With his back turned to the street, he lifted the receiver off the cradle and dialed "0".

A very young sounding woman answered on the second ring. "Operator. What number, please?"

Jesse immediately hung up as his nerves got the best of him. His hands were shaking and his throat was dry.

He briefly considered leaving, but the thought of pocketing three thousand dollars prevailed. Instead, he stepped out of the booth, walked over to his tractor, reached up and grabbed the brown sack, opened the jar, took a small swig of the brew and returned to the booth.

Feeling less anxious, he lifted the phone off the cradle and dialed "0". Once again, a young sounding but different woman answered. "Operator. What number, please?"

"NOrmandy 3-1212. The poster says it's s'posed to be a free call."

"I'll connect you. Please wait."

Operators in the four small rural telephone exchange offices located in Chambers and Lee Counties had been issued specific instructions on how to handle calls to that particular number. They were to use a special plug to make the connection and immediately notify their supervisor of the call. The special plug had been designed by Southern Bell engineers during an earlier rash of false fire alarms to freeze the mechanical switches allowing the supervisor to trace the origin of the call.

The young operator did as she had been instructed.

The wait for the connection was almost too long. Jesse was just about to hang up when he heard a male voice answer.

"Pine Mountain Police Department. Missing persons. Sergeant Phillips speaking," answered Lewis who was covering the three to seven evening shift. Broome who had heard the phone ring sprang from his desk and was standing behind Lewis before he had the words *missing persons* out of his mouth. Lewis held the phone away from his ear so that both he and the chief could hear the caller.

"Uh … I got that boy in the poster and want to git the reward money," said Jesse as calmly as he could.

"Are you saying you have Tommy Harrison?"

"Yes sir. I mean not right here next to me, but he's at the farm."

Broome's face lit up even though he knew the call might be a hoax.

"Where do you live?"

"I ain't tellin' you that. I ain't stupid."

"I'm sorry. I didn't mean it that way. But you said Tommy's at your farm?"

"Yes sir. Safe and sound. So how do I git the money?"

"First, we have to make sure that the boy you have is Tommy Harrison. So I'm going to ask you a few questions about Tommy if that's alright with you."

"Yes sir. But it's Tommy, alright. He looks jest like the picture in them posters excepting his hair is shorter."

"I understand. Now … can you tell me Tommy's middle name?"

"No sir. I don't even know his last name. We jest call him Tommy."

"Do you know where he was born?"

"No sir."

"Do you know his favorite golfer?"

"No sir."

"Tommy has a birthmark. Can you tell me where it is and what kind of fruit it looks like?"

"No sir."

"Do you know the name or color of his dog?"

"No sir. I know he and Vernon talked about a dog named Buck, but that's all I know."

"Who is Vernon?" asked Lewis straying from his scripted Q & A list.

"He's Tommy's friend."

"Does Vernon live on your farm?"

"This ain't about Vernon. This is about how do I git the reward money."

"You're right. Just a few more questions. What is Tommy's birthday?"

"I don't reckon I know that neither."

"Where did you find Tommy?"

"I didn't. I ain't had nuttin' to do with finding Tommy. My daddy found him out on the highway." Then remembering what Turner had said about the police and possible jail time. "Now this best not git me or my daddy or nobody in no trouble. All I want is the money and you can have the boy."

Lewis didn't know how to respond to the caller. If he told the truth that prison time would be involved, they might never see Tommy again. So he didn't say anything.

"Just to let you know, we've had a number of calls from people just like yourself claiming to have Tommy Harrison. So far, they have all been fakes. I'm afraid that you don't know enough about him for us to consider you as a legitimate caller. I …"

"What do you mean?" asked Jesse, cutting Lewis off mid-sentence. "You got that all wrong. We got Tommy. And I ain't no fake," barked Jesse, angrily.

"Is there any way you could call us again and bring Tommy with you. That way, we can ask the boy these same questions that only *he* would know the answers."

"I ain't bringing Tommy nowhere. But I can git them answers from him and call you back. Jest you don't give that money to nobody else."

"We won't. When do you think you'll be able to call us back?"

"Tomorrow."

"What's your name so we will know you're the same caller."

"Uh … uh … Eddie," answered Jesse, the only name to come to mind. Then, he hung up. Lewis didn't. As long as one caller didn't end the call, the supervisor at the rural telephone exchange in Lanett could track down the phone where the call originated.

Broome patted Lewis on the shoulder.

"Good job. I have a real good feeling about this one."

"Chief, it's the only real caller we've had."

"True. But I think he's our man."

"So what do we do next?" asked Lewis.

Before the chief could answer, the main office number rang.

Broome went over to Betty's desk and picked up the receiver.

"Pine Mountain Police Department. Chief Broome speaking."

"Chief, this is Ellen Michael, Southern Bell supervisor in Opelika, Alabama. We've been able to track down the location of that last call. It was made from a payphone in Willis, Alabama. I checked our records and there is only one payphone in Willis and it's on highway 15, near Benson's Feed & Seed. I hope that helps."

Broome grabbed a pen and piece of paper from Betty's desk and wrote the information down.

"You have been most helpful. Thank you very much. And thank the operator who recognized our missing person telephone number."

Broome went back over to Lewis.

"You asked what we're going to do next. We're heading back to Willis. That call was made from the only pay phone in the town. The caller said he would call back tomorrow and *we're* going to be there when he does."

CHAPTER 60

After finding the courage to make the phone call about the reward money, Jesse figured by now he'd be heading back to the farm to pick up Tommy and then drive him over to the Pine Mountain Police Department. There, the money would be waiting for him. But that wasn't going to happen, not without him knowing more about the boy. What was most disturbing was that the sergeant who answered the call wouldn't say whether or not he or his daddy might be in trouble. Maybe Turner was right. Maybe he, as mayor and constable, should be the one who turned in the boy. A finder's fee, regardless of the amount, was better than jail time.

Within minutes, he was back at the Willis Cotton Gin's office building.

Becky was surprised to see the somewhat handsome, one of the few eligible young men in town, walk back into the office. With quitting time so close, she immediately assumed he had come back to take her up on her offer. As before, she stood and smoothed down the non-existent wrinkles on her waist high denim jeans and checked her highly teased bouffant for any misplaced strands.

"Hello, Jesse," she said as sweetly as possible. "I'm glad you ..."

"Is your daddy still here?" he asked, interrupting the young receptionist.

"If they're still weighing cotton at the scales, what do you think?" she said curtly, disappointed that Jesse had come back to see her father and not her.

Without asking permission, Jesse pushed open the counter-high wooden swing door and headed straight to Turner's private office and knocked on the door a couple of times. Being that this was his second time at the office and his courage emboldened by Turner's brew, his raps were not quite as timid as his first visit.

"Come in," barked Turner from the other side of the door.

When Turner saw Jesse, the frown on his face at the thought with having to deal with another cotton farmer's problems immediately turned to a smile. Obviously, the finder's fee had peaked his daddy's interest.

But the more he thought about it, Jesse couldn't have gone to the farm, discussed the offer with his daddy and returned to the gin. He hadn't been gone that long. He had to be acting on his on. This was working out better than he thought.

"Have a seat, Jesse, my boy."

Without asking, Turner opened his desk drawer, grabbed the same two glasses he'd used during Jesse's previous visits, filled both glasses with his illicit brew and shoved one over to Jesse.

"So … what's on your mind?"

Jesse took a big sip. Talking to Turner was always intimidating even though Turner was much smaller and he only had one good arm.

"When I left here, I seen one of them posters on the pole at Benson's. I took a good look at the picture of the boy and it come to me that it was the long hair that done fooled me. Then I got to thinking about what you said about that finder's fee … you know … splitting the reward money in halves."

"Yes … I believe I said *something* like that." Turner took a small sip of the brew. He never over imbibed. Too much drinking dulled the senses, confused the mind and made one vulnerable.

Turner continued. "If I'm not mistaken, I believe you said your daddy knows about the reward money?"

"Yes sir."

"But I'm guessing he doesn't know you're here talking to me about turning that boy in for the money and you getting the finder's fee."

"No sir. He wants to take the boy back to where he stole him from and turn him loose. He don't want the money. Like I said before, he says it's a sin. Devil's money."

"And you're *absolutely* sure it the same boy in the posters? I don't want you bringing me no boy that ain't worth nothing. You hear?"

"Yes sir. It's Tommy alright, in them posters,"

"Well … son … you've done the right thing coming to me. Your daddy can't be of right mind if he's willing to turn his back on that kind of money. When is he planning on taking the boy back?"

"Monday … I think before he goes to the bank."

"Then we've got to act fast. Let me think." Turner watched Jesses take a small sip of his brew.

Nothing was said for a few minutes as Turner thought of his options which were few considering the time constraints and who he was working with.

"I want you to bring me the boy tonight. Can you do that?"

"I ain't real sure he'll go willingly. He don't trust me."

Not sure I do either, thought Turner. He picked up the poster that was laying on his desk and pushed it in front of Jesse.

"Show him that there poster," said Turner, sharply tapping his index finger at Tommy's picture. "Tell him your daddy don't want the money. That he just wants to keep him there picking cotton. Then you tell him you know a man who will get him home, but he wants the money on that poster. You also tell him that you're gonna get a share of the money. Otherwise, he won't believe a word you're saying."

"I don't know, Mr. Turner. That boy ..."

"Ga'dangit, Jesse," yelled Turner. "From the picture of that boy on them posters, he can't weigh over 100 pounds. If he won't go willingly, pick him up and carry him."

"Yes sir. You're right about Tommy. He's a scrawny little fellow. Ain't no bigger than a minute." Jesse folded the poster into quarters and slipped it in his back pocket. "What time are you thinking?"

"You got a watch?"

"Yes sir." He pulled out a pocket watch from one of the many pockets of his bib overalls. "It's my granddaddy's on my mother side."

Turner checked his watch, an A-11 military Spec Bulova he had gotten while he was in the service.

"The sun sets in a couple of hours. Just before it sets, say around 6:20, I want you and that boy standing next to your mail box. You got that?"

"Yes sir. Me and Tommy will be there."

"When I get there, y'all get in the backseat and then you push the boy to the floorboard so nobody sees him."

"I got it. Put him in the backseat on the floorboard."

"Good. Now get out of here before you get stuck waiting for the train to pass. And whatever you do, don't tell anyone. You hear me, boy?"

"Yes sir."

Jesse left and headed back to his tractor. As he did, Turner walked over to the window and watched him drive off. He looked at his watch.

4:33. Five minutes later, Jesse might have been waiting at least fifteen or twenty minutes while the Chattahoochee Valley Railway picked up four or five freight cars filled with bales of cotton and left empties, assuming it was on time.

Turner returned to his desk where he sat down, placed his hands behind his head, leaned back and smiled. He just figured out his plan.

CHAPTER 61

"Can we trust him?" asked Lurleen as she reached for her glasses that hung from her neck by a thin gold chain.

"I ain't got much choice. It's Jesse or nothing. Henry is planning on taking the boy back to Georgia, come Monday. Said he didn't want the money. So he's not an option. It's gotta be Jesse."

"How are you going to get the boy?"

"Jesse's bringing him to me. We're supposed to meet at his mailbox a little before sundown."

"What if he doesn't come? What if he decides he wants all the money for himself?"

"Ain't gonna happen. Jesse came to me. He needs me."

"What does Jesse get out of this? I know he's not doing it out of the kindness of his heart."

"No. He's getting a finder's fee."

"And *how much* is that supposed to be?"

"He thinks I told him half."

Lurleen was obviously not happy.

"That's not going to happen, Jimmy. A finder's fee is usually a percentage of the total amount. Say ten percent. You can give him three hundred and no more. Do you understand?"

"Yes, Lurleen. Three hundred dollars. Take it or leave it. That's what I'm gonna tell him."

"How are you supposed to make all this happen?"

"Actually, it's pretty simple. First, I get Jesse to call the number on the poster and tell them he has the boy. I can't call because if Chief Broome or that sergeant answers the phone, they might recognize my voice. Then …"

Lurleen held up her hand stopping Turner in mid-sentence.

"And you think they're going to believe Jesse just because he *says* he has the boy? As far as they know, he could be some jackleg trying to cheat them out of the money. They're gonna want to talk to the boy or at the very least, they will want Jesse to have some proof that he has the boy."

"I was just about to say that when you interrupted me," lied Turner. "If they want to know something about him, they can ask Jesse and he can ask Tommy. I ain't letting that boy out of the car or out of my sight."

"That'll work. Continue."

"Once they know we have the boy, I will tell them to drop the money off inside the phone booth, here, in Willis tomorrow morning, no later than 7:45 and instructions will be left …"

Lurleen raised her hand again, interrupting Turner again.

"Jimmy … tomorrow is Sunday. Banks are closed on Sunday. How are they going to get the money on a Sunday?"

"I know tomorrow is Sunday. That's part of my plan. Ain't no store gonna be open and ain't nobody gonna be on the roads 'til church time. If them folks try to bring in extra people, we'll know. And as far as getting the money … this is Pine Mountain, Georgia we're talking about. Not Columbus or Atlanta. They ain't much bigger than Willis. They know the local banker. If they want that boy, they can get the money."

"I guess you're right. Go on."

"Let's see … where was I? Oh yeah. When Jesse calls them, he tells them to bring the money tomorrow morning, no later than 7:45 a.m., Alabama time. Only small bills. They are to leave it in the payphone across from the bank. There will be instructions in the coin return for them to wait in front of the bank until the train passes. Now this is where I need *you*."

"*Me?*"

"Yes. You. You asked me if I trust Jesse. I don't think we can take that chance. That's why I want you to be with him when he gets the money and drops off the boy. He doesn't have a car, so he'll have to take mine. I want him to drive and you and the boy ride in the front seat next to him."

"Why can't you do it?"

"'Cause I'm going to be watching everything from my office, making sure there ain't no shenanigans going on." Turner pronounced the word with a long sheeee.

"I'm listening."

"As you know, on Sundays, the train always passes through town at 8:05 a.m. Jesse, you and the kid will be in the car at County Road 272 waiting for the train. Once Jesse sees it coming, he's to pull out onto the highway and drive along side of the last engine staying about three car lengths behind. As the train approaches Willis, it always slows down to about fifteen miles per hour. It takes about two to three minutes for it to pass in front of the bank and through the town, depending on the number of freight cars. That will give Jesse enough time to get the money from the phone booth and dump the kid off on the side of the road. Then Jesse will drive y'all up to the still. After about an hour, y'all will come back to the gin and park behind the office. I will let y'all in and we will divide up the money."

"What if there *is* no money in the phone booth?"

"You keep the kid. Go to the still, wait an hour, then come back to my office and we can figure out what to do next."

"What happens if you see that things aren't going as planned? Say … what if they have officers hidden behind Benson's or Millie's? How will I know that something's wrong?"

"I've already thought of that. As you approach the town, look at the flag in front of your store. If it's at half mast, do not stop for any reason. Head straight for the still, wait an hour, then come back to my office and we can figure out what to do next. But I don't think anything's gonna happen. They want that boy real bad. Not only that, these are small town cops. Not much smarter than some of them farmers you deal with."

"I hope you're right. I do like your plan. It's well thought out. But I don't want to be up at the still with Jesse and the money. Not alone. I need some protection. I want you to put that German gun you have at the office in the glove compartment of the car, loaded and with the safety off. If Jesse even looks at me the wrong way, I won't hesitant one bit about putting a bullet in him."

The gun Lurleen was talking about was a German Luger that Jimmy had removed from a dead German soldier's body during World War II … when he had both arms.

"Good idea. It'll be there. No way we're gonna lose that money. Plus, I might need it when I tell him he's only getting three hundred dollars."

"While we're talking about the money," continued Lurleen. "I think we should ask for $5000. If they can come up with three, they can come up with five."

"Now let's not be too greedy, honey."

"Jimmy ... do you want my help or not. If you do, you ask for $5000. You hear me? I'm sick and tired of working in that store ten hours a day, worrying about paying the bills, collecting money from the farmers who owe us but can't pay us, keeping track of the inventory, worrying about the taxes and a daughter who's more interested in who's coming through the door than watching those dirty little sharecropper kids as they steal us blind."

"Then five thousand dollars it is," replied Turner knowing Lurleen wasn't being totally truthful with him.

"Now ... what about the boy?" asked Lurleen quickly changing the subject. She couldn't believe she had run her mouth like she always accused Jimmy of doing. "He can identify Jesse who can identify you and me. How do you plan to handle that?"

"Don't worry about the boy. He'll fall in line. I'll make sure of that."

"If you don't, I will."

CHAPTER 62

Once Jesse had the tractor separated from the cotton wagon and parked in the barn, he stopped by his room long enough to slide his brown sack under his bed. He then ran up to the main house where he found both parents sitting in their favorite chairs by the dormant fire place. Henry had his Bible out preparing his Sunday sermon for the boys and Sarah had the Sears Roebuck catalog in her lap with it opened up to the appliance section where she was admiring all the new washing machines. If wishes were horses …

"What took you so long, boy?" asked Watson watching his son walk over with check in hand.

"Long lines today and the train caught me," lied Jesse who sat down in a chair far enough away from his parents that they wouldn't smell Turner's brew on his breath.

"This should be a good'un," said Watson as he opened the envelope.

Jesse watched his daddy as he pulled out the check. The look on his face showed that it was a good'un as he said. But it wasn't three thousand dollars like he could have had. Jesse felt guilty taking the money. But he was ready to quit farming, ready to leave Willis and ready to get him a real job at the factory. He wanted the city life. The reward money was his way out.

"Daddy … you ain't still thinking of taking Tommy back to where you stole him, are you?"

Watson looked up from the check and gave his son the stink-eye.

"You watch your mouth boy," said Sarah slamming the Sears Catalog shut. "Your daddy *found* that boy on the highway and that's where he's going back."

"But Mama, you saw that poster. They want to pay three thousand dollars fer him. Three thousand dollars." Jesse elongated the amount the second time. Before he shared that money with Jimmy Turner, he decided to give his folks one more chance at the money, his way of easing his guilt.

Jesse continued. "If Daddy got that reward money, he could buy him that cotton picker he's been wanting. Then he wouldn't need them boys no more."

"Devil's money," said Watson. "I done wrong by taking him in the first place and I ain't gonna make things worse by taking money that ain't mine."

"But Daddy …"

"Don't Daddy me, Jesse. My mind is made up."

So is mine, thought Jesse who jerked himself up from the chair and headed out of the house slamming the screen door as he did.

CHAPTER 63

Jesse looked in on Caleb before he entered his own room. He was sound asleep, snoring relentlessly. The sound normally grated on his nerves but, tonight, for some reason, the steadiness of the heavy breathing was calming. Even so, out of habit, he closed the door behind him and immediately knelt down by his bed and pulled out the sack containing the mason jar. He sat down on the edge of his bed, opened the jar and took a couple of big swallows. Large enough that he could actually feel the numbing effects on his brain. He pulled out his watch to check the time. He had a little over an hour to meet Turner.

As he sat there, he thought about his future. By Monday, he would be heading off to Macon, Columbus or West Point, Georgia. He was nervous but excited at the same time. This was something he'd wanted to do for a long time. But he never had the money or the resolve. The time he had spent in his room after the confrontation with his dad gave him time to think. He realized that as long as he stayed on the farm, he would always be under his daddy's control. Never his own man. He realized it was time. And now he had the money.

His thoughts drifted to his family. Would his daddy ever forgive him for leaving *and* taking the money? What about his mama? She was going to be devastated. He had always been her favorite and she had protected him. Even Caleb would miss him, but not for long because he was such an idjit. Jesse laughed at the thought but it was a sad laugh. Then there were the boys. They would be glad he was gone, but he wouldn't miss them either.

To rationalize his actions while at the same time trying to ease his guilty conscience, he figured if he didn't turn in the boy, his daddy might go to jail. Turner had said so and he should know, being the constable and mayor of the town. Even the police officer he'd talk to on the phone never gave him a direct answer about getting into trouble. His daddy wasn't thinking straight. He had to do this for him. Forget the money … well, maybe not.

While his mind pondered the unanswered questions, he continued to drink until he had finished the entire jar. All of those unanswered questions didn't seem so important now.

He wiped his mouth with the back of his hand and rolled the mason jar under his bed where it found a home near the other empties. He checked the time again. Even with his vision somewhat blurred, he could see that he less than an hour to have Tommy by the mailbox. As his daddy would have said, *time's a 'wasting.*

* * * * * *

On Saturdays, Caleb was always in charge of 'Lights Out.' But with the boys not having to work on Sunday, Caleb oftentimes let them turn out the bunkroom lights themselves. With him already fast asleep, tonight was one of those nights.

With the main hall completely dark, Jesse made his way towards the bunkroom on the right using its door's illuminated outline as a guide. He carried a cane fishing pole in his left hand, but he wasn't going fishing.

The closer he got to the door, the louder the boys' jabbering became. Had he been in charge of Saturday's 'Lights Out," this wouldn't have been allowed. But he wasn't in charge. Not only that, by then, he was already asleep or more likely, passed out.

When he reached the door and flung it open, everyone expected it to be Caleb, happy and smiling. The friendly banter immediately ceased when they saw who it was.

"Lights out means lights out," barked Jesse. He slapped the door with his cane to make his point. "Tommy … I want you to come with me. JoJo, git the light."

"Y … ye … yes … s …"

"Ga'dang it. Wayne … *you* git the light. Everybody … asleep. Now."

Both boys did as they were told.

Before Tommy left the bunk area, he gave Vernon a quizzical look. Vernon only shrugged his shoulders which meant that neither one had any idea of what was happening.

To confuse the boy even more, on the way to Jesse's room, they stopped by the pie safe where Jesse pulled out some fresh work clothes.

Once they had reached the end of the building, Tommy headed straight towards the front door, expecting that he was being taken back to the storm cellar and possibly a beating. Instead, Jesse shoved him into his room. Tommy was surprised by what he saw. The bed was disheveled and the room was in complete disarray. *Do as I say, not as I do*, he thought.

Jesse closed the door, threw the fresh work clothes on his bed and turned Tommy around so he was facing the boy.

"Tommy ... how would you like to go home to your mama and daddy?" he asked.

Tommy was taken completely off guard by Jesse's question. He had no idea of what Jesse wanted when he pushed him into his room, but it certainly wasn't this.

"Yes! Yes! I would like that," he responded, his eyes wide with excitement.

"Tommy ... me and Daddy done had a fallin' out. I don't want to live here on the farm no more. Now Daddy ... he wants to keep you here pickin' cotton 'til you done growed up. But I know a man who can git you back home. But they's money involved. And jest so you know, I git some money, too. That way you and I both can leave the farm."

Tommy was confused. Had Jesse and another man sent his parents a ransom note?

"My mom and dad don't have any money. They can't pay ..."

"Somebody's got money," interrupted Jesse. He then pulled the poster from his back pocket and showed it to Tommy.

Tommy's eyes first went to his picture; one that could have only come from his parents. Then he saw the amount of the reward.

"Three thousand dollars!"

"Yessiree. Me and this other man are going to turn you in and git the money. All you has to do is come with me."

Tommy handed the poster back to Jesse who slipped it into his back pocket.

"Who is this man you're talking about?"

"Ain't none of your business. You want to go home or not?"

"Yes sir. When?"

"Right now. But first I need to make sure I ain't got the wrong boy. Take off your t-shirt."

"What? Why?"

"Boy … if you …"

"Yes sir. Yes sir." Tommy did as he was ordered.

Jesse looked for a birthmark on the boy's chest and then down the front of his legs. Nothing. He grabbed Tommy by the shoulders and turned him around and examined the boy's back and legs. Again, he saw nothing.

"Something ain't right here. I ain't losing that money. Pull down them drawers,"

Tommy shook his head.

"I ain't asking agin," said Jesse, slightly popping Tommy on the leg, just enough to get his attention.

Tommy shoved his underwear down to his knees, covering himself with his hands as he did.

Jesse looked at Tommy's butt cheeks for a birthmark, but saw nothing.

"You ain't got no birthmark. You ain't the right boy," said Jesse, knowing Turner was going to be furious, not to mention there would be no money.

"Why didn't you just ask me? It's on the back of my neck, real close to my hair. It looks like a strawberry."

Jesse looked and saw the fruit-looking mark. An immediate relief came to his face.

"Thank you, Lord. Thank you."

Without waiting for an okay from Jesse, Tommy began pulling up his underwear. As he struggled using just one hand while using the other as a privacy shield, Jesse watched.

The sight of the half-naked boy aroused Jesse, putting other ideas in his head other than looking for birthmarks.

"Ain't you the cute little thing. You too pretty to be a boy. Kinda like Little Eddie."

While Tommy continued to work his underwear up his legs, Jesse released the bibs to his overalls, let them fall to the floor and slid his briefs down to his knees. He surprised Tommy by pushing him to the bed and crawling on top of him.

"Heeeeeeelp! Help! Help me!" yelled Tommy as Jesse became more aggressive.

Jesse reached around with his hand and tried to cover Tommy's mouth, but Tommy kept shaking his head to prevent it. Every now and then he was able to call out for help.

Without warning, Jesse's door flung wide open.

"What in tarnation!" yelled Caleb upon seeing his brother's partially naked body on top of Tommy's.

"Git off that boy," he ordered, but like a dog in heat, his brother ignored him and continued his assault.

Having seen enough, Caleb bolted over to the top of the bed, wrapped his arm around Jesse's neck and pulled him off of Tommy with both men falling to the floor...

"You stupid moron," yelled Jesse as he turned to his left side and with his right hand began pummeling Caleb's face.

The boys in both bunkrooms had heard Tommy's cries for help. It was eerily reminiscent of the time that Little Eddie had been ordered to Jesse's room. Only, that time, Watson, Sarah and Caleb were in Macon for the funeral of Sarah's only sibling, a spinster, ten years older than she. Unlike then, when everybody was afraid and nobody dared challenge Jesse, every boy from both bunkrooms headed towards the cries for help.

The first three boys to get to the room were Vernon, Eugene and Sammy. They saw Tommy sitting on the bed, in the corner of the room, as far back as he could, wearing only his underwear and his knees bent in front of him for protection and cover. They saw Jesse, his underwear still down to his knees, now crouched over his brother pounding him unmercifully. Blood was pouring from Caleb's nose and his right eye was partially swollen shut.

They watched until Jesse began lifting himself off the floor while hitching up his briefs. That's when Sammy, the largest of all the boys at the farm, pounced on him, shoving him back to the floor next to Caleb. Even with Sammy on his back, Jesse immediately began pushing himself off the floor until Caleb crawled on top of him. The weight of the two was more than enough to force Jesse back to the floor.

When the other two boys saw Jesse sufficiently constrained, they ran into the room and began punching him anywhere they could. Soon all of the boys from both bunkrooms had arrived. As if it were a game, each one began running up to the helpless man and either punching or kicking him, then stepping back to allow another boy to take their turn.

But Jesse was too strong. Either his adrenalin had kicked in because he was mad or because he could see his portion of the three thousand dollars slipping away or both. Regardless of why, he slowly crawled to his knees causing Sammy to fall to the floor. He then elbowed Caleb in his stomach causing him to release his hold.

With both Caleb and Sammy on the floor, Jesse stood and looked poised for another attack. The sight of him with his arms extended, his hands balled into fists and his bib overalls down around his ankles would have been funny had this been nothing more than horseplay instead of a sexual assault, which it was.

"Okay… who's next?" he yelled.

No one was willing to take him up on his offer. Sammy crawled backwards and joined the other boys who had begun backing up into the small hall that separated the two brother's rooms. Jesse took the opportunity to pull up his overalls. By then, all of the boys had gathered into the dark main hall, whispering among themselves. The attack was over. At least for now.

Jesse looked over at Tommy who was still tightly balled up in the corner of Jesse's bed.

"You need to come with me now if you want to go home. We ain't got much time."

Tommy shook his head, his fear of another attack outweighing Jesse's most likely lie of going home.

Jesse didn't ask again. He reached down to grab Tommy's feet. When he did, Tommy kicked back hard, his heel hitting Jesse just under his chin, knocking him out cold and causing him to fall on top of the boy.

"Help! Get him off me," yelled Tommy.

Caleb who had remained on the floor in fear of another attack by his brother pushed himself up, ready to do battle again. He couldn't let his new friend suffer through another assault. When he saw Jesse laying on Tommy, he reached down, grabbed him by the back straps of his overall and jerked him off the boy. To his surprise, Jesse offered no resistance but simply fell to the floor, his eyes rolled back into his head.

Vernon and at least half the other boys who had also heard Tommy's cry for help came running back only to see Jesse lying on the floor, passed out.

"What happened?" asked Vernon.

"He came at me and I kicked him in the face with my feet and he just fell on me. He's so big, I couldn't get him off."

"He ain't dead, is he?" asked Caleb, scared and forgetting about his new found English.

"No," answered Vernon quickly to assuage Caleb's fears. "Tommy just knocked him out. But he won't be that way long."

"I need to go tell Daddy."

"No Caleb. I want you to wait until Tommy leaves."

"Where's Tommy going?" asked Caleb.

"He's going home."

"I … is h … h … he run … run … running away li … like Lil … Little Eddie?" asked JoJo who was standing behind Sammy and Vernon.

Vernon looked at Jo Jo and all the boys who were in Jesse's room, waiting on an answer.

"Yes. Now all of y'all hurry back to bed before Jesse wakes up. Caleb, go get the clothes out of Tommy's foot locker that he wore when your daddy picked him up. And make it fast.

Everybody left with Caleb prodding the boys to move faster.

Vernon reached over and pulled the keys from Jesse's neck and then led Tommy out into the main hall where they both found a seat.

"Are you okay?" asked Vernon, his voice almost to a whisper so not to be overheard.

"Yes, but it was awful," said Tommy softly.

"Were you violated in any way?"

"No. Thanks to all of you."

"Now I know why Little Eddie killed himself."

"I thought you said he ran away," said Tommy, surprised at the revelation.

"I know that's what I said. I didn't want any of the other guys to get any ideas. Suicide is often contagious and it is an easy way out of bad situations. If I had *only known* what had happened …" Vernon paused for a second in reflection. It was too dark for Tommy to see the sadness in Vernon's eyes. "He must have been embarrassed and kept it too himself. In retrospect, we should have come and helped him when he cried out for help. But without Caleb or Watson around, we were all too scared. Look … it won't be long before he wakes up. Do you remember the way back to the highway?"

"Yes. I've gone over this in my head more times than you want to know. Once I'm out of the farm, I turn left at the road at the mailbox. When it dead ends, take the next left. That's highway 15 and I'm heading away from Willis."

"You got it."

Caleb saw the silhouette of the two boys created by the light from Jesse's room and brought over Tommy's clothes plus some clean socks and work boots. In less than a minute, Tommy was dressed in his green and white striped, short sleeve polo shirt, khaki shorts, socks and boots.

Once he had his boots laced up, Vernon handed Tommy, Jesse's keys and put his arm around him like a big brother. "Here … you'll need theses."

Tommy slipped them in his pocket.

Vernon had hardly released his friend when Caleb threw his arms around Tommy giving him a big, long hug. "I'm gonna miss you. You're my bestest friend." Tears were streaming down both Caleb and Tommy's faces.

Once Caleb released Tommy, Vernon led him to the front door.

"We'll see each other again," said Vernon, tears welling up in his eyes. "That's a promise. Now get out of here."

Tommy ran from the workers' cabin and never looked back. He was going home.

CHAPTER 64

"What happened?" asked Jesse groggily as he rubbed his aching chin. He was talking to Caleb who had stood watch over his unconscious brother ever since Tommy had left.

"Tommy plumb knocked you out cold. He done it with his feet. I thought you was dead." said Caleb laughing nervously. He paused for a second, then continued. "Jesse ... what you done to Tommy ... that weren't right. You ought to be ashamed of yourself. Daddy says ..."

"Shut up, fool. I'm trying to think and you're making my head hurt."

Jesse had been out for only a few minutes, but it took another couple of minutes for his brain to readjust. That's when he remembered his meeting with Turner. And he was supposed to bring Tommy. He reached for his watch, but his overalls were still around his feet.

"What time is it?" he asked.

While he waited for Caleb to retrieve his watch, he sat up in bed and tried to put his feet on the floor only to find his right leg in shackles and attached to the bed frame.

Caleb immediately backed away expecting Jesse to explode. Instead, he asked for the time.

Caleb quickly pulled out his pocket watch and closely examined the face of his time piece.

"Uh ... uh ... Six something. I think 6:10 ... no ... 6:11. Yes. 6:11. That's the time," he said beaming.

"What a ga'dang idjit," mumbled Jesse. "So where's the boy? Where's Tommy?"

While waiting for an answer, Jesse reached under his mattress, pulled out his spare set of keys and unlocked the shackles.

"He ain't here. That's all I'm gonna say."

Jesse pulled up his bib overalls, fastened them at the top and without warning, grabbed Caleb's jaw and squeeze it while pulling it so close to his face that Caleb could smell the foul odor coming from his brother's breath.

"Caleb," Jesse yelled ignoring the ache in his head. "Where is Tommy?" He then squeezed his twin-brother's jaw even harder. Caleb's swollen and now black eye was hard for Jesse to ignore.

"Jesse … stop. You're hurting me," muttered Caleb as he tried to pull Jesse's hands away from his face.

As if someone had flipped a switch, possibly the short-term effects of his head trauma, Jesse let go of Caleb's face and began to cry.

"I'm sorry, Caleb. I didn't mean to hurt you." He then wiped his eyes. "But I hate it here. I hate farming. I don't hate you or Mama or Daddy, but I don't want to live here anymore. I want to go live in the city where I can be free to be myself. You know … git a job in the factory. And all I had to do was to bring Tommy to Jimmy Turner and he's gonna give me enough money so that I could leave."

He pulled the folded-up poster from his back pocket and showed it to Caleb.

"You see, Caleb. I ain't lying," he said, excitement in his eyes. "Somebody wants to pay three thousand dollars to git Tommy back. Me and Jimmy Turner was going to do that and go in halves on the money. So I need to know where he is or I ain't gonna git any money and Mr. Turner is going to be real mad."

"What about Tommy? He ain't no better off with Mr. Turner."

"No Caleb. You don't understand. Mr. Turner ain't gonna keep him. He's a good man. He runs the gin and, not only that, he's a constable, so Daddy won't git into no trouble with the law fer taking the boy. Else, he might have to go to jail. Me, too. Don't you see … this is a good thing fer me and Tommy."

"But Jesse … I don't want you to go." Caleb began to cry.

"Caleb … I have no choice. I've got to. If I stay, I might do more bad things."

"No, Jesse. No. You can't go. You're the good brother. What will me and Daddy and Mama do without you?"

"Caleb … you're better at farming that I ever was. And the boys like you the best. Remember. Caleb yes. Jesse no. Everything will be jest fine. Now I need to know where y'all put Tommy so I can git him and go meet Mr. Turner."

"He ain't here. He done run away to West Point."

Jesse checked his own watch for the time. Tommy couldn't have gotten too far.

"Thank you, Caleb. I love you," he said, wiping the newly formed tears from his eyes. "You take care of Mama, Daddy, Tippy, the farm and them other boys. I'm sorry I ever called you idjit. I'm the idjit."

Then he left.

CHAPTER 65

Within fifteen minutes, Tommy had made it to highway 15. It had been faster and easier than he had expected. And there had been no sign or sound of Jesse or Watson or Tippy. He felt free. He had just begun his journey to West Point when he heard a vehicle approaching from his rear. He turned to see a car coming from the direction of Willis. It was not Watson's tractor or his truck. The timing couldn't have been better. He stepped out onto the road and began frantically waving his hands, trying to flag the vehicle down.

Tommy watched as the car slowed and pulled off to the side of the road. Once it stopped, he ran over to the open window of the driver's side where he saw a pleasant looking man staring at him.

"Is everything alright?" he asked.

"Yes sir. I was wondering if I could catch a ride."

"Where are you heading?"

"West Point, Georgia. I need to get to a telephone and call my mom and dad."

"Are you lost? What's going on?"

"No sir. I'm not lost. I live in West Point, Georgia. I got angry with my parents over something really stupid and ran away," lied Tommy not wanting to get the Watsons in trouble. "But now I just want to go home. They've got to be worried sick over me. If you don't' mind driving me to the West Point police department, I would *really, really* appreciate it. Then I could call them and let them know I'm safe. Then they could come and get me."

"I … uh … I was heading over to my mama's for a visit, but she ain't got a phone. The closest one is back in Willis. Maybe five minutes away. West Point is more like twenty-five … thirty minutes away. I can't drive you that far. I can either take you back to Willis and drop you off at that phone booth or drive towards West Point and drop you off at County Road 270 which is kinda in the middle of nowhere. You could try and catch a ride there. Or … I could drop you off at the constable's house. He's got a phone."

Tommy thought about his options.

"What's a constable?" he asked, never having heard the word.

"Kinda like the po'lice."

"Yes! Yes! Can you take me there … the constable's place in Willis? Please?"

"That ain't no problem. Hop in. My mama will understand. Anyways, she ain't expecting me 'til around seven."

Tommy ran around to the passenger's side of the car and climbed in. When he saw that the good Samaritan was driving *away* from Willis, his mind immediately reverted back to his kidnapping.

"Where are you going? Willis is back there!"

"Just hold your horses. I got to find a good place to turn around."

A little way down the road, he made a big U-turn and headed back towards Willis.

Tommy relaxed. Two abductions within a week with the same boy? He laughed to himself. Then, without warning, he slid down to the floorboard.

"What you doing down there, boy?" asked the man, stopping his car and looking down at Tommy who had fear in his eyes.

"It's got to be him."

"Him, who?"

"That man on the tractor, driving this way. I think it's that mean man who tried to hurt me. You need to drive away. Fast."

The man looked up to see that the tractor had stopped in front of his car on his side of the road.

"That's Jesse Watson, Henry's boy," said the driver, looking confused. "I don't know what's going on, but something ain't right. Maybe he seen you get in my car 'cause he's stopped on the highway, blocking my lane. You stay down while I go talk to him. He ain't gonna do you no harm if I have anything to do with it. Stay down 'til I get back."

The man left and after a short while returned.

"He says he's looking for a boy that was trespassing on his property, but I don't trust him. I told him I ain't seen no boy on the road. You just stay down until he leaves."

"Yes sir," said Tommy, keeping his head down.

He could hear the tractor's engine grow faint as the tractor seemed to drive away.

When there was no tractor sound at all, Tommy asked, "Is it safe to get up?"

Before the one-arm man answered, the passenger door opened.

"Hello Tommy," said Jesse.

CHAPTER 66

Tommy's eyes never left the road as the one-arm man drove back to the small town of Willis. He sat in the middle of the car's bench seat between him and Jesse. Turner talked the whole way. As they approached Willis, he pointed out the first of many missing person posters that hung on telephone poles. They were the same as the one that Jesse had shown him.

"Tommy."

"Yes sir."

"If you play your cards right, you'll be on your way home tomorrow. *And we will have three thousand dollars in our pockets,* Turner thought. "The first and most important thing is *not* to remember who we are and what we look like. You hear me. You will *not* remember who we are, what we look like or where we live. If you say one word … one word to your mother, father, the police, the FBI, anybody, we know where you live and *we will kill* you and *both of your parents.* Do you understand me?"

"Yes sir," said Tommy. "I won't say anything. I promise."

"Good. Also, if you try to run away, *we will kill you.* Do you understand me?"

"Yes sir. I … I just want to go home."

"Mr. Turner ain't kidding," added Jesse. "You best do what he says."

Turner gave Jesse the evil eye.

"And you ain't never heard that name. Understood?"

"Yes sir. No one has mentioned any names. Not a one. I promise."

Even though Turner was threatening him and his family, he felt less afraid being around him than Jesse. He had no plans to tell anybody about the Watsons knowing that his friends at the farm … the boy workers … the bobbing heads … Caleb … had no place to live if the Watsons were taken away to prison.

"Then we have a deal. You go home. We get the money."

Turner slowed to 25 mph as he entered the town and at the corner of Lee and South Main, he turned right onto Lee Street and made a left into Benson's Feed & Seed's parking lot and parked next to the phone booth, leaving the engine running.

Turner leaned across Tommy and handed Jesse a small piece of paper with the telephone number from the poster written in large numbers.

"Jesse … I want you to call this number. You tell them that you have the boy. Whatever you do, don't give them our names. Understood?"

"Yes sir, Mister … uh … yes sir."

"Good. Now they're probably gonna ask you some questions to make sure you ain't some jackleg trying to cheat them out of the money. When that happens, you ask me the question and I'll ask Tommy boy. Then I'll relay the answer back to you and you tell the police. Understood?"

"Yes sir." Jesse had already been through the drill, so this was nothing new to him.

"Once they know we got the kid, tell them to have the money in Willis tomorrow morning by 7:40. And not to be late. Tell them they will find written instructions in the coin return inside the only phone booth in Willis. Now this is important. You tell them we want $5000 … not $3000 … $5000 in small bills no larger than twenties, if they want the boy back alive and no cops or funny stuff. Don't wait for a reply. Just hang up. You got that?"

"Yes sir."

"Before you leave the booth, I want you to stuff these instructions in the coin return."

He handed Jesse a small piece of paper with the instructions.

"Now … if you get nervous for any reason, hang up and we'll call back. Understood?"

"Yes sir."

"Make sure you leave the door to the booth open so I can hear what you're saying."

"Yes sir."

Tommy listened with interest to the entire conversation. What he didn't understand was why Watson himself wasn't trying to collect the money. Why Jesse and this Turner man? He wanted to know, but more than anything, he just wanted to go home.

Jesse stepped out of the car, made his way over to the phone booth, leaving the folding door open as directed. Turner watched his every move.

Having done this once before, he wasn't as nervous when the young sounding operator answered.

"Operator. What number, please?"

"NOrmandy 3-1212. It's a free call."

Turner was most impressed by Jesse's confident manner.

"I'll connect you."

The operator recognized the number and used the special plug to connect the call and immediately notified her supervisor.

"Pine Mountain Police Department. Missing persons. Corporal Galloway speaking," answered Bob who immediately covered the mouthpiece and yelled out, "Chief … we've got another call."

But Broome had already left his desk as soon as he heard the phone ring. He stood behind Bob who held the phone away from his ear so he and the chief could hear the caller.

"I have that boy in the poster."

"Ask if this is Eddie," whispered Broome.

"Is this Eddie?"

Jesse was taken aback at first when the officer asked if he was Eddie. Then he remembered his earlier phone call where he said his name was Eddie.

"Yes sir. It is."

"How is the boy?"

"He's doing real good. I've got him in the car."

"As you know we need to ask you some questions to make sure this isn't a crank call."

"Yes sir, I do."

"Can you tell me Tommy's middle name?"

"Wait a minute." He leaned outside the booth towards Turner who had remained in the car with the window down. "They want to know Tommy's middle name," he whispered.

Turner looked at Tommy who had heard the request.

"Powhatan," said Tommy loud enough for Jesse to hear. So not to be misunderstood, he repeated the name, breaking it into three syllables.

Jesse repeated what he thought he heard.

"It's Powder can."

Bob had to muzzle the phone as he and the chief couldn't help but laugh.

"Tommy has a birthmark. Can you tell where it's located what fruit it looks like?"

Jesse answered without repeating the question to Turner.

"Up there, on the back of the neck. It looks like a strawberry."

"Do you know the name or color of his dog?"

Again, Jesse leaned out of the booth, relayed the question and Tommy answered. "Rusty. The dog's name is Rusty and he's red colored."

As before, Jesse gave the police the correct answer.

"Who is Tommy's favorite golfer?"

This time, Tommy wasn't sure, so he gave two.

"He said it'd be Ben Hogan or Sam Snead."

The chief gave Bob the thumbs up. By now, both he and Bob were convinced that the caller had the boy.

"One last question. When is Tommy's birthday?"

After the same ritual as before, Jesse answered, "September eighth."

"Okay Eddie. We believe you have the boy. When and where can we meet to exchange the money for the boy?"

"The instructions will be in the coin return inside this here phone booth. It's the only one in Willis. Be there by 7:40 tomorrow morning with the money. And we want $5000 … not $3000 … $5000 if you want Tommy back alive. We don't want no large bills. Twenties and under. And no po'lice or funny stuff."

As directed, he hung up and got back into the car.

"You did mighty fine, Jesse. Mighty fine. Couldn't have done it better myself."

Turner looked over at Tommy and patted him on the leg.

"We ain't gonna kill you, son. That's just how you're supposed to scare them. That's all. At least, unless you make us." He then laughed.

Tommy was not convinced.

CHAPTER 67

As soon as the call with 'Eddie' ended, Chief Broome went to his office, sat down at his desk, looked up the home phone number of Ray Parker, city president of the local branch of Farmers & Merchants Bank and placed the call.

"Ray, I hope I'm not interrupting anything, but I just got a call from the person who has our boy."

"Alive, I assume?"

"Yes. The caller was able to answer questions about Tommy that only he would know and if he were alive."

"That's good. When do you need the money?"

"I'm afraid that's the problem. The abductor wants $5000 … not three … and in bills no larger than twenties by 6 a.m. tomorrow at the station. Can you make that happen?"

Being the local branch that handled Callaway Gardens, the bank was never short of cash.

"We have the money and in small denominations, but who's going to make up the $2000 shortfall? I can tell you what my boss will say. *We're not a charity.*" The banker used a gruff sounding voice supposedly imitating his boss.

"I understand."

"I'm sorry. You know I'd help if I could." Broome could hear the real concern in the tone of Parker's voice.

Then a thought occurred to Broome. "Ray … can I call you back in about five minutes? I might have a solution."

"Of course." And the call ended.

Broome immediately called home.

"Ruthie … Good news. We've talked to the person who has Tommy, but we have a slight problem." He then went on to explain the money situation.

"Jim … you didn't need to ask my permission. If we can get this boy back to his family, it's worth every penny."

Broome hung up and called Ray Parker.

"Ray … Here's what I want you to do. I've got a savings account that …"

"Jim, I don't mean to interrupt you, but we've got the whole $5000 covered. After I talked to you, I got to thinking and I called our biggest depositor … and you know who that is. I explained the situation and they said they were glad to front the money and asked why I hadn't said something earlier. I will have the money at your office by 6 a.m. And I will inform J. N. Rutledge that we will be returning his deposit."

"That is wonderful. But can you wait until this is over to call him? I want to have the boy with me, safe and sound, before we start spreading any joy. Just in case. You understand?"

"Yes sir. I do." The call ended and Broome immediately called Lewis and Betty at home and had them come back to the office.

While he waited for his staff to return, he called the Sheriff of Lee County and requested the assistance of two patrolman in unmarked cars. He proceeded to tell the sheriff where and why he needed the officers. The sheriff offered more help, but Broome didn't want to compromise the exchange with too many strangers or unfamiliar cars in town. Broome also inquired about the train that ran through Willis and its schedule of which the sheriff was most familiar.

Broome then called Jimmy Turner at his house. Lurleen answered and told Broome that Jimmy wasn't at home. He left a message with her requesting Jimmy's presence tomorrow morning. He gave her the time and place for them to meet. Before they hung up, she promised the list of Old Gold smokers, but Broome let her know that it was no longer needed and thanked her for all her hard work. The veiled insult did not go unnoticed.

Within thirty minutes, Bob, Betty and Lewis were standing in front of Broome's desk where he reviewed the phone call from 'Eddie' including the time, the place and the increased amount of money demanded.

"I think this is it," said Broome looking at each one. "Let's hope by tomorrow evening, Tommy Harrison will be safely home with his parents. I am very proud of all the hard work you all have done. We make a great team. Tomorrow, we need to get an early start. It takes about an hour to get to Willis assuming no stops. To be on the safe side, we will leave here by 6:45 a.m., 5:45 Alabama time. Betty … even though the office is normally closed on Sundays, I want you to cover the missing person's phone just in case the abductors call with a change of plans. If that happens, you are to call Sheriff Nick Carson of Lee County." He then handed her a piece of paper with the sheriff's name and telephone number. "Tell him what the abductors want. He can reach me on my mobile radio. I'll keep my patrol car close by, all the windows open and the speaker on its highest volume."

"Yes sir," replied Betty who was writing down everything the chief said on a small notepad.

Bob …. Lewis … I want you both to drive your trucks tomorrow with your shotguns on the back rack, loaded. I want y'all to wear your hunting gear but carry your badge. Lewis, bring Buddy, just in case we need him. Make sure your trucks are filled up. Save your receipt and we'll reimburse you for the gas and the mileage."

Broome looked up and saw a nod from both men.

He continued. "The abductors said that they want us to have the money in Willis by 7:40 tomorrow morning and there will be instructions in the town's only phone booth. When Lewis and I were in Willis, yesterday, we scoped out the town. It's not very big. Only five businesses and one church. A train track splits the town right down the middle with roads on both sides of the track. South Main and North Main. The phone booth the abductors are talking about is on the corner of Lee Street and South Main. After a little research, I found that a train passes through the town on Sundays around 8 a.m. I believe these abductors … and it's pretty obvious they are not professionals ... I believe they plan to use the train as a barrier between us and them. If you are on the North Main side of the tracks, your only way out of the town is Lee Street east. If you are on the South Main side of the tracks, you have four different ways of leaving Willis. Alabama State Road 15 North or South, Lee Street west or Jackson Avenue. So my suspect is the abductors will want us, me and Mayor Turner to be on North Main. That way they have more options to leave town. Is everybody with me so far?"

"Why do we need the mayor?" asked Lewis.

"Not only is he the mayor and he's the constable of Willis. I want to have local law enforcement present."

"Makes sense."

"Are we going to try and take down the abductors?" asked Bob.

"Good question. No. I just want the boy back. They can have the money. If the FBI, GBI or Alabama's equivalent want to pursue the abductors after this exchange, they have my blessings. We don't have the time, money or manpower to try and track down these people. And we don't know how dangerous they are," answered the chief thinking mainly about the moonshiners Turner had talked about.

Broome paused for a second to hand out a sheet of paper to each of his officers with hand-drawn map of the town.

"There's always a chance that things will go haywire, so we have to be ready. That's why I want you two to be in your trucks. Now … look at your maps. Lewis, I have you covering Jackson Avenue. Bob … I want you on Lee Street. Both trucks should be parked inconspicuously off the side of the road about a quarter of a mile from South Main Street. Make sure that once you're parked that no one can see your license plates. As for highway 15, the Sheriff of Lee County is providing me one officer to cover the highway heading towards Opelika and another officer to cover the highway heading towards Lanett. So not to compromise the exchange, these officers will leave from Opelika and Lanett, respectively at 8 a.m. and travel to Willis stopping any car coming their way. However, I suspect the abductors will choose to stay off the main roads. Any questions?"

Both men shook their head.

"Once you're parked, you are to remain at your location until 8:15 then return to the phone booth. Hopefully, we will have Tommy back, safe and alive. But … if you hear gunshots of any kind, you are to immediately pull your truck into the middle of the road blocking both lanes. Stop any vehicle that approaches your truck. If it appears they will not stop on their own accord, you stop them using any means necessary. If after fifteen minutes and there's been no activity your way, drive back to the phone booth but be prepared for anything when you get here. Does everybody understand their role tomorrow?"

All nods or 'Yes sirs.'

"Then I'll see y'all tomorrow morning. I'll have the coffee already made and will bring some of Ruthie's ham and sausage biscuits. When it's time for us to leave, we will space out our departures, leaving a ten-minute window between vehicles so we won't look like a convoy."

The meeting was adjourned and everybody went home.

CHAPTER 68

Turner slipped the gear shift into *Drive* and pulled out onto South Main Street. On Jackson Avenue, the first street past Benson's Feed & Seed and just before Willis Free Will Baptist Church, Turner took a hard right turn and traveled for about three miles where he turned right onto a dirt road. Like the Watson's farm, the road was not meant to be seen as it was almost totally hidden from view by overgrown bushes and weeds. Unlike the Watson's farm, there was no mailbox, no *Keep Out* signs or anything to draw attention to the entrance.

Once Turner had driven a few hundred feet up the winding, hilly and bumpy dirt road, he came to a stop.

"Don't move," he ordered and got out of the car.

Hanging from two pine trees was a long rusty chain that blocked further entry up the road. Turner unfastened the lock on the chain, let it drop to the ground and returned to the car.

A couple of miles up the road the car's bright headlights revealed an old, weathered, clapboard house with the roof caved in, a crumbled chimney and a collapsed porch. Off to the right and to the back of the dilapidated house was a small wooden shed with an overhang. Turner drove straight towards the shed and parked about five feet away from the front door. He turned off the ignition but left the headlights shining on the door.

"Where are we?" asked Tommy, a question that Jesse wanted to ask but chose to keep his mouth shut.

"That was my mama and daddy's old house," said Turner, pointing to the old wood-sided structure. "They died about fifteen years ago, three days apart. Both had consumption. That's why the old place is falling down. Daddy was too weak to hold a job, much less keep up the repairs. And I was a one-arm man with a wife and two children, so I was no help. This shed is all that ain't fallen in."

Realizing he had said too much, Turner ended his story with a caveat.

"But you never came here. Understood?"

"Yes sir."

"We'll be staying in this old smoke house, just for tonight. You go home tomorrow if …"

"I understand," said Tommy, feeling less and less anxious about the situation.

"Jesse … get that box of supplies out of the back of the car."

"Yes sir."

"Tommy … you come with me."

"Yes sir."

Turner removed the key from the ignition,

Jesse made his way to the back of the station wagon while Turner and Tommy headed to the front door of the shed. Turner pulled out a ring of keys and unlocked the three padlocks that secured the building. As a one-arm man, he had no trouble with the locks giving proof he had done this many times. By the time Turner shoved the door open, Jesse had arrived with the box of supplies.

"Jesse … grab a couple of them lanterns off that table in there. Get 'em lit and bring me one. Leave the other one on the table. Matches should be right next to them. If not, I brought extras. They should be in the bottom of the box."

Jesse found the matches, lit the lanterns, left one on the table as directed and brought the other one out to Turner.

"Good. Now turn out my headlights and come in the shed with me and Tommy. We can't be having that battery go dead. Not if we want to get our money." Then looking at Tommy, "And you get to go home."

"Jesse. Make sure those lights are turned out," yelled Tommy, then laughed as did Turner. Jesse didn't.

Once inside the shed, Tommy looked around. The small building had a dirt floor and no windows. It reminded him of the storm cellar but with a door in its proper place and one that would open. Wooden barrels and big sacks took up most of the sides of the building except for another table which sat against the wall to the left of the door. On top were open boxes of mason jars and some cooking pots.

"Y'all make yourself comfortable. Privy's out back," said Turner.

"Oh … I forgot. Tommy, if you do decide you want to take off into the forest, there's bears, snakes and coyotes out there just looking for a good meal." Turner laughed again.

"No sir. I'm not going anywhere tonight. I just want to go home tomorrow."

"You will. You will. Just don't do nothing stupid. I know me and Jesse must have scared you when we picked you up. But you best be thankful that *we* got you and not some bounty hunter. Them people are bad. Real bad. They'd soon shoot you as look at you. Once they get their money, their victim … meaning you … they ain't never seen alive again."

"Thank you, sir. I'm glad you're not a bounty hunter," replied Tommy, feeling most calm.

Jesse had hardly listened to the banter between Turner and Tommy. Instead, he had checked out the shed and its contents.

"So is *this* where you make that good whiskey of yours?" he asked.

"Jesse … we ain't here to discuss nothing but getting that money and getting Tommy back to his family. Now … both of y'all … have a seat on them sugar bags. I want to go over what we are supposed to do tomorrow. Then we eat and sleep. We got a big day tomorrow."

CHAPTER 69

"What do you mean Jesse's gone?" asked Watson, his question directed at Caleb who was standing in the kitchen of the main house. Sarah had stopped making biscuits to listen in on the conversation, her arms folded across her chest.

"He took off after Tommy and he said he ain't never coming back home."

"What do you mean he took off after Tommy?"

"Tommy run off last night after Jesse done had his way with him. Then …"

"Boy … what are you talking about?"

Before Caleb could answer, Sarah spared her son the embarrassment of having to explain himself.

"Henry. *You know* what Caleb's talking about. Jesse ain't exactly like the Lord intended him to be. He has thoughts that jest ain't right. When he were a young'un, he used to talk to me about these things. I tried to help him. Don't seem like I done any good. I guess I weren't a good mother."

"Sarah … we've had this discussion before. The Lord don't make mistakes. And the Lord made Jesse. Jesse is who Jesse is. Ain't nuttin' you, me or Jesse could do about it."

"But it ain't right to force yourself …," began Sarah.

Watson held up his hand like a school safety patrol officer but without a 'STOP' sign. "Leave us not discuss this in front of Caleb," said Watson.

Sarah wasn't happy about being interrupted but understood. She and Henry would talk about this later. Right now, she was more concerned about the whereabouts of Jesse and Tommy.

Watson continued, almost yelling. "Caleb … you ain't telling me everthing. How come you and Jesse didn't stop the boy from running off? What was y'all doing? Why wasn't the front door locked? And what do you mean Jesse ain't never coming back home?"

Frustration got the best of Caleb and he began slapping his head with his hands. Only in rare instances had Henry and Sarah ever seen Caleb act this way. Mostly when he was a teenager and when Henry had gone off to War. Neither Sarah nor Henry knew for sure how to calm him other than remaining calm themselves and heaping love and praise on the boy. It had been years since his last episode, so this one caught the Watsons off guard.

"Caleb, your daddy's sorry he yelled at you. He's jest worried about Jesse and Tommy. You done real good in coming and telling us. You want your mama to fix you some biscuits and sausage gravy?"

"No Mama," said Caleb, tears forming in his eyes. "I need to tell Daddy about Tommy and Jesse."

"You're a sweet boy. They don't none come any better." Sarah then gave her son a kiss on his forehead.

"Daddy … the best I recall, I were fast asleep but woke straight up when I heard somebody crying real loud fer help. I jumped out of bed, ran out in the hallway and I seen Jesse stooped over Tommy, hurting him. Me and the other boys tried to stop him but Jesse … he were way too strong. He knocked me to the floor and went over to git Tommy, but that little, tiny boy kicked him straight in the mouth and knocked him out cold. Tommy got real scared and he run off. When Jesse woke up, he got real mad. He said that Mr. Jimmy Turner was s'posed to give him lots and lots of money fer Tommy. That's when he took off looking fer Tommy. Before he went, he said he ain't never coming back to the farm and that he loved you, Mama, Tippy and me."

"Caleb … you done the right thing telling me and mama what done happened," said Watson. "You're a good son."

Watson was devastated. Jesse was supposed to take over the farm. He was the only heir that he felt could run the farm and continue the Watson legacy. Unless he could find him and bring him back home, that wasn't going to happen. He should have known the money was too great a temptation for his son. And Jimmy Turner had taken advantage of his boy's greed. The Devil was taking its toll.

"Caleb … you come with me."

"Where are we going?"

"To see Jimmy Turner."

CHAPTER 70

It was a little after 7 a.m. when Turner arrived at the general store with Tommy and Jesse riding in the back seat. With it being Sunday, the trip had been uneventful with no foot traffic or vehicles along the way other than a truck parked on the side of the road with a hunter inside.

Turner saw Lurleen standing outside the front door with her hands on her hips and an aggravated look on her face.

"Is everything alright?" asked Turner through the open driver side window.

Lurleen looked at Tommy, giving him the once over to make sure they had the right boy. She then looked at Turner.

"No. It's not alright. That Chief Broome from Georgia called last night. He was looking for you."

"Why was he looking *for me?*"

"Why do you think? He said that they had a call from the people who had the boy. He said they were supposed to do the exchange today ... this morning. And he wants you there because you're the town's constable, the local law enforcement. He said he would meet you here, this morning, around 7:45."

Tommy's heart leaped when he heard the words, *this morning.* Maybe he was really going home.

"That makes sense. What'd you tell him?"

"I had to make something up on the spot. I told him you were out playing poker with your buddies and wouldn't be back until real late."

"That's good, Lurleen. Real good. I guess I shoulda known he was going to call."

"Yes, you should. I hope everything else goes off as planned. You know I don't like surprises."

"Everything will be just fine. By the way, that's Tommy back there."

"I've already looked." Then she leaned in the window as close to Turner as she could and asked quietly, "Did you do what I asked?"

"Yes. It's there."

"Then we should probably go before anybody sees us."

Turner looked over his shoulder in the back seat.

"Okay boys. It's showtime."

What happened next looked like a Chinese fire drill. Turner opened the front door and stepped out of the car while Jesse and Tommy exited the back seat. Jesse crawled into the driver's seat while Tommy slid into the middle of the bench seat, right next to Jesse, leaving room for Lurleen.

Turner followed Lurleen over to the passenger's side of the car, watched her get in and afterwards shut the door.

"You can still back out if you want," he whispered, leaning into the open window.

"Oh no. I'm all in. All five thousand dollars' worth. I hope *you're* not getting cold feet."

"No ma'am. Uh … you know what to do if things don't work out as planned?"

"Yes. Worse case, I have my own backup plan. Jimmy, I love you, but nothing … and I mean nothing is coming between me and that money."

"Me neither. Look … I need to go change my clothes. I need to look like a constable."

"You do your part; I'll do mine and everything will work out."

Lurleen turned towards Jesse.

"Do you know where you're supposed to go?"

"Yes ma'am."

"Then drive."

CHAPTER 71

Jimmy Turner was wearing his CONSTABLE badge pinned to a yellowing white shirt as he paced back and forth in front of his wife's general store. He was armed with a Colt 38 Special, holstered to his right side and was carrying a Remington 721 bolt action rifle which had an effective range of three to five hundred yards. More than enough fire power to protect his and Lurleen's five thousand dollars.

He was about to check his watch for the fourth time when he saw Broome's patrol car come driving up North Main, not down South Main. Hopefully, that meant he had dropped off the money in the phone booth as instructed.

Turner stopped his pacing, lowered the shotgun muzzle towards the ground and watched the car turn into dirt and gravel parking area of the general store. By the time the car had come to a full stop, Turner was standing by the driver's side of the car.

"Lurleen said you made contact with the kidnappers. That's good. Real good. You bring the money?" He then looked over to the passenger's seat where he expected to see Lewis, but no one was there.

"Yes. There were instructions to leave the money in the phone booth and that's what I did. We're not here to create a disturbance. We just want the boy back, safe and sound. But I see you're loaded for bear."

"My town. My rules," laughed Turner, but he meant it. "Where's your buddy, Lewis?"

"It's Sunday. He's off. He's either going hunting or going to church."

"That's good," said Turner, thinking the less people, the better. "What happens next?"

"We're supposed to go to the bank building and wait there until the train passes. When it does, Tommy is supposed to be standing by the phone booth."

"Do you believe them?" asked Turner, trying to act as if he knew nothing about the exchange or the note.

"Yes. I believe they are the ones who kidnapped Tommy. Oh … and by the way, they asked for $5000 not three."

"Well ain't that something. I'd have taken three and been happy. Where'd you come up with the money so quick and on a Sunday?"

Broome looked at his watch. This was not a time for idle chitchat.

"It's getting late. I think we need to get on down to the bank."

"You mind if I ride with you? Lurleen has the car. She and the girls have gone down to see her sister in Opelika. I didn't want them to be around in case there was any trouble."

"Good idea. Hop in," said Broome, wondering why Turner had lied. Lurleen had made a point to tell Broome that she was an only child and sole owner of the general store. Hopefully, Turner wasn't going to be a problem.

CHAPTER 72

Seeing his tractor parked just off the road on the corner of highway 15 and County Road 271 in a field of weeds was like a wake-up call for Henry Watson of Jesse's true intentions. He wanted the money and was not coming back to the farm. The angst had been building in Watson since leaving the farm and seeing the gate at the twin lakes left wide open and the chain to the entrance of the farm laying on the ground.

"Ain't that our tractor?" asked Caleb as Henry parked his truck next to their only decent piece of farm equipment.

"Yes. Caleb. Now git out and look around and see if you see anything."

"Yes sir. Uh … what am I s'posed to be looking fer?"

"I ain't sure myself," said Watson praying it wasn't Jesse's body that they would find.

They had only been searching for just a short while when Watson heard the Chattahoochee Valley Railway train approaching while braking it's speed down to twenty miles per hour as it neared Willis. When he looked up to watch the train pass by, he saw a blue Ford station wagon approaching the intersection where he and Caleb stood among the weeds. The car was traveling slow enough that he recognized the vehicle and two of the front seat occupants. The car was Jimmy Turner's car and sitting in the passenger's seat with the window down was Lurleen Turner. Sitting next to her, perched on the front edge of the seat and peering out the front windshield was Tommy. He couldn't see the driver, but if it wasn't Jesse, where was he? And where were they going with Tommy? He had no answers, but he planned to find some.

"Caleb," yelled Watson over the noise of the train. "Come here!"

Caleb stopped his search and immediately ran to his father.

"What's the matter, Daddy?"

"Any chance you know how to drive this tractor?"

"Yes sir," said Caleb proudly. "I know'd how to drive it fer going on five years."

"Then drive this thing back home. I got some business to attend."

He removed his tractor key from his keychain and gave it to Caleb. He waited long enough to see his son start the engine and easily back it out of the weeds and onto the road heading back to the farm. Until then, as far as Watson knew, only he and Jesse had driven the tractor, too scared to let Caleb drive. Evidently, the boy had taught himself. He smiled. Not something he did too often.

With Caleb on the way back to the farm, Watson ran to his truck, cranked the engine and did a right turn onto highway 15, heading towards Willis.

By now, both Turner's car and the train were out of sight.

CHAPTER 73

At 8:07 a.m., the CVR train and its sixty plus freight cars began to slowly make its way through the town of Willis, traveling at about fifteen miles per hour. It was two minutes late, but by train standards, it was ahead of schedule.

As it slowed, so did Jesse who, as directed, had stayed about three car lengths behind the second of the two locomotives.

Excitement was in the car. Tommy was going home and Jesse and Lurleen could almost feel their new found wealth. The posters of the boy along the way had only added to their anticipation.

"Missus Turner … I see the phone booth up ahead. I believe Mr. Turner said I was s'posed to park the car, git out and git the money? Ain't that right?"

"Yes, Jesse," said Lurleen worried that Jesse might somehow botch the job.

"Jest checking."

"Make sure you leave the car running. This has got to be quick."

"Yes, ma'am."

Lurleen then looked at Tommy who had been watching both Jesse and her, depending on who was talking.

"Tommy … when Jesse gets out of the car, don't you go anywhere until he brings the money back and everything checks out. If there's no money, or they try to pull a fast one, you don't go home. You understand?" asked Lurleen.

"Yes ma'am," said Tommy politely, but all the while thinking, *Money or no money, I'm going home.*

* * * * * *

With the abductors and hopefully Tommy just on the other side of the train as it rambled through town at what Broome thought was an unusually slow speed, he and Turner tried peering through the small space between the freight cars as they passed. But even at the train's slow speed, everything seemed to be a blur to Broome's dismay and Turner's delight.

"I don't see nothing," said Turner. "Looks like them abductors knew what they were doing. Any chance you got some of your folk on the other side? I'm the only lawman in this town. Otherwise, I'd have the place crawling with folk."

"No. We don't want to spook them," lied Broome. "We just want Tommy back."

"I don't know what I was thinking," said Turner, also lying but happy with Broome's response. Otherwise, he and Lurleen might be spending their golden years looking through bars.

Turner rambled on. "If them people kill little Tommy, ain't no amount of money gonna bring him back."

Broome had no response for the inappropriate comment. Instead, he checked his watch. Only thirty seconds had passed, but it seemed like thirty minutes.

* * * * * *

Jesse turned right onto Lee Street, slowed and then turned left into the Benson's Feed & Seed's parking lot, being careful to avoid the roadside drainage ditch just in front of the phone booth. The car had hardly stopped when Jesse threw open the door and headed straight to the phone booth. When he pushed back the bi-fold door, he saw a Farmers & Merchants Bank bag on the booth's metal seat. It was much smaller than he had expected. He wasn't supposed to open the bag, but curiosity prevailed. His knees almost buckled upon seeing the two bundles of twenties and one bundle of tens. He pulled one out and fanned it. So much money. *Three ... no five thousand dollars.* For a fleeting moment, he thought about running away. Maybe grabbing hold to one of the freight cars and riding it to the next town and taking all the money.

Jesse's dreams of leaving the farm, leaving Willis, and heading to the big city came to an abrupt end when he heard the screeching sound of a vehicle as it came to a sudden stop just outside the booth. He turned around to see his daddy's old truck in the street, stopped only a few feet away from him.

Watson bolted from the truck, jumped the small ditch and stood face to face with Jesse as he left the booth with his hand firmly gripping the bag of money.

"Jesse … I done told you that nobody's taking that money. It's the Devil's money."

"But Daddy …"

Before he could complete the sentence, Watson grabbed the money bag.

* * * * * *

Lurleen had seen Jesse bend down to check out the money. Not something he was supposed to do and it cost them precious seconds. As she looked down at her watch to check the second hand and mentally calculate how much time they had left, she heard the sound of a vehicle coming to a sudden stop. When she looked up, she saw Henry Watson getting out of his truck, jumping the small ditch and come running over to Jesse where he grabbed the money bag. She immediately thought, *double-cross*. The Watsons had planned on keeping all the money for themselves and they had tricked her husband into making it happen.

The intense rage that filled her body was like nothing she had ever felt before. Her head was pounding, her heart racing and her hands were trembling. That was her money they were taking. Not theirs. Reacting rather than thinking, she jerked opened the glove compartment and pulled out the Luger. With gun in hand, she flung open the car door and ran around to the phone booth where she confronted both Watsons.

"I should have known better than to trust you," she screamed pointing the gun at Watson but directing her words to Jesse.

Then, looking at Watson, she yelled, "Give me that money."

"This money ain't yours. Ain't nobody …"

Before he could complete his sentence, Lurleen raised the gun and fired at Watson but not before Jesse rushed the gun, taking the bullet in his neck which pierced his carotid artery. The bullet passed through Jesse but just missed Watson as it exited the body. The force of the round knocked Jesse backward into his father and both men fell into the ditch.

* * * * * *

Turner saw Broome check his watch for about the third time. He, instead, looked to see if he could see the end of the train. All he saw was freight cars, no caboose.

"Won't be long. I hope everything goes as planned," commented Turner. He paused and thought about what he had just said, and added, "You know … that we get that boy back, safe and sound."

"I understand."

Even the roar of the train could not drown out the sound of the gun shot coming from the other side of the tracks. Broome immediately drew his weapon. Turner flipped the safety off his bolt-action rifle. Then the two men moved towards the tracks while staying a safe distance away from the passing train.

Different scenarios played out in each man's head as to what might have happened on the other side of the tracks, none of which were good. Regardless, all either of them could do was to wait for the train to pass.

* * * * * *

Lurleen rushed over to the phone booth and looked down to see the money bag lying in the ditch next to Watson's outreached hand. She carefully worked her way down into the shallow ravine, grabbed the bag and climbed back out just in time to see her blue Ford drive away.

That little booger just stole my car.

She looked over at the train and knew she only had a few seconds left to make her escape. With her car gone, Watson's truck was her only option.

To save time, she ran around the phone booth to the truck rather than trying to navigate down and up the ditch. The front door of the pickup was open and the engine still running. She tossed the money bag and gun onto the bench seat and climbed in.

Stick shifts were not foreign to Lurleen, but it had been years since she had driven one. Like riding a bicycle, she hadn't forgotten but needed to think. Before shifting the gear from neutral to first gear, she looked back at the train and saw the caboose. She knew then the end was near. Once she had the gear shift properly pulled down into first, she eased out the clutch and hit the gas. Even though the caboose had just passed her by, leaving the truck totally visible, she felt she was sitting far enough back in the seat that nobody could tell who was driving. She had the money and that's all that mattered. Nothing could stop her now.

* * * * * *

Tommy watched in horror as Lurleen shot Jesse. He wasn't sure why she had done it, but he couldn't take a chance on being next. Once he saw the woman ease herself into the ditch, he slid over to the driver's side of the car, positioned himself on the front edge of the seat, slipped the gear into *Drive* and stretched his leg so the toe of his shoe reached gas pedal, but just barely. While he wasn't able to get the car going full throttle, he could give it enough gas to put him and the car out of Lurleen's reach.

Once he had driven the length of Benson's parking lot, he made a hard right onto Jackson Avenue, in front of Willis Free Will Baptist Church. He didn't know where he was going or how far. But he was free. At least that's what he thought until he saw a pickup truck, a few hundred yards ahead, blocking the road.

Instinctively, he stopped the car, threw open the door and ran towards the woods. He was free and he planned to remain that way.

* * * * * *

As soon as the last car of the train had passed, Broome and Turner raced across the tracks looking at the phone booth, but there was no Tommy. Instead, they saw the toe portion of a black boot sticking out of the nearby roadside ditch and a gray truck driving away. Broome immediately thought, *Tommy,* and ran towards what he thought was the fallen boy. He was aware of the truck getting away, but knew it couldn't get very far knowing that the sound of the gunshot had signaled all four officers to close all outbound exits.

Turner on the other hand not only saw the boot and the gray pickup truck but he also saw the tail section of his blue station wagon as it headed towards Lee Street. He immediately thought, *Watson ... double-cross* with no consideration for Tommy or his fate. He just knew he had been duped by the Watsons. Jesse never had any intentions of taking a finder's fee. Henry Watson wanted all the money. All five-thousand dollars.

As Turner saw his car slowly driving up Lee Street, he realized it wouldn't take long for Watson to overtake Lurleen and steel *their* money. *That ain't gonna happen*, he thought as he raised his Remington 721 bolt action rifle, balanced it on the stub of his left arm, and fired off a single shot at the driver's side window of the old pickup.

The truck immediately slowed, swerved to the left and hit the railroad tracks causing the truck to come to an immediate halt but not before Turner had pulled another cartridge from his pocket, reloaded and fired another round at Henry Watson's truck.

The sound of more bullets coming from behind and to the left of Broome caused him to immediately take cover in the nearby ditch, covering his head. Memories of his time in Belgium during the Battle of the Bulge flashed through his mind. As he assessed his surroundings, he saw two men lying only a few feet from him. He immediately leveled his gun at the older one … just in case. Were these the abductors? If so, who shot them. And who was in the truck? And most importantly, where was Tommy?

* * * * * *

"I'm sorry, Daddy," whispered Jesse as Henry Watson tried desperately to stop the blood from pouring out of his son's neck. "I … I hope you ain't mad at me. I done you and the Lord wrong." Tears fell from the corner of his eyes.

"No son. I ain't mad at you," said Watson failing to hold back his tears or the blood draining from his dying son's body. "I love you."

Within minutes, the pain was over for Jesse. Not for Henry.

* * * * * *

After Lewis had heard the first gunshot, he immediately drove his truck out into the middle of the road as he had been instructed. When he heard two more gunshots, he grabbed both shotguns from the truck's gun rack, checked to make sure they were loaded and laid them on the truck's running board. He didn't know what was going on in Willis, but he was ready for anything that came his way.

That 'anything' came sooner than later as he saw a blue vehicle approach his truck and stop about a hundred yards away. When he saw the driver's side front door swing open, he pulled his handgun and took aim.

Fleeing from the car, towards the woods was a kid. Lewis had studied the missing person posters enough to know it was Tommy Harrison. But was he running from the roadblock or was he running from someone in the car. He waited a few seconds then rushed the car. There was no one.

By then, Tommy had made it to the woods, never looking back until he heard his name called out.

"Tommy Harrison. Stop! This is the police."

* * * * * *

Once the shooting had stopped, Broome checked on the two men lying beside him in the ditch. Seeing that one man was dead and the other one crying, he holstered his gun. He then peered over the top of the ditch only to see Turner slowly walking across the highway heading his way. His rifle was pointing safely to the ground and he had a big smile on his face.

Broome immediately stood and began shouting at Turner, not hiding the anger in his voice, "Who or what in God's name were you shooting at?"

Turner pointed to the truck that sat motionless against the train tracks.

"That's Henry Watson over yonder. When I saw his truck … and I know his truck because I buy his cotton … anyways, I figured he was the one who stole Tommy. So I just took aim. Bam. He ain't going nowhere." Then quickly thinking about the purpose of the mission, he added, "Tommy with you?"

"No. Now get over here. I need your help."

Turner promptly picked up his pace. Until he had reached the ditch, he was totally unaware that Henry and Jesse Watson lay at the bottom. When he saw the two men, he turned and looked back at the truck.

"Do you know who …"

Before Broome could complete his sentence, Turner had dropped his rifle and was running over to the gray truck.

There he found Lurleen, slumped down on the bench seat. Blood was everywhere. Even for a one-armed man, Turner was an excellent marksman and his aim was true.

* * * * *

Broome pushed the dead body off the old man. He then extended his arm and helped pull the old man off the ground and helped prop him up against the ditch.

"Is this your boy?" asked Broome his voice hushed with sorrow.

"Yes sir. He's … he's my boy … Jesse."

Broome remained silent while the old man buried his head in his hands and continued to cry.

Deaths like this one was not foreign to Broome who had served in two wars. The grief, sorrow and suffering that followed was something that only the callous and heartless could dismiss. As he leaned against the ditch, his thoughts focused on the young man in the ditch. One father had forever lost his child. He prayed there weren't two.

When Broome saw the old man's tears begin to subside, he waited a few minutes then asked, "Do you feel like talking?"

Watson looked down at Jesse then at Broome and nodded while once again wiping away the tears.

"My name is Jim Broome. I'm the chief of police from Pine Mountain, Georgia."

There were no handshakes between the two, only another nod in acknowledgement from Watson.

"Henry Watson."

"Mr. Watson, do you live here in Willis?"

"Yes sir."

"What happened to your boy? Who shot him and why?"

"Lurleen Turner shot Jesse. She meant to shoot me, but she done shot Jesse instead. My boy saved my life." Watson then broke down in tears again.

Broome gave the man time to recover.

"Why did she shoot him?" asked Broome, putting off the question whose answer he feared the most: *Where's Tommy?*

"She kilt him fer the reward money. The Devil's money, I tell ya'. The Devil's money. Weren't nobody was s'posed to take any money fer that boy. He was s'posed to go home Monday. Now Jesse is dead." The tears began to flow again.

Broome waited patiently before asking another question.

"Who was driving the gray truck?"

"That'd be me. That's my truck."

"Right after you were shot, somebody tried to take it. Do you have any idea who would take it?"

Watson took a quick look around and saw that his truck was gone. When he did see it, the truck was stalled and resting against the railroad tracks. Jimmy Turner was sitting on the running board, his arms crossed and his head bowed.

Before he answered, Watson pulled out his pack of cigarettes, stuck one in his mouth, lit it and offered the pack to Broome. The chief looked at the pack of unfiltered Old Golds but declined the offer.

Watson took a few calming puffs and then answered, "I can't be certain, but I reckon it's got to be Tommy seeing that Lurleen who brung the boy here in her car ain't here and neither is her car. Tommy must of tried to git away and drove my truck straight into them train tracks."

Watson had hardly gotten the words out of his mouth when Broom climbed out the ditch and began running towards the truck while screaming at the man who sat solemnly on the running board.

"What have you done? Oh God! What have you done?"

* * * * * *

Tommy stopped for just a second to look back at the person who had called out his name. He didn't look like a police officer nor was he dressed like one. He was wearing hunting clothes. And sitting beside him on a leash was a dog. One like Tippy who could probably track down anything.

He then remembered what Turner had said earlier. *You best be thankful that we got you and not some bounty hunter. Them people are bad. Real bad. They'd soon shoot you as look at you. Once they get their money, their victim … meaning you … they ain't never seen alive again.*

He had already been fooled by Watson and Turner. That wasn't going to happen again. He turned and ran as fast as he could into the dense forest. He had gotten himself into this mess and he planned to get himself out.

* * * * * *

Broome's heart was pounding when he reached the truck. Turner looked up at the chief. Tears were in his eyes. Broome said nothing. Instead, he pushed Turner off the running board and stepped up and looked in the cabin of the truck. Laying on the seat was Lurleen, not Tommy with a large bullet hole in her head and blood splattered everywhere. A sense of relief came over the man and then a feeling of remorse at how he had yelled at Jimmy and shoved him aside.

Broome scanned the truck's interior and saw on the floorboard the bag of reward money and a German Luger. Broome left everything in place. A lesson he'd learned from Dr. Barrineau.

After stepping down from the truck, he lifted Turner up off the ground and both men sat down on the truck's running board.

"I'm sorry," said Broome.

"All because of that ga'dang money," said Turner with tears welling up in his eyes.

Broome said nothing. He let Turner do all the talking.[3]

By the time Turner had finished, Broome was quite certain that Henry Watson was the Old Gold Man and that he had taken Tommy. He also learned of Jimmy and Lurleen Turner's involvement in the exchange of Tommy for the reward money as planner, coordinator and facilitator with Jesse Watson, not Henry Watson, a co-conspirator.

When Turner finished talking, the intermittent tears had finally ceased, but his face still bore the look of a defeated and saddened man. He had lost everything. His wife, his job, his status and the five thousand dollars.

---

[3] Note: Miranda Rights were adopted after the Supreme Court Case, Miranda v. Arizona, June 13, 1966.

Broome felt he knew the who, what, why and when of the abduction and the botched money exchange. But not the "where" as in where was Tommy.

* * * * * *

Approximately fifteen minutes after the first shot was fired by Lurleen Turner, the two officers from the Lee County Sheriff's department and Corporal Bob Galloway were parked at the lone phone booth in Willis, Alabama as instructed. None of the men had seen any vehicles, including farm equipment, traveling on their assigned roads before or after the barricades. With it being Sunday and blue laws in affect, seeing no one was not unusual.

Broome looked at his watch. He decided to give Lewis five more minutes. If he didn't show by then, he and Bob were going to find out why.

While they waited, Broome relayed to Bob and the two Lee County officers of what he thought had happened. Because the commission of the crime had occurred in Lee County, the two officers had orders to take control of the crime scene. Broome gladly consented. He was more interested in finding Tommy.

Once the wait time had expired, Bob and Broome were in Bob's truck speeding across Benson's Feed & Seed parking lot, with the truck's tires spitting out gravel as they drove towards Jackson Avenue.

* * * * * *

While Tommy couldn't see the bounty hunter, he could hear his dog and they were getting close. It was only a matter of time before he was caught. He had to think of something and quick. If he continued running into the woods, the dog would eventually find him, just as Tippy had found Clarence. He didn't want to die. His only option … his only way out was to return to Turner's blue car. He wished he'd never left it in the first place.

Keeping a steady pace, he did an immediate left turn, ran about a hundred yards and then did another hard left. He was far enough away from the hunter that neither one of them could see the other. He ran as fast as he could, heading back towards the road he had once traveled. It wasn't long before the woods were thinning out, offering him glimpses of the asphalt road up ahead. It was none too soon as he could feel the hunter and hear the dog closing in.

Once the old blue Ford station wagon came into view, he knew he was going to make it.

As he reached for the car's chrome door handle, he looked back towards the woods and saw that the man had stopped running and the dog was sitting by his side looking up in anticipation of another command. He had given up!

Tommy flung open the door, slid in behind the large steering wheel and slammed the door shut, locking it as he did. There was no time to lock the others. Through the window he could see the bounty hunter and his dog as they slowly walked towards the road.

A sense of relief came over Tommy until he reached for the ignition key. It was gone!

With the hunter and his dog closing in on the driver's side of the car, Tommy slid across the seat, and exited from the passenger's door only to see another truck pull up behind the station wagon and another hunter exit the vehicle.

There was no place for him to run or hide. They had caught him. Resigned to his fate, he leaned back against the car, his head bowed in defeat.

* * * * * *

It wasn't just the man's kind sounding voice; it was what he said.

"Are you Tom Powhatan Harrison, the third?" A name no bounty hunter would know.

Tommy looked up to see a big, burly man, dressed in a dark blue police uniform wearing a peaked cap.

"Yes sir. Yes I am," said the young boy with tears of joy streaming down his face.

"Do you know we've been looking for you for over a week?" asked Chief Jim Broome, he, too, with tears welling up in his eyes.

"Well … here I am."

THE END

EPILOGUE

There was a sense of relief on Tommy's face as he slid into the passenger seat of Chief Broome's patrol car and locked the door. He was safe ... at last.

As they drove away from Willis heading to the Pine Mountain Police Department where he would be reunited with his parents by phone, Tommy remained silent. Broome wanted to hear what had happened at the farm but chose to leave the boy alone. He would talk when he was ready.

They had driven only a few miles out of town when Tommy yelled out, "That's the road ...the one that leads to the Watson's farm."

Then he began to talk. Almost nonstop.

Broome expected to hear a tale of horror. Instead, Tommy talked about the new friends he'd made, how hard they worked and the good meals that Sarah Watson prepared. He told Broome how he had learned to pick cotton, milk cows, and most of all he learned never, never, never to get in the car with strangers, having done it twice. Once with Henry Watson and the second time with Jimmy Turner.

He said that Henry Watson was very strict but fair. He preached discipline as well as the Bible. He told him about Caleb and how kind he was and how different he was from Jesse. Never once did he mention the shackles, the ear pullings or Jesse's aborted sexual assault. When Broome broached the subject of the possible abduction, Tommy said, at first, he thought he had been kidnapped. But then he learned that Watson thought of him as a runaway who had stolen the golf clubs and shoes. And that when the old man had learned the truth, he had planned to bring him back to Pine Mountain and drop him off, but that the Turners and Jesse had other ideas. He said he had no hard feelings towards Mr. Watson. That he was a good man.

He then told how Jesse Watson and Mr. and Mrs. Turner plotted to get the reward money. He told Broome how Henry Watson had tried to stop the money exchange and how Mrs. Turner shot Jesse. And that's all he knew.

By the time he and Broome pulled into the police station, Broome was convinced of Henry Watson's innocence. And Tommy had kept his promise to Vernon. The boys would always have a home at the Waston's farm.

Dorothy Harrison answered Broome's long-distance call. He could hear the apprehension in her voice as she called her husband to the phone, so they both could listen. They prayed it wasn't bad news, but with Tommy being gone so long, they feared the worst.

When they heard Chief James Broome say, *we have Tommy. He's safe and unharmed*, their living nightmare was finally over.

Tommy Harrison and **David Rutledge** would remain close friends for the rest of their lives, even though their careers would take them separate ways. Tommy attended Georgia Tech on a golf scholarship and would later become a professional golfer, winning on the PGA tour a number of times, finishing in the top ten in the Masters three times.

David Rutledge graduated from Georgia State College[4] with a degree in Political Science and a Law degree from Emory University. He became a successful lawyer and, at the age of 39, became the mayor of Decatur, Georgia. He remained in office until he retired.

Chief James (Jim) Broome retired from Pine Mountain Police Department the following year at the age of sixty-five. While he and Ruth Ann never had children of their own, they adopted two of the boys from the farm: **Vernon Martin** and **Eugene Barfield**. They spent their golden years playing with their grandchildren and traveling the world.

* * * * * *

THE FARM BOYS:

Vernon Martin graduated from LaGrange College with a major in English and a minor in criminology. Following his adopted father's footsteps, he became a police officer, working for the Atlanta Police Department for three years before moving to the Washington D. C where

---

[4] In 1969, Georgia State College became Georgia State University.

he would later become captain of the 5th District, Washington D.C. Metropolitan Police Department.

Eugene also attended LaGrange College with Vernon. After graduating with a degree in History, he attended Emory University, Candler School of Theology, after which, he became a United Methodist minister serving many United Methodist churches in the South Georgia Conference.

Leroy entered the army as a private at Fort Benning, became a drill instructor and rose to the ranks of Sergeant Major.

Wayne, Ronnie, Clarence, JoJo, Billy, Sammy, Claude and Charlie continued to live on the farm. Eventually, each of the boys except Sammy and Claude married into other Alabama farming families. Sammy and Claude never left the Watson farm but continued to work with Caleb and fish.

* * * * * *

THE WATSONS:

Henry Watson was arrested and charged with kidnapping and extortion. At his trial, he chose not to testify. Fingerprint evidence clearly showed that he was the Old Gold Man. Tommy Harrison was the key witness, but he refused to say that he had been kidnapped or abducted. Instead, he said the whole incident was a misunderstanding and that the Watsons were very kind to him. The jury found Henry Watson innocent.

Sarah Watson was not charged with any crime as she was unaware that one had been committed. She and Henry were married fifty-eight years before Henry passed away from emphysema. Two weeks after his death, she died in her sleep.

Caleb Watson became heir to the farm. Henry was hesitant to leave Caleb in charge of the boys, the crops, the weigh-ins, the weekly hauls, but he had no choice. Given the chance, Caleb blossomed. Without the fear that Jesse imposed, production from the boys grew. At Caleb's insistence, the locks and the iron bars were removed from the boys' cabin and the shackles were thrown into the nearby pond.

Jesse Watson was buried in the family cemetery on the Watson's farm near the old plantation. His tombstone read: *Died a Hero.* His and Little

Eddie's graves were on opposite sides of the fenced in area with a weeping willow tree separating the two.

* * * * * *

THE TURNERS:

Jimmy Turner was arrested and charged with voluntary manslaughter and extortion. The voluntary manslaughter charge was dropped by the district attorney because Turner was the Constable for the Town of Willis and was legally bound to protect the people. However, he was given two years in prison for extortion, stripped of his job as mayor and constable and lost his job as manager of the cotton gin.

Once he was released from prison, he returned to Willis and was given a job at the cotton gin as the scale operator. He continued to make his illegal whiskey, drinking most of it and died of cirrhosis of the liver twelve years later.

Lurleen Turner was charged with the murder of Jesse Watson. With both the accused and the victim dead, there was no trial.

Embarrassed by the notoriety, the Turner's two daughters, **Becky** and **Rachel Turner** moved to Mobile where both found husbands.

* * * * * *

THE REWARD MONEY:

With the reward money not being claimed, the benefactor chose to set up a trust fund for each of the boys on the farm, including Tommy with each one getting an equal share once they turned eighteen.

* * * * * *

POST SCRIPT:

Two weeks after the trial, Dr. Gordon Barrineau personally returned Tommy's golf clubs and Kangaroo golf shoes.

Acknowledgements

I would like to thank my wife, **Lou**, my daughter, **Shannon Waites** and my best friend since the third grade, **David Paul Burnett** for proofreading this book. They have been very helpful, supportive and honest!

Also, a big thanks to **T.B** for his help with all farming related questions.

Thank you for reading my book. I hope you enjoyed it as much as I enjoyed writing it.

John Thomas